"Terry Brennan's new release is an engrossing ride into the dark world of political corruption that feels too close to home. In the epic unfolding of biblical prophecy, *Ishmael Covenant* catapults you across a landscape you've only imagined—on both a global and personal scale."

—**Cher Gatto**, award-winning author of *Something I Am Not*

"A master storyteller, Terry Brennan has created an exceptionally well-researched backdrop for this end-times novel along with believable characters and an action-packed plot that kept me turning the pages. *Ishmael Covenant* is for anyone who wants substance rather than fluff and novels with a greater purpose than to simply entertain."

—**Marlene Bagnull**, director of Write His Answer Ministries

"James Rollins meets Joel Rosenberg in Terry Brennan's *Ishmael Covenant*, first of his new trilogy, the Empires of Armageddon. An only-too-plausible, high-octane plotline, superb research, and a powerful spiritual message make this a must-read for any fan of end-times thrillers—or student of current-day global politics. My only complaint is that it ended too soon. When do we get the sequel?"

—**Jeanette Windle**, award-winning author of *CrossFire*, *Veiled Freedom*, and *Freedom's Stand*

"Terry Brennan has done it again with *Ishmael Covenant*. Terry combines faith, suspense, and adventure in such fun and entertaining reads, you just can't put it down once you start!"

—**Grant Berry**, author of *Romans 911*

ISHMAEL COVENANT

EMPIRES OF ARMAGEDDON

Ishmael Covenant

Persian Betrayal

Ottoman Dominion

THE JERUSALEM PROPHECIES

The Sacred Cipher

The Brotherhood Conspiracy

The Aleppo Code

ISHMAEL COVENANT

Empires of Armageddon #1

TERRY BRENNAN

Ishmael Covenant

Published by Kregel Publications, a division of Kregel Inc., 2450 Oak Industrial Dr. NE, Grand Rapids, MI 49505.

Apart from certain historical facts and public figures, the persons and events portrayed in this work are the creations of the author, and any resemblance to persons living or dead is purely coincidental.

ISBN 978-0-8254-4530-9, print
ISBN 978-0-8254-7497-2, epub

Printed in the United States of America
20 21 22 23 24 25 26 27 28 29 / 5 4 3 2 1

To my wife, Andrea:
Thanks for being the best part of me
and, after forty years,
for the sweetest season of our marriage

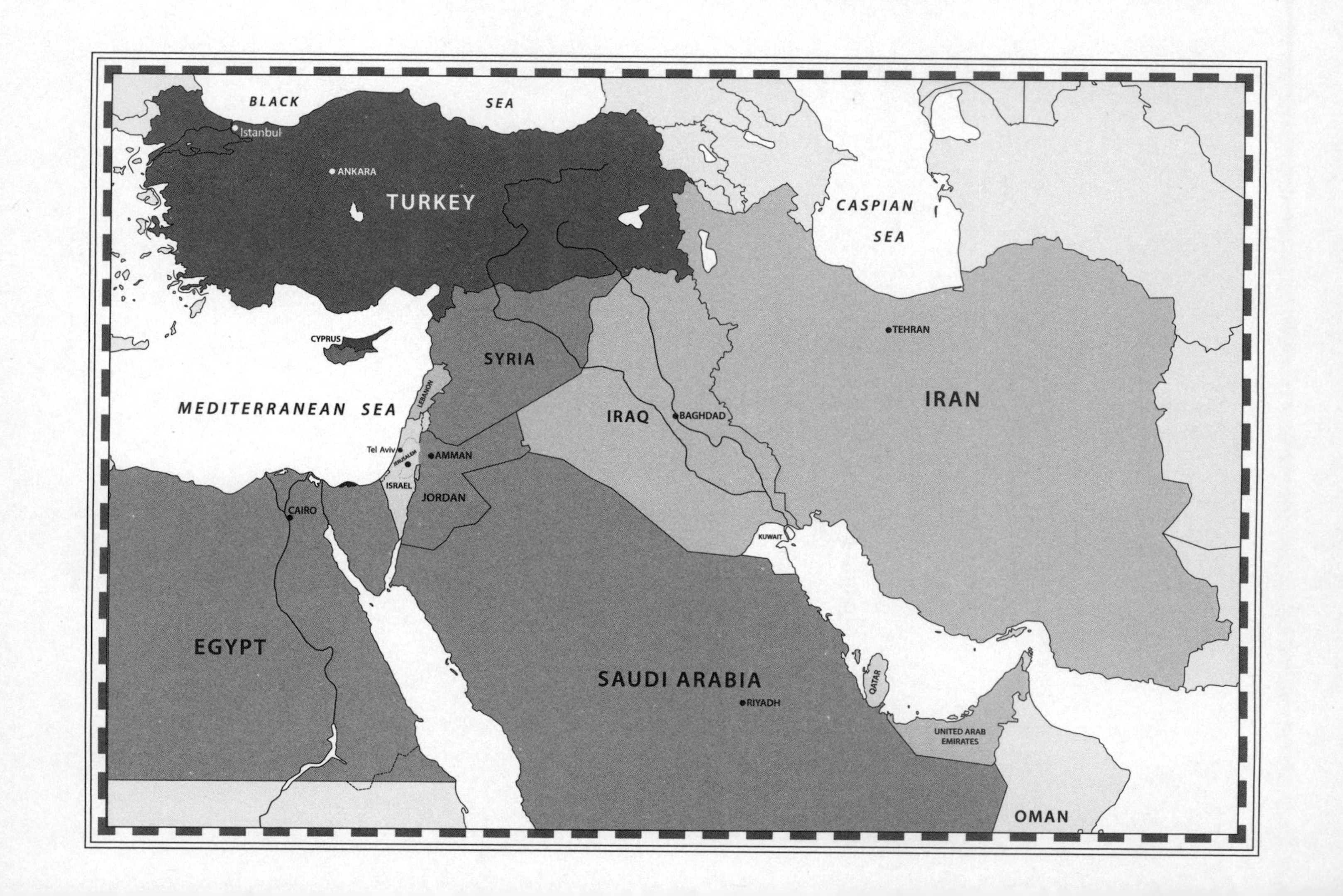
BLACK SEA
Istanbul
ANKARA
TURKEY
CASPIAN SEA
TEHRAN
IRAN
CYPRUS
SYRIA
MEDITERRANEAN SEA
LEBANON
IRAQ
BAGHDAD
Tel Aviv
AMMAN
ISRAEL
JORDAN
CAIRO
KUWAIT
EGYPT
SAUDI ARABIA
QATAR
RIYADH
UNITED ARAB EMIRATES
OMAN

CAST OF CHARACTERS

United States

Brian Mullaney—Diplomatic Security Service (DSS) agent; regional security officer overseeing the Middle East; chief of security for Joseph Atticus Cleveland, the US ambassador to Israel

Abigail Mullaney—Brian's wife and the daughter of Atlanta-based financial giant Richard Rutherford

Joseph Atticus Cleveland—US ambassador to Turkey transferred to Israel

Palmyra Athena Parker—Ambassador Cleveland's daughter

Tommy Hernandez—DSS chief for Ambassador Cleveland's security detail in Istanbul; transferred with Cleveland to Israel

Lamont Boylan—President of the United States

Evan Townsend—US secretary of state

Noah Webster—Deputy secretary of state for management and resources; oversees DSS

George Morningstar—Deputy assistant secretary for DSS

Arthur Ravel—Deputy secretary of state

Jarrod Goldberg—Deputy chief of mission, US embassy, Tel Aviv

Jon Lin—Head of FBI office, US embassy, Tel Aviv

Ruth Hughes—Political officer, US embassy, Tel Aviv

Jeffrey Archer—Cleveland's secretary at the ambassador's residence in Tel Aviv

Senator Seneca Markham—Former chair of the Foreign Relations Committee, now retired

Richard Rutherford—Billionaire Georgia banker and DC power broker

Israel

David Meir—Prime minister of Israel

Moshe Litzman—Minister of the interior of Israel

Benjamin Erdad—Minister of internal security of Israel

Turkey: Ottoman Empire

Emet Kashani—President of Turkey

Arslan Eroglu—Prime minister of Turkey

The Turk—Otherworldly pursuer of the box and the prophecy

Iraq and Iran: Persian Empire

Samir Al-Qahtani—Deputy prime minister of Iraq; leader of the Badr Brigades

Muhammad Raman—Chairman, Iran Expediency Council

Saudi Arabia, Egypt, Jordan, and Palestine: Islamic Empire

King Abdullah Al-Saud—King of Saudi Arabia

Prince Faisal ibn Farouk Al-Saud—Saudi defense minister; son of King Abdullah

Sultan Abbaddi—Commander of the Jordanian Royal Guard Brigade, personal bodyguards of the king and his family

PROLOGUE

Konigsberg, Prussia
1794

This time evil came riding on shafts of lightning, thunder its rapacious roar—torrents of pounding, cold rain hurtled out of the blackened sky for hours on end.

Yehuda pulled his fox-lined cape more tightly around his body, his left hand gripping it securely against his neck, his right hand throbbing in pain as his mule jerked against the reins with every bolt and bellow from the skies. "Papa . . . please. We should seek shelter from this storm."

The dark shape ahead of him, nearly obscured by the downpour, wrestled his mule to a stop on the narrow, muddy path through the tall pine forest. As Yehuda came alongside in the enveloping blackness of the storm, he didn't like the look of his aged father—fiery determination in his eyes, yes, but a sallow, sunken exhaustion in his face.

"We push on, Yehuda. We cannot, we must not, turn back again. Tonight, we cross the Prieglius."

A chest-rattling cough was muted by his expansive white beard as he turned away from his son and kicked his mule forward.

His father was as stubborn as this mule. Yehuda knew his father feared this would be his last opportunity, his last chance to make his desperate pilgrimage to Jerusalem. But the hounds of hell were surely unleashed against them. Evil had stalked their days and threatened their nights ever since they left Vilna, only eight days past. Hooded bandits on black stallions hunted for them in the dense Lithuanian forest, and thieving Gypsies swept down on their camp in the blackness before dawn. Only the sharp eyes and ears of Itzak, his father's servant, allowed them to escape unharmed. But this rain . . . this rain would not relent.

And neither would this Talmudic scholar.

Yehuda's aged father was no ordinary pilgrim. Renowned as the Vilna Gaon, or *genius of Vilna*, Rabbi Elijah ben Shlomo Zalman was a Torah prodigy from the age of seven. As a result of his great wisdom and his extraordinary comprehension of both Torah and secular knowledge, the often reclusive Gaon spent forty years writing voluminous corrective notes to the ancient texts of his people, particularly the Talmud. Now approaching seventy-four years, Yehuda's father was regarded as the most influential Jewish writer of his time. There was almost no ancient Torah text that did not bear his notes.

But about a year earlier, the Gaon received a vision—a visitation—that turned his focus from the past to the future. The words he wrote down on two sheets of parchment were a pair of prophetic utterances he was convinced were delivered directly from the throne of Yahweh. And all life changed around the Gaon.

Twice before Rabbi Elijah had set out for Jerusalem, and twice he had been forced to retreat back to his home in Vilna, nearly losing his life in each attempt. Yehuda feared this attempt might . . . no, put away those thoughts . . .

Itzak, ever watchful, reached a bend in the path and raised his hand for them to stop. Leaning forward, he inched his mule ahead and disappeared from sight.

Sitting in the darkness, soaked through to his skin, Yehuda's mind conjured up a picture of the hearth at home, his wife, Khana, stirring a huge pot of lamb stew, his seven children and their myriad cousins creating an uproar like the rumble of an avalanche in winter. Wait . . . that sound, that roar was in his ears, not his mind.

"Father, what is that sound?"

The Vilna Gaon hunched his shoulders under his thick cape and seemed to shrink in size. "It is the sound of defeat, I fear."

"Come!" Itzak's urgent command was nearly buried by the mixture of thunder and distant tumult.

Yehuda followed his father's mule around the bend. On the far side he pulled slightly to the right so he could see past his father into the gloom where Itzak stood, holding fast to the reins of his mule.

Behind Itzak, Yehuda could just discern the northern cliff edge of the Prieglius River Gorge, southeast of Konigsberg. Yehuda slid from his mount and stepped quickly to the Gaon's side. With Itzak's help, they eased Rabbi Elijah to the muddy ground. All three turned and, with great care, approached the edge of the cliff.

Several hundred meters below them, the Prieglius River Bridge bellowed prolonged groans, like a great beast trying to give birth. The river boiled over the bridge in massive, riotous brown waves that crashed and ebbed with growing ferocity. At times, the broad planks of the bridge were thrust to the surface of the raging torrent, at other times the middle section of the bridge disappeared under the rampaging river.

Itzak pointed, fear frozen on his face. "Is that the bridge we plan to cross?"

The Gaon closed his eyes and leaned into Yehuda's chest. "There is no other bridge . . . not for hundreds of kilometers in either direction. Either we cross that bridge now, or we go home. Again."

The faces of his children passed through Yehuda's mind as he envisioned trying to cross the savagely swaying Prieglius River Bridge. Once more its planks arose, awash with tree limbs and bubbling brown water. "We can try."

His father rested his head against Yehuda's shoulder. "Thank you, my son. We . . ."

The bridge was lifted high once more by an onrushing wave of floodwater. The massive braces of the bridge bent toward the gorge, their thick support ropes screeching as they pulled against the wood. In an instant, like a sail driven by gale force winds, the middle third of the bridge blasted down the gorge on the back of the raging water. Carried by the flood, the Prieglius River Bridge disappeared into the darkness.

Three hundred meters above the river, Yehuda felt his father's body sag against his chest. He grabbed the Gaon under the arms to keep him from falling.

"Itzak, help me. We need to get my father to shelter."

With Itzak's assistance, Yehuda lifted the Gaon onto the mule. As he considered how to secure his father in place, the Gaon opened his eyes. His voice was shallow, but clear.

"Take me to the house of Abraham Rosenberg, rabbi in Konigsberg. He is the son of Rabbi Chaim of Volozhin."

"Your most loyal and learned pupil," said Itzak.

"Yes." The Gaon nodded. "And a man we can trust. One of the few."

On the mantle, the clock was just short of midnight. Outside, the storm raged unabated, as wild and clamoring as two hours ago when they first had reached the Konigsberg Synagogue and the home of Rabbi Rosenberg, hard against the synagogue's western wall. Changed into dry clothes and fed a hearty soup, a thick mug of hot tea warming his hands and a welcoming fire heating his body, the Vilna Gaon was thankful to God for saving their lives once again and for bringing them—exhausted and despondent—to the home of this good man.

Yet his heart was heavy with failing to fulfill his vow . . . to bring his prophecies to the leaders of Jerusalem. No, not his prophecies. Never his prophecies. He was just an instrument. The prophecies came from the heart of God. His job was to deliver them. Again, he had failed.

"You didn't fail, Rebbe."

Rabbi Abraham Rosenberg rested in a chair facing Rabbi Zalman, his left side toward the crackling fire that faced the Gaon. His eyes reflected the comfort of his words.

"No man was going to pass through the Prieglius River Gorge tonight," said Rabbi Rosenberg. "From what Yehuda tells me, you have been spared death many times on this journey. Yet the demons of hell continue to come against you. Praise his holy name, the Lord of Hosts has brought you safely to my home. I do not think it coincidence."

Leaning forward in his chair, Rabbi Rosenberg closed the distance to the Gaon to just more than an arm's length. "Tell me, honored one, how may I be of assistance?"

They were alone, Yehuda and Itzak retired for the night. Doubt assailed the Gaon's mind as he considered the impact of his coming request. But he set his heart upon the Lord, closed his eyes, and recited the Shema.

"Hear, O Israel, the Lord our God, the Lord is one."

After the first two words, Rabbi Rosenberg joined in the traditional opening to Jewish prayer.

The Gaon raised his head, looked into the fire, and then turned to his host.

"Other than my sons, your father is probably the one man nearest to my heart," he said. "No disrespect to you, Rebbe, but if he were closer, it would be his home in which I would be resting. Because what I have to share with you tonight is from the throne of God himself. Its importance transcends the ages, and its meaning shakes me to my soul."

Reaching to his neck, the Gaon lifted a stout leather cord from his shoulders and pulled from under his robes a leather pouch that was attached to the cord. He fixed his attention on the rabbi, the pouch held between them.

"As my son will attest, I sleep only two hours in a day," said the Gaon, "never more than thirty minutes at a time. My hours are filled, and my stamina supplied, by studying the words of the Torah. Just over one year ago, with Yehuda in the room, I slept for seven hours straight. During that time, my spirit was lifted into a different realm, a place of living light and exquisite peace. That place was not of this earth."

Rabbi Elijah ben Shlomo Zalman looked over his shoulder to make sure the door to the room was securely closed. "I received two prophetic messages that day, both of which are written on parchment in this pouch. This journey—the last, I fear, of three attempts—was intended to take these prophecies to the Rishon LeZion, the chief rabbi in Jerusalem, and allow them to be safeguarded there. The messages in these prophecies must be protected and preserved until the day comes when they are needed."

"You honor me, and frighten me, at the same time, Master," said Rosenberg. "What should I ask first—what is in these messages, or why are you sharing this information with me?"

His long, thick white beard bobbing on his chest, the Gaon nodded his head and looked at Rabbi Rosenberg from under his eyelids, like a teacher pleased with his pupil. "Well spoken, my young friend. First, I will tell you what. Then I will tell you why. And then you will have a fateful decision to make."

Rabbi Elijah reached into the pouch and withdrew two pieces of parchment, each one folded over. He allowed the pouch to fall back upon his chest as he held the two pieces of parchment before him in his right hand.

"On that day, the first words the Voice of the Light said to me were, *'Son of man, listen to my words and write them down for the days to come. When you hear that the Russians have captured the city of Crimea, you should know that the Times of Messiah have started, that his steps are being heard.*

'And when you hear that the Russians have reached the city of Constantinople, you should put on your Shabbat clothes and not take them off, because it means that Messiah is about to come at any minute.'"

The Gaon watched Rabbi Rosenberg closely. First, Rosenberg's eyes widened in wonder. Then he sat back, the first of many questions flashing across his countenance. He stirred, raised his hand to speak, but held his tongue. A sigh lifted his shoulders, then appeared to be released from every part of his body. He shook his head, and the Gaon felt a twinge of fear and despair.

"Rav," Rosenberg said, expressing respect for the great rabbi, "my mind is spinning in a torrent that my words cannot yet express." Rosenberg spread his hands. "No man knows the hour of Messiah's appearance. Many have issued unfounded predictions and been proven fools. But you . . . many revere your knowledge and your wisdom. Master." He leaned toward the Gaon. "Are you certain?"

A jab of indignation stabbed at the Gaon's heart. "That I heard a word from the Lord? That the light which spoke to me was heavenly? Was Isaiah certain . . . Jeremiah . . . Ezekiel? I think, not certain. But confident? Yes, I am confident that I was called into the throne room of the Lord and that these words were from the Holy One."

"Forgive me, Master, but I . . ."

"No!" The Gaon held up his left hand. "Judge me . . . not yet. There are two pieces of parchment, no?" He separated the two sheets, holding one in each hand. "It is the second one"—he motioned with his right hand—"that gives me confidence in the providence of each one. But first . . ." He placed the pieces of parchment back in the leather pouch and pushed himself more erect in his chair. "Let me tell you why I am sharing these secrets with you tonight. Tomorrow, Yehuda, Itzak, and I will begin our return journey to Vilna. No more will I attempt to reach Jerusalem. Clearly it is not yet God's timing for these prophecies to reach that city. So when we depart, I *will* leave something behind."

His host pulled his hands back into the folds of his robe as if he were terrified at the thought of what the Gaon might ask him to accept.

"You are wise to be cautious," said the Gaon. "There is a covenant anointing on these prophecies, the same heavenly power of God that filled and flowed forth from the mercy seat of the ark. The vengeance of God will fall upon any who touch these prophecies without first receiving the anointing of God.

"If you agree to my request, Abraham, first you need to be blessed and protected by the anointing of God. And before passing this prophecy on to another, you must cover and protect him with that same anointing—the Aaronic blessing—or the angel of death will come through your door."

Rabbi Rosenberg's chest heaved under the weight of the deep breaths that preceded each sigh that sprang from his lips. He was looking at the floor, avoiding the Gaon's eyes.

"Abraham," the Gaon whispered, "are you willing to help me carry this responsibility?"

An old wooden clock in the corner clicked away the seconds. With one last deep breath, Rabbi Rosenberg squared his shoulders and sat back in his chair. "Yes."

"Then for your own protection, Abraham, recite with me now the Aaronic blessing. Give me your hands."

Rabbi Rosenberg's hands trembled, but his grasp was firm.

"God of heaven, God of our fathers, I place my brother Abraham into your care as I bestow upon him the task of guardian for some of the words you spoke to me. Defend him as you have defended me. Protect him with this anointing as you continue to protect me, as long as these prophecies are in our possession. May we both remain under the shelter of your anointing. Now, join with me, Abraham."

Rosenberg joined in as the Gaon recited the blessing. "The Lord bless you, and keep you. The Lord make His face shine on you, and be gracious to you. The Lord lift up His countenance on you, and give you peace."

The Gaon, eyes closed and head bowed, held onto Rabbi Rosenberg's hands a few moments before releasing them. Opening his eyes, he reached for the pouch and once again withdrew the two pieces of parchment. He looked at them, separated them one into each hand, then turned his gaze upon the rabbi.

"My son, the Lord of Israel is One, but he is also Alpha and Omega—the beginning and the end—is he not? All things are in balance, which is one of the first laws of kabbalah. Beginning and end. This first prophecy"—the Gaon held up the sheet in his left hand—"any man can create words like these out of his own mind. But this"—he took the parchment in his right hand and placed it on Rosenberg's knee—"this is proof that the words are not mine."

Rabbi Rosenberg looked down at the folded sheet on his knee but did not move to touch it. "What is written on this document of yours?"

Ah, does he now begin to believe?

"The document is no longer mine if you accept it. It is yours. I leave it in your safe keeping," said the Gaon. He placed his hand on Rosenberg's arm to stifle his objection.

"My son, I am convinced these two prophecies cannot remain together. I am now assured it is the power of the words on these sheets that draws demonic opposition. Keeping them together, none of us will be safe. I will keep the first prophecy with me. If you accept, the second will stay here with you. Hide it well. Once we return to Vilna, I will dispatch Yehuda and his entire family to move to Konigsberg. He will become your yeshiva master and teach your scholars. I charge you that, between the two of you, one of your descendants will be chief rabbi of Konigsberg for all years to come. When the day is right, you or your seed must reveal this prophecy—without fail."

Rabbi Rosenberg was shaking his head. His hands came out of his lap and grasped tightly to the folds in his robes just below his neck. He began to rock back and forth in his chair as if reciting a prayer. The Gaon's heart sank.

"What, Master, is written on this second document?"

The Gaon picked up the piece of parchment from Rosenberg's knee and held it out to his host. "It is a warning to our brothers in Palestine. To Jews the world over. And it also reveals the identity of the great deceiver, the man of violence. The one who is sent from hell to overcome Messiah, if that were possible. Here . . . open it."

Rabbi Rosenberg's rocking continued. Now his lips were moving frantically. The Gaon kept his arm outstretched. Rosenberg pulled in a deep breath and took the parchment from the Gaon's grasp.

"Praise the holy one of Israel," said the Gaon. "Now it is under your care."

As if he were opening a cage of vipers, the rabbi pried apart the paper and looked at the writing on the surface. His head tilted to the side and a grimace creased his cheeks. "I can't read this. What does it say?"

A great burden was already partially lifting from the Gaon's shoulders, a relief that would allow him some measure of peace. He smiled for the first time in weeks. "You are not meant to know, my friend. The words on these pieces of parchment have one purpose—to warn and prepare the people of Israel on the day determined by God for their revealing. Until that time, these prophecies are to be hidden and protected. There are forces in this world and the next that are diabolically opposed to the revelation of these prophecies. We must keep them safe.

"One way to keep them safe," said the Gaon, "was for me to transcribe them into a code that would be inscrutable to most people on this earth, a code that none but a Talmudic scholar can understand, only the Rishon LeZion in Jerusalem."

"The second way, I see now, is to keep them separate from each other, hidden by time and protected by distance until the determined day for each is reached."

Rabbi Elijah ben Shlomo Zalman rose from his chair and placed his hand on Rabbi Rosenberg's shoulder. "When the day comes, Abraham—and that day will be when this first prophecy is revealed—you or your seed *must* immediately take this second prophecy to the chief rabbi in Jerusalem. If this second prophecy is not revealed in its right time, not only is it likely that all Jews will be enslaved or murdered, but the eternal destiny of all men will also hang in the balance."

Rabbi Rosenberg's eyes had grown wide during the Gaon's instructions. "Rabbi . . . you make me fear for my children's children, that judgment day may soon be upon us."

"I know not of when comes judgment day," said the Gaon, his voice soft and reassuring. "Only that God has a purpose for the words on these pieces of parchment. But believe me, Abraham, I may have failed to reach Jerusalem, but I will not fail in this. We will guard these prophecies. We will hold them sacred and secret. And in that day when it is decreed from heaven, we must reveal these prophecies. If we do not, this world, and all those who live in it, will be doomed."

A log snapped and fell into the fire, sending a shower of sparks onto the hearth. The Gaon gave Rabbi Rosenberg's shoulder a squeeze. "Take heart, Abraham. Our God is with us. Let us pray for our success and your safety. Hear, O Israel: the Lord our God; the Lord is One. Now, we need a secret place that is safe."

Can a person think they are dead?

Death flashed across the Vilna Gaon's mind as a supernatural light burrowed through his closed eyelids. *I'm in heaven?*

When he opened his eyes, he knew he was dead.

The tongues of fire in the hearth were silenced. Candles on the mantelpiece flickered and were extinguished. But the light in the main room of Rabbi Rosenberg's home only grew in intensity, warming the room in spite of the extinguished fire.

Before the Vilna Gaon stood three men. They were tall and regal, cascading brown hair falling well past their shoulders. They were dressed like ancient warriors, gleaming silver breastplates covering their chests, massive broad swords in scabbards hanging from their hips. Their wings were one-third again taller than their bodies, furled tightly behind their shoulders.

Yes, I am dead. But . . . how do I know this?

The angel in the middle pointed to the left, to the door through which the Gaon connected his last concrete memory—Rabbi Rosenberg exiting on the way to his toolshed. *Was that seconds ago? Was I asleep? Am I dead?*

"Delay him," said the angel in the middle.

The angel on the left moved toward the door like fog drifting over snow, reached out, and placed his left hand against it.

Rabbi Elijah ben Shlomo Zalman—honored Talmudic scholar—returned his gaze to the angel in the middle.

The angel nodded his head toward the rabbi. "I am Bayard. We have been with you since you left Vilna. Your servant, Itzak, has sharp eyes. But it was our sharp swords that rescued you from the hooded assassins who sought your life in the forest."

"And I am not dead," said the Gaon, as much to himself as to these apparitions who looked so much like flesh-and-blood warriors. If he were not dreaming or hallucinating, then these were angels standing in Rabbi Rosenberg's home. The Gaon bowed his head in respect. "I am grateful for your protection," he said, "but why are you here . . . now?"

Bayard rested his right hand on the hilt of his sword. "We are here to help you complete your mission."

He raised his head to meet the gaze of Bayard. "I have failed. My mission has failed. Three times I have endeavored to reach Jerusalem and deliver the prophetic messages to the chief rabbi." His hand felt for the leather pouch that was concealed under his robes.

He waited.

Bayard crossed sharply muscled arms over his shining breastplate. "Evil has opposed you," he said, "but evil has not triumphed. Your mission is neither a failure nor complete."

Bayard unfolded his arms and took a step toward the Gaon. "The words you received during your vision of the living light," said Bayard, "they have power. You were warned about that power, the need to protect it and the need to protect yourself from it with the blessing of Aaron. Nothing you received from the living light has changed, can change."

A year earlier, when the Vilna Gaon had spent seven sleeping hours in a different realm, his spirit had lifted into that place of living light and exquisite peace. During that vision, the Gaon was aware of other holy, immortal ones—other angels—warriors like Bayard. The warriors who were engaged in a supernatural battle.

"The messages themselves have power to change the course of history," said Bayard, "power to rescue your chosen people from those sworn to your destruction . . . those who stand against the purposes of God."

"The evil agents of the Great Deceiver also have power," said the Gaon. "The same power that is above the order of human nature and resides in immortal beings like yourself. It will take the power of the holy immortal ones to thwart the power of the fallen immortal ones."

The intensity of Bayard's scrutiny created tiny fissures of doubt in the Gaon's resolve. Had he overstepped?

"What you ask is rarely given," said Bayard. "You are requesting to bring immortal power into the mortal world."

The Gaon measured his words carefully. "It appears to me that it may not be God's timing for these prophecies to be delivered. That their day has not yet come. But it also appears to me that, when they are together, these prophecies have attracted the wrath of hell. It was my thought to keep the first prophecy with me and pass it down to my sons until the day it is to be revealed. The second I intended to leave here with Rabbi Rosenberg.

"So I ask again. Why are you here?"

"We are here to serve," said Bayard.

"I believe you are here to help," responded the Gaon.

Bayard smiled, and pulsing waves of light surrounded his head. The Gaon felt as if his cheek had been kissed. "Yes," he nodded, "and it is help we bring."

Bayard turned his head and the angel on his right stepped to his side.

"You are correct," said Bayard. "These prophecies must no longer stay together. They must be preserved and protected until their time comes. While there is divine power in the messages, the prophecies themselves do not possess the power to hold back and deny the intentions of the immortal evil ones. You will need immortal power to combat immortal enemies . . . the power of kabbalah and the power of heaven, lethal power protecting the words themselves."

Bayard lifted his right hand from the hilt of his sword and held it out to the angel on his right. From within the folds of his cape, the angel withdrew a small metal box. It looked like bronze. He handed the box to Bayard, who moved it to his left hand.

"Stand."

The Gaon pushed the robe off his lap and wrestled his legs into a standing position. The angel reached out his right hand.

"Take my hand."

With a sharp intake of breath, the Gaon placed his left hand into Bayard's palm.

"This is the box of power," said Bayard. "It is anointed from the throne room of heaven. No evil shall stand against it. And no mortal being may touch it and live." The Gaon felt a shiver in his bones, and it was not because of his age. "Except those under the blessing. The same blessing that protects the guardian from the lethal nature of the message will protect the guardian from the lethal nature of the box. But know this . . . the box has a mission of its own. Do not deny the box from its intended purpose."

Bayard's hand gently pulled the Gaon closer to him. The angel released the Gaon's hand and placed his hand on the Gaon's head. "The guardian of the box may only touch it under the anointing of the blessing. And there can be, at any one time, only one guardian. This blessing must be given intentionally, one guardian to the next, until the time of the prophecies is revealed. If any mortal touches this box without the anointing of the blessing, they will die a hideous death."

Bayard looked deeply into the Gaon's heart. "Do you still want this power?"

The Gaon nodded his head. His voice, when he found it, was a whisper. "We need it. All the guardians will need it."

"Very well, then."

A gasp leaped from the Gaon's mouth as Bayard unfurled his wings. The wings encircled the Gaon as the angel pressed closer.

"The Lord bless you, and keep you," said Bayard, his words a chant of power as they recited the biblical Aaronic blessing. "The Lord make His face shine on you, and be gracious to you. The Lord lift up His countenance on you, and give you peace."

The Gaon could actually feel it . . . years of decline purified from his bones; richness infusing through his veins; strength filling his muscles. He realized his eyes were closed. When he opened them, Bayard stood before him, the box of power held outstretched, in both hands.

"Take it," said Bayard, "and hammer a warning into its lid using the symbols of kabbalah . . . the Merkabah in the middle; two mezuzahs in the corners opposite each other; the Hamsa in one corner, the Tree of Life in the other. To touch this box, or the message that rests within it, is to sever the tree of life."

A question flooded into the Gaon's mind, sparking anxiety. "Will our enemies have the ability to decipher the warning . . . perhaps avoid the power of the box?"

Bayard stretched out his arms and held the box closer to the Gaon. "The weapons that we fight with are not mortal. And not everything that is immortal is visible to the enemy. Take this box and place the second prophecy inside it. Leave it here. Each has an appointed time. We will protect you and the first prophecy. The box of power will protect the second. And the plans of God will not be denied."

It was well after midnight, and the Gaon's frail body was aching for rest. He was startled out of his slumber when Rabbi Rosenberg returned to the main room with the tools he had retrieved from the shed adjacent to his home.

"Oh, you were asleep?" said Rosenberg. "Forgive me, it took me much longer than I expected to find the tools."

Rosenberg looked at the Gaon's hands, resting in his lap. "That is a fine metal box," he said. "Did you bring it with you?"

The Gaon's gaze moved from Rosenberg, past the fire in the hearth, to the bronze box in his hands. "It was a gift," said the Gaon. "Do you have a hammer and an awl in your tool box?"

Rosenberg took a small hammer and an awl and laid them on the table next to the Gaon's chair. Selecting a maul and chisel, he started digging into the mortar around the stones in the bottom left corner of his hearth.

Reciting incantations cherished by Jewish kabbalah mystics for centuries, the Gaon opened the bronze box, rubbed his fingers over the underside of the lid and gently began working the metal with the awl and hammer. He hammered five cryptic symbols into its lid. Working in from the bottom side of the lid, the symbols projected from the top in three dimensions. One symbol, in the center of the lid, looked like a three-dimensional Star of David.

His work completed, the Gaon took the parchment given to Rosenberg, wrapped it in linen and leather, placed it inside the box, and sealed it with wax on all four sides, the Gaon's seal pressed into the wax. Rosenberg had removed three large stones from low on the left corner of the hearth. The Gaon leaned on Rosenberg's arm as he lifted his aching body from the chair and moved to the corner of the hearth. Both of them reciting the Aaronic blessing, the Gaon took the box, turned it on its edge, and squeezed it into the opening. Rabbi Rosenberg replaced the stones and then mixed some mortar with dirt and pressed it into the openings between the stones. A casual observer would never notice the difference.

As the sun rose the next morning, the Gaon of Vilna and his party mounted their mules and set off for Lithuania. Twisting awkwardly in his saddle, the Gaon cast a glance back to Rosenberg who stood silently in the doorway to his house. He breathed a sigh of relief. Now only one remained his responsibility. But the box, and the prophecy, would never be far from the mind of the rabbis of Konigsberg.

Konigsberg, Germany
November 8, 1938

Relentless, like a dagger carved from a glacier, the wind made a mockery of Dr. Hugo Falkenheim's thin wool coat. It was a fashionable coat, well befitting the owner of the Konigsberg Pediatric Clinic, but poorly suited to the bitter blasts that ricocheted off the buildings on Synagogenstrasse. Holding down his hat,

Falkenheim bruised his knuckles knocking feverishly on the heavy wooden door of the stone building adjacent to the Old Synagogue.

Driven more by urgency than the bone-rattling wind, Dr. Falkenheim pushed through the door, and its attendant, as soon as it opened a crack. "Forgive me, I must see the rabbi immediately." Chairman of the Jewish Congregation of Konigsberg for the last ten years, Hugo Falkenheim often visited with Rabbi Lewin. Seldom had he arrived uninvited—never demanding an audience. But today was different.

Rapping once on the door to the rabbi's office, Falkenheim burst in without waiting for a response, taking off his hat and shoving the door closed in his wake as a warning erupted from his lips.

"They are coming, Reinhold—tonight or tomorrow," said Falkenheim, gasping for breath. "They are coming and they will burn the synagogues, all of them. We must get the box to safety. We may have waited too long, but it can't remain in Prussia any longer."

Reinhold Lewin, chief rabbi of the city's Old Synagogue, turned in his chair to face Falkenheim, a look of doubt replaced by resignation. "Yours has always been a voice of reason, Hugo." The rabbi got up and walked to the small window that faced the street. "You believe," he said, turning back to the room, "the Nazis would do such a thing? Burn all the synagogues? It sounds barbaric—and insane."

He had been loath to believe the report himself. But Falkenheim knew its source was impeccable. His bald head steaming in the warm room, he stepped alongside the rabbi and gripped his arm. "It is barbaric and it is insane, Reinhold. That is true. But it is also true that Hitler is fomenting a hatred of Jews that will only end in a pogrom, or worse. The Brown Shirts are coming. I know this for a fact. And they will destroy and burn not just the synagogues, but everything that is Jewish in Konigsberg."

Falkenheim locked his eyes on the rabbi's. "But not only Konigsberg, Reinhold. This atrocity will occur across all the land that is under the swastika's shadow, all on the same night. We Jews are no longer safe here. And neither is that document. We must get it to safety."

The rabbi bit his lip. He looked unconvinced. "And what do you propose?"

"I leave within the hour," said Falkenheim, hoping his words would persuade the rabbi to action. "I will drive to Warsaw and then take the train to

Istanbul. I have friends there. It is a strong, safe, and stable Jewish community. I know a place where the Gaon's message will be secure until . . ."

"Until the day it is needed. Yes, I know." Rabbi Lewin stepped away from the window, and away from Falkenheim, pacing across the small room he used as an office. "Five generations have closely held the Gaon's secret. Five generations, father to son, entrusted with its safety here in Konigsberg. Since I have no son, the responsibility became yours and mine. But . . . perhaps this Hitler is the man of violence that legend tells us is in the prophecy." He turned to face Falkenheim. "How are we to know?"

"Because the Gaon's first prophecy is yet to be fulfilled," said Falkenheim, his voice low but urgency in his words. "This is not the time for the prophecy to be revealed. But it is time for us to act, to protect the Gaon's message."

Lewin stepped toward Falkenheim and placed his hands on both shoulders. *"May Adonai bless you and keep you; may Adonai make his face to shine on you and show you his favor; may Adonai lift up his face toward you and give you peace."*

Twenty minutes later, Falkenheim stood at the door to Rabbi Lewin's office, a calfskin bag in his left hand.

"Thank you, Reinhold. Thank you for your courage."

Rabbi Lewin shrugged his shoulders, his hands held palms up. "Eh, I should be the one thanking you," he said. "For being a man of wisdom . . . and action. Be careful, my friend."

Falkenheim rested his right hand on the rabbi's arm. "I'll be back, my rabbi. We must convince our people to escape this place, before it is too late for all of us."

Lewin nodded his head then lowered his chin. "Hear O Israel . . ."

1

Fairfax, Virginia
April 21, 2014, 4:13 p.m.

Joy flooded Brian Mullaney's soul. Released for a moment from the bondage of his memories and regrets, he basked in joy's glorious freedom. So sweet. So rare.

"Are you here?"

Mullaney opened his eyes and glanced to his right where his brother, Doak, sat in one of the folding canvas chairs that are the ubiquitous havens for moms and dads at youth sports events across the country.

His hat pulled down and his jacket collar up around his ears, Doak Mullaney nodded his head toward the soccer field just below them. "I thought you liked this game."

Brian turned his attention back to the soccer field where his girls were competing for their school, a smile curling the corners of his mouth and warming the outer reaches of his heart. "No . . . I love this game."

"So stop snoozing. You might miss Kylie score a goal."

"Not snoozing, little brother. Just happy."

"Well, that's about time."

Keeping his eyes on the tangle of ponytails racing up and down the soccer field, Mullaney reached out and touched his brother's arm. "I know . . . I'll take it."

The pine trees behind them captured some of the wind blowing through Lawrence Park. At six foot two and 225 pounds, Mullaney had the build of a football player. He wrapped his arms across his chest, pulling his wool coat closer, as much to keep the warmth in his heart as it was to keep the cold from his bones.

"I remember when they first started to play," said Mullaney, "running around in a pack, all of them trying to kick the ball at the same time. The very serious looks on their faces as they tried to remember what their coaches told them. Then to see the growth, the maturing of their skills. The best part . . ." Mullaney inclined his head and shot a quick glance at his brother before returning his attention to the game. "The best part is watching them run—free and wild, abandoned to the speed and the thrill of the game. I sit here and watch them, and all the cares of the world lift off my shoulders. I'm free with them . . . uninhibited, running with them . . . the joy of being so full of life and oblivious to what's out there beyond the park. It's glorious."

"Sounds like a religious experience," said Doak.

"You're almost right. You know—Yes! Great shot!" Mullaney was up out of his chair, his arms and fists raised above his head, so much a Rocky pose. "Way to go, Kylie!" he shouted across the field. "Way to go!"

"She hates that, you know."

"All kids hate that, Doak," said Mullaney, easing back into the chair. "And all kids love it and would wither away if they didn't get it. It's affirmation. We all need affirmation, right?"

"Well, I never—"

"Look at them, will you." Mullaney pointed to the joyous scrum at the end of the field, hugging and jumping together, smiles as broad as the Potomac. "They love being part of a team. There is something about women and girls on a team that men just don't share. Did you ever watch the women volleyball players in the Olympics?"

"Yeah, they—"

"They congratulate each other after every point—whether they won or lost the point. Get together for a group hug and encouragement. I think it's because they just love playing a game together. Sure, they want to win. Kylie and Samantha are fierce competitors, both desperate to make the playoffs. But they are also fierce teammates. And they love their team. I only felt that once. I helped coach a Little League Baseball team when I was in college . . . you remember, Phelps Insurance. Our kids were terrible the first year—really bad. Then they became competitive the second year. But the third year . . . all the kids still together on the same team . . . the third year we went undefeated."

The score of the soccer game was still only 1–0 for Lawrence School, but the opposing Draper Park Falcons had an awesome front line, so Mullaney never took his eyes off his girls in the Lawrence green and white, wishing them on to another goal.

"Undefeated. That is hard to do in any sport, at any level," he said. "You've got to be really good, and you've got to be lucky too. I'll never forget those last few games. They were so intense and emotional. The head coach lost it one day and threw a baseball soaring over the opposing stands. Got ejected. Nearly got kicked out of the league. The kids were stunned . . . shocked. Then they laughed. They were having too much fun to let anything get in their way. Those kids loved each other for what they accomplished."

Mullaney pointed toward the soccer field. "But that was nothing compared to what these girls experience. For them, team is life. It's all about relationships. In a lot of ways, the game is only the vehicle to the relationships."

"Until you get one game from the playoffs."

"Okay . . . okay, that's true. They love the game and they are driven to win. But it's all based on their relationship together. I just love watching them. And at some level, I envy them for something I didn't have—we didn't have. Not with Dad. Not with other guys outside the service. That emotional commitment, that heartfelt camaraderie." The words tumbled out of Mullaney without conscious thought. "Guys don't go that deep. It's the task, the game, the score. It's not so much about the other people. That's why I'm so grateful, so fortunate, to have Abby. She's the only one . . ." As the significance of what he was saying fell from his lips to his heart, Mullaney's thoughts left the field and looked inward. His last words were whispered, as if directed to himself. "And I'd be lost without her."

The first half came to an end, and the girls huddled with their coaches on either side of the field.

Mullaney held up a thermos toward Doak. "Coffee?"

"No thanks." Mullaney's brother held his gaze. "You mentioned Dad. How are you with that?"

Brian Mullaney focused on the thermos. Nothing was going to ruin this day. The coffee was still hot, and the cup warmed his hand as he filled it. *Stay in the moment.* But that was so difficult when the past hit you with the bite of April wind.

"Which part—the part that he just died a week ago, or the part that he got lost in his mind for the last ten years, or the part where he never forgave me for leaving the force?"

"Yeah, that part," said Doak.

Mullaney sipped his coffee, looking at the empty field and feeling as empty inside. *Yeah, that part.* John Mullaney, 1946–2014, Captain, Virginia State Police (Ret.). Left this earth in 2004 and never came back. Betrayed by his eldest son in 1995. Held onto his bitterness like it was a life preserver. And that's probably what ended up killing him. Unforgiveness. And it was Mullaney's fault. *Yeah, that part.*

"You know, Doak . . . sometimes you just need to grab hold of your own life and come to a decision about where you're headed. Abby and I prayed long and hard to know God's will about that choice. It wasn't easy to go against tradition, go against Dad's wishes. But we were certain it was God's plan for me to join the State Department. It's a shame Dad could never understand or accept that decision."

The girls were running back on the field for the second half when Mullaney turned to his brother. "You know, it's ironic. Or too sad to comprehend. You remember Dad's favorite phrase when he was miffed?"

"'Don't be useless! Get up and do something!'" said Doak. "Yeah, how could either of us ever forget?"

Mullaney watched as the game progressed and his Lawrence School Crusaders increased their lead. But the joy was gone.

"Sad that he ended up the way he did, curled up in a fetal ball on a nursing home bed. I remember whispering in his ear that last day. 'God loves you, Dad. And so do I.' But he wasn't there. He hadn't been *there* for ten years. It would have killed him to know how it ended for him. Probably better . . ."

"Yeah, probably better," said Doak. "Listen, I've got to report in. This one looks like it's in the bag. Give Abby and the girls a hug for me and tell them I'll do everything I can to be at the playoff game." He stood up, stretching in his gray-and-black Virginia State Police uniform.

Mullaney felt a stab of remorse. "That bar looks good on you, Lieutenant."

"Thanks," said Doak. "Now if they would only get rid of these Smokey the Bear hats, I'd be fine." He laid his hand on his brother's shoulder. "Be careful out there, Brian."

Mullaney added his hand over his brother's. "Be careful out there, Doak."

Mullaney watched his brother walk up the hill toward his squad car. And he missed the Crusader's last goal.

Washington, DC
April 23, 6:06 p.m.

Down the hall was his regular office. But it was empty tonight. Diplomatic Security Service agent Brian Mullaney was on a different assignment, picking up a shift in the operations center because he lost a bet. Georgetown going down to defeat in the first round of the Big East basketball tournament would do that.

In the home stretch of his forty-fourth year, Mullaney was naturally calm in demeanor, fluid and graceful in his movement, with ever watchful, knowing eyes. Doing this job he often felt older than his years. The laugh lines at the corners of his eyes told one story, but the wisps of gray at the temples of his thick, black hair gave a more accurate statement. Walking into ops, he knew he was early. His shift as diplomatic security watch liaison officer didn't officially start until six thirty. But it had been awhile since he was on duty in ops. Mullaney wanted to make sure he was up to speed.

The US State Department operations center—ops to everyone in the business—was a monitoring and information hub that essentially kept track of everything important that was happening in the world twenty-four seven. On the seventh floor of the Harry S. Truman building on C Street in the District of Columbia, ops was just down the hall—and past several armed guards—from the secretary of state's suite and the offices occupied by State's upper echelons of leadership. That is where Brian Mullaney belonged.

A nineteen-year veteran of the Diplomatic Security Service, Mullaney was adjutant to George Morningstar, the deputy assistant secretary for diplomatic security. Morningstar was a bigwig, two steps removed from the secretary of state himself, but a regular guy. Mullaney was blessed by the trust he and Morningstar shared. But tonight the lights in his office were dark, and Mullaney found himself in the middle of one of the most critical links in the chain of his nation's security.

In many ways, DSS fulfilled a similar mission to that of the US Secret Service—protecting American ambassadors and consular staff overseas, in nations around the world. But DSS also set up task forces to provide security for things like the opening sessions of the UN General Assembly each fall in New York City, or for the Olympics and World Cup every four years. It also supervised security for the foreign diplomatic corps when those officials were on US soil. Lately, DSS had been deeply involved with international law-enforcement activities, hunting human traffickers and drug lords.

But it was overseas where DSS made its bones, protecting the thirteen thousand men and women of the US Foreign Service on assignment in other countries. Overseas was also where DSS agents were most at risk.

And ops was at the center of that mission. Teams of sixty-five—including forty-five watch officers—rotated on eight-hour shifts to effectively manage the two hundred and forty-four telephone lines that handled three hundred forty thousand annual calls to ops. Live video feeds from nearly every US embassy and consular station in the world fed into a wall of television monitors, and ops staff members were required to maintain active, open lines of communication not only with the secretary of state, but also with nearly every level of the executive branch of government.

Mullaney wasn't responsible for directing the activity of this sixty-five-person cohort. His job was to make split-second decisions in cases where American lives or property were at risk, to get those decisions right, and to communicate those decisions immediately and accurately to State's top-echelon leadership.

Mullaney walked along the back of ops, past the gray cubicles with signs hanging from the ceiling announcing each person's title, toward the watch commander's desk. The further Mullaney stepped into ops, the sharper his focus became, and the more precise his thoughts. Just in case. Over the last fifty years, six United States ambassadors on foreign duty had been murdered by armed attackers. Every year over a dozen American overseas installations were attacked in one way or another. Crises didn't happen every day . . . but sometimes it felt that way.

"I've got a report of an explosion at the compound in Ankara!" came a shout from one of the gray cubicles that spread out over the main floor of ops.

Mullaney bolted upright. Voices, adrenaline, and action all accelerated.

To his left, Senior Watch Officer Gwen DeBerry pointed to her deputy. "Locate the secretary, but hold off on the call for a moment." She turned to the ops floor. "Pull it up on the monitors," she called to the watch officer controlling the video feed. Mullaney scanned the wall as a number of screens faded and then refocused with views of the US consulate in Ankara, Turkey, from several different angles.

The main gate of the embassy was a tangle of concrete chunks and twisted steel. Hooded men in the street were firing what looked like rocket-propelled grenades and automatic weapons at the embassy's defenders. Bodies lay on the ground on both sides of the gate.

"Make the call," DeBerry said over her shoulder. "Heavily armed attackers at the main gate in Ankara. More to come."

Mullaney was at DeBerry's side in two strides. "Who's that on our side—marines or Turks?"

DeBerry shook her head and broke away from the feed to face Mullaney. "Turkish contracted agents, I believe. I haven't seen any marines yet. Probably getting the embassy staff to safety. But my biggest concern"—she looked up as another blast assaulted the embassy gate—"is that we don't know where the ambassador is. He had a meeting scheduled in the city this morning. We were not yet alerted about what time he planned to leave. So he may be on the streets or in-house. We don't know yet. And Tommy is there too."

Mullaney turned his attention back to DeBerry at the mention of his best friend's name. Tommy Hernandez and Mullaney went through DSS training at Quantico together and remained close even as their placements took them to far-flung outposts worldwide.

"I've got the incident process checklist started," said DeBerry.

No time . . . stay focused . . .

"Can you check to ensure the comm protocol is instituted?"

"Sure . . ." Mullaney looked at the screens and the firefight lighting up the dimness of early dawn at the embassy's main gate. "I'll be right back."

With half a dozen long strides, Mullaney entered the soundproof communications room at the rear of ops where the voice, video, and data recorders were kept and monitored twenty-four seven. Stuffing his anxiety for the moment, Mullaney raced through the communications protocol with the watch officer on duty. "Okay, looks good." He turned to give the watch officer a thumbs-up, but the agent was on a secure phone that he now shoved in Mullaney's direction.

"It's the ambassador."

In a heartbeat Mullaney was across the floor. "Mr. Ambassador? Brian Mullaney. DSS . . . Are you safe, sir?"

US Embassy, Ankara, Turkey
April 24, 6:17 a.m.

"We're good at the moment, Mullaney," said Joseph Atticus Cleveland, US ambassador to Turkey. Cleveland swept a quick glance around the underground bunker filled with frightened embassy staff and edgy, armed marines. "All the embassy staff members are secured in safe havens with marines on guard. Sounds like a terrible fight going on out there. Who's winning?"

"Hard to say at this moment, sir, but the bad guys have yet to gain entry to the compound. Things are pretty brutal around the main gate right now. We've got local reinforcements on the way."

"Mullaney? You're George Morningstar's adjutant, right? Hold a moment . . ."

Cleveland inclined his ear toward the chief of his DSS security detail. Underground and as secure as they were, the reverberating sounds of explosions still shattered the silence in the bunker. "Okay . . . Listen, Mullaney, I'm informed you are a man we can rely on."

"Thank you, sir."

"So Tommy wants you to know that you still owe him twenty bucks on the Final Four."

Ops Center, Washington, DC
April 23, 11:18 p.m.

Mullaney laughed to himself. The scuttlebutt on Ambassador Cleveland was simple; he was a solid, stand-up guy who was very rarely shaken. "Yes, sir. Tell Tommy to keep his mind on your game. The money will be waiting when he gets home."

There was some muted conversation on the other end of the line. "Okay," Mullaney could barely hear Cleveland's voice. "Give me some space for a moment . . . Mullaney, you there?"

"Yes, sir."

"Where's the secretary?"

"Geneva, sir. Deputy Secretary Roberts is in California, but Deputy Secretary Webster is on his way."

"Okay, but somebody needs to hear this . . . just in case," said Cleveland. "Our plans changed here this morning. Original plan was to head into the city to meet with the Turkish president. That got switched in the early hours of this morning. President Kashani was coming here."

"Sir?"

"An agent was looking out the window when this started. As the president's motorcade was pulling through the main gate, a vehicle drove up from the opposite direction and detonated just outside the gate, followed closely by a van that unloaded a whole swarm of heavily armed guys. This was a coordinated assault on the main gate of a US embassy facility. Somebody knew about the change in plans, Mullaney. Somebody knew Kashani was coming here. Get me?"

Mullaney glanced over at the communications watch officer, who turned away from the other phone with a puzzled look on his face. "Yes, sir," said Mullaney. We've got it. And it's on the recorder. What's happened to Kashani?"

"I'm not sure," said Cleveland. "Before we were hastily escorted into the safe rooms, one of the staff took a quick look out the window. There are some charred and mangled vehicles by the gate, some of the motorcade still in the street. Hard to tell who belongs to what, but the attackers are firing into the embassy grounds."

"Sounds like Kashani probably made it into the compound," said Mullaney.

"I don't know," said Cleveland. "Now, look . . . it's getting a little warm in here, and we certainly would like to get some breakfast. But get some people out here quickly and help those guys outside. It doesn't sound too good for them from where we're sitting."

"Our guys are on the way, Mr. Ambassador. Sit tight."

"Oh, we're not going anywhere, Mullaney. Not just yet. Okay," said Cleveland, "we'll keep the line open . . . as long as we can. Thanks, Mullaney. Good man."

US Embassy, Ankara
April 24, 6:20 a.m.

"Roger that."

Tommy Hernandez, DSS chief of security for the ambassador and the embassy, turned away from his shoulder mic toward Cleveland. "Three of the guards are down."

"How many attackers?"

Hernandez shook his head. "Don't know, sir. But the captain is taking half of the marine detachment to add firepower at the front gate. The rest are staying to guard . . ."

An explosion rocked the compound, bigger than the one that started the attack.

"That is not good." Hernandez got up off the bunk where the ambassador was sitting, pulled his Heckler & Koch MP5 submachine gun close to the body armor on his chest, and joined the marine sergeant flanking the door. He looked at the frightened faces in the hardened room. "Find something to get behind, to protect yourselves."

Their safe haven wasn't soundproof. Ambassador Cleveland and his staff could hear the incessant rattle of automatic weapons and the occasional explosion. So once again he walked around the small room, touching a shoulder here, whispering comfort there. Cleveland didn't know what was going on outside, but he knew how to be a leader that others willingly followed.

Without warning, the gunfire stopped. It was as gut-wrenching a moment as when the first explosion detonated and their orderly world unraveled.

Cleveland turned toward the door. "Tommy?"

Hernandez had his head cocked to one side, over the mic on his shoulder, as if that would make it easier to hear the voice on the other end. "Roger that. We'll wait for you." He stood up straight. "Five attackers . . . all dead. None of them penetrated the embassy's perimeter. President Kashani's motorcade was halfway through the gate when the first explosion hit. Kashani's vehicle made it inside. He's okay. But we're not going anywhere yet. Some Turkish military just showed up. A bunch of them are escorting Kashani back to his palace at warp speed. The marines are going to sweep the compound, and the remaining

Turkish military are going to secure the streets and make sure there aren't any more surprises out there."

Cleveland's chin dropped to his chest. "Thank you, Lord." When he looked up, several heads were nodding in agreement. "Tommy . . . what about our guards?"

Hernandez flexed his chin and shook his head. When he spoke, it was a whisper that carried thunder. "Three of our guards are dead. Two more are badly wounded. "Four of Kashani's security detail were killed in the first explosion. The marines are okay. The captain will give us the all clear when they know it's safe." He looked at the ambassador. "Looks like we dodged a bullet today, Mr. Ambassador. God is good."

Ops Center, Washington, DC
April 24, 12:57 a.m.

Noah Webster, deputy secretary of state for management and resources, was realistic and sensitive about two things ever since he went to high school—his height and the color of his skin. The needling he took about being short was blatant harassment, defeated somewhat when a growth spurt pushed him to five nine during his senior year. But the prejudice and discrimination he endured as a black man was more subtle, though no less real. Webster never outgrew his resentment of the constant discrimination against a black man in a white man's world.

But Webster fed on that resentment. He converted his anger into a catalyst that drove him not only to excel in the classroom and on the athletic field, but to prove himself better than—superior to—all the white kids who had looked down at him and treated him as if he were someone . . . less.

Webster may have been slight in stature, but he was tall enough to project command and require obedience. Since the Diplomatic Security Service and the State Department's operations center were directly under his authority, Webster stood in a small office in the rear corner of ops, surrounded by a cohort of his key staff. The postmortem of the Ankara attack was well underway. A new watch team was on duty in ops, the earlier crew split into several segments as the debrief was rigorously pursued in rooms throughout the Truman building.

Watch Liaison Officer Brian Mullaney leaned against a desk in a corner of the room, alongside his boss, George Morningstar, deputy assistant secretary for diplomatic security.

"Paul, please get Secretary Townsend on a line in my office," said Webster, referring to Secretary of State Evan Townsend. "I'll be there in moment." Nodding to his executive assistant, Webster turned back to his waiting staff. "I want a draft press release on my desk in five minutes. Ryan, alert the press corps we'll have a press conference"—he looked at his watch—"at fourteen hundred hours. Lydia, get CIA on a line and find out if they had *any* hints of a threat in Ankara. And Paul, wait, see if you can reach Ambassador Cleveland and get an update on him and the staff."

"Mr. Secretary," Morningstar interrupted, "as of eleven forty our time, the ambassador was safe and secure and so were all the embassy staff. They were all in safe havens with armed security during the attack. Mullaney talked to Ambassador Cleveland in the middle of the action and he was fine. But there is something . . ."

Webster was always disciplined and calculating, a survivor in the jungle that was Washington. Every move, every word, had a purpose and a message. He turned slowly to his right and faced Morningstar, cutting short his sentence. Webster's words were silken and spiked. "*Mullaney* spoke to the ambassador?"

It never failed to give Noah Webster a thrill when he could wield power. A delicious iciness embraced his heart, bringing the hint of a smirk to the corners of his lips as he allowed Morningstar to dangle on the implication of his question.

"Yes, sir."

Morningstar did not appear flummoxed. *Hmmm . . . unfortunate. I'll have to try harder next time.*

"Mullaney was on duty as watch liaison officer when the call came in. During the conversation, Ambassador Cleveland expressed his concern that the attackers may have received some inside information about President Kashani's change of plans. Cleveland was scheduled to meet Kashani at the palace this morning, but that changed at the last minute. It appears the attackers knew that Kashani and the ambassador were at the embassy and not at the palace."

"And the ambassador relayed these concerns to Agent Mullaney?"

"Yes, Mr. Secretary."

Within his chest, a lance of dread pierced Webster's heart. For a fraction of a second, doubt coated his confidence. Was he in danger? He was deep into a clandestine, unsanctioned, high-stakes play with the prime minister of Turkey, a scheme he was certain was in the best interests of the United States. But a scheme he was also certain must remain a secret.

"All right. We'll deal with that. But for the moment, I want our best available medical team flown into Ankara immediately. Find one of our people on the ground there who isn't too shaken up, and make contact with the families of the dead and injured. Lydia, prepare a crisis management team to deal with the embassy staff—get them all the help they need. And now let's get ready for that press conference."

Webster started walking toward the door, but looked back over his shoulder. "And Morningstar," Webster said, the smile of a snake on his face, "would you and Mullaney please step into my office for a moment, as soon as I complete my call with the secretary?"

2

Fairfax
April 24, 4:13 a.m.

He could see the flickering blue light of the television set reflecting through the drapes over the front window before he got to the front door of his house. Brian Mullaney didn't know what he longed for more, Abby's company or solitude. But he wasn't going to have a choice.

Abigail was at the door as soon as he started turning his key in the lock.

"Oh, my God, Brian, when will these attacks stop?"

Before her words ended, her arms were around his shoulders, pulling him against her. The smell of strawberry that always flowed from her hair filled his nostrils as—

Abby pulled back to arm's length as if she had just violated some unspoken rule.

"Are you okay?" Her question was more probing and cautious than a genuine concern for his well-being. There was no welcome to the tone of her voice.

Years ago, she would have held him close and pressed her softness against him, her warmth finding the numbness of his heart. But those days seemed so far away.

They were casually introduced at an unremarkable Washington soiree in a Georgetown trophy house. But the connection was immediate—sensually electric as they consumed each other with their eyes, and spiritually satisfying as they quickly discovered the faith at the root of their peace.

She actually liked and understood the game of baseball. And he had already developed a genuine fondness for the melodies of Puccini's operas. When she found a well-worn CD of *La Bohème* resting alongside his stereo equipment, Abby felt her heart skip.

There soon followed weekends where a day game watching the Baltimore Orioles at Camden Yards would be followed by an hour's drive south on I-95 for an evening of opera at the Kennedy Center for the Performing Arts followed by a midnight run for the best barbecue in DC. Bliss was not a strong enough description.

The darker side of Brian's Irish personality, the insecure part that wanted to hide its feelings from public view, found refuge, respite, and resurrection in the spontaneous eruptions of joy that poured out of Abby like a newly discovered sun. Her smile warmed places in his heart he didn't even know existed. She loved so *fully* that he was entranced, spellbound.

And she found in Brian strength of character that was not dependent on wealth or position but which was spawned by faith, duty, and honor. Abby relished the peace and comfort she drew from Brian's physical power and the singular, unshakable focus of his loyalty.

He loved the way she looked in a summer dress, that tingle of warmth that rippled along his flesh and brought a smile to his lips as his heart drank in her ravishing beauty. When with a flip of her curly auburn hair, she would turn to him and bless him with a look that said *I belong to you, and it makes me so happy.*

She loved the safety of his arms around her, the strength rippling beneath his shirt. And she loved to push her fingers into the thicket of hair at the back of his head and pull his lips to hers.

When they weren't in the stands at Oriole Park at Camden Yards, or in the seats listening to the Washington National Opera, they loved to curl up on Brian's sofa—his back to the sofa and his arms encircling her shoulders—whispering their dreams of the future.

Their courtship was relaxed, ebbing and swelling with the languid contentment of a summer stream, prodded in one direction or another by the demands of their budding careers . . . hers in the corporate offices of privilege, his in the sterile halls of national service. And they both loved the work they were created to do.

But her devotion to PR—polishing the public personas of DC's power brokers, the people in the same orbit as her wealthy father—disintegrated under the weight of her loneliness when Brian was assigned overseas. Their relationship got serious, and more passionate, when he returned from Yemen. The altar followed in close order.

The only daughter of Richard Rutherford, an obscenely rich Southern financier, Abigail joyously transferred her loyalty and commitment from her power-banker father and the swirl of Washington society to her new, globe-trotting husband and walks along the Potomac. They counted each child and each assignment that came their way as a new adventure to be savored.

For the first ten years of their marriage, they were a great team. Then Mullaney was rotated back to Washington for a two-year tour on home soil. Daddy was overjoyed to have his Abby back home. And Abigail found herself overwhelmed by the seemingly endless parties, crowded cruises on Daddy's yacht, and serving as Daddy's "date" at DC's mega social events for the proud and powerful.

This world, the world she was raised in and raised to inherit, was intoxicating and, over the past six years, Mullaney watched as that world began to seize territory. There was no one moment of decision, no conscious abandonment of one life for another. But power is pervasive and persistent. And intoxicating. With Abigail's renewed appetite for the kind of life she'd left behind, its perks and power, Mullaney and his children saw less and less of her. Cracks showed; loyalties were no longer common; disappointment replaced devotion and mutated into criticism.

His last two tours overseas were a family and relationship disaster. His marriage was surviving on fumes. He didn't know what to do to rescue it. But he was honest enough to admit that he contributed as much to the problems they faced. This distance between them was not entirely Abby's fault. It was Mullaney who worked a demanding and unpredictable schedule, who was often out of town and away from home, chasing the power of a career he had chosen. It was Mullaney who, like any law-enforcement officer, faced the possibility that a life-or-death moment could confront him at any time. And Abigail who waited for the call or the knock on their front door. The glue that held these opposing orbits in place had simply dried up.

Abby had dutifully served during Brian's many years of shuffling around the globe, eleven times picking up hearth and home—and children—to his next assignment. But always with the clearly articulated expectation, to which he agreed, that one day, sooner rather than later, Brian would receive and accept a permanent assignment in Washington. And there they would stay—benefiting from "Daddy's influence"—as Brian advanced his career and Abigail gained sway in the intoxicating world of society among the most powerful people on earth. It was a role Abby was born into and one in which she expected to live the rest of her days.

With a desperate longing to return to her embrace, Mullaney looked into Abby's worried eyes. "Am I okay? Honestly, I don't know. Three of our guards dead. Two others badly wounded—we're not sure if they'll make it. And four of Kashani's security detail were killed in the explosion."

"I know," she said. Abigail led him into the house and closed the door to a neighborhood where only some homes were dark. "I've been watching CNN for hours, ever since I got your first call. What a tragedy."

"What a screwup, you mean." Mullaney's thoughts and emotions were thrashing about like a lava cone about to explode as he followed Abigail to the sofa. She grabbed the remote to turn off the TV. Mullaney laid his hand over hers. "Leave it on, okay? Just in case."

Sitting on the sofa, Abby by his side, exhaustion settled into Mullaney's bones. He laid his head back and closed his eyes. "George warned them until his voice, and his capital, were exhausted. Ever since that suicide bomber in February, he felt we needed to tighten security. And not just in Ankara."

Mullaney could feel Abigail's eyes on his face.

"Was there anyone we know in Ankara?"

He turned to face his wife, and once again was bewitched by the depths of her eyes, azure like the color of the sky on a clear morning. "Tommy was there. He's right hand to Ambassador Cleveland. They're both okay. I don't think we know anyone else."

Abby searched his face. "There's something else. What is it?"

This is where it always got tricky. As a sworn officer of the federal government, Mullaney had clear orders about with whom, what, and how he could share information. Most spouses probably knew more than they should—that was just human nature. But Mullaney was determined and confident. He would never tell Abby anything that would be dangerous or illegal for her to know, and he would never burden her with information that was in the gray area—information that someone like her politically rapacious father would love to get his hands on.

"It appears there's been a breach in security," said Mullaney, measuring each word. "Cleveland's plans changed at the last moment. Kashani decided to come to our embassy instead of Cleveland going to the palace. It appears the attackers knew where to find them anyway."

Abigail's eyes widened. "But . . . but that would mean . . ."

Mullaney sat up, rested his elbows on his knees, and held his head in his hands, running his fingers through his thick, black hair over and over. "Yeah

. . . there's been a breach in security somewhere, either here or in Turkey. We don't know enough yet. The attackers could have been after Kashani, could have been after Cleveland. The attackers could have been ISIS—Kashani's been threatening to bring Turkey into the fight against ISIS in Syria. There's a lot we don't know yet. But there's a strong possibility that somebody's been flipped—and pretty high up. Webster, however, went through the roof for a different reason. He called Morningstar and me into his office after the debrief and ripped us up one side of the room and down the other. Said this assault came very close to penetrating into the embassy compound itself. Told George he had failed to maintain a properly trained and effective force . . . that *his* officers should have seen the car bomber coming and stopped him before he got to the gate. He called it 'an abysmal failure of security.' It was brutal. And I think Webster loved every minute of it."

Another ripple of tension seeped into the room. Mullaney could feel his wife stiffen.

"Brian," her voice a whisper, "what's going to happen now? We both know . . ." Her voice trailed off. Mullaney could read her mind.

He nodded his head without opening his eyes. "Right. We both know Washington. Somebody is going to take a huge hit for this, but it won't be Webster. Probably more than one somebody. Careers are going to crash and burn . . . some right away. Others maybe after committees and investigations release their reports. That could be a year or more. But heads are going to roll. It's going to be ugly."

Mullaney didn't move or open his eyes, even when the secretary of state came on TV at the start of a press conference from Geneva. He pushed the Mute button on the remote. He was more concerned with Abby's unspoken fears than what the secretary was about to hand-feed the press. He knew what his wife wanted to hear. His heart ached that he couldn't say the words she desperately craved.

"I don't know." Mullaney opened his eyes and turned to his right to get Abigail into his gaze. "I'm sorry, but I don't know if we're going to be okay. I wish I could promise you that we're safe—that my position is safe. But right now, I can't promise anything."

Abby pulled herself farther away from him.

"Oh, Brian . . . no, please." Abby's eyes desperately searched his face. "We can't move the girls again, not at this age. We've only been here two years. You told me . . . you promised . . . that we were done moving. That you had put in your time and we were here to stay."

Mullaney understood the events of the last twelve hours threatened to eradicate the last vestiges of Abby's patience and his family's security. He was in the wrong place at the wrong time working for the wrong guy. Morningstar already bore the crosshairs of a scapegoat on his back. Secretary Townsend was not going to take this hit; neither was Webster or those in his closest circle. But somebody had to take the fall. Somebody needed to be responsible. And Morningstar was the likely candidate. Mullaney's career was on life support and out of his control. It was a subject he was much too tired to discuss now.

"I've got to get some sleep. I don't have much time."

"Okay," Abby yawned, stretched her neck and looked at Brian. "But you remember I have the luncheon for Senator Markham's wife this afternoon, right?"

Abigail was looking for his agreement. "Okay," he said, understanding beginning to break through the gathering fog in his sleep-deprived brain.

"And today is the girl's playoff game. You promised to pick them up. And I'll try to meet you at the field—if at all possible. Right?"

If Mullaney's heart could fall any farther today it would have landed at his feet. *Not today.* "Abby, I'm sorry. I don't know if . . ."

Abigail Rutherford Mullaney was as Southern as pecan pie and as sweet as a Georgia peach. Most of the time. But not if she felt betrayed—in thought, mind, or deed. Then her honeysuckle charm turned to poison darts directed with a lethal accuracy. And Mullaney knew he was on the edge of becoming a target.

"Oh, no. No, no, no."

Abigail jolted to her feet, hands on her hips and fire in her eyes. She was just about to let fly . . .

"It's four in the morning. The girls are asleep."

Her eyes narrowed. She dipped her chin and tried to pierce his brain with a withering look of warning. Without diverting her eyes, Abigail settled at his side on the sofa, her face so close he could feel the heat of her breath on his right ear. "All right, I'll keep this low, but let me make it clear."

Mullaney steeled his spine for what he expected and ratcheted up his patience.

"I've been working on this luncheon for six months. It took me a year to get on her calendar. Seventy of the most important and powerful women in Washington will arrive at the George Town Club in"—she looked across the room at the clock on the wall—"eight hours. You will not mess this up, Brian Mullaney, and neither will the State Department. I don't care how many terrorist attacks there are. If you don't want to experience a terrorist attack in this room, this very minute, you will pick up your daughters at three this afternoon and get them to Lighthouse Field in time for the three-thirty game time."

Not too bad. Could have been worse.

Abigail stood up with a pert crispness and shook her auburn hair.

"I'm going to bed," she said, looking at Brian. "I need some rest. And you? Please, just be there."

He woke up on the sofa. The clock said 6:36. Good. The girls weren't awake yet.

Brian Mullaney unpeeled his aching body from the microfiber marvel, picked up his shoes, and paddle-footed up the stairs of their prewar, center-hall colonial, keeping his weight to the outside of the wooden treads. He cast a glance inside as he passed each of the girls' rooms . . . always vigilant . . . and managed to get through his bedroom door, gather up a full change of clothes, and exit the room without making a sound or waking Abby.

Which was also a good thing.

What wasn't a good thing was that he was heading back to State with no clue. No clue about a lot of things, particularly about his future. But he was on duty. He would serve well. Serve his country and serve his family. Beyond that, well, the rest was out of his hands.

Washington, DC
April 24, 6:22 p.m.

Outside the windows of Noah Webster's seventh-floor office, Nora Carson could see a beautiful panorama of the Lincoln Memorial and the Potomac River. But she wasn't there to sightsee. She was there to save her job as undersecretary for management and Webster's chief of staff.

"What happened, Nora?"

"One version is another attempt on Kashani's life. Coincidence that it occurred in front of the embassy."

"I don't believe in coincidence. Neither should you." Webster sat behind his desk, which rested on a raised platform, about eight inches off the floor. A short man's affectation . . . the desk was raised so he could look down on anyone in his office. Carson tried to ignore the cultivated atmosphere of intimidation.

"You're right, but that is the swill your friend Prime Minister Eroglu is trying to sell to his boss, Kashani. The president had an appointment to meet with Cleveland at the Cankaya Mansion, but a protest march descended on Cankaya. Turkish opposition is livid about how much it's costing to build Kashani's new presidential palace. So Kashani offered to come to the embassy. Kashani's staff told his driver to get the car ready, that there was a change in plans."

"So many questions, Nora. Why our embassy? Why today?"

Webster had still not invited her to sit, and Carson's resentment was rising. But she kept it in check.

"According to the story Eroglu is pitching, the driver's brother was a sleeper member of the People's Liberation Front. He wasn't on anyone's list. The driver left home and said he had to go to work, that Kashani's plans changed and he had to drive the president to the American embassy. Supposedly, the brother saw an opportunity. Kashani is so fearful since the failed coup and the other attempts on his life, that he never allows his driver to take the same route anywhere. You never know what streets he's going to travel, but the brother knew he had to enter the embassy from the front gate. It was the only predictable spot. At least, that's the official story at the moment."

"You don't sound convinced, Nora." Webster pushed himself forward and planted his elbows on the desk, his hunched shoulders a barometer of growing anxiety. "What do *you* think happened in Ankara?"

Carson measured her options and weighed her words. But she was already all in with Webster.

"When I looked at the tape," she said, "I saw a military action. Could it have been a couple of bozos from the Liberation Front? Sure. They are an unpredictable group of communist terrorists committed to chaos and doing all in their power to drive Turkey closer to Russia's orbit. We had no clue, no chatter before their suicide bomber ripped a hole in our outer wall last February either. Who can predict what they'll do? But what I watched today was not a bunch of amateurs fumbling their way through a raid. These guys were precise professionals. What do I think? I think Eroglu is blowing smoke . . . and it makes me wonder why. If it wasn't the Liberation Front outside the embassy today, then who was it? I think Kashani's inner circle has sprung a leak."

Carson could almost see Webster's mind racing through a myriad of possibilities, pursuing what could be a threatening truth. And she fully understood why Webster was specifically concerned about this day. It had not been that many hours ago when Webster executed a wire transfer of half a million dollars through a tortuous maze of Cayman Island banks and into Eroglu's hidden Swiss account—dollars intended to finance their attempts to thwart the emergence of Persia.

That was all she had at the moment. But she was fully aware of what Webster really wanted to know. So she waited. Her next answer would likely determine her future.

"Who knows, Nora?"

Ahh . . . there it was. Webster needed to know the extent of his vulnerability. This man was walking a very thin line for a very high prize. *I'd be worried too*, thought Carson. Only time would tell if Noah Webster would be remembered as patriot or something a lot more damning.

Webster had ascended into this post at the State Department through his long history and close association with now-retired Senator Seneca Markham. And it was Senator Markham who was still manipulating Webster's strings behind the scenes. Markham was in league with a consortium of American bankers, led by Atlanta's Richard Rutherford, who had benefited richly from the Iranian assets seized by the US government in 1979 and held by their banks ever since.

It was always about money.

Markham and his allies were vocal and ardent foes of President Lamont Boylan's overtures to the Iranian government. Boylan was determined to consummate an agreement that would curtail Iran's nuclear development program in exchange for lifting the economic sanctions against Iran and returning its assets that were seized thirty-five years before. Boylan envisioned this proposed agreement with Iran as the legacy of his presidency. Markham's bosses saw the agreement as the loss of one hundred million dollars a year in revenue—the interest spun off by the languishing Iranian assets.

With his eyes fixed on the further accumulation of political power and office, and the financial backing that Markham's consortium could provide, Webster became a willing and effective impediment to the negotiations with Iran. And he soon discovered an eager ally in opposing the Iranian deal.

During a NATO summit in Reykjavík, Iceland, Webster was introduced to Arslan Eroglu, prime minister of Turkey, the nation's second-in-command and appointed to his position by Turkish president Emet Kashani. In Eroglu, Webster found a powerful man with an equal zeal to keep the Iranian government impoverished and in the shackles of international sanctions. Eroglu's stated motivation was to maintain what little balance of power remained in the Middle East. But Nora Carson suspected Eroglu, and the government he represented, also harbored more self-serving motivations.

The math of the Middle East was simple. There were three primary people groups in the region: Persians, equivalent to the current residents of Iran and Iraq; Turkomans, residents of the land mass that linked the continents of Europe and Asia; and Arabs, those nomadic desert dwellers whose tribes roamed from the Arabian Sea to the Anbar Desert to the walls of Jerusalem. Each of those people groups had spawned an empire. Each of those empires had occupied essentially the same land mass—and each of them wanted it back. Even though each of these groups were now believers in the Islamic faith, their hatred for and fear of each other spanned millennia. It wasn't going away.

The Turkish government of President Kashani was both active and vulnerable. The easternmost bulwark of NATO, a member since 1952 and part of NATO's nuclear sharing program since 2009, Turkey had its eyes and its treasury fixed on the West. But the heart of Kashani's personal politics was firmly fixed in an Islamic East. Kashani was not only faced with the challenge of maintaining at least a semblance of balance between Turkey's NATO responsibilities and the lure of an ascendant Islamic world to his east, but he was also faced with an unstable domestic political environment that had nearly toppled his government a year earlier.

Kashani was head of the Turkish Justice and Development Party (AKP), a long-time ally and supporter of the Muslim Brotherhood. Although giving lip service to the West, Kashani's personal philosophy was a neo-Ottamanism, reestablishing Turkey as a regional power in the Middle East on the footprint of the old Ottoman Empire. While the AKP grew in power and influence from its creation in 2001, gaining seats in the Turkish Parliament in each of the last three elections, Kashani was blindsided by events in 2013, when the military coup in Egypt overthrew the Muslim Brotherhood government of Mohammed Morsi and put Turkey in direct conflict with the governments of both Egypt and Saudi Arabia.

Kashani quickly and ruthlessly crushed a similar coup attempt by a clique of centrist generals who opposed his close ties to the Muslim Brotherhood and embraced the secular democracy that had defined Turkey since the great reformer Ataturk.

With a national election scheduled for August, Kashani was steering a delicate course between this existing secular democracy and a growing Islamic activism in his people.

While President Kashani was encumbered by Turkey's delicate balancing act on the international scene and the crucial upcoming election, it was Prime Minister Eroglu who was assigned by Kashani the vital task of thwarting the rebirth of Persia—the ancient empire where what is now Iran and Iraq marched under the same flag. A reborn alliance of Iran and Iraq, a new Persia, would be a direct threat to Kashani's dream of a new Ottoman Empire. Both the Ottomans and the Persians would covet the same territory: all of the Middle East, land each empire had once ruled.

Noah Webster not only found himself in collusion with an agent of a foreign power, but also financially and politically supported in that collusion by a shadow cabinet of bankers and power brokers. If this scheme were to be uncovered . . .

So who knew? That was a good question. Noah Webster's future and freedom may depend upon the answer. Carson wasn't sure if her answer was entirely accurate. But it was the only answer she could give him and remain this close to real power.

"Three—you and I, and Eroglu."

"Are you sure?" Webster stood up from his chair, leaned his knuckles on top of his desk, and glared at his chief of staff. "Cleveland told Mullaney that somebody must have had inside information on the fact that Kashani's plans and location had changed. Morningstar brought it up at the debrief. You know that nugget will get back to Kashani . . . that he's probably been betrayed by someone in his inner circle. When the Turks start looking for the traitor, what will they find? Are our conversations with Eroglu secure? Any disclosure at this point would destroy us. And Cleveland is no fool. What else might he know? If he were to suspect . . ."

Carson didn't flinch. She kept her eyes fixed on Webster. "Our conversations with Prime Minister Eroglu are secure. Nobody knows about them except you and me . . . and whomever you may have informed."

Webster held her gaze so long, Carson felt her concentration waver. Then he turned and faced the windows behind his desk. "And Cleveland has no suspicions?"

"I can't speak as to what is in Ambassador Cleveland's thinking."

"No." Webster's word hung suspended in silence. "No, you can't, can you."

Webster stood silently at the window, his hands clasped behind his back, rocking gently on the balls of his feet.

"You and I are risking everything, Nora," said Webster. "But if we succeed, our country will avoid a disastrous mistake, our world will be safer, and the peace of our nation more secure. Then my friends become your friends. And where I go, you go. And we could go a long way."

She knew the dream in Webster's mind. It was nearly palpable as he gazed down on Washington's beauty. Carson understood and shared that longing.

Webster turned away from the windows. With a crisp, determined gait, he stepped up to his desk. "So . . . two things. First, just as a precaution, you will get rid of Joseph Atticus Cleveland and you will get rid of him now. I want him sent to Mongolia if possible."

Nora Carson fumed on the inside at the self-centered arrogance of Noah Webster. How had she come to sell her soul to this man? Ordering her to have Joseph Atticus Cleveland relieved of his duties after thirty years of exemplary service? And facing a deadlocked Senate with a huge backlog of waiting appointments? There was no way to engineer Cleveland's demise. But there was a solution.

"Mongolia is filled. Cleveland is too senior for that post anyway. But remember, Harley Carnes is planning to . . ."

"Yes," snapped Webster. "That's perfect. Tell Harley he's getting an early vacation. Israel is even in Cleveland's area of expertise, and we already have somebody on the ground in Tel Aviv who can keep an eye on him. But we need to get this appointment fast-tracked and past the backlog."

Her high heels making her ankles ache, Carson shifted her portfolio binder from one hand to the other, but Webster didn't get the hint. Arrogant . . . "Shouldn't be a problem," said Carson. "The Senate always acts quickly on Israel, and Cleveland is respected on both sides of the aisle. We can make it a package deal . . . put the president's crony Dyson in Azerbaijan and transfer Bruce Brown to Turkey. He's a protégé of Basil Thornwood," Carson said, mentioning the cochair of the Foreign Relations Committee.

Webster tilted his head to the right and gave Carson a quizzical look. "Well done, Carson. You're even beginning to think like me. We'll get Thornwood to run the idea up the pole to the White House tomorrow. He'll be thrilled with the idea and so should the president. How long do you think it will take? I want to make the announcement and get Cleveland packing for Israel. I want him out of Turkey as soon as possible, and I don't want to see his face for the next hundred years."

"Hyperbole for dinner? You should—"

"And tell Cleveland that if he doesn't remain a team player, then we *will* send him to Mongolia."

"That won't scare him. Cleveland's been around too long, and he's nearly earned career ambassador rank. He knows the rules. He should—"

Webster pounded his right fist on the padded top of his desk chair. The veins in his neck twitched and tightened, and his voice carried the threat of damnation. "Then tell him something that *will* scare him. Tell him we'll make sure he's disgraced and dismissed from the service. That we will revoke his pension and that we'll send that wise-mouth daughter of his to jail for tax evasion."

"We can't do that." Carson shifted her weight and smoothed down her dark blue business suit. "That would be illegal. We can't touch his pension."

Leaning forward, Webster looked like a predator. "We can do anything we want, Nora. Who will stop us, Congress? Those fools can't even tie their own shoes. We can always throw some outlandish plan at Congress and get their brains freaked out for months while we do what we want to do." Webster's left hand gripped the top of the chair as if he was strangling an intruder and he thrust his right index finger in the direction of Carson's forehead. "Tell him . . . shake him to his soul."

Nora Carson knew it was her soul that was being shaken. Another flicker of doubt ignited for a moment.

"And Nora . . . the second thing . . . we need a diversion. Something to keep prying eyes away from our involvement with the prime minister. So I want you to keep alive the story that there was a massive security failure at the embassy in Ankara . . . a failure of responsibility. Saturday, leak that to the press so it hits the Sunday papers and talk shows. And then we throw Morningstar to the dogs. Which reminds me. Send Mullaney to Israel with Cleveland. Mullaney knows too much and too many people. So get him out of here too. Send them both to the desert."

There was a smile on Noah Webster's face that chilled Nora Carson to the marrow.

Washington, DC
April 25, 12:22 a.m.

A town house in Georgetown was the stereotype for the Washington powerful. Noah Webster didn't care about stereotypes. He loved his nineteenth-century brick town house more than he cared for most people. It was a perfect blend of character, elegance, and peace—three personality traits he envied, but knew he didn't possess. So the house was his alter ego, his perfect mate.

Deputy Secretary of State Webster wandered into his library, filled with leather-bound books he would never read, a goblet of California cabernet in one hand and an encrypted satellite phone in the other. It was critical his conversations with Turkish prime minister Arslan Eroglu remain short and private.

"Good morning, Noah. I've—"

"Tell me you didn't have anything to do with it," snapped Webster. Normally he was fascinated by Eroglu's British-tinted accent. It had character. But not this morning. Now it was just annoying affectation. "Tell me you wouldn't—"

"Please, Noah, allow me to begin by apologizing for the near disaster of two days ago. I was quite relieved to hear that neither the ambassador nor his staff were injured in any way."

Webster gripped a tenuous leash on his rising fury, shaking his head at Eroglu's empty apology.

"The president's chauffer, Arslan? Are you kidding? You should have come up with a better story," Webster said, not bothering to temper the rebuke in his voice. "The people over here aren't stupid. Deluded, perhaps, but it wouldn't take long to pierce that threadbare excuse if someone were to test it out. We can't afford this, Arslan. The attack on the consulate was foolhardy. And dangerous. How could you—"

"Mr. Secretary." Now Eroglu's voice had an edge. "You may lose your position and your ambition if our secret were known. But I would most certainly lose my life."

Take a breath. Stay in control.

"I must confess," said Eroglu, his words once more draped with silk and lace, "I firmly believe our future would be more secure with Kashani out of the picture. But I was not the orchestrator of the attack on the embassy. At least . . . not intentionally."

Webster's mind parsed the meaning between the words at the speed of an atom in a giant collider. He was sure Eroglu had his own agenda, but this . . . "You have another scheme in the works, don't you? That could prove to be a deadly risk for both of us."

"Perhaps you don't understand the Eastern mind as fully as you believe," said Eroglu. "Our logic is often labyrinthine; our plans often inscrutable. But . . . I am certain you also have in place what you call a Plan B, yes? You see, I've been involved in an ongoing dialogue with some our army's key generals, men who are devoted to the secular democracy and the memory of Ataturk. Just in case. I'm sure you understand. I was speaking to one of these generals and may have mentioned the president's change in plans. I'm afraid that general misconstrued my intentions, took advantage of the information, and was a trifle imprudent in his response."

Imprudent? Fear and insecurity mocked Webster's choice of coconspirator. But that decision was long past. So Webster wrestled his doubts into submission and hunted for a solution.

"I had a suspicion your hands were dirty when I heard that lame story about the driver," said Webster, determined to keep the responsibility squarely on Eroglu's shoulders. "So now that you've lit this match, how do you plan to keep it from igniting our destruction?"

"Well . . ." Eroglu's voice was as slippery as black ice on a February morning.

"Following this fiasco, I took some extraordinary measures to ensure our security continues. I have had the driver arrested on suspicion of treason. And the general has taken, shall we say, an early retirement. A permanent retirement. His body will never be found. You would be unwise, Noah, to underestimate my devotion to our plans and my determination that they remain secret."

Webster pulled in a long, cleansing breath. He lifted the goblet, swirled the wine, and drank in its aroma. *Good. The hook remains deeply set.*

"How it happened is no longer germane," Eroglu continued. "I have done what was necessary to return the cloak of darkness to our efforts."

The wine was excellent. It had character. But first, he needed to turn this conversation back to business—his business. He needed to impress Eroglu with the depth of his inside knowledge, particularly knowledge of what was happening in Iraq, under Eroglu's nose. "Al-Bayati will win the upcoming election in Iraq, with the help of his Shia brothers from Iran," said Webster. "He will appoint Al-Qahtani to his cabinet."

Like a boxer landing a powerful blow to the midsection, Webster heard an abrupt intake of breath through the receiver. It was a well-timed and well-placed shot.

"That will bring the Badr organization into power," said Eroglu. "And it will be a significant impediment to our plans."

Once known as the Badr Brigades, Al-Qahtani's Shiite Militia—forefront in the rebellion against the Sunni-led Iraqi government in the years following Saddam Hussein's overthrow—was a decade later the only effective Iraqi military force arrayed against ISIS and the only remaining defender of Baghdad. A double-edged sword, since the Shia Badr organization was financed and directed by Shia elements in Iran and more loyal to its religious brotherhood than to the unstable and unreliable government of Iraq.

Webster's thoughts drifted to the geopolitical quagmire of the Middle East. So much was happening, so quickly, it was easy to overlook the basic drivers of the region's politics and conflicts: that the people of this desolate land—Jews, Arabs, Persians, and Turks—had been at war with each other for most of the last fourteen centuries. Out of the Muslim faith of Islam was born a fundamental fracture, the schism in the middle of the seventh century that created the Sunni and Shia factions of Islam. Their hatred and distrust of each other enflamed a conflict that remained unquenched. Arabs, Turks, and

Persians—Muslims all, but implacable enemies who each dreamed of restoring an ancient empire. And all three harbored a merciless hatred of the Zionist invaders of Israel. Now the madmen of ISIS had inserted an unprecedented chaos into the region. Someone needed to impose order. Webster believed he was the answer.

"Once inside the Iraqi government, it won't take long for Al-Qahtani and his organization to increase their influence," said Eroglu. "He will insert his Shia supporters into every level of government."

"And Al-Qahtani is being hailed by Shia and Sunni alike," said Webster, "as the savior of the Iraqi people from the onslaught of ISIS. The intertwining of Iraq and Iran is occurring much more quickly than we had anticipated, Arslan. Once Iran signs a final nuclear agreement with America and its allies, possibly sometime next year, a Persian confederation won't be far behind."

Webster eased himself into the plush pleasure of a wingback chair, his feet feeling the heat from his gas fireplace. He sipped on the cabernet and allowed the silence to stretch into discomfort for Eroglu. He relented. "What's happening with the Kurds?"

"President Kashani is dragging his feet on allowing the Kurdish rebels to truck their purloined Iraqi oil through Turkey to the coast." Eroglu paused. "We need the Kurds, Noah. ISIS is preparing for another offensive this summer. Despite my president's fear of the Kurds and their Peshmerga militia, currently the KRG are the only reliable ground fighters opposing ISIS except for Al-Qahtani's Shia soldiers. And your president continues his misguided support for this agreement with Iran."

Webster sighed. It was true. President Lamont Boylan saw a nuclear deal with Iran as a legacy maker. His California peace-and-love, surfer-boy persona might win votes, but it was a tragic foreign policy. "One would think that Russian tanks in the Ukraine and the Russian annexation of Crimea would knock some good sense into Boylan's head," Webster said. "But I don't see it happening. It's up to us, Arslan. Arm the Kurds. Arm ISIS. Arm the goats of the Anbar if necessary, but we need to keep Syria and Iraq in crisis. I'll continue to sabotage the talks with Iran."

"Noah." Eroglu's voice held an edge of urgent insistence. "We must destroy even the idea of a new Persia. Our president Kashani is an Islamist radical. He will continue to push Turkey into the camp of the jihadists. But the future of my nation is with NATO, with the West. That is our only hope. Somehow, you and I must stop that agreement. A nuclear-armed Iran is unthinkable."

Unthinkable, yes. But possible. So in Webster's assessment of the Middle East, a strong Turkey, even a resurgent Ottoman empire, was one of the few viable options to thwart the malevolent intentions of a Shia-led coalition of Iraq and Iran, potentially a new Persia.

"Keep stirring chaos into Syria and Iraq, Arslan. That's phase one. And open the door for the Kurds to get some oil revenue. A Kurdish state is phase two. One step at a time. We can still slay the Persian beast before it unleashes its wrath upon the earth. But we need to stay the course. We'll speak again soon."

The cabernet was rich and crimson as it eddied around the inside of the goblet. *If only the stakes weren't so high, I'd get out now.* But Webster knew that was not true. It would take character to turn his back on selfish ambition. And the only character in this room was on the inside surface of the crystal goblet in his hand.

Washington, DC
April 25, 8:14 a.m.

Secretary of State Evan Townsend stretched. His day was only two hours old, and he was already exhausted. Thus far, the fallout from the Ankara attack had been minimal. Perhaps he would catch a break with this one. He swept his eyes around the conference table, the morning huddle with his deputy secretaries nearly complete.

"Anything else?"

Noah Webster caught his attention from the other side of the table.

"Yes, sir. I was thinking . . ."

Great. The last thing I need is Webster thinking.

"Harley Carnes has been asking to be relieved for months and—"

"Yes, and the Senate's backed up, and we haven't found a suitable replacement, and . . . yes?" A breath of regret floated through Townsend for his rudeness, but it didn't last. Noah Webster had been dumped into his office because of strong-arming by then senator Seneca Markham. Townsend didn't want him then, and he didn't want him now. He needed diplomats, not water boys for powerful politicians pulling in one more favor. *Take a breath. Get through this meeting.*

Noah Webster was staring bullets at Townsend, his mouth still half open.

"I'm sorry, Noah . . . not getting enough sleep. What's your point?"

Webster set his chin, clearly not satisfied with the secretary's apology. He tapped the papers in his hands on top of the table. "A suggestion, Mr. Secretary. We need a seasoned hand in Israel. Why not move Bruce Brown to Turkey—he's a protégé of Senator Thornwood, which would help move things along. And then move the president's friend Warren Dyson into Azerbaijan. That would free up Joseph Atticus Cleveland for Israel. Cleveland is well liked and well respected across party lines, and he's got the maturity and experience to handle the Israelis."

It was a good idea. Still, Townsend was no political neophyte. There was some benefit here for Webster. He couldn't see it, but he knew it was there. Well, it was out on the table now.

"Ambassador Cleveland might appreciate a change of scenery. And he's a perfect fit for Israel. That's a sound idea, Noah. We—"

"Thank you, sir. We could ask Senator Thornwood if he would like to present the idea to the White House, if you think that would be helpful."

Evan Townsend felt the door close. He knew he had just walked into something that was not of his own making. This was going to be a long day.

3

Arvand Island, Persian Gulf
May 7, 6:57 p.m.

Dusk was being swallowed by darkness over the Arvand Naval Surveillance Base. The only light visible to Samir Al-Qahtani from his perch on the balcony were the running lights on the bow and stern of the Iranian Moudge-class frigate *Janamar* as it slipped into a berth at the far end of a distant dock. Positioned in the Persian Gulf at the mouth of the Shatt al-Arab River, the border between Iran and Iraq, Arvand Island was the Iranian military's forward listening post over Iraq. This night Arvand would host a clandestine but friendly meeting between Muhammad Raman, chairman of the Iranian Expediency Council—the actual rulers of Iran—and himself, the newly appointed deputy prime minister of Iraq.

To many in the outside world, Al-Qahtani knew, this meeting would have been considered impossible. Fifteen years earlier, Iran and Iraq had reached the end of the longest war of the twentieth century, the eight-year Iran-Iraq War that—depending on whose estimate you believed—killed between four hundred thousand and one million military and civilians with an equal number of wounded.

Since the seventh century, the Muslim world had been divided between two sects of the Islamic faith—Sunni and Shia Muslims. The division erupted from a disagreement about who should lead the religion after the Prophet Muhammad's death . . . a disagreement that, for fourteen hundred years, had all too often flashed from bitterness to violence. Even though both Iran and Iraq were nations with vast Shia majority populations, they had waged a brutal, often inhumane, war because of the hatred that dominated the relentless conflict between the Sunni-dominated Baath party of Iraqi dictator Saddam Hussein and the religious Shia mullahs who ruled the Islamic Republic of Iran.

But in the aftermath of Saddam's overthrow and the Allied occupation of Iraq, a new, Shia-led military and political power began to exert growing influence in Iraq. Thousands of Iraqi military abandoned Saddam during the Iran-Iraq War and fled to asylum in Iran, where they were trained by Iranian officers and reconstituted into anti-Saddam militia units. When the US-led Allies invaded Iraq to depose Saddam in 2003, the Allies quickly adopted these Shia militia units as allies.

The Badr Brigades, led by Samir Al-Qahtani, were the largest, best organized, and most powerful of the Shia militia. They were also the fiercest and most feared by Iraq's suddenly beleaguered Sunni minority. In the years since the Allied invasion, Badr, still under the control of Iran, also became a political party. Al-Qahtani took his fight against the Sunni minority not only to the streets in an ongoing eruption of sectarian violence but also to the Iraqi parliament and the halls of its government. His Badr Organization Party had won more than twenty seats in parliament in the last election. And its popularity and power were growing daily.

With the religious fanatics of the Islamic State overrunning vast areas of western Iraq, routing the inept Iraqi army, Al-Qahtani's Badr Brigades—along with the Kurdish Peshmerga—were the only military forces standing against an ISIS invasion.

Al-Qahtani's Badr Brigades were led by military officers from Iran who were loyal to the Iran-based Shia Islamic party, the Supreme Council for Islamic Revolution in Iraq (SCIRI). The Shia brothers in Iraq and Iran were finally joining forces. And their ultimate goal was coming within reach.

Chairman Raman entered the room, a private reception area on the top floor of Arvand's headquarters building, and bowed at the waist, a sign of respect. Raman was slight of build, fully unremarkable in his appearance. He was dressed in the plain black robes adopted by members of the ruling Iranian clergy, a round, black pillbox hat on his head, and a long, bushy white beard projecting from his chin. Only his eyes commanded respect.

"*Salaam aleichem*, my brother," said Al-Qahtani, his head bowed as expected of a guest. Where Raman was an indistinguishable cipher, Samir Al-Qahtani dominated any room he entered. A massive man by any standards, but particularly among his Persian brothers, Al-Qahtani stood six foot five and carried 250 pounds of muscle and sinew with the rippling potential of a notched arrow in a fully extended bow. He was always only a finger flick from unleashed aggression. No robes for this warrior. Al-Qahtani wore his battle fatigues with dignity, like a general's hand-sewn uniform, and the scars on his face like medals of valor. He was a professional soldier, ruthless, loyal only to his faith and his Shia brothers.

Raman crossed the room, and his right hand touched the Iraqi's outstretched arm. "*Wa' aleichem salaam* . . . and God be with you also. I thank you for your courtesy, but there's no rank here tonight, my brother. We have enemies on all sides and weighty matters to discuss. Our hearts should beat as one."

A small cup of thick, black coffee suspended in his hand, Raman turned to his guest. "No, Minister. We cannot lose focus. There are many tasks before us, but the first and most important is to destroy this so-called Islamic State of ISIS and restore Iraqi sovereignty over the Anbar Province." Raman placed his cup on the side table. "You have made significant inroads into Al-Bayati's government."

Al-Qahtani was already dismissive of Raman, who was all motion and gestures, never still. Al-Qahtani displayed the patience of a soldier. Despite his imposing bulk, he was comfortably relaxed on one of the room's cushioned divans, his strength and energy coiled, prepared, waiting.

"Once one of our party was appointed minister of transportation," Al-Qahtani said of his military commander, "it became easier to keep the door open to bring more of our organization into positions of influence—soon a high-ranking member of Badr Brigades was minister of human rights, and last week we added the Interior Ministry to our portfolio. An ally was even elected governor of Diyala Province. So yes, we have more influence. But it is not enough."

Raman gathered his robes to stand and started pacing around the spacious but intimately furnished meeting room. "Listen, my friend," he said, as if he were speaking to himself, "we have an opportunity to do something that hasn't been accomplished in over two thousand years: the restoration of the greatest Persian Empire of all time. Think of it." He turned to face Al-Qahtani. "Persians ruling from India to Egypt to Eastern Europe, surrounding the Mediterranean Sea. Not since the days of the Eranshahr have Persians controlled the Levant. And now it is again possible." Raman pointed in Al-Qahtani's direction. "We must make it possible."

Robes sailing in his wake, Raman was off again, fast-stepping around the room as if only motion could satisfy his passion. Al-Qahtani stifled a disparaging chuckle at Raman's histrionics because the Iranian's words were stirring a passion he harbored in his own heart. "First we wipe out the stain of ISIS and make Iraq secure. We continue to increase our influence in the Gulf to frustrate the Saud—perhaps instigate some instability on his border to get his attention. But the second step is to lure the American president and his sycophantic allies into a binding agreement that would preserve much of our nuclear capability while lifting the murderous Western sanctions from the necks of our people. Then, released from the bondage of those sanctions, we can use our oil—Iraqi and Iranian oil—as a weapon."

Raman came to a jolting halt, his shoulders thrown back as if he had collided with an invisible wall. He turned toward Al-Qahtani.

"That is when the trap is sprung." He moved to the divan where the deputy prime minister was seated and perched on its edge, his voice as smooth, quiet, and deadly as a razor-thin stiletto. "Our Syrian friend and ally in Damascus—whom we've barely been able to keep enthroned—will have no warning and no place to hide when Hezbollah turns against him, and our combined forces, triumphant over ISIS, establish protectorates that surround Damascus. Within a year, all of Syria will be annexed into the New Persian Empire."

A smile hinted at the corners of Al-Qahtani's lips. This man might be slight in stature, but his passion was contagious.

With a wave of his hand, Raman regained Al-Qahtani's attention. "And you and I, my brother Samir, will be at the center of the empire's power. Perhaps we will be the ones honored to push the button that will annihilate Israel once and for all time. Yes"—Raman put his hand on Al-Qahtani's shoulder, and his gaze bored into the Iraqi's soul—"our time is almost here. Destroy ISIS. Destroy the Arab economy. Destroy the Assyrian. And then wipe the Jew from the face of the earth."

Al-Qahtani was thirty years old in 1980 when Saddam Hussein sent his troops into Iran and started the eight-year bloodletting that took half a million lives on each side of the Iran-Iraq War. But that war was birthed from the heart of a Sunni madman who ruthlessly wielded power over a Shia-majority nation. On this day, Shia brothers with Persian blood were finally standing in unity against their common enemies.

Tomorrow—or one day soon—there would be no more Iraq or Iran. No more Syria. Certainly no more Israel. Only one all-encompassing Persia. And their mortal enemies, the Arabs, would be ground into the sand.

Eilat, Israel
June 23, 3:13 p.m.

Moshe Litzman and Benjamin Erdad, Likud Party loyalists and trusted advisers to Israel's prime minister David Meir, sat side by side on one side of the table in the Crowne Plaza Hotel. The hotel sat directly on the beach of Eilat, the year-round resort city at the southern tip of Israel. The view from Eilat's beach across the Red Sea was stunning. To the right the Sinai Peninsula of Egypt, to the left, the shoreland of Jordan leading to the highlands of the western coast of Saudi Arabia. Perhaps the heavily armed agents of Shin Bet surrounding the hotel would have a moment to enjoy the view. But not Litzman and Erdad. They were not in Eilat to vacation. They were in Eilat to receive a miracle.

Erdad, minister of internal security, couldn't see Litzman's face and wondered if it revealed the same depth of conflicting emotions—doubt and hope—that surged through his thinking.

"I can see that you find this hard to believe. I can understand your doubt completely. It is the same emotion I felt not so many hours ago. Doubt, but hope as well." Prince Faisal ibn Farouk Al-Saud, defense minister for the Royal Kingdom of Saudi Arabia, spread his hands wide above the table. "But my father is confident it is time to put doubt aside, to put mistrust and enmity aside. He believes, and he has convinced me, that hope and courage will ensure our future. Mistrust and enmity will lead to the utter ruin of us all."

Benjamin Erdad was fifty-four, a career officer in the IDF—Israel Defense Force—rock-solid in body and commitment to his nation. Transferred to Shin Bet for a temporary assignment at the outbreak of the first intifada in 1988, Erdad remained with Israel's domestic security agency, rising in rank and influence. Colonel Erdad laid aside his uniform for a time to join David Meir's cabinet. With a fragile ruling coalition to keep in check, Meir was desperate for the help of those he could trust. Now that trust was in even greater demand. If what the prince shared with them was true . . .

Israel had been at war off and on with its Arab neighbors since the nation was first established in 1948. Sometimes the war was violent, military conflict, as in 1948 and 1967. At other times it was a bitter conflict about land or refugees or housing or freedom. Sometimes only a war of words but, Erdad was fully aware, always a war, nonetheless. Egypt was the only Arab nation to sign a peace treaty with Israel, acknowledging its right to exist. In theory, and often in practice, Israel's other Arab neighbors refused to accept the legitimacy of the Israeli state.

It was an enmity that stretched back thousands of years to the first two sons of the biblical patriarch Abraham—Ishmael and Isaac.

In a story recorded in the Jewish Tanakh, the Islamic Koran, and the Christian Bible, God promised Abram he would be the father of a chosen people but also the father of many nations. Even though Abram was ninety-nine years old, and his wife, Sarah, was barren, God had promised that Abram would be the father of a great nation and that Sarah would bear him a son. But after many years of waiting, Sarah was frustrated enough to arrange for Abram to sleep with her maidservant Hagar. Hagar birthed a son, named Ishmael, who was Abram's firstborn son, thus heir of all he possessed. But Ishmael was not the result of God's sovereign plan for Abram—to birth a people of promise who would enter into covenant with God as his people.

For fourteen years, Ishmael was honored and recognized as Abram's heir. One day after Abram experienced a visitation of angels, he slept with his wife, Sarah. She became pregnant, as God had promised. It was through Sarah's son, Isaac, that Abraham—whose name was changed by God—was told he would father a great nation which would occupy the promised land. Isaac was the son of promise—God's chosen line to bring forth God's chosen people from whom would spring Messiah, the redeemer, through whom everyone's sins would be forgiven.

When conflict arose between Sarah and Hagar over which son would be considered Abraham's firstborn, Sarah convinced Abraham to send Hagar and Ishmael away into the desert.

Hagar and Ishmael were cast out of Abraham's household—divorced—and sent into the desert. There God spoke to Hagar's distress and told her Ishmael would also become the father of a great nation, but that "he will be a wild donkey of a man, his hand will be against everyone, and everyone's hand will be against him; and he will live to the east of all his brothers." From Ishmael sprang the Ishmaelites, the men of the desert . . . all the Arab tribes.

During the thousands of years since the day Hagar and Ishmael were abandoned, the sons of Isaac and the sons of Ishmael had been in constant conflict. Now, Prince Faisal announced, the nations of the Arab world were offering Israel a peace treaty. The end of war.

Erdad had known Prince Faisal for nearly twenty years. Their paths crossed several times by necessity, twice in crisis. The man had proven himself honest and trustworthy, willing to engage in spirited debate about the geopolitical realities of an area they both called home. His arguments were passionate but never aggressively belligerent. Today he presented a proposal that would change both of their futures.

"What about the Palestinians?" Erdad asked. "What about Jerusalem?"

Faisal nodded in acknowledgment. Dressed in a black business suit more appropriate than his royal Saudi robes, Faisal was no less regal in bearing and presence. "Yes, Benjamin, you come straight to the crux of the problem as you always do. My father, the king, has a simple remedy—though it may not be so simple to implement."

He held up his right hand. "Pen . . . paper." An aide stepped from the side of the room and placed a pad and pen in front of the prince, who drew a straight, vertical line down the middle of the page ("The Jordan River," Faisal explained) ending in an elongated oval ("Dead Sea"). He then drew a circle, about three-quarters of the way up the vertical line. To the left of the line, a shape that looked like a kidney bean—the land occupied by Israel after its 1967 war with the Arab states.

"The solution is this. We will not insist on the boundaries from before 1967. You can have the Jordanian territory you captured during the war. We will recognize Israel as a nation and recognize your right to exist. In fact, we will ask you to consider a mutual defense pact with the other signatories as part of the treaty. But . . ."

Erdad knew there was a "but" coming.

"Jordan is willing to contribute the land you, shall we say, liberated in sixty-seven. So we believe Israel must also provide land for a free, sovereign Palestinian state. The Palestinian issue is an obstacle to lasting peace, and it must be addressed.

"So this is what we propose in general terms. Establishment of a Palestinian state from Abu Dis south, for the most part south of Highway One and east of Highway Sixty, to the Dead Sea. This way the Palestinian state can claim East Jerusalem as its capital—but Jerusalem itself remains as it is, unified under Israel. We think it essential that Bethlehem and Hebron be included within the boundaries of the Palestinian state."

Faisal looked up from his rough sketch. There was no defiance in his glance, only a question.

"You are asking a lot, Your Highness," said Moshe Litzman, minister of the interior. He leaned into the table and jabbed his finger into the middle of the Palestinian state drawn by Prince Faisal as if he were trying to slay the idea. "Do you know how many Israeli families will have to be moved to create this state?"

Erdad took a deep breath. Prince Faizal silently stared at Litzman, refusing to take the bait. Likewise, Erdad was determined not to respond out of emotion.

"If we were to announce this agreement, Your Highness," said Litzman, "our hard-liners would be up in arms over the issue of settlements alone. The government would fall within hours. I don't believe your suggestion is viable."

Faisal sat back in his chair. "I agree. The questions of who will live where, of citizenship and ownership—these are thorny problems that will require careful consideration and compromise from both sides. Yes, a threat to an agreement, if that was all the treaty contained. But there are two additional points that I would ask you to consider. First, the mutual defense pact would require all parties to guarantee Israel's security. Which means the signatories to this agreement will commit to fight alongside you and to squeeze Hamas out of Gaza and remove Hezbollah as a threat from your northern border. We will stand with you if ISIS dared an incursion through the Golan Heights. Perhaps even more important, we would be united and determined in our opposition to Iran."

Erdad desperately wanted to light up one of the cigarettes in his pocket. He fought to keep his legs from bouncing. "Prince Faisal," said Erdad, "just who is the 'we' you speak of?"

Thick, black-rimmed spectacles perched on his scimitar nose, a smile filled Faisal's eyes as well as his face. "My father has spoken in substance to the leaders of Egypt, Jordan, Kuwait, Oman, and the United Arab Emirates. All are willing to sign a treaty and a mutual defense pact with Israel. I confirmed that personally before embarking on this mission."

"If you can deliver," said Erdad, "well, this is an offer I'm confident Prime Minister Meir would seriously consider. What is your second point?"

Faisal got up from his chair and stepped toward the only window. One of his bodyguards moved between the prince and the open glass before he could get very far. "Yes . . . thank you." He turned back to the Israeli ministers.

"My father, the king, said—and these are his words—'I want to enter into a new covenant with our brothers in Israel. For too long have the sons of Jacob and the sons of Ishmael been in conflict with each other. It is time for Ishmael to reach out and offer a covenant of peace to his brothers. So as part of this Ishmael Covenant, we promise to assist Israel in constructing a new platform, an extension of Temple Mount, reaching out from the Eastern Gate in the Old City wall over the Kidron Valley. So that the Jewish people can finally build a temple on Temple Mount and restore ritual sacrifice to Israel.'"

Erdad glanced to his left. Litzman, his arms folded across his chest, looked like he was being sold a lame donkey.

"Why now," said Litzman, "this covenant of yours will ignite a regional military conflict before we even get near peace. *We*—all of us—will have to take out Hamas. *We* will need to eliminate or neutralize Hezbollah. *We* will likely find ourselves in armed conflict with the Muslim Brotherhood at some point. And I believe we'll all be at war with ISIS—sooner more likely than later. So why now, Prince Faisal? Why is this Arab confederacy ready and willing to stand up for Israel now? It's got to be more than just the Palestinians."

Faisal returned to the table and leaned on the back of his chair. "Of course you are correct, Minister Litzman. This covenant offer is more than simply a desire for peace—though peace is what we truly desire. The Iranians are liars, and the American president is either blind or foolish or so desperate for a legacy . . ." He threw up his hands. "Well, it appears the West is determined to conclude a nuclear deal with Iran. But Iran will not stop its enrichment program. Deep underground at Fordo, or Natanz, or some still-secret facility, the Iranians will continue moving toward nuclear weapon capability. The sanctions will be removed, Iran will have billions of dollars in assets returned to them, and their oil fields will pump once again. And I'm sure you see the same thing we see—that the Shia brothers in Iran and Iraq are now allies instead of enemies. One of the Iranian generals on the ground in Iraq to fight ISIS said this is the start of a *new* Persia."

Looking first at Erdad, then at Litzman, Faisal pushed back from the chair. "Please, tell your prime minister that we . . . all of us . . . face only two possibilities. A nuclear-armed Persian Empire determined to annihilate not only Israel and the Jews, but the Arabs as well. Or a regional power, united by covenant, dedicated to protecting our freedom and committed to doing everything necessary to destroy Iran's enrichment capacity and prevent the emergence of a new Persia. While there is still time."

4

Baghdad, Iraq
July 9, 8:14 a.m.

Abdul Kafir's bookstore and café was practically indistinguishable from the dozens of similar bookstores and cafés that once again lined Mutanabbi Street in the old quarter of Baghdad. Just off the intersection of Al Rasheed Street, Mutanabbi Street was the historic center of Baghdad bookselling, a street often referred to by locals as the heart and soul of the Baghdad literary and intellectual community. Named after the iconic, tenth-century classical Iraqi poet, Al-Mutanabbi, the street's heartbeat was crushed in 2007 when a car bomb exploded, killing thirty people and wounding another one hundred—and destroying or severely damaging the majority of bookstores.

This street of books was reopened in 2009, but it took years not only for the booksellers to reestablish themselves but also for the citizens of Baghdad to once again feel comfortable picking through its open stalls and musty smelling stores.

Samir Al-Qahtani emerged from the glare of the early morning sun on Mutanabbi Street and strode purposefully down the main aisle of Abdul Kafir's bookstore, his two bodyguards only two paces behind each shoulder. Al-Qahtani was tall, with wide, strong shoulders and rock-solid muscles from his wrists to his ankles. His dark hair cropped close to his scalp, Al-Qahtani was dressed in black slacks and a short-sleeved white shirt—a far cry from the military fatigues he favored as the leader of the Badr Brigades, Iraq's infamous Shiite militia which was now a bulwark against the advance of ISIS not far to the west of Baghdad.

Only two months into his new role as deputy prime minister of Iraq, Al-Qahtani was dressed for a more delicate but no less dangerous mission.

With a nod of his head toward Abdul Kafir behind his wooden counter, Al-Qahtani forged past the small, smoke-filled café at the rear of the shop, through a bead-covered doorway, and up a flight of steps to a large room on the second floor. Sitting at a small table by a window, a cigarette in one hand, diminutive coffee cup in the other, sat Muhammad Raman, chairman of the Iranian Expediency Council.

"*Salaam aleichem*, my brother," said Al-Qahtani as he pulled a straight-backed chair up to the table. "Forgive my rudeness, but I have not much time."

"So I guessed, my brother." Raman nodded his head. "Please proceed."

"Prime Minister Al-Bayati no longer has the ability to govern my country. His Sunni-dominated caretaker administration is a shambles. Parliament can't even decide when to have their next meeting. Meanwhile, ISIS has overrun Tikrit, Fallujah, and Mosul with Iraq's farce of an army running in retreat."

Al-Qahtani paused for a breath, Raman nodding in agreement. "Yes . . . and nature abhors a vacuum."

"We cannot wait for the next election," said Al-Qahtani. "We do not have the time to build political power. So we must take that power. You need to know. You need to tell the council and be prepared."

"A coup?" said Raman. "The Americans won't like that."

"To the devil with the Americans," Al-Qahtani spat. "First we need to save Iraq—from itself and from ISIS. Then we need to join with our Shia brothers in Iran . . . form a new confederation and squash this rabble army of murderers and thieves."

Raman inhaled deeply, then flicked the glowing butt out the window. "When?"

"I will be ready in ten days, two weeks at the most," said Al-Qahtani. "Time to call more of the militia to arms, some to send west against ISIS, but the bulk of the brothers to station strategically here in Baghdad to control the city, the media . . . and the Americans. Very soon, my brother, we will need Iran to stand by the side of our new government. From there, we build the new Persia together."

Raman lifted his half-empty coffee cup. "To the new Persia, my brother. May she reign forever."

Istanbul, Turkey
July 15, 10:40 a.m.

Cleveland was surprised, and blessed, by the outpouring of heartfelt emotion he received from the Turkish government, its officials, and its people after the announcement of his impending transfer to Tel Aviv. Like any capital in the Middle East, Ankara—and this global crossroads of Istanbul—was a shifting bog of intrigue, half truths, hidden agendas, and outright deceit. It was a tough place to discern friend from foe, particularly in light of the very real cultural chasm between Western and Eastern thinking. Yet not only had he survived his three years as ambassador to Turkey, he had also forged some honest and lasting relationships with powerful people who valued integrity above personal gain.

Regardless of the vibes, the threats coming his way from Washington, Cleveland was satisfied . . . no, encouraged . . . by a job well done. Then he heard a whisper in his spirit. *Another job well done.*

"Thank you, Lord."

"What's that, sir?" Tommy Hernandez glanced in the rearview mirror. Even though he was the senior agent and chief of the DSS security team protecting Ambassador Cleveland, Hernandez always drove.

Cleveland looked up at his driver, a sideways smile creasing the left side of his face. "Sorry, Agent Hernandez. Thinking out loud."

Tommy Hernandez shot a quick glance to Jack Nelson on his right. "Praying again, eh, Mr. Ambassador?"

Now the smile engulfed all of Joseph Atticus Cleveland's face. "Yes, Tommy. You caught me once again."

"Well then, pray for me and Jack, okay? I'll wager we need your prayers more than anyone else in this country. We have to live with Buster Brown for the next two years."

"Mr. Hernandez, Ambassador Brown is a fine man of character and integrity. I'm sure he'll be a joy to work for."

"Yeah, I'm sure. Just as sure as my mother was a shot-put champion." Hernandez cast another glance toward Agent Nelson. "Actually, my mother was a shot-put champion, so that's not a very good—"

"Keep your eyes on the road, please, Mr. Hernandez," said Cleveland, his heart warmed by the banter and its sentiment. "We don't want to lose our escort, or mow down a dozen Turkish nationals my last few days here."

"Yes, sir. Eyes on the road."

Cleveland settled back into the comfortable leather of the armored Crown Victoria. He was happy his official car wasn't one of those fancy Lincoln Town Cars or an armored tank. A Ford was more his style. And he was comfortable in his style.

Joseph Atticus Cleveland was old-school State Department. His thirty-plus years of diplomatic service to the United States were an advantage he sometimes wielded as a weapon but mostly as a tool. He was only the sixth African American this century who had been assigned to an ambassadorial level position in a country that was predominantly white. Following tours on three continents, Cleveland's longevity on the diplomatic scene was a result not only of his legendary effectiveness at diffusing crises, but also because he had the character and integrity of a man who devoutly lived his Christian faith on a daily basis. The ambassador nourished the political savvy to harbor big secrets and barter big favors with sovereign leaders the world over. He talked to people others wouldn't talk to and made good come of it.

A widower, fifty-eight years old, Cleveland walked a lot when he had the time and the freedom, got on the exercise bike when he could. He was three years removed from a real scare—triple bypass. But he'd come back stronger. Sure he needed to lose a few more pounds, but he had good stamina, strong legs, and a bald head that gleamed like a setting sun. His shirts monogrammed at the cuff, he wore his Brooks Brothers suits with authority and treated his only daughter, Palmyra, like a queen.

Palmyra. He would soon see his daughter for the first time in four months, since the funeral for her husband. She probably needed the company. Cleveland knew he did. The next few years would test his mettle. But first he had precious little time to wrap things up here in Turkey. He had a packed agenda today in Istanbul, including an invitation from Rabbi Moische Avi Kaplan, leader of the nation's Jewish community and an ally and friend during Cleveland's three years in Turkey.

Neve Shalom Synagogue, situated in the old city once called Constantinople near the tip of the Golden Horn and the Bosporus Strait, was the central and largest Sephardic synagogue in Istanbul, currently home to the largest—but shrinking—Jewish population in the Muslim world. Originally invited in the fourteenth century by Sultan Bayezid II to emigrate from Spain to Turkey to escape the Spanish Inquisition, the Jewish population in Turkey flourished to half a million souls during the growth of the Ottoman Empire. But the last several decades witnessed an increase in Islamic fervor and a growing apathy among Istanbul's officials that put the community on edge. Three recent terror attacks against the sixty-five-year-old Jewish synagogue of Neve Shalom didn't help.

The ambassador's Crown Victoria was inching along the narrow, one-way, cobblestoned Buyuk Street from the direction of the square surrounding the Byzantine-era Galata Tower. What little parking might have been available was blocked by three-foot steel poles along both sides of the street.

"I can pull into this small cutout across from the synagogue," said Agent Hernandez, "but the guys behind us won't be able to stop. The SUV will have to circle the block. Is that okay?"

"That should be fine, Mr. Hernandez," said Cleveland. "I don't expect I'll be that long."

Ankara
July 15, 10:48 a.m.

In the darkness to his right, outside the halo of light around his desk, the untraceable mobile phone rattled to life.

"Yes?" said the Turk.

"He is at the synagogue."

"Did he enter empty-handed?"

"Yes."

"If he leaves with a package, your men know what to do." It was not a question.

The Turk placed the mobile back on the table in the twilight. *And so it begins.*

Istanbul
July 15, 10:49 a.m.

Rabbi Moische Avi Kaplan was waiting just inside the iron gates. "So good of you to come, Mr. Ambassador. I truly appreciate your graciousness in meeting me here."

Cleveland and Rabbi Kaplan—with Agent Nelson in their wake—walked through the central part of the synagogue, beneath the massive round chandelier. "Your invitation sounded urgent, my friend. For you, it was the least I could do."

Seated in the rabbi's office, Agent Nelson outside at the door, Cleveland declined the obligatory offer of coffee. "Rabbi, you look in distress."

Spreading his arms out across his carved wooden desk, the rabbi looked as if he were trying to get his hands around a vapor. "Atticus, my friend, I know you don't have much time, but I have a great favor to ask and quite a story to tell. I'm concerned you may decline my request if I can't explain myself fully or clearly. But I will attempt to be succinct.

"You and I have spoken many times about the dangerous impact of Russia's incursion into eastern Ukraine and its annexation of Crimea. We share the concern that, if not stopped, Russia not only wants to increase its influence but also its territory into the Mediterranean basin. But there are other implications to this current Russian aggression.

"Over two centuries ago," said the rabbi, "one of the greatest and wisest Talmudic scholars of Jewish history lived in Vilna, Lithuania. He was revered as the genius of Vilna—the Vilna Gaon. In the last years of his life, the Gaon received two prophetic messages from the voice of our Creator."

"I've heard about this," said Cleveland, sitting forward in his chair. "Didn't his great-great-grandson recently reveal the contents of the prophecies? Something about the Russians and the return of Messiah?"

The rabbi nodded in agreement, but raised his hands. "Yes . . . but let me be precise. In March, the Gaon's great-great-grandson, who is a member of the Chief Rabbinate Council in Jerusalem, revealed only the first prophecy. It reads:

> When you hear that the Russians have captured the city of Crimea, you should know that the Times of Messiah have started, that his steps are being heard. And when you hear that the Russians have reached the city of Constantinople, you should put on your Shabbat clothes and not take them off, because it means that Messiah is about to come at any minute.

"We understand Christians are waiting for the second coming of Jesus," said Rabbi Kaplan, "but for the Jew, our Messiah is yet to come. This message, written in a cryptic code that took months to decipher and has been a guarded secret for centuries, is a warning to the Jewish people that—with the Russians now in Crimea—our Messiah's coming is at hand."

The rabbi folded his arms upon the top of his desk and leaned closer to Cleveland. "Atticus, if the Russian aggression were the only indicator, well, there may be some doubt about the validity of the prophecy. But more than most men, you understand the rapidly shifting geopolitical reality in the Middle East and the wave of chaotic instability we are all riding. At this moment, any outcome is possible. If the Gaon's prophecy is true, accurate—and knowing its source I have every reason to believe it is genuine—then we both know its implication. According to both Jewish and Gentile Scripture, the fulfillment of this prophecy is a signal that what is known as the end of days is upon us. Everything changes."

Cleveland's heart was racing while his mind was methodically dissecting what the rabbi had revealed. Could they really be having this conversation?

Trying to shake loose his conflicting thoughts, the ambassador studied the design in the rug at his feet. "You and I, Moische, we both know the clock started ticking in 1948 when the nation of Israel was created, fulfilling a prophecy that, in effect, turned on the countdown to the end of humanity's days on this earth."

Cleveland looked across the desk at his host. "There have been wars and rumors of wars for thousands of years, other markers that are mentioned in the Tanakh and our New Testament—hurricanes and earthquakes and famines. And throughout the ages, many have foretold the coming of the end of the world, but they were obviously mistaken. It appears to be the height of foolishness, of pride, for a man to try to predict God's timetable.

"Yet"—Cleveland spread his hands wide—"yet I find myself looking at this world we're in, at the state of this world we're in, and wondering how much time is really left."

For years, Cleveland had found himself convinced that a new age was coming for the Christian church. For the first two thousand years of monotheism, the core of that "one-God faith" was in the covenant relationship between the nation of Israel and its omnipotent God, Yahweh. For the second two thousand years, the core of that faith rested in the church established by Jesus Christ and his disciples.

Barely remembered in these modern times was that during the first three or four centuries of the church age, the Christian church struggled with its identity, evolving from a predominantly Jewish church—a synagogue of Messianic Jews—into an ethnically diverse community united by their belief that Jesus of Nazareth was in fact the Son of God.

But in the fourth century, the Roman emperor Constantine, a convert to the Christian faith, not only legally protected the church after decades of persecution, but also stripped it of much of its Jewish heritage. Constantine imposed many changes on the church, such as hierarchical clergy, but he also laid the foundation for a church where the Jews were no longer the carriers of The Word; they were now the enemies of The Word. And the world changed into open, often bloody, conflict between Christian and Jew—those people "who killed Jesus."

When Cleveland read Scripture, however, he was shown in the book of Romans that a day would come when Jew and Gentile would once again be joined together, when "the fullness of the Gentiles has come in." And with that day, Cleveland believed, would come another portent of the last days—the countdown to Messiah's second coming. Just as the creation of the Israeli nation in 1948 started the last-days clock ticking, just as the return of ritual sacrifice to a restored temple if it ever occurred would accelerate that timetable, Cleveland was convinced that once Christ's church became a "completed church" of Jew and Gentile, where the Jewishness of the early church was embraced by today's believers, the days of Revelation could not be far behind.

And he saw in each day's headlines and in the minutiae of his daily work, the inexorable march of humanity to the brink of Armageddon. Because of this, Cleveland was caught in the claws of both foreboding and expectation.

Finding his voice, Cleveland asked a question he knew would have an answer. "You said there were two prophecies?"

"Ah . . . yes . . . good." Rabbi Kaplan rose from his chair and crossed the room to the wall on his right. He moved aside a table on which sat a large, twin-chambered silver ark holding the Torah scrolls and then the curtain behind it. The wall that this revealed was covered with large squares of carved olive wood. Kaplan pressed his fingers against the side of one of the squares and a four-square section slid up into the wall, revealing a large safe with two tumbler locks. Twisting in the combinations, freeing the safe's door, the rabbi withdrew a large wooden box about ten inches square. He carried the box to his desk and laid it in front of Cleveland. With the care of a nurse with a newborn, Rabbi Kaplan raised the hinged lid of the wooden box and revealed overlapping folds of purple velvet. Peeling away the velvet cloth, Kaplan revealed a smaller metal box inside.

Cleveland was intrigued with the metal box before him. He guessed it to be bronze, weathered by many years, about six-inches square. He could not tell its depth. But most fascinating were the symbols on what appeared to be the lid. Rather than being etched into the metal, the symbols were hammered from behind into raised, three-dimensional shapes. In the middle of the lid was what looked like a three-dimensional Star of David. At each of the corners of the box were other symbols, only one of which Cleveland recognized.

He looked up at the rabbi. "What are the symbols?"

Rabbi Kaplan stood beside Cleveland and swept his hand above the lid and its symbols. "These are kabbalah," he said. "Symbols of the ancient discipline of Jewish thought that, essentially, tried to explain the relationship between the eternal and the mortal, between God and God's creation. This symbol in the middle is the Merkabah, a three-dimensional representation of the Star of David. Worn as a talisman, it is believed to access both blessing and protection. Meditating on the Merkabah brings a person into the spiritual realm where wisdom and knowledge of the eternal can be found. Again, the heavenly and the earthly."

"And these symbols in the corners? These two opposite each other are mezuzahs, correct?"

"Yes," said the rabbi, "they are mezuzahs. The other two . . . the one with the intersecting lines and circles is called the Tree of Life." Kaplan looked at Cleveland to get his attention. "Very complicated. The other is Hamsa, the five. Like a hand."

Cleveland turned toward the rabbi. "So what does it mean?"

Rabbi Kaplan walked back around his desk and took his seat, leaning back. "Inside the box is the parchment with the Vilna Gaon's second prophecy. This box was sealed at the end of the eighteenth century, hidden, and protected by the chief rabbis in Konigsberg, Prussia. Two days before Kristallnacht, when the Nazis began their reign of terror against Jews in November of 1938, the box was brought here to the relative safety of the large Jewish population in

Constantinople. The knowledge and safekeeping of the box has passed from one chief rabbi to the next, awaiting its appointed time."

Cleveland's mind was already tracking ahead of the rabbi's words. "Which is now, because of the Russians taking over Crimea, correct? And you are telling me all this because you need to get the box to Jerusalem, to the chief rabbi and the Rabbinate Council."

Kaplan was nodding his head. "Yes. My hope and expectation is they will know what to do with it. They will know how to read and understand the message."

"And you believe you can't take it yourself because you fear it won't be safe for you to travel with it. So you want me—and my diplomatic immunity—to carry the box back to Israel and get it in the right hands. Correct?"

The ambassador tried to bring his discernment to bear on the conflicting emotions he witnessed in Kaplan's response. "And there is something else, isn't there, Moische? What have I missed?"

Succumbing to his curiosity, Cleveland stretched out his right hand toward the top of the box.

Faster than he could imagine, the rabbi lunged across the desk. Kaplan's left hand clamped onto Cleveland's right wrist and held it, suspended as if it were locked in cement. Off balance, the sudden action caused the rabbi's shoulders to dip toward the desk. He reached out to steady himself and his right hand landed square on top of the Merkabah pounded into the lid of the metal box.

"No, Atticus! You must not touch the box."

At that moment, Cleveland felt torn: one part of him wanted to leave the room as quickly as possible, while another wouldn't leave the room for love or money. At least, not until . . . "All right, Moische, now that my heart rate is a bit more normal, I'm all ears."

Rabbi Moische Avi Kaplan pulled closer to his desk and reached his hands toward the box. "The mezuzah is a talisman of protection," he said. "It's a warning to messengers of evil, like the angel of death in Egypt, that God is watching. The word *mezuzah* is a combination of *maveth* and *zaz*, which together mean 'Death, remove thyself.' The use of two mezuzahs indicates that this is more than just a warning."

Cleveland held the gaze of the rabbi. "Pretty melodramatic stuff."

Kaplan took a deep breath. "Beyond melodrama, my dear Atticus. The five kabbalah symbols are a message to those who understand. The dual mezuzah is only part of the warning. If a hand, the Hamsa, touches this box, the Tree of Life will be severed. But the Merkabah, the Star of David, is protection."

"Okay . . . now I'm confused," said Cleveland. "Warning and protection at the same time?"

"Let me put it this way," said Rabbi Kaplan. "For generations, the rabbis guarding the Gaon's prophecy have passed down a belief that it's the messages themselves that are imbued with the deadly promise on the box." He pointed at the metal container. "I don't believe this box itself has any power. Like the ark of the covenant, it's what is inside the box that has the power. But like the ark, only those who are consecrated, anointed for that purpose can touch the box without losing their lives."

"Like a curse."

"No, not like a curse," said Kaplan. "Like the power of God. The tablets of the Ten Commandments were in the ark, as was Aaron's staff and the jar that held manna. Objects touched by the hand of God, through which the power of God flowed. And only the priests, the anointed ones, could touch the ark without invoking the deadly wrath of God. I've been taught all my life that the power of God resides within this box and to touch it without the anointing of the Aaronic blessing is sure death. That anointing and protection has passed from generation to generation. And I will pray that anointing over you, Atticus, to preserve your life, if you accept this task."

Cleveland's mind raised what he thought was the obvious question. "So Rabbi, what is in this message that requires the protection of God's wrath?"

Rabbi Kaplan raised his hands, palms up toward the ceiling, and shrugged. "No one knows for certain, Atticus. All I can tell you is that the belief passed down from father to son for more than two hundred years is that this prophecy of the Vilna Gaon contains the identity of the man of violence . . . God's adversary in the last of days."

"And you think that's why this synagogue has been attacked so many times over the years? Because of this prophecy and its adversary?"

"Yes. And my heart breaks for the task I am asking you to accept."

Part of Cleveland was afraid to say the words, because saying the words would make it true . . . make it real. "If the Gaon's prophecies are accurate and the Jewish Messiah is *about to come any minute*, as it claims, then the man of violence is already here on the earth."

"Yes, Atticus, that is also what I believe."

"Moische, are you speaking of the Antichrist when you say the man of violence?"

The rabbi shook his head with such emphasis that his ears were quivering. "Honestly, Atticus, I don't know for certain. All I know is what my father told me and what his father told him. Through the generations, our rabbis have believed this prophecy will reveal the name of the man of violence. Is he your Antichrist? I don't know."

Cleveland felt his stomach turn over. "If this man of violence walks this earth, then I expect there's a good chance he probably knows where the second prophecy lives . . . here. He may even suspect what it says. And he will move heaven, if he could, and hell to keep that secret from being revealed."

"Yes, Atticus, that is what I believe."

Getting up from his chair, Cleveland began to pace around the rabbi's office, having a hard time trying to extricate his State Department responsibilities from his understanding of Scripture. The scriptural implications of everything he was hearing were overwhelming his thought patterns. And muddied thinking was dangerous for a diplomat.

"Moische, forgive me if I oversimplify all that you've just told me, but whether you slice this revelation of yours with an Old Testament knife or a New Testament knife—from a Jewish perspective or a Christian perspective—the end result is the same. I trust you and respect you, so I expect all that you have told me is true. If that conclusion is correct, then we are entering a time that has been predicted for more than two thousand years. On that front, I'm awestruck and I don't know what to think or feel or hope.

"But there is another side to this that I need to consider." He turned to face Kaplan. "Rabbi, I value our friendship and all your assistance these last three years. So I apologize for being blunt. But . . . why would I do what you ask? Why would I take possession of this potentially deadly box, which is probably sought by determined agents of evil, and carry it under the auspices of our flag into another sovereign nation? I represent the United States of America. Why would the US government allow me to take this task upon myself?"

His eyes closed, his head nodding down onto his chest, it almost looked as if Rabbi Kaplan was asleep. Cleveland wondered whether the rabbi had heard his questions. When he responded, it was as if his voice came out of a dream. "Atticus . . . as I said, no one knows what is written in this prophecy. But I believe"—his eyes opened—"and ten generations of rabbis before me believed, that this second prophecy *also* speaks of the coming Messiah. His coming will change everything, for every living soul.

"Tell me, my friend, if you don't agree with me. But when our Messiah comes, or when your Yeshua H'Mashiach comes again, everything changes—for Israel first, and most completely, yes. But also for Israel's neighbors . . . for those who give Israel their wholehearted support and for those who hate Israel with a black-hearted vengeance. I would think, Atticus, that you and your government would benefit mightily from knowing, in advance of everyone else, what is written on the parchment in this box."

Rabbi Kaplan rose from his chair, came around to the front of his desk, and placed a hand on Cleveland's arm. "Take this message to the leaders of the Rabbinate Council in the Hurva Synagogue," he said, his voice the plea of a parent for a child. "They will know what it says. And you, my friend . . . there are few men in this world I would entrust with this task. You, Atticus . . . I am confident that you will know the right thing to do once you hear the Gaon's prophecy."

The rabbi's argument was valid. If all they had discussed today was true, having the information first would be a vital advantage for his country.

"And you are expecting me to walk out of here today with this box under my arm?"

"No . . . no," Rabbi Kaplan waved his hands in front of him. "No. I will give you a leather satchel. And a very important anointing."

It was a solemn moment. Rabbi Moische Avi Kaplan recognized the gravity of what he was doing. For the first time in more than two centuries, a rabbi would no longer be responsible for protecting the box of prophecy. He felt he had no other choice. But a piece of his heart broke, nonetheless.

He placed his hands on Ambassador Cleveland's shoulders, then moved his right hand to the top of Cleveland's head. Kaplan looked over at the box of prophecy sitting atop his desk; the purple velvet was still pulled aside, the kabbalah symbols visible on its lid. *I hope I am doing the right thing.*

"The Lord bless you, and keep you." Rabbi Kaplan spoke the words quietly, with the reverence of a personal prayer. "The Lord make His face shine on you, and be gracious to you. The Lord lift up His countenance on you, and give you peace." Kaplan looked down at Cleveland, whose eyes were closed. "Be safe, Atticus. Bring the prophecy to the rabbis at the Hurva, but please . . . be safe."

Without waiting for Cleveland to open his eyes or raise his head, before the rabbi had a change of heart, he turned to his desk, took the wooden box in his hands, and pulled it closer. Wistfully, Kaplan traced the outline of the Merkabah with his index finger. A current of warmth emanated from the metal. Taking a breath, he folded the purple velvet back over the metal box, attached the wooden lid, pushing it down tightly so it sealed. Kaplan picked up the wooden box and slid it inside a large, leather satchel he had fetched from a closet.

When he turned, Cleveland was already standing alongside the chair. The dark skin of his face looked ashen. Grasping it by its sides, the rabbi lifted the leather bag and held it out toward the ambassador. The clock on the mantel in his office ticked away the seconds as he waited. Pulling in a deep, short breath, Joseph Atticus Cleveland reached out his hands. With great care, he took the handle of the satchel in his right hand, put his left hand under the bag, and lifted the weight . . . from the rabbi's hands, from his heart, and from his shoulders.

Cleveland knew that Agent Nelson was miffed. But he was going to carry this bag himself. He didn't plan to leave it out of his sight until the day he handed it over in Jerusalem.

"He has a bag . . . he's carrying a bag, like a leather briefcase."

The Turk blew the acrid smoke out of his lungs. "Get it. Kill him. Kill them all if you have to. But get it."

Holding the leather satchel against his chest, Cleveland slipped into the back seat of the limousine as Agent Nelson closed the door.

"Gifts, Mr. Ambassador?" asked Hernandez, still at his station behind the steering wheel.

"In a manner of speaking."

"Any chocolate in that—"

"Tommy, we are leaving for the airport now and returning to Ankara," Cleveland said crisply. "Get the escort around here pronto. Agent Nelson, contact the crew and tell them to get the plane ready. Then call my secretary and have her cancel the rest of the day's meetings. Tell her I'll send personal notes."

Agent Hernandez had the car started. "The SUV is halfway down Kule Street, parallel to us. They'll swing through Tower Square and come up behind us."

Cleveland's escort vehicle, a hulking black SUV, edged its way down a narrow street of retail shops and markets. Behind the blacked-out windows, four DSS agents were outfitted with body armor and big-punch automatic weapons.

"Radio Hernandez," the driver said. "Tell him we're coming into Tower Square."

The agent riding shotgun turned his head to the right to speak into his shoulder mic, just in time to see the massive tow truck hurtling toward them like a missile. "Incomin—"

The tow truck T-boned the SUV, picking it up off two wheels and driving it across the narrow confines of Kule Street at the intersection with Tower Square, up onto the sidewalk, and into the corner pillar of the Anemon restaurant.

In his last instant of consciousness, his hands still firmly gripping the steering wheel, the driver managed one word into his mic. "Move!"

DSS Agent Tommy Hernandez mashed the gas pedal, laid his hand heavy on the horn, and accelerated wantonly over the cobblestones of Buyuk Street. There was no pity in his driving, and no levity in his voice.

"Buckle up, Ambassador. This isn't going to be pretty. Jack, alert the marines at the airport. We'll be coming in hot."

"Catch him. He'll have to slow at the circle."

The white van bolted out of a side street as the ambassador's car hurtled past.

From the passenger seat, the leader looked into the back of the van to the five hooded men dressed in black. "Prepare."

The Ford shot into the Isekender circle, Hernandez ignoring the traffic and using his horn for leverage. He pulled the car into a tight right, just missing a milk truck, cut across the traffic coming into the circle from his right, and jammed his foot on the gas, fishtailing out of the circle on the other side.

"Where are you going?" Nelson was hanging on, one hand on the dashboard, the other against the door, as the car swung through traffic like a towel snapping in the wind.

"Fastest way to the Ataturk Bridge and the airport," breathed out Hernandez. "Get in the back and get the ambassador on the floor."

The van driver muttered a Turkish epithet as the ambassador's car disappeared amid the clogged traffic at the circle.

"Don't lose him."

The van driver muttered another Turkish epithet, weaved left behind a bus, cut between two trucks parked along the hub of the circle, and drove with two wheels on the sidewalk.

Hernandez wrestled the black Crown Victoria past the Daru Sultan Hotel onto a tight access road. Traffic was backing up.

"Red light!" Nelson yelled.

"Hold on."

Cars were standing still in the street, backed up from the red light. With a veteran's calm, calculated assessment, Hernandez identified a wide grass-and-dirt plaza at the far end of the street. It was on the left, just short of the intersection . . . an escape route. But first he had to get there.

A low, stone divider to his left ran down the middle of the street, separating the traffic running in opposite directions. The divider sloped downward from their travel lanes to the lanes of oncoming traffic and continued all the way to the grass-and-dirt plaza. In the flick of an eyelid, Hernandez yanked the car left. The Crown Victoria jumped the curb, sliding down the incline of the barrier. The Ford bounced hard into the lane of oncoming traffic. Hernandez strained to keep the car against the inclined divider, ignoring the rising wail of car horns. He muscled the car halfway up the stone divider before the car hit the dirt plaza. *Turn green!* A tall, steel light pole sent sparks in the air as it scraped against the left flank of the Crown Victoria. *Turn green!*

"We have company," warned Nelson.

Hernandez couldn't risk a glance in the rearview mirror. Didn't matter. He had no choices.

They could see the large black car, sliding along the stone divider in the middle of the street. The light was red.

"Get beside him." He looked in the back. "Open the door."

The side door of the white van slid open, and the barrels of three automatic weapons peeked into the sun.

"Cover him, Jack."

The intersection they were hurtling toward was the six-lane highway to the Ataturk Bridge—three lanes going onto the bridge on the far side of the intersection and three lanes exiting the bridge on the near side of the intersection. The ambassador's Crown Victoria slalomed through the dirt plaza, avoiding traffic signal poles and steel utility boxes. And still the light glowed red. *God help us.* Hernandez mashed the gas pedal and aimed for the intersection.

"He won't make it," said the driver.

A taxi exiting the bridge must have seen the Ford plowing into the intersection. In the traffic lane closest to the rampaging automobile, the taxi driver instinctively pulled his car to the left, into the path of a small truck. The chain reaction started. One of the spinning vehicles slammed into the left rear quarter panel of the Ford, but that just drove the car through the three exiting lanes with even more force. Hernandez's hands fought the steering wheel against a deadly combination of too much speed and not enough room, causing him to doubt . . .

The light finally turned green as the ambassador's car skidded across two of the far-side lanes—lanes now suddenly empty of traffic—its back end fishtailing so it was facing toward the bridge. Out of his peripheral vision, Hernandez saw two things as he tried to keep the Crown Victoria traveling in a straight line: dozens of pedestrians scattering in all directions from the intersection's crosswalks, and a white panel van, its side door open, slamming headlong into the steel pole of a traffic signal.

"Stay down, Jack. But see if you can raise our escort team on the mic. I'll call the marines."

Still accelerating, Hernandez flexed his fingers, stretched his shoulders, and took a quick glance into the rearview mirror. No van. No pursuit. *Wow . . . that was a miracle.*

"And Jack . . . see if you can get some of that chocolate from the ambassador, eh?"

5

Ankara
July 16, 9:15 p.m.

The location of Medir's "office" was as cloaked in secrecy as the smuggling business he conducted from it. Off tree-lined Ileri Street in Turkey's capital city, it was found by climbing a rear, outdoor stairway behind the busy Dedem coffee shop on Ordular Street, just south of Anitkabir, the sprawling, massive mausoleum to Ataturk, the father of Turkey's republic.

The Turk sent his bodyguards into the room first, as was his custom. And his customs were singularly eccentric.

He neither ate nor drank in public, which could be discerned as caution. His hands were forever folded up within the voluminous sleeves of his jubba, the ankle-length, robe-like garment he wore over the traditional baggy trousers, the salvar. When offered a hand to shake, the Turk would smile, bow, but refrain. He didn't touch others and expected none to touch him. Caution, perhaps.

But along with his penchant for the ancient dress of Turkey, the Turk practiced other peculiarities—peculiarities that often caused Medir considerable anguish. And fear for his soul.

Like repeating back to Medir the smuggler's most private personal thoughts. After one such revelation, Medir had dispatched his three mistresses and no longer skimmed a few lira off the top of any transaction that came his way. Like inquiring as to the health of Medir's wife and twelve children with sweet words that appeared to carry evil, lethal intent that chilled Medir's blood and froze his corpulent fleshy folds.

Most peculiar of all were his eyes. Or what was behind his eyes. Medir could not tell for certain, since he no longer looked into those eyes. Medir had looked once, at their first meeting, and felt his heart shrivel in his chest. One more moment of those eyes, he believed, and his heart could have stopped altogether. Forever. But it was one look he would remember. Forever. The Turk's eyes were black, his pupils a pale yellow, the space around his irises swirling like a gray fog. In Medir's one look, the yellow pupils appeared to swell, pulse as if they had a life of their own—or they were the portent of death.

Medir sat silent, immobile behind his desk as the bodyguards circled the room, opened the door to the closet, and ensured the windows were shut, latched, and covered by their curtains. Who this man really was, Medir didn't know. At the prices he was willing to pay, Medir didn't care. When he was first contacted, Medir was told to expect the Turk the next afternoon. As if there was only one Turk. Well, there certainly was only one of this man . . . perhaps only one of him in the entire world. For his own peace, Medir called him only "Excellency." He hoped that was deference enough.

The bodyguards completed their circuit of the room and stood, flanking the door, one facing Medir, one facing the small alcove beyond the door that opened onto Kale Kapisi Street in the Old Town of Ankara. The Turk entered, his silent, unnamed aide in his wake, and approached the desk. While there was movement under his salvar where his legs would be, the Turk appeared more to glide over the floor rather than walk. For a man who radiated an incredibly powerful aura, the Turk's physical presence seemed as formidable as the morning fog. His voice was a sibilant whisper that seemed to emanate from the lips of a serpent. Medir lowered his eyes and bent from his shoulders. "Excellency, how may I serve you today?"

"Good afternoon, Medir." The Turk's words slithered into Medir's ears and defiled his thoughts. Medir kept his eyes fixed on the amulet at the base of the Turk's throat and tried to empty his mind. "How is the health of your wife and children?" The Turk slipped into the chair on the opposite side of the desk. "May their good health continue."

"Thank you, Excellency." Medir was perspiring in rivulets, snaking down his body and soaking his clothes, including the expensively tailored French suit that still looked like a wet potato sack.

"Forgive me for my lack of courtesy today, Medir, but I have little time and many pressing matters. May I get directly to the issue at hand?"

"Yes, Excellency."

"Do you have what I requested?"

"Yes, Excellency." Medir focused his attention on the amulet at the Turk's throat—an infinity symbol carved into the face of the earth. "The convoy is ready to move, well hidden in the mountain valleys south of Lake Van. Some heavy weapons, including two tanks and a half dozen mortar and rocket launchers, four thousand assault rifles, and an abundance of ammunition. The Peshmerga will be delighted."

"The Kurdish militias in northern Iraq are fighting a lonely battle against ISIS. They will only be delighted if we can put these weapons in their hands. Can you get them safely to our destination?"

"Yes, Excellency, without a doubt. We have traveled the route many times. Our connections are effective and reliable. We will succeed."

Eyes diverted, Medir waited. No response came. The longer the silence, the stronger the compulsion to look up once more and see if those eyes were truly as he remembered. But that was a risk he would not take.

"Medir . . . I have long admired your smuggling enterprise in the east. The operation has reaped great wealth for you. I hope it continues to flourish. It would cause great hardship, for both of us, if the government were to intercept your shipment . . . shut down your means of trade."

Medir shuddered at the veiled threat.

Without appearing to move, the Turk withdrew a large leather pouch from the folds of his jubba. He tossed the pouch onto the top of the desk, where it hit with a thud and the invigorating crinkle of gold coins. "Half now . . . half on delivery."

Medir gazed at the leather pouch. This operation would earn him twice the normal yearly income on all his other smuggling combined. If only he didn't feel like he was dealing with Satan himself.

Medir lifted his eyes from the bag of gold coins to address the Turk once more. But the chair was empty. The specter-like aide and the bodyguards were gone. The Turk had silently disappeared. And Medir felt like he needed to bathe—both his flesh and his spirit.

Ankara
July 17, 5:55 a.m.

"I despise that pink monstrosity. All of it! I hate living in Ataturk's museum." Turkish president Emet Kashani walked slowly through the long greenhouse of the Pink Palace, the presidential residence built for Kamal Ataturk, the revered father of Turkey's republic. His fingers caressed the velvety leaves of one bromeliad after another. "It's as if I sleep with his ghost every night and walk with his memory every day."

The sun was barely up, the greenhouse tolerable at this time of day. Still, Kashani's short-sleeved shirt was already streaked with sweat stains. Arslan Eroglu followed in his president's wake, as he always did.

"You won't be here much longer," said Eroglu, prime minister of Turkey and Kashani's closest confidant. "The White Palace will soon be finished."

"Not one day too soon." Kashani was wearing the pants of a farmer, soiled and stained from digging in the greenhouse—one of the safer ways to vent the anger he could not expose in public. And the greenhouse was one of the few safe places to keep certain conversations unheard. Kashani turned toward Eroglu. "What of our other plans, Arslan? How do they proceed?"

How to respond? How much truth could he tell Kashani?

"It is as we expected, Mr. President. All our enemies are committed to the same quest for the same land. It's one of the few things we, the Persians, and the Arabs agree on, the unalterable truth that once Islam controls some part of the earth's surface, that land is forever under the rule of Islam. Our conflict arises from the question of whose Islam will rule.

"The Islamic State controls over eighty thousand square kilometers of Syria and Iraq, from the Mediterranean Sea to south of Baghdad. Its leader, the Sunni usurper Al-Baghdadi, has declared the caliphate. Now the Shia brethren of Iraq and Iran are moving inexorably toward a reincarnation of the Persian Empire, first to crush the stain of ISIS and then to reclaim all the territory once ruled by Persia.

"We know our enemies. And unfortunately, no one controls ISIS any longer." Eroglu reached a bench in an alcove of the greenhouse and settled himself into its cushions.

"We were fools to think we could ignite that spark and keep it from scorching our fingers," said Kashani. He walked over and joined Eroglu on the bench. "Are we being fools again by arming the Kurds?"

"The enemy of my enemy is my friend," Eroglu recited. He leaned closer to Kashani. "Our task remains threefold: obstruct and cripple the advance of Persia, or dismantle it altogether; destroy ISIS as a military force; and cut the legs off that heretic pig in Damascus to absorb Syria into the new Ottoman

Empire. An empire ruled by Sultan Kashani . . . where Turks are masters of the caliphate."

Kashani nodded his head. "Yes. Keep my eyes on the ultimate goal, Arslan."

If you only knew the ultimate goal.

"So, my president, we use the weapons at our disposal," said Eroglu. "We secretly arm the Kurds to fight ISIS. As we know too well, after fighting against their rebellion for the last decade, the Peshmerga are relentless enemies. And we offer to unlock the flow of fresh water back into Iraq and send our military to strengthen the corrupt Syrian government—with one stipulation. That Syria and Iraq join Turkey in contributing the territory necessary to create an independent Kurdistan, our bulwark to the east. When Syria and Iraq agree to those terms, the resurrection of the Ottoman Empire will be assured. Emet Kashani's Ottoman Empire."

Eroglu bowed his head to his president, and set his final hook. "And the ghost of Ataturk shall be banished, forever."

6

Tel Aviv, Israel
July 18, 11:46 a.m.

His iPhone powered up, Brian Mullaney was scanning the online sports section of the *Washington Post*, his mind completely enthralled by the roller-coaster reality that was the Washington Nationals, as he sat in Ben Gurion International Airport, waiting for Tommy Hernandez to arrive on the flight from Istanbul.

"Excuse me, sir. Do you know of any good barbecue joints nearby? Or maybe a Taco Bell?"

"Hello, Tommy," Mullaney said, even before he looked up.

"So I've blown my cover already? I'd never make a good spy." Hernandez flopped into an uncomfortable plastic seat alongside Mullaney.

Mullaney forced a smile to his face as he looked to his right. Tommy Hernandez and Mullaney had survived DSS training together under the relentless battering of the marines at Quantico, both of them honing rare skills in life-and-death management. After nearly two decades of friendship, Hernandez was closer than, and knew Mullaney better than, even his brother, Doak.

Raised in Texas of Mexican American heritage, Hernandez was five ten, broad shouldered and barrel chested. His body thick with muscle, a flat-top crew cut bristling like porcupine quills, Hernandez radiated restrained power packaged in an expensive suit. He looked like a throwback NFL fullback or a phys ed teacher from the fifties. Except for his brown eyes, where a jester cavorted and mischief watched for opportunity.

"How are Abigail and the girls?" Hernandez asked.

"You knew the answer to that question before you asked, correct?"

"Yeah . . . sorry. I guess that wasn't the most tactful way to stick my nose in your business."

"She told me she didn't sign up for this."

Hernandez shook his head and looked at the cowboy boots on his feet. "What happened to 'for better, for worse'?"

"It all looked pretty ugly there for a while . . ."

"Ugly? It was a festering pus bucket," Hernandez snarled. "The media were ravenous for someone to fry after that debacle in Ankara, and somebody conveniently leaked George Morningstar's name. Morningstar got kicked into a basement office with no chance for parole, and you were banished to the land of the eternal sand wedge—for doing your job. Is that when your friends abandoned you? Is that the way loyalty works?"

"Back off, Tommy." Mullaney turned off the iPhone and stuck it in his pocket. "Still too sensitive. Abigail moved eleven times during our marriage, packing up the house and the kids and heading off to another assignment. And the constant upheaval was acceptable because each return home improved my position and returned her to the Washington diplomatic and political circles she grew up with. I promised her one day we would be home for good. We both thought this was the time."

Mullaney's mind and heart drifted back to their center-hall colonial home and the soccer fields of Fairfax, Virginia. He was brought back to Tel Aviv when Hernandez laid a hand on his arm.

"Brian, I love Abby. You know I do. But . . . but"—Hernandez's hands were waving in circles in front of him—"this is not the time. I mean, you just lost your dad, and all the stuff that went with that. And now your career has been hijacked from underneath you. Hey . . . I can tell by looking in your eyes at how deeply this has shaken you."

"Look, Tommy . . . all I want to do is get this assignment over with and get back to Washington as soon as possible. There's still time to put this family back together again. I just need to be there to make it happen. But this"—Mullaney swept his hand, taking in the whole airport—"none of this is Abby's fault."

"Okay, okay," said Hernandez, throwing up his hands. "I get it. I'll be like Zorro's butler—mute and cute. So how are the girls holding up?"

A wistful smile found its way to Mullaney's lips. "Well at least I'm good with the girls. We had a week alone at the cabin in the mountains before I had to get over here. They understand what's happened—and they are blissfully confident that Dad can fix all things. We have a great bond, thank God."

"Are you thanking God now?"

The frustration and resentment roiling just below the surface of Mullaney's defenses punched a hole in his heart. "Don't start on me, okay?"

"I'm sorry. My mouth sometimes does the thinking for my brain."

Hernandez turned sideways in the seat. "It's just that, well, you weren't doing that—thanking God—at your dad's funeral. And Brian, I'm worried about you."

Mullaney took a deep breath. It was hard holding everything in, trying to keep it together when so many anchors in his life were being ripped out at the same time. "I don't see how God can be involved in any of this. I've always done things the right way, Dad's way." Mullaney's downcast eyes studied the design in the tile floor. "I'm an honorable man, trustworthy, honest. God's supposed to protect honorable men, right?"

Taking a blue paisley handkerchief out of his pocket, Hernandez held the question at arm's length while he cleaned his sunglasses.

"That's a bigger question than we have time for right now, don't you think?" said Hernandez.

"Okay, then," said Mullaney, pulling himself up to look squarely at his partner. "Let me ask you another question. What happened in Istanbul? I've read the report, but I don't buy half of it. Something doesn't add up. A Turkish terror cell waits until President Kashani is at the gate of the embassy to launch an attack? And Cleveland just happens to be in the line of fire? And less than three months later another unknown group attacks Cleveland and his escort in Istanbul, and the threat analysists are telling us there's no connection? That's the kind of head-in-the-sand analysis that got us Benghazi. Our investigators should be all over both of these incidents until we do find the connection. You were there. What do you think?"

Hernandez grimaced as he tried to stretch the kinks in his body, the unforgiving chair giving him no help. "At this point, what I think appears to be irrelevant. I tried to give my opinion to Nora Carson, and she smiled but ignored me. Said it was local unrest with Kashani's growing authoritarian rule. Right, and my next-door neighbor Santa Claus took a night job as the tooth fairy.

"Listen, Brian, I think we've got a leak inside the department. They—and we better figure out who *they* are real quick—they knew Atticus was at the embassy when he was scheduled to be at Kashani's Palace. And *they* knew the ambassador was heading to the synagogue in Istanbul long before he got there. And *they* knew what he left the synagogue with, which is why they tried to whack us when we left. We've got an enemy that is two steps ahead of us . . . and we don't even know who that enemy is. That's why I convinced Nora that

I had to come here a day before Cleveland—so I could bring you up to speed and we could start planning our defenses."

As Hernandez paused to position the aviators back on his nose, Mullaney had an opening.

"So what *did* Cleveland get at the synagogue that triggered the attack?"

Hernandez slapped his hands down on his knees. "That, my friend, is a good question. And its answer is one the kind ambassador has declined to share with me, despite countless inquiries over the last three days. He walked into the synagogue empty-handed and came out carrying a leather satchel that he held so tightly I thought he was going to climb inside the bag. He wouldn't let me or Jack Nelson touch it. He's got marines stationed just outside the door of his office since the recent attack, so the bag's either been in his hands or locked behind armed marines the whole time. Honestly, Atticus is so anxious to get to Israel I think he would have walked here days ago, but he's obligated to do the ceremonial transfer of station with Buster Brown tomorrow morning and then the introduction to President Kashani. But the way he treats that bag, you would think it contained the launch codes."

"For our nukes?"

"No, for Candy Land." Hernandez shrugged his shoulders and threw up his hands. "Who knows? All I can tell you is that Atticus accelerated his departure schedule to the bare minimum. I left the ambassador with a double guard and didn't like it one bit. He wanted you and me to prepare for a trip into Jerusalem at the earliest possible moment. And he promised to fill us in completely when he gets here. But listen, I know tensions are high and things are already heating up around here. My gut tells me we'll have little time for personal conversation. So let me get this out now."

Hernandez pulled off the sunglasses, turned to his left, and waited for Mullaney to look up. "Brian, there are an awful lot of people in all levels of the department—both lefties and righties—who know you and believe in you. You're getting a raw deal here, just like Morningstar. You know it and I know it. I just want you to know I'm here for you. Anytime, anywhere, any way—you are the brother I never had, and I'll never quit on you." Hernandez lowered his voice. "But if you start crying, the offer's off the table."

In a long litany of bad days, Tommy Hernandez brought Mullaney a ray of hope. And the knowledge that he wasn't alone after all. His prayer life had evaporated, pushed aside by the growing anxiety on so many levels. He no longer felt close to God. So Tommy's encouragement felt like dew in the desert.

"Congrats, by the way," said Hernandez. "RSO is a nice bump."

A grimace twisted Mullaney's mouth, broadcasting the turmoil in his heart.

The Diplomatic Security Service had the world divided up into regions. In each of those regions, individual DSS agents were under the authority of a regional security officer (RSO), a senior officer with higher rank and pay than individual agents. The RSOs were also granted a great deal of operational freedom and authority—the tools necessary to respond instantly to any threat in their region.

He shook his head. "The title goes with the Israel posting. I wouldn't call it a promotion, and it's little consolation for banishment."

Mullaney got up, stretched his six foot two frame, and pulled the car keys from his pocket. "C'mon, we need to get cracking. You're right . . . things are getting hot, fast. This morning we got word that the IDF was calling up a huge chunk of its reserves. We don't know why, but I think we'll keep you busy."

"Well, I'm glad you requested me to stay on the ambassador's detail," said Hernandez, grabbing his bag and getting to his feet. "Otherwise, I could have been steering a desk now, looking down the sites of a computer screen and going nuts. I'm not ready to retire."

"I've heard good things about Cleveland," said Mullaney as they walked toward the exit.

"You're going to like Atticus," said Hernandez. "Just don't call him that to his face. He's a man of character and integrity. You can always count on him to tell you the truth and to watch your back. In our business, you can't get better than that." He hesitated. "But there are times when it seems to me that he's carrying some great weight, something that reaches to the depth of his soul. I want to reach out and hug him when I see it."

"Probably not a good idea."

Hernandez stopped in the middle of the busy terminal, throwing up his hands. "Hey . . . you should commune with your feminine side once in a while, right? Go with the emotions, you know?"

"You should go to the psych team and get some help."

As Mullaney neared the exit, he turned to face Hernandez. "I'm glad you're here, Tommy. I'm going to need you. Something has stirred up a hornet's nest the last few days, and it seems like everybody is on edge. Besides"—Mullaney reached into his pocket, then held out his hand to Hernandez—"I owe you this twenty."

Hernandez took the twenty dollar bill and rubbed it between his thumb and forefinger. "All right . . . let's go find that Taco Bell!"

Washington, DC
July 18, 2:53 p.m.

It was the kind of car he had once commanded—a long black Cadillac stretch limo with a stern-faced driver in front and blackened windows all around. The car radiated wealth, power, and influence—the three currencies of the nation's capital. Currencies he had once enjoyed in abundance. Now? He was too proud to give up his position and too foolish to surrender to time and reality.

Senator Seneca Markham spent more than forty years of his life in the intoxicating halls of Capitol Hill. Former chairman of the United States Senate Committee on Foreign Relations and a senior member of the Committee on Appropriations, Markham was more than simply one of Washington's most powerful politicians. Before declining health forced his retirement two years earlier, Markham had lived the life of a feudal lord. His estates were the cotton fields of Alabama, his manor house an antebellum, white-columned beauty of the Old South, his vassals the uncountable thousands who had benefited financially from Markham's undeniable reputation as a dealmaker.

Now he was just an old man living beyond his means. A man whose debts were being called to account.

The limo eased up to the underground entrance of the Savoy, high-priced condos on the edge of Washington's downtown. The driver came around and opened the door for Markham . . . took his elbow to help him into the spacious back seat. Each day his body betrayed him even more.

The welcome air-conditioning and the sumptuous leather upholstery embraced him at the same time.

"Good afternoon, Senator." The heavy southern drawl momentarily transported Markham back to his family home in Dooly County, the cotton king of Georgia. "I am truly grateful that you would allow me the honor of your company today."

The limo pulled out of the Savoy and turned left, toward central DC. To Markham's left sat Richard Rutherford, chairman of the Georgia National Bank—his state's largest bank—founder of the Savannah Roundtable, a monthly invitation-only gathering of Georgia's most wealthy families and, for decades, Markham's largest and most reliable campaign funder. Rutherford was a vibrant and strapping sixty-three-year-old financial dynamo who, from behind the scenes, had dominated and directed the state's politics and government for more than twenty-five years.

"Good afternoon, Richard," said Markham, both of his hands resting on the top of his ivory-handled cane. "I appreciate the ride . . . and the time to talk. And how is your family, your daughter, Abigail?"

"We are blessed, thank you for asking, Senator."

Rutherford had the looks of a Hollywood heartthrob, tall and muscular, his skin tanned and flawless, and his thick hair graying in dramatic sweeps that accented the ruddy gold highlights. Markham hated him for his health.

"Martha is content with her church socials and bridge club in Atlanta," said Rutherford. "Robert E. is prospering in Berlin. Honestly, I think he'll soon end up owning half of Germany. And Abby? Well, it's been glorious having Abby and her girls here in Washington the last two years."

"You and Abigail, it appears, have become the center of Washington society." Markham turned his head to the left to give the coming compliment even more weight. "You must be very proud of your daughter, Robert. She is a delightful, beautiful woman . . . an honor to the Rutherford name."

Rutherford was nodding his head, but his eyes were staring into space. "Yes, Seneca . . . it's been wonderful." Like a man jolting awake as his train home was *leaving* his station, Rutherford gave a quick shake to his head and squared his shoulders. "But we have business to discuss and not much time to do it. You are on your way to speak to young Webster. How is our young man holding up? Can we still rely on his loyalty and commitment?"

Ah, the language of political deals. Seneca Markham had made a living, and a small fortune, using words like *loyalty* as an incorrect but justifiable substitute for *is he still in our control*. Sadly, a small fortune wasn't near enough to support the life of a feudal lord.

"There is no reason to concern ourselves about Noah Webster," said Markham. "He knows his future, and his freedom, are irretrievably intertwined with our purposes and good will. And he is a willing ally."

"Good, we need him." Like a scythe through sugarcane, Rutherford's voice took on an edge and urgency. "That fool Boylan is causing a great deal of concern among our friends, Senator. He appears determined to forge ahead with this handout to Iran."

"It is their money, Richard."

His chin tucked down to his neck, Rutherford slowly turned his head. He was looking down his nose at Markham, like a disappointed teacher in the wake of a foolish question. "Possession, Senator. Possession is nine-tenths of the law. It was the shah's money anyway, which he got from us in the first place. Regardless. We both know the most important truth about those funds, don't we, Seneca?"

Yes . . . the most important truth. Money. But not only money. This was unencumbered money, a torrent of cash that remained mostly invisible. The Iranian assets seized by the government during the 1979 hostage crisis now hemorrhaged interest at an inconceivable rate, the clandestine flow of money that had at one time kept Senator Seneca Markham living in the luxury to which he had become accustomed but could no longer afford. And a flow of money that held great promise for Noah Webster's ambition.

"If we are forced to return Iran's assets and lose the income from those funds," said Rutherford, "all our lives will abruptly change for the worse. Senator, I would hate to see you destitute at this stage of your life."

Senator Markham squeezed the ivory handle of his cane, his knuckles turning white around his age spots. *There was a time . . .*

"No, Seneca, my friends and I are honored to help you live in the manner and comfort you deserve. And we will continue to do so . . . if young Webster can prove his value. Please, ensure he understands just how important his effectiveness is to those of us who care for his future."

The car began to slow as it approached the river walk along the Potomac. Senator Markham attempted to push himself more erect . . . to regain some measure of dignity before he faced Noah Webster.

"Oh . . . by the way, Senator. There is one thing you can do for me." Rutherford's words had morphed from sharp edged to sweet tea. "Perhaps you can bring my son-in-law back from his unwarranted banishment. It would make my granddaughters undeniably joyful to have their father back in Washington. I would be personally grateful if you could rescue Brian from that desert in Israel."

Senator Seneca Markham endured the pain in his hips and turned toward Rutherford. He nodded his head in agreement. "Very well, Richard. I will see what I can do." The car stopped. In a moment the driver was opening Markham's door. "Thank you for your kindness of bringing me here. I'm sure we will be speaking again soon. Good day, Richard."

As the driver helped Markham to his feet, the senator had a smile on his face. Rutherford had just made a deposit into Markham's currency account of power and influence. Rutherford wanted his son-in-law home. Fine. Markham would put in a word . . . when it suited his time and his purpose. This was one ace he would not play until absolutely necessary.

He walked along the Potomac promenade leaning on a cane, Noah Webster trawling to his right. Senator Seneca Markham's body might be more feeble than it had been during his days on the Hill, but his mind and his will were as sharp as ever.

He had a message to deliver to Webster. And he would deliver it with conviction and purpose. Much depended on his former pupil.

"Seven hundred million dollars a year, and compounding by six percent each year—that's a lot of loose change, Noah. Do you think we're going to give it away?"

A wide-brimmed fedora shaded Markham's balding head from the summer sun. But his eyes still calculated the meaning of Webster's every move as he shuffled along the shade-dappled promenade. "Don't think our friends are concerned only with the money," Markham cautioned. "Most of these men had their worldviews refined by the shah's overthrow and the national angst of the following hostage crisis. Here . . . let's rest on this bench."

Webster held Senator Markham's elbow, steadying his former boss as he lowered himself to the green, wood-slat bench. The senator had been a dictator then, when Webster served as Markham's chief of staff in the mid-nineties . . .

but always a benevolent dictator when it came to Webster. Nearly two decades later, the senator still held Webster's future firmly in his grasp.

"It was only a few years after the shah was kicked out that Iran's Islamic jihadist government was responsible for the murder of 241 marines in the bombing in Beirut," Markham continued. "In the thirty years since, Iran continues to be identified as the world's leading state sponsor of terrorism." Markham turned to his right, his face in shadow under the fedora's brim. "Our nation has three relentless enemies, Noah—Russia, China, and Iran. All three of those nations have a similar endgame . . . to replace the United States as the most dominant military and political power in the world. It is to our own peril if we choose to ignore that truth. Sadly, it's something our president has conveniently forgotten."

There was little traffic on the Potomac in the afternoon heat, less on the promenade itself. Some bees buzzed in the background as the mere promise of a breeze briefly stirred the air.

"It's not just the money." The senator's rheumy eyes held a hundred-year gaze as he looked out over the river. "Our friends are dedicated patriots and fierce foes of our enemies. But make no mistake." He turned to face Webster once again. "Two billion dollars in Iranian assets were frozen in American banks thirty years ago. That two billion sitting in American banks has gained over ten billion in interest over that thirty-year span. That's a lot of money." The senator placed his hand on Webster's arm. "Richard Rutherford urged me to remind you that it's more than enough to finance a successful run for the Senate in two years, more than enough to finance a presidential election bid in ten years."

Senator Markham waited while the words sunk in, but Webster's dreams had already advanced down those roads.

"ISIS is on the offensive in Sinjar Province," said the senator. "Over three hundred thousand people, mostly Christians and Yadzikis, have been driven from their homes. We need to strengthen the Kurds and continue to push for a free Kurdish state as a bulwark against Iran's plans for expansion. You cannot allow our president to give in to the Iranians. I don't care how you do it, but block that Iranian treaty. If you want the support of our friends, Noah, you need to stand with them now. Before it's too late."

7

US Ambassador's Residence, Tel Aviv
July 19, 7:38 a.m.

The sun was on the front of the residence this early in the morning, so the patio to the side of the building, well shaded by palm trees and hedges, was washed by cool breezes coming off the Mediterranean Sea. Brian Mullaney, a hot mug of coffee in one hand and his suit jacket in the other, stepped off the stone veranda and moved into the shadows. He set his blue embassy mug on a square white table, draped his jacket over one of the padded white wrought iron chairs scattered throughout the large patio, and settled into the cushions like a man in need of comfort.

There was nothing small about the US ambassador's residence in Israel. It was perched on a cliff in the Herzliya Pituach neighborhood, just north of seaside Tel Aviv. A sprawling complex with an expansive, multi-level lawn overlooking the sea, the residence building had a modern white California-like exterior designed with the Spartan squareness of Israeli architecture. In most years, the staff would still be recovering from the ambassador's annual Fourth of July party—an all-American extravaganza where over two thousand guests filled the lawn and filled themselves with McDonald's burgers, Domino's pizza, and Ben & Jerry's ice cream. But outgoing ambassador Harley Carnes canceled the event, partly out of respect for the mourning period for three Israeli teenagers who were kidnapped and murdered, but mostly just to avoid the embarrassment of answering the question of his sudden departure two thousand times.

Mullaney pulled in a deep breath and stretched out his long legs. The air was sweet and mild but edged with the tinge of salt. He drained half his mug, determined to focus his mind on all he needed to accomplish in anticipation of Ambassador Cleveland's arrival that afternoon. For the time being, it was necessary to find a compartment in his mind in which to stash his thoughts of Abby and the girls back in Virginia. He closed his eyes and breathed deeply once more. The scent of flowers floated . . .

"Good morning, Agent Mullaney."

He looked over his right shoulder.

"Please, don't get up."

Palmyra Parker was a stunning woman. Tall and regal, with the grace of a professional dancer, she slid into the chair opposite. Unable to break his training and upbringing, Mullaney was on his feet. "Good morning, Mrs. Parker."

As part of the ambassador's team overseeing the transition, Mullaney knew before he arrived in Israel two weeks earlier that Cleveland's daughter would be joining the ambassador in the residence, taking on the role of hostess for her widowed father. He had seen her in passing in the two days since her arrival but had had little opportunity to speak with her.

What he knew from his briefing was that Parker, who performed with the Alvin Ailey Dance Theater while an undergrad at NYU, had traded a short but accomplished tenure as a linguist at the United Nations for a law degree from Fordham University and ten years as counsel for the Children's Defense Fund. Four months ago, her world ruptured when her husband was killed in an automobile accident. Childless and grieving, Parker welcomed her father's invitation to make a home for them both in Israel.

What he hadn't been told was that Palmyra Parker, in addition to being a knockout, emanated a presence of both confidence and competence. Dressed in a white cotton dress with a turned-up collar, she wore her black hair in a short but elegant style. Her eyes were a shade of pale green that seemed translucent, framed by a café au lait complexion that added depth to her beauty. *Wow!* crossed his mind, followed immediately by an image of Abby's smiling face and a certainty that only one woman had his heart. Abby might not be pleased that a woman as stunning as Palmyra Parker was in residence, but she had no reason to doubt Mullaney's faithfulness . . . and he was not about to give her one.

Mrs. Parker extended her hand across the table, and Mullaney caught a scent of what smelled like hyacinth. "I was happy to see you out here, Agent Mullaney. Give us a few minutes to talk in private."

Her handshake was deliberately strong and firm, sending a message.

"How can I be of service, Mrs. Parker?"

But her voice was welcoming. "First, I want you to know up front that I am very grateful to have you as head of security for Dad's team here in Israel. I did a little homework before I got here, called a couple of friends. You are a highly respected man, both as an individual and as a professional in your work. I know you weren't planning on this assignment, but selfishly, I'm glad you're here. Second, Brian, my name is Palmyra. If we have to call each other by our titles, it will be a long two years. Maybe we can lighten up when it's just us?"

"Palmyra?"

"My Dad was inoculated with the Greek classics by his mother," she said. "She was an English teacher in a very run-down school in North Carolina. Don't ask what my brothers are named."

"Androcles, which means *glory of a man*," said Mullaney, "and Kleitos, which means *splendid* or *famous*. I've done some homework too."

Her eyes were the color of Caribbean shoals, a sparkling and fresh green, and they washed over his face with inquisitive assessment. A smile brushed the corners of her mouth. "And what do you know about me? Perhaps I should call you Agent Mullaney after all."

Tickled by her playfulness, Mullaney reclined farther into the cushions and returned her smile with one of his own. "I know what I read about you in the brief, the sterile stuff. But I'm happy to see that your heart confirms what I discerned—you love your father enough to set your life aside to serve him. And I can tell now that you're somebody I want on my side. I would not want to cross swords with you, Mrs. Parker. Oh"—Mullaney leaned into the table and banished his smile—"I'm sorry about your loss. I can only imagine how painful it must be."

Parker searched his countenance once more, as if she were probing for signs of false sincerity. "Thank you, Brian. I appreciate your kindness."

Mullaney picked up his blue coffee mug and stared at the lukewarm contents. "I could use your help," he said, looking up from the mug. "From what I've read about your dad and from what Tommy Hernandez has shared with me—"

"I am *so* glad you got Tommy back on Dad's detail," she interrupted. "Tommy saved his life back in Istanbul."

Mullaney nodded his head. "Tommy's rescued me more times than I care to remember. But listen. My experience has shown me there are two types of ambassadors—one is a posturing empty suit with too much pull in Washington, and the other is a guy like your dad, who has worked his way up and earned his post by staying three steps ahead of everybody else in the room. Guys like your dad are great to work for—until they decide to go off the reservation and try to do something on their own without proper security, because they've got the chutzpah to take a great risk for a greater reward."

Parker smiled. "That's Dad."

"Then I need your help, Palmyra . . . I need you to help me keep him alive over here."

Mullaney rested his elbows on top of the table and leaned closer to Parker. "Your father came under attack in Istanbul, and I'm not convinced that President Kashani was the only target of the attack on the embassy in Ankara. That's twice in the last three months that your father's life has been threatened. My gut tells me whoever means him harm will likely try again. I'm going to know where Ambassador Cleveland is every minute of every day—until he decides to pull a Lone Ranger on me. And I need you to warn me when that's coming. Because I believe you will know—probably even before Atticus knows—when he's planning a stunt like that."

"Atticus? Are you part of the family now, Brian?"

Mullaney relaxed. He knew he had found an ally in Palmyra Parker . . . an ally who would be invaluable for whatever amount of time he was in Israel. "Closer than a brother, Palmyra."

A mischievous twinkle lit up the corners of her eyes. For some men, Palmyra Parker would be irresistible. Mullaney would not allow himself to be one of those men.

"Well, I guess it's appropriate we're already on a first-name basis." Parker pushed back her chair and stood, looking up into the blue sky. "Going to be hot again." She turned to face Mullaney and reached out her hand once more. When Mullaney took it, her grip was still like hardened steel. "Thank you, Brian. I've lost my mother. Now I've lost my husband. I love my brothers, but"—her eyes bored into his—"Atticus is all I have. I am not going to lose my father, not to this job and not to those crazies out there who long to take his life. I think, together, we can keep him alive, but . . ." She let go of his hand and stepped back.

"Brian . . . I know you didn't plan to be here, and I know this assignment has caused upheaval in your family, and I'm sorry about that. Sorry you've been separated from your wife and daughters. And I'm pretty sure you'd like to get back to Washington as soon as you can. But I hope you're here for the duration of Dad's assignment. Please don't hold that against me."

Standing, Mullaney shook his head. He picked up his jacket. "We both want what's best for your dad. And we're both here to serve—however long that's required. Let's just take it one day at a time. Tomorrow's about as far ahead as I can look. And now I need to get to the embassy."

Parker started walking toward the residence. "Duty calls us both. Thank you, Brian. And be careful out there today."

What? The same words he and Doak spoke to each other almost every day when they were both with the state police. Mullaney stopped, watching Parker's back. *That's weird.*

US Embassy, Tel Aviv
July 19, 11:12 a.m.

Mullaney's empty stomach was just starting to send signals about lunch when Jarrod Goldberg knocked on his open door. Jon Lin was at his shoulder. "Got a minute?" It wasn't a request.

As deputy chief of mission for Israel, Goldberg was the ranking State Department officer in the absence of the ambassador and, as such, was in charge of the entire mission staff. He and Lin stepped into Mullaney's office and closed the door behind them.

"Half of our situation board just went red," said Lin, a bespectacled MIT grad. He and Goldberg stood, ignoring the chairs in front of Mullaney's desk. Lin, head of the FBI office in the embassy, reached across the desk and handed Mullaney a one-page report. "In the last twenty minutes Israel, Egypt, Jordan, Saudi Arabia, and a handful of Gulf states all raised their threat levels to the maximum. Israel has called up one-third of its military reservists. Jordan and Egypt have mobilized military units."

Mullaney glanced at the paper. "Doesn't make sense." He looked up. "Ever since the Palestinian Authority turned over those suspects in the teenagers' murders, everything's been quiet. We've picked up no evidence of pending conflict anywhere. What's happened?"

"We don't know," said Lin, "and that's both frightening and humiliating."

A myriad of possibilities raced through Mullaney's mind, but the reality was clear. America's diplomatic and security agencies had suffered a colossal failure. The governments of the Middle East were suddenly poised for a third Arab-Israeli war. And no one assigned as part of the US Diplomatic Mission to Israel or of any of its extensive intelligence corps had any clue it was coming.

Washington must be in an uproar. And the ambassador was scheduled to land at Ben Gurion Airport in less than an hour. The men in this room were on the cusp of disaster.

"We are not anticipating a military conflict between Israel and its Arab neighbors," said Goldberg. "And that is the message we delivered to Washington." A Foreign Service veteran with an illustrious record, Goldberg's demeanor was as neatly pressed as his suit. "What we do not know is why. What has precipitated this unexpected activity? Jon and I are twisting as many arms as we can find, but no one is willing, or able, to enlighten us.

"You've been here before, Agent Mullaney, during your tour in Amman. Are your contacts still viable?"

"Yes, sir. I believe so."

"Good," said Goldberg. "Utilize promises or threats, whatever is effective. But find out what is happening. We need answers."

Mullaney felt another rumble in his stomach. But this time it wasn't hunger.

Scrolling through the contacts on his iPhone, Mullaney stepped out of his office and stopped at the first door on his left. "Tommy . . ."

Hernandez dropped the blue-covered daily CIA briefing to the top of his desk. "Yes, Boss?"

"Get ahold of the ambassador's daughter. She should be at the residence. Tell her we'll be picking her up in about thirty minutes."

"Are we going on a date? Brunch on the Tel Aviv beach?"

"No. And it's no use trying to hide the crossword puzzle," said Mullaney, his smile admonishing. "Ask her if she's willing to accompany us to the airport to meet Ambassador Cleveland. Be polite, but it's not a request. You and I are bringing Cleveland straight here from the airport—threat levels have just gone through the roof in Israel, Egypt, and Saudi Arabia. We need to be mobile. And we need Mrs. Parker to take on the responsibility of getting Cleveland's belongings to the residence. So get a second car and a driver to the airport to help Mrs. Parker. And Tommy, let's double the escort detail for both the ambassador and his daughter."

"You got it, kemo sahbee. And Brian?"

"Yeah?"

"What's a seven letter Farsi word for vacation?"

Mullaney took one step into Hernandez's office. "Try *U R Fired!* How's that fit?"

Hernandez threw up his hands. "Like a glove, Boss. Like a glove. I'm movin'."

"Good," said Mullaney as he walked back through the door. "We all are."

He hoped the number was still active. You never knew for sure in this business.

"Yes?"

The voice was unfamiliar, the tone tense and wary. Not surprising, since so few had access to this phone number.

"Is this the office of the Guard?"

Silence.

"This is Brian Mullaney, regional security officer for the US State Department, stationed in Tel Aviv, Israel. Please tell Sultan that I'm looking for him . . . and tell him he still doesn't know how to play Texas Hold'em."

More silence. "This is Captain Lubayd Nasari of the Jordanian Royal Guard Brigade. In spite of your calculated rudeness toward my superior officer, I will inform Commander Abbaddi of your request. How may he reach you?"

"He has the number, Captain. Thank you for your—"

The click and dial tone ended the conversation before Mullaney could finish his sentence.

8

Ankara
July 19, 11:58 a.m.

The Turk was resting on a divan, slipping into slumber. The room was in twilight, two small lamps offering limited light from the corners.

His reverie was cut short when his aide entered the darkened room. He lifted his right hand and waved it toward the door. Assan was dressed in a long black robe, a black cowl over his head. He was as thin as a cadaver, bony hands tucked into the robe's voluminous sleeves, and he moved into the room like ice on a warm plate, sliding up to the divan's side.

"Tüm güçlü," said the aide in Turkish, bowing deeply from his waist. *All Powerful.* It was the Turk's favorite form of address.

"Yes?" The Turk replaced the hose onto the hookah. "Why do you disturb me?"

"Master." He bowed low once more. "The ambassador's plane is landing momentarily. He has the case in his possession. We have two teams of disciples at the airport, another outside the embassy, and a fourth watching the residence."

"Very well." The Turk stretched the muscles of his legs. "Keep the package in sight at all times. If they see an opportunity to seize the package, do it. Let no one stand in their way."

"Yes, Master." The aide hesitated. The Turk waited for the words he knew would follow. "May I ask a question?"

"Proceed."

"Master . . . once we have the box . . . will it not be a death sentence to touch it? How will we determine the contents of the Gaon's second prophecy?"

The Turk smiled. It was a smile without mirth or life, a smile that could freeze a flame in mid-flicker. Assan was once an eminent professor of philosophy. His dabbling in the occult opened a portal which the Turk accessed to exert dominion in mind, soul, and spirit. Assan was one of his most devoted disciples. Still at times, his mind functioned a bit too independently.

"I require the box," said the Turk, "because I require the prophecy. The Lithuanian knew how to destroy our plans. We believe that is the lethal nature of the message. It is imperative—it is worth any risk, any cost—to prevent others from knowing its message and using its power."

Assan bowed his head but withdrew one withered hand from the sleeve of his robe, turning it palm up. "Yes, Master. Your disciples are determined to frustrate and prevent the fulfillment of Jewish prophecy. If we can change the promises in the book, we can change its ending."

Soon, the Turk mused, *I may need to consider Assan's further freedom of thought. But for the moment . . .*

Like a man who longed to continue in slumber's embrace, he drew his legs over the side of the divan and sat before his aide. "The prophecies of the Jew's book, the Christian's book," said the Turk, "foretell the end of man in the great conflict for control of this world. Those prophecies are interconnected. If one fails, all the others collapse . . . lose their relevance and authority. I intend to write a new ending to history, Assan. An ending that is not in the book. An ending that enthrones us as rightful rulers of this world. There is one prophecy in the book that, when destroyed, will abolish all the rest."

The Turk rose, stiffly, but his leaving was stalled.

"One prophecy, Master? Which one is this?"

Lowering his chin, the Turk turned his head to the left and leveled his withering gaze upon his aide, who wisely averted his eyes. "You ask many questions this day, Assan."

The words were rapidly mumbled past trembling lips. "Forgive me, Master. I do not wish to offend."

Utilizing his silence as a weapon, the Turk willed his consciousness into Assan's captive mind. *Benign curiosity. No threat. Very well, once we have completed . . .*

"It is Jerusalem, Assan. It is always Jerusalem. The book falsely labels the One as a usurper. That is the prophecy we will defeat. We will ensure that the One enters the gates as savior. And he will enter the temple as ruler, ruler of this world in body, mind, and soul."

The Turk turned away from his aide and slowly moved toward the corner of shadows. "But this so-called prophecy of the Lithuanian dreamer," he said over his shoulder, "is not contained in the book. It would be irrelevant to us, but for one thing. Stealth is our ally, Assan. Darkness is our cloak." Blackness enveloped the Turk as he turned once more to his aide. "And the Gaon's message will shed light where darkness must reign. It must be obliterated. See to it."

Ben Gurion Airport, Tel Aviv
July 19, 12:09 p.m.

After a discreet stop at the Ben Gurion Airport office of Shin Bet, Israel's internal security agency, Mullaney, Hernandez, and Palmyra Parker stood on the airport's tarmac, under the front fuselage of a Boeing 737, the four embassy vehicles idling quietly behind them. Following the direction of a Shin Bet officer, workers hustled a mobile stairway up to a door in the Jetway while the plane's crew kept the passengers in their seats.

Within moments, US Ambassador Joseph Atticus Cleveland's perplexed face appeared in the open doorway, a leather bag suspended in the grip of his left hand.

"There's the bag," said Hernandez. "I better go give him a hand."

The Shin Bet officer came up beside Mullaney as Hernandez offered a hand to the descending Cleveland. "We'll unload the ambassador's luggage from the plane and make sure it all gets to the vehicle."

"Thanks."

"A rather unorthodox welcome, Agent Mullaney—though I'm not complaining." Ambassador Cleveland was past him before Mullaney could respond, moving quickly to his daughter. He wrapped his right arm around her shoulders and pulled her close, the leather bag still in his left hand. "Palmyra," he spoke into her hair, "I've missed you. I wish I could have stayed longer with—"

"That's okay, Dad," said Palmyra. She stepped back from his embrace and looked into Cleveland's face. "I know where your heart is."

A long, intimate silence made Mullaney feel like he was intruding on a family's grieving. Cleveland reached out his right hand and caressed Parker's cheek. "We'll catch up back at the residence," said Cleveland. "Unless"—he turned toward Mullaney—"I see we have increased security. Are there other plans?"

"Forgive me, Mr. Ambassador, but we need to go directly to the embassy. We can discuss this on our way. Mrs. Parker will see to your belongings."

Cleveland searched Mullaney's face, glanced toward his daughter, then turned back to his regional security officer. "Very well. Just give me a moment." The ambassador moved to his right, gently grasped his daughter's arm, and guided her—not toward his waiting limousine, but toward the second vehicle that would take his daughter and his belongings to the ambassador's residence.

In the back seat of the car, Cleveland placed his hand over Palmyra's and gave it a squeeze. "Sweetheart, I wish I had more time to go into more detail with you, but I think our time here is limited. Allow me to get directly to the issue."

How could he emphasize the critical importance of what he was going to tell her without unduly frightening her? No . . . she should be frightened.

Cleveland hefted the heavy leather satchel sitting on the floor at his feet. "I received this from the chief rabbi in Istanbul four days ago, and it has seldom been out of my sight since. Inside the bag is a small wooden chest that contains a sealed metal box. Inside the metal box, the rabbi believes, is a 250-year-old message . . . the second prophesy written by an eighteenth-century Jewish scholar, the Vilna Gaon. The first prophesy came to light several months ago. It said when the Russians annex Crimea then Messiah's coming was imminent."

Palmyra tucked her leg up onto the seat in order to face her father directly. "And the Russians are now in control of Crimea," she said. "So the clock may be ticking. What's in the second prophecy?"

"Nobody knows, not even the rabbis who have protected it. It is assumed the message is written in code. I've promised the chief rabbi in Istanbul that I will deliver this bag and its contents to the Gaon's disciples at the Hurva Synagogue in Jerusalem. But none of that is why I needed to speak to you alone." Cleveland took a deep breath and met his daughter's gaze. "Possession of the box inside this satchel is very dangerous. It could be deadly."

He was alarmed by the sparkle that entered her eyes.

"Now, that sounds interesting."

"This is nothing to trifle with, Palmyra," he snapped. Cleveland tried to slow his heartbeat. "There are two critical points. You are not to touch the metal box inside this bag under any circumstance. Anyone who touches this box without the proper anointing will lose their life. I know it sounds like a bad movie plot, but I assure you this is a warning we need to heed. Second, as soon as the box was in my possession, my car and my security team were attacked.

The synagogue in Istanbul suffered three terrorist attacks in the time the box resided there. I believe there are forces at work here that are determined to prevent this bag from reaching the Rabbinate Council at the Hurva."

"And you want me to take this bag back to the residence?"

Cleveland struggled under a growing burden of fear for his daughter and guilt for asking her to take this risk. Mullaney and Hernandez would be traveling with him to the embassy. There was no one else to trust with the package. "Yes."

"Cool," said Palmyra. Cleveland's heart plummeted to the floor of the car. "What about this anointing? Do you have it?"

When there was a knock on the window, Cleveland nearly jumped into the front seat. "Forgive me, Mr. Ambassador. We need to get moving."

"One moment, Mullaney." Cleveland closed the window and redirected his attention to his daughter. He took his right hand and laid it on the crown of her head. "I'm taking the rabbi's word on this, and his word has not been tested. So don't touch the box. But just in case . . ." He closed his eyes and willed whatever power was in him to flow over and into his daughter "The Lord bless you, and keep you. The Lord make His face shine on you, and be gracious to you. The Lord lift up His countenance on you, and give you peace."

Palmyra covered her father's hand with her own. "The Aaronic blessing, that's appropriate," she said. She pointed to the leather bag at his feet. "What do you want me to do with it?"

Cleveland nodded. "When you get to the residence, find a place that is totally secure and out of the way. Hide this well. We'll talk about it more when I get home. And we'll make sure the box gets to the Rabbinate Council as soon as possible. But for now, we need to keep both you and the box safe. Promise me, Palmyra"—he took both of her hands in his—"you will not open this satchel and you will not go near the box inside. Understood?"

She squeezed his hands, but Cleveland felt anything but comforted. "Don't worry, Dad. You've left this package in good hands. I'll keep it safe."

Tommy Hernandez was at Mullaney's side.

"What is that all about?" said Hernandez.

Through the smoked-glass windows, with the sun behind the car, Mullaney could see the outlines of the ambassador and his daughter. The ambassador had his hand on top of her head.

"Either she's been grounded," said Hernandez, "or Atticus just bequeathed her all his earthly possessions. I'd bet on door number two."

"I'd bet your lame attempts at—"

"Oops . . . sorry, they're getting out."

Mullaney glanced at his watch as Hernandez helped Cleveland out of the car. It wasn't until later that Mullaney realized that the ambassador got out of the car—but the leather bag didn't.

Parker stood next to the car and watched the ambassador's limo and security escort make a right turn at the end of the terminal as her driver loaded luggage into the trunk.

From his vantage point in the terminal, the Turk's watcher could not see the leather satchel. But the ambassador had exited from the car empty-handed. The bag must be in the back. It would ride with Cleveland's daughter.

He brought the cell phone to his cheek.

"There has been a switch. The package is no longer with the ambassador," he said. He expected no reply. "The package is with his daughter, in a second embassy vehicle, a dark blue Ford. It is leaving now. She has two guards with her, and two more in an escort vehicle behind her."

9

Jerusalem, Israel
July 19, 12:39 p.m.

Colonel Benjamin Erdad slammed his fist on the table so hard the prime minister's water glass tumbled sideways. Luckily, there were no important documents sitting before David Meir. No one was taking any notes for this unusual but necessary Sabbath cabinet meeting.

"Blind? Blind! We have no choice but to accept," Israel's minister of internal security raged, his anger directed at the cabinet members from Yesh Atid, the most conciliatory party in Israel. "Do you think we don't understand the reality here? I trust that Prince Faisal is a man of good conscience. But Prince Faisal does not rule the Muslim world. We can never take these men at face value. I have no faith in their proposed covenant. If it were in force for ten years, I would not trust in it for ten years and a day. If we lose our focus, our determination for one day, Israel may be only a memory. But in spite of my utmost skepticism, we must accept this treaty. There is no other choice for Israel. Are we going to refuse to sign a peace treaty with a mutual defense pact with nearly every one of our closest Arab neighbors when they are the ones proposing this peace? We would be excoriated, standing alone. Even the Americans, with this president, would turn their back on Israel."

David Meir, prime minister of Israel only as long as he could hold together a fragile coalition of mismatched parts, was grateful. Erdad was taking the offensive, taking point on an issue where it would be much too easy for Meir to get dangerously ahead of his cabinet. The Ishmael Covenant, as Faisal called it, put the Israelis in a devilish position, caught in a trap of their own making. The Arabs were offering everything the Israeli government had for years claimed as prerequisites for a two-state solution to the "Palestinian question." Recognition of the state of Israel without a demand to return to the boundaries from before sixty-seven, a mutual defense pact that tied their security together, joint offenses against Hamas and Hezbollah to guarantee the safety of Israel's borders, and Jerusalem—intact and under Israel's dominion. They even offered a space for the Jewish temple connected to Temple Mount.

In return they asked only for East Jerusalem, Bethlehem, and Hebron—and the eternal wrath of thousands of transplanted Israelis who now lived in settlements the world condemned as illegal, settlements that would now exist in a new Palestinian state or cease to exist at all.

Still, as far as Meir could see, there really was no option for the government. Israel must accept.

"Israel must accept," Erdad concluded.

"What is this 'must,' Benjamin?" asked Moshe Litzman, minister of the interior and fellow Likud party member. "Since when is Likud willing to accept a 'must' in connection with an independent Palestinian state? And do you think there will ever be peace with Hamas?"

Meir looked around the large oval wooden table and considered the odds. If he couldn't get the cabinet members from his own party to support the treaty, what chance did it have with the members from other parties?

"Thousands of Israeli citizens will feel abandoned." Avi Lentz, leader of the Jewish Home, an ultra-right wing party, leaned into the table, his right index finger pointing at Erdad as if it were an Uzi. As the minister of housing, Lentz was a relentless evangelist for expanded Israeli settlements in the West Bank and draconian methods of dealing with the Palestinians. "We've asked them to risk their lives, their family's lives, and now we're going to toss them into the hands of the terrorists?"

Down at the end of the table, another of Meir's coalition "partners" stood from his chair. "This Faisal thinks us fools?" said Menachem Herzl. "He offers peace with one hand while he protects Wahhabi clerics with the other—clerics who preach the annihilation of Israel." Leader of the orthodox religious party Shas, Herzl was the ultimate power broker. With twelve active political parties holding seats in the Knesset, and another twenty political parties presenting candidates in each election, it was nearly impossible for one party to win a majority of the 120 seats in the Knesset. Shas was the glue that for decades held together the tenuous governing coalitions for both Likud and Labor governments. And Herzl played that card to its fullest.

Meir was about to answer when Erdad stepped to his defense once more.

"You know me," Erdad announced. His voice was as rock-solid as his build, commanding attention and respect. A career officer in the Israel Defense Force, Colonel Erdad's temporary assignment to Shin Bet was entering its twenty-fourth year when Meir invited him into a cabinet position two years earlier. "I would take no step that would weaken our defense or put Israel in jeopardy. All of you," he said, his eyes sweeping the table in challenge, his close-cropped steel gray hair standing up like a porcupine on alert, "know me."

Erdad focused on Menachem Herzl. "Every settler in the West Bank knew they were taking a risk with the future. Those settlers may not want to hear it now, but the settlements were always expected to be a bargaining chip." Erdad swept the table again. "I understand your concerns, your reluctance to trust the Arab states. Believe me; I don't trust them, either. But ministers, Israel has no choice. If we decline this offer of peace, this offer of recognition and Arab solidarity in destroying Hamas and Hezbollah, the nations of the world will turn against Israel in a heartbeat. *We* will be the villains."

"Better to be villains to the world than asleep in our beds when the Arab tanks start rolling again," thundered Lentz. "This fool's errand of a treaty can only result in a less-prepared Israel. We join in this mutual defense pact, who will guard our border with Syria? Jordan? Who will ensure that the jihadist groups in the Sinai Peninsula are beaten into the sand? Egypt? And what happens when the Muslim Brotherhood rises again in Egypt? Or when ISIS controls Northern Africa? No! There is only one of us. There are many of them, only one of which needs to have a bad day and start throwing missiles into Haifa or Eilat. You, Erdad, from you I would expect more."

Meir could see where this discussion was going—nowhere. There was no unity in his cabinet. How did he ever imagine to get this proposed treaty through the Knesset? Impossible. But he must. Somehow he must. *There is no other choice for us.*

"In less than twenty-four hours," said the prime minister, "all the Arab nations of the Middle East except for Syria will offer Israel a peace agreement that our nation has pursued for more than six decades. I suggest we all ratchet down the rhetoric, take a deep breath, and think about the nation we want to hand off to our children and grandchildren. An Israel always at war, or an Israel finally at peace? There are risks with each scenario, and regardless of which path we pursue, Israel must be forever vigilant. We will never again rely on others for the future of our people. But we have before us an opportunity to accomplish what was once unthinkable—not only an independent Jewish state, but a secure, independent Jewish state at peace with all its neighbors."

Meir stood from his chair and regarded the men and women of his cabinet. "I would like us to meet again this evening. Please . . . think of your children."

Highway One, Israel
July 19, 1:03 p.m.

Cleveland's mind strained to stay engaged with the briefing Mullaney was delivering, but his heart, his anxiety, resided with Palmyra.

Hernandez was driving a specially modified, two-year-old Mercedes-Maybach sedan, Agent Wiley Coates riding shotgun, Mullaney in the back seat with the ambassador. Hernandez was ignoring nearly every motor vehicle rule on the Israeli books as the sedan—often referred to as a limo because of its luxurious appointments—hurtled west on Highway One toward the American embassy in Tel Aviv.

One of the finest luxury cars money could buy, the Mercedes-Maybach 57 sedan—at three hundred fifty thousand dollars each—was the flagship of Mercedes's S-Class. The Maybach they were riding in was a modified, heavily armored version of the classic sedan, retro-fitted by State Department engineers. Outfitted so that both its body and windows could withstand hardened steel-core bullets fired from assault rifles, all the Maybach's safety features were integrated into the car itself, using certified ballistics protection.

The American engineers designed a layer of protective plating between the inner frame and the outer shell of the sedan and then added overlapping protective material in the joints and seams where the armored plates met to prevent any weak points. All the reinforced windows were coated with polycarbonate to prevent splintering. And the Maybach, its entire underbody fitted with armored plating, was capable of surviving a bomb blast whether the explosion was under the car or alongside it.

After the attack on his car in Turkey, Cleveland was grateful for the engineered safety of the Mercedes limo, but his thoughts were elsewhere—bouncing between concern for his daughter and confusion about the events transpiring around him.

"Why," Cleveland asked Mullaney, "did Deputy Chief Goldberg believe there was no hostile intent to this mobilization?"

"He's betting his reputation on one piece of information that might be telling," Mullaney answered. "It's true both Israel and Egypt have mobilized a portion of their military. But in neither case are those units moving toward the borders. Our assets on the ground tell us they are deploying around cities and other heavily populated areas. We should have a satellite pass in the next hour or so. The pictures will tell us a lot."

Cleveland looked at the floor beneath his feet. Odd, now that there was no leather bag, he felt more fearful. He turned his mind back to Mullaney.

"Why is Jordan mobilizing, Agent Mullaney? If there was some flash point or offense occurring that we didn't know about—some fracture about Gaza, for instance—I could understand heightened tensions between Egypt and Israel. But why Jordan? And the Saudis? Riyadh appeared to be opening conversation with the Israelis on several fronts. This mobilization doesn't make sense. I wonder . . ."

Mullaney's mobile phone clamored to life. "Excuse me, sir."

There was no caller ID on the screen of Mullaney's phone.

"Yes?"

"Two aces in the hole last time, remember? Cost you one thousand of your dollars. I'm sure you remember that."

Relief washed over Mullaney's anxiety, bringing a smile to his face. "Nearly cost my kids their Christmas gifts. How are you, Sultan? Well, I hope."

"Probably better than you and your newly arrived ambassador at this moment, I would venture. Tell Ambassador Cleveland he can relax . . . there is no war about to erupt."

"Can I put you on speaker?"

"Certainly. It would be my pleasure to reassure the ambassador."

Mullaney turned to Cleveland, the iPhone held in front of him. "Sir, this is Major Sultan Abbaddi, commander of the Jordanian Royal Guard Brigade."

"Personal bodyguards to the king and his family?" said Cleveland. "Highly placed."

"And a good friend," said Mullaney. He pushed the speaker button and handed the phone to Cleveland. "Sultan? I'm with the ambassador."

"*As salaam u aleiykum*, Mr. Ambassador . . . peace be upon you."

"*Wa aleiykum as salaam,*" responded Cleveland. "On my first day, I wish us all peace, Commander Abbaddi." Cleveland glanced at Mullaney, who nodded his head. "Perhaps you can enlighten us somewhat regarding the heightened threat levels and mobilizations in the region? I would be indebted for your counsel."

"Yes . . . well . . . with respect, sir, there is a limit as to what I am free to share," Abbaddi said through the phone. "First, I am requested to share with you the pleasure of our government with your appointment." Mullaney pulled a pen and small notebook from his jacket pocket and started to write. "You have consistently provided understanding and compassion to all in the Middle East. For that, we are grateful."

Mullaney showed his notebook to Cleveland. *He speaks for the king.* Cleveland nodded in agreement.

"Thank you, Commander. I truly appreciate your welcome. But," said Cleveland, "what can you tell us about today's activities?"

"Mr. Ambassador, I can assure you that the actions taken today by my country, Egypt, Saudi Arabia, and the Gulf States are not the first steps in an armed conflict between our nations and Israel. We apologize for their abruptness. There was little option. What I can share with you is that there is a seismic shift of power and influence—toward a lasting peace—about to take place in the Middle East. An announcement is imminent that will change the world as you know it."

Cleveland grabbed the pen and pad from Mullaney's hands.

"It is in anticipation of this announcement that our nations are taking precautionary steps," said Abbaddi.

A peace treaty? Cleveland wrote. *Why? Why now?*

"Forgive me, but that is the extent of the information which I can share with you," said Abbaddi. "We hope it will soothe any concern at the seat of your government."

Cleveland shrugged his shoulders in a question, but Mullaney had no answers.

"Well, Commander Abbaddi," said Cleveland, "I'm grateful for your information. I'm sure many of us will sleep better tonight. But forgive me, your information raises more questions than answers. Can't you help us out here?"

"Truly, I wish I could . . ."

"Hey, Sultan," Mullaney interrupted. "Enough of this diplomatic dance we're doing. Okay, so there's no holocaust about to descend on us, and we sure are relieved to hear that. But what's really going on?" Cleveland reached out a cautionary hand. "You're helping us out here, but we still feel like we're walking in the dark."

The silence from the other end of the phone made Mullaney concerned that he had overplayed his hand. Abbaddi had shown them one ace. Maybe he still had another in the hole.

"Officially, I've told you all that I can," said Abbaddi. "I wish you peace."

The car slewed violently to the left as Hernandez avoided a slow-moving truck.

"Tommy! Watch the road and not the back seat."

"Yes, Boss. Slowing it down."

Mullaney was frustrated as he and Cleveland looked at the phone and the "Call Ended" screen. Then his phone rang a second time.

"This call never happened." It was Abbaddi's voice. "I'll be brief. Regardless of what is announced tomorrow, do not trust the Saudi king."

"Commander," interrupted Cleveland. "I must know. Is this you speaking or your sovereign?"

"For more than a decade," said Abbaddi, ignoring the question, "the house of Saud has lavishly financed the nuclear weapons development program in Pakistan. Some of those weapons were developed specifically for the Saudis and are held in storage by Pakistan.

"King Abdullah sees his mortal enemies, the Persians, joining together to his north. He sees the probability of a nuclear-armed Persia. The king is cashing in his chips. He's placed his order with the Pakistanis. The nuclear weapons will soon be shipped to Riyadh. I repeat: do not trust the Saudi king. What you hear announced tomorrow is historic. What is being done in secret could be catastrophic."

Hernandez was driving the car like a rodeo rider on the back of a Brahma bull, bucking back and forth from one lane to another. Still, there was time before they could reach the US embassy in Tel Aviv, and Mullaney had a question gnawing at the edges of his consciousness.

"Mr. Ambassador," he asked, twisting in the seat to look at Cleveland more directly, "I can understand the Saudis would feel vulnerable if Iran develops nuclear weapons. They would be in the same boat as Israel. So the idea of a treaty makes sense. What I can't figure is why Pakistan would sell nuclear weapons to Riyadh. Why make the arms race in the Middle East worse than it already is?"

Cleveland set his hands on the car's seat and pushed back, squaring his shoulders. Mullaney could tell he was trying to revitalize his body after the long flight.

"There is a twelve-round heavyweight bout going on in Washington right now," said Cleveland. He took a handkerchief from the inside pocket of his suit jacket and wiped it across his face for a moment before stuffing it back in his pocket. "The main event is between those for and those against any nuclear deal with Iran. But there are any number of side slugfests going on over ancillary issues. One conflict is between those who believe an Iran deal will slow down nuclear proliferation and those who believe an Iran deal will accelerate nuclear proliferation because everybody else will want the bomb. A second theater of conflict revolves around the whole issue of Pakistan, which is really the most important wild card in this entire saga."

Other than worrying about his daughter, the one thing that caused Cleveland to lose sleep each night was the dangerous morass that was the government of Pakistan. While most of the world wasn't watching, Pakistan had devolved into the most dangerous nation on earth. Not Iran and its nuclear hopes. Not North Korea and its maniacal leadership. Neither the resurgent Russian bear nor the military and economic behemoth in China. Pakistan, a nuclear-armed Muslim nation with a population of two hundred million people, a government and military—often the same thing—both densely populated with radical, Islamic jihadists and a propensity of going to war with little provocation. One result of the Afghan war and America's crusade against the killers of al-Qaeda was that the US and Pakistan became uneasy allies. Cleveland knew it was an alliance that could never be sustained.

"The military of Pakistan is rapidly becoming radicalized," said Cleveland, "which is a threat to every nation on earth. Pakistan has somewhere north of 120 nuclear weapons. We don't know where they are. We don't know how secure they are. And we don't know who has access to them.

"After 9/11, President Musharraf was terrified that elements of his military might just walk off with all 120 nukes. So he ordered the weapons be *de-mated*—the fissile cores are stored separately from the nonnuclear explosives packages, and the warheads are stored separately from the delivery systems. Then he ordered the parts to be randomly shuttled around between at least fifteen different storage sites throughout the country." Cleveland raised his hands and shook his head. "They use commercial delivery vans to move nuclear weapons. Like bread trucks. No military escorts, no security convoys. Just a couple of guys in a truck with parts of weapons that could destroy nearly any city on earth.

"The greatest nightmare for the West is not whether Iran will get nuclear weapons," said Cleveland, looking out the car's window, "or even whether a Muslim country like Saudi Arabia gets nuclear weapons—both potentially catastrophic events in themselves—but whether Pakistan can keep from losing one, some, or all of the nuclear weapons it already has."

"Pakistan is the worst kind of ally for the US to have . . . one you can't trust," said Mullaney. "So what can we do about it?"

The ambassador lowered his head for a heartbeat, then lifted his shoulders. He turned back to Mullaney. "Ever heard of JSOC?"

"Yeah, aren't they the guys who run the Olympics every four years?"

Cleveland winced. "Thank you, Tommy, for your insight."

"Joint Special Operations Command," said Mullaney. "Yeah, I've heard of those guys. Tough bunch, very elite. I wouldn't want to tangle with that outfit."

"That would be wise," said Cleveland. "Well, JSOC maintains rotating deployments of specially trained units in the Persian Gulf region, most of them Navy SEALs and Army explosive ordnance disposal specialists. If any of Pakistan's nuclear weapons were to fall into the wrong hands, JSOC teams would be assigned to carry out a render-safe mission—finding, capturing, and disabling any weapon of mass destruction.

"They already pulled one off back in the nineties. CIA told JSOC that a North Korean ship had just left port with an illegal weapon. Our guys, a SEAL Team Six component, were able to find the ship, sneak aboard, find the weapon, and immobilize it in a way that left no trace of their presence or their mission. Extremely resourceful individuals."

"Hey, Boss." Hernandez was trying to keep one eye on the road and one eye in the rearview mirror—and failing. "How do you know so much about these super commandos? I'd think a lot of that info would be stamped *Secret*."

"Most of that information is not classified," said Cleveland. "Let's just say I have a very good friend closely connected to JSOC and its mission in Pakistan. And that mission gets more challenging every day.

"In the event of a jihadist coup, civil war, or other catastrophic event in Pakistan, JSOC would be tasked for a disablement campaign—capturing and/or dismembering Pakistan's entire nuclear arsenal. A most dangerous mission. JSOC has been preparing for such an operation for years—how to breach the inner workings of nuclear installations and what to do with any live weapons they find there. Delta Force and SEAL Team Six squads practice deep underground shelter penetration at a secure site northwest of Las Vegas. They've also built simulated Pashtun villages at a site on the East Coast for special ops training.

"In the event of a coup, our forces would penetrate Pakistan's borders in several ways. They already have the necessary equipment stored nearby. Our guys would secure known, or suspected, nuclear-storage sites, disabling the tactical nuclear weapons first. If necessary, they also know how to destroy a nuclear weapon without setting it off. If we're not certain we've located or contained the entire arsenal, there's a standing order to launch precision missile strikes on nuclear bunkers, using special hard-target weapons. "We have lots of arrows in our quiver," said Cleveland. "I wouldn't want to be in Islamabad when those arrows were launched."

10

Ankara
July 19, 1:22 p.m.

The man who entered had neither an ounce of fat on his muscles nor an ounce of doubt in his soul. He was the leader of the Disciples, the far-flung but tightly knit cadre of operatives devoted to the Turk and his calling, his mission, his destiny. Dressed in a suit and open-collared shirt, entirely in black, the man moved with the confident purpose of one trained to use his body as a weapon. He stopped six feet short of where the Turk rested on a divan.

"Praise and honor to you, Emissary of the One," said the man, bowing at the waist. When he straightened up, his eyes were fixed on the Turk. "How, All Powerful, may I be of service?"

The Turk pointed to a straight-backed chair to the left of the divan. The man went to the chair. *There is something unique about this man. He has never been afraid to look into my eyes.*

"Bring it closer," said the Turk. As the man lifted the chair and brought it to within a body length, the Turk thought quickly of the man's father, and his father's father, who had also served faithfully and effectively as leaders of the Disciples. Countless generations, father to son, had served the Turk in this critical role. Now, finally, the day of the One was closer than ever before. The Turk was confident that he and his disciples could engineer the coming of the One and his glorious reign. It was time to put into motion the harbingers of the end.

"Tell me of the Disciples," the Turk said as the man sat in the chair.

"There are 186 equipped, trained and ready," said the leader. "Forty here in Turkey, twenty-four in Iraq and Syria, ten well-placed in Iran. Two dozen remain in Israel and as many are in Palestine. Twenty on their way to Pakistan. The others established in Lebanon, Jordan, and Egypt. Waiting for your orders and ready to move at your command, All Powerful."

"Very well. You understand the goal?"

The man bowed from his waist as he sat in the chair. "Yes, All Powerful. First, destroy the message and the box of power. And those who may stand in our way. At your command, seize the weapons from the infidel's airbase at

Incirlik. Do all in our power to ensure neither the Persians nor the Arabs get control of the weapon. Manipulate Israel, by whatever means necessary, into a position of vulnerability. Above all—destroy the book and its prophecies and hasten the dawn of the age of the Mahdi, the One of Allah."

A torrent of heat flashing through the blood in his veins, for a moment the Turk struggled for control. Close . . . so close. Once the threat of the Lithuanian was finally destroyed, he could focus on his ultimate goal. "Yes . . . and this is what I wish you to do."

Watching the leader's departure, Assan floated into the light from a darkened corner of the room. "He still does not suspect."

"No . . . he speaks of the One, but knows not which One."

"There is a great day of reckoning coming," said Assan. "Many will be astonished when the bedrock of their truth turns to sand."

Once again, Assan's independent thinking triggered an alarm in the Turk. Another task to be dealt with.

No signs of life were visible in the basement of the house on Alitas Street, a solitary cul-de-sac down the hill from the Ankara Castle. The only light came from the flame of the small oil lamp which the Turk carried with him down the stone steps. His soft-soled slippers made no sound as he descended, the temperature of the air falling more rapidly with each step deeper into the darkness. No cobwebs, no skittering of small, clawed rodent feet. No life.

But a fleeting trace . . . a nauseating sweetness of decay . . . tinged the air, thickening as the Turk reached the basement floor.

The lamp cast a pale halo around the Turk as he crossed a large subterranean room. On the far side was a wooden door. The Turk withdrew an iron key from the pocket of his jubba. He pushed the key into the keyhole, and despite its age and condition, the lock opened quickly on well-oiled tumblers.

The Turk leaned his shoulder against the formidable door, forcing its bulk open inch by inch. He was assaulted by an overwhelming putrid reek of rot and decay, but one to which he was so accustomed that it gave him no pause. As he pushed through the opening, the flame of his lamp was snuffed out. Impenetrable darkness engulfed him like a wet, black blanket. The door groaned with a mournful dirge as—on its own—it sealed the Turk within the room, the lock falling back into place.

He waited. The dark held no fear for him. It was home.

In the midst of the blackness, a pinpoint of light, red and pulsing, flickered and began to grow beat by beat. The air temperature rose quickly as the light expanded in size and intensity. The Turk stood immobile, the light and heat pressing upon him like the open door of a blast furnace. Two yellow dots appeared within the red light. As the light grew in size, the yellow dots also grew. A gray swirl, like clouds driven by the wind, flowed across the surface of the yellow dots.

They were looking at the Turk.

The Turk lowered his head, bowed from the waist, then got on his knees, his forehead pressed against the stone floor. "Exalted One."

A voice slithered from the darkness in the corners of the room, closing on the Turk from all sides. The voice thrummed with sovereign power, held the Turk in an embrace like a constricting python.

"Rise."

The Turk pushed up from the floor. A pair of gibbous, yellow eyes hovered in the midst of a dim, indistinct, and shifting countenance—like a face constructed of smoke rings distorting and dispersing in the heavy air. He could feel the power of the yellow eyes probing for his brain, searching for his thoughts, seeking for his knowledge.

"Does anyone, other than your servant, know of our plans?"

"No, Exalted One."

The red halo flared behind the piercing eyes.

"You must protect the secret!"

Pride suffused throughout the Turk's consciousness. He was entrusted with this awesome responsibility. The One was relying on him.

"The secret is safe. No one suspects," said the Turk. "Eroglu and Kashani believe our support is for a transcendent Ottoman Empire. The Disciples believe we pave the way for the emergence of the Mahdi. They believe we serve the spirit of jihad."

"Excellent." The pleasure of the voice was soft, liquid, warm, sliding across the floor. But like a rolling swell on the ocean, it now grew in stages of size and power. "And that is what we will allow them to continue to believe until the armies of Islam have followed me and conquered all the earth. We will establish a new world order, a global Islamic empire. Even Jerusalem will fall beneath our battle flags. And then our day will come. We will demolish the Quran and destroy the Bible . . . annihilate all false prophets who claim to foretell of another."

The Turk returned the gaze of the countenance with confidence, without fear, and with the same malevolent yellow eyes. "You," proclaimed the Turk, "will rule, Exalted One."

"Over all the earth!" The voice crested, the thunder of roiling sea. "There will be one government, one law, one religion, one time—the time of power, the time of wealth, the time of dominion. Our time. A time we have pursued for ages. Now we see it. Now we see the opportunity before us. We will use the forces of Islam. We will use the armies of Persia. We will use the hordes of the Ottomans. All together. All to forge one world order. Not only are the times of the Gentiles complete, but the times of the Jews are complete and the times of the Muslims. All three—these three self-proclaimed great religions—will swear fealty to me . . . or they will lose their heads and their lives. We are so close.

"This time"—the yellow eyes closed to pinpoints, the voice a venomous whisper—"we must not falter."

In mockery of the heat on his face, a chill ran down the spine of the Turk as he recalled the failures of the past.

How many ages had they waited? How many empires had they corrupted? Each empire proclaiming its power and permanence, pursuing and persecuting Jew and Christian alike. Each time their treacherous schemes and design for global domination had collapsed. Each time, the Turk had failed.

"The time is yours, Exalted One. Everything points to your ascendancy. You will finally prevail." *And I will ultimately succeed*, thought the Turk. *And I will rule with you.*

"What of the box and the prophecy? Have you recovered the Lithuanian's message?"

Raptures of glory were vomited from his brain. The Turk's reverie came crashing back to reality.

"No, Exalted One. It eluded us at the residence."

The rings of smoke surrounding the countenance whirled like dervishes preparing for battle.

"Do not forget!" The Turk's eyes grew wide as the power of the voice squeezed more urgently against his body, driving breath from his lungs. "The Lithuanian knew how to stop us. He was given the knowledge and the power and the words by those who seek our annihilation, the other immortals, our sworn enemies. You must destroy the message before it destroys us!"

Like a hot poker scalding his skin, the Turk's memory returned to that awful night over two hundred years ago. His riders of the storm had come so close to snatching the message. The roiling, flood-stage Prieglius River was prepared to swallow up the Lithuanian and his companions. But the Lithuanian had found refuge in the home of that Jewish cleric. And then their enemies appeared. When the Lithuanian returned home, this lethal message, now secured in a bronze box, remained in Konigsberg, protecting a secret that could destroy the plans of the Exalted One. Centuries had passed, and still his task remained the same. He must destroy the message and the box, or those carrying it.

"The Disciples will locate and destroy the box." The words croaked from the Turk's throat. "Of that I am confident."

"The box?" declared the voice. "That box is not our enemy. It is the message that threatens us and the message we must destroy. The prophecies of the Lithuanian have power. The box only receives power from what rests inside."

Heavy lids fell across the hypnotic yellow eyes, the intensity of heat and light waning for a moment. "It appears that the Jew and the Arab will help pave the way for us. This new covenant that will be proclaimed gives the Jew permission to once again build a temple—and it's the temple we desire. If the Lithuanian's message is revealed, then our future plans are threatened. The temple might not be built, the treaty might not be signed. Our opportunity to thwart prophesy could be lost. The message *must* be destroyed."

As if a supernatural hand had grabbed the throat of a volcano, clamping it shut to snuff out an eruption, silent stillness joined the darkness.

Moments passed like eternal heartbeats.

The Turk stood his ground. He forced his heart to keep a steady beat. He knew the Exalted One could not read his thoughts. But he could smell fear. The Turk waited.

"What of these new intruders . . . these new obstacles. You have not eliminated their threat."

"They know nothing," countered the Turk, feeling confidence return. "We have encountered this kind of ignorant opposition for centuries. They know they are in a battle, but they know not who or what they fight. Or why. The ambassador is a formidable follower of the Nazarene. He would be difficult to corrupt. And his chief protector—also a follower, but troubled and insecure—is proving resourceful. They have both been difficult to destroy."

"I want them dead!" As if awakened, the invisible constrictor surrounding the Turk's body flinched. "Now!"

The coils squeezed harder. Breath fled from his lungs like pumped water. The Turk fought for control, fought for air.

"Destroy all opposition!" The voice grew in menace. "Take no mercy and waste no more time. Their very existence is a risk *you* cannot afford to survive. Destroy them. Destroy the message. Destroy them all!"

Like the scales of a serpent, the heavy lids closed over the yellow eyes. The red light in the middle of the room vanished and blackness reigned. The Turk began to sweat.

US Embassy, Tel Aviv
July 19, 1:47 p.m.

Israel's road system was fine as long as a car remained on the main highways, which were wide and fast and well designed. Once off the highways? Well, that was another story.

After driving the ambassador around the urban anarchy of Ankara and Istanbul in Turkey, Tommy Hernandez figured he could handle the streets of cosmopolitan Israel. Until he discovered that street names could, and did, change every few blocks.

He exited the Ayalon Highway at the HaShalom Interchange and made a left onto Derech HaShalom, which turned into Giv'at HaTahmoshet Street, past the Azrieli shopping center, which turned into Eliezer Kaplan Street—all within three blocks. He was ecstatic by the time he reached Bograchov Street which ran straight, with the same name, for twelve blocks toward the sea. The US embassy building was just off to his left when he reached Ha-Yarkon Street, but the street was one-way north so Hernandez drove the loop, around the Dan Hotel, and came up on the rear entrance to the embassy on Retsif Herbert Samuel Street. To their right lay the broad, sweeping sands of Tel Aviv's perfect beach and the deep blue waters of the Mediterranean.

Once past the infamous Mike's Place, a favorite watering hole and hangout for embassy staffers, Hernandez stopped at the anti-tank barriers that blocked the only entrance to the embassy's rear parking garage.

"Not much to look at, is it Mr. Ambassador?" said Hernandez.

The American embassy to Israel resembled a fortress—or a prison, depending on your point of view. It was big, square, solid, and ugly. Utilitarian would be kinder. Like the majority of the architecture in Israel, the embassy was designed to serve a purpose. Exterior frills? A waste of time and money.

In the midst of a busy downtown neighborhood, just off the beach promenade, the building hulked over its flanking streets. No buffer, no grass, no garden existed between the front entrance of the embassy and the civilians walking past on the wide sidewalk. Just across narrow Ha-Yarkon Street, behind a flank of parked motorbikes, were a car rental office and an internet café. Two civilians, the same size and build as the half dozen security guards scattered along the front of the embassy, reclined in chairs in the shade of the internet café.

There was a time, in the distant past, when the embassy sported a ground-level, columned portico on its front side, along with over a dozen diagonal parking spaces just outside the front door. Security soon trumped convenience. This day, the ground floor of the embassy was a solid, windowless stone. Four-foot high, round steel pillars—bollards—were stationed along the edge of the sidewalk every few feet, the bollards connected and spanned by a steel I beam that ran the entire length on both the front and back of the massive building.

Along both Ha-Yarkon Street at the front of the building and Samuel Street to its rear, men in civilian clothes stood under small metal awnings spaced at various intervals along each sidewalk. Part of the embassy's security force, these men were Israeli—locally hired security professionals who were the first line of defense for the embassy. They would also be Diplomatic Security's eyes and ears on the local community.

"I think the architect must have spent part of his youth living near Alcatraz," said Hernandez. "Welcome to your new home."

When Hernandez pulled to a stop at the "active vehicle barrier" at the rear of the embassy—large, thick steel rectangles that lifted from the street level like huge yawning mouths—three of the civilian security agents walked slowly toward the car, one to the driver's window, the second holding back a few feet, the third wielding a round mirror attached to a long, metal pole, scanning the undercarriage of the vehicle. The two who approached the car wore large, loose-fitting shirts, unbuttoned, not tucked in, a lanyard and ID tag hanging from their necks. One hand was visible, the other near their belt line. Hernandez powered down the window.

"Hey, Yakov, who's your tailor?" said Hernandez. "Where can I get some cooler clothes for this desert?"

His left hand out, the security guard waited for their IDs and passes. "Only your second day here and already you're harassing the local citizenry? You'll get a bad reputation, Agent Hernandez. Isn't that right, Mr. Ambassador?" The agent bent down to look through the window to the back seat. "Welcome to Israel, sir. Agent Mullaney." He nodded to the regional security officer. "We're here to be of assistance, sir. If there is anything we can do for you, please ask. For him," he pointed a thumb at Hernandez's back, "not so much. Have a good day, sir."

Yakov lifted his left hand and flicked his fingers toward a small, block building attached to the back wall, its many windows smoked and impenetrable from the outside. The vehicle barrier descended to street level, allowing access to the underground garage.

"Look out, world . . . the eagle has landed." Hernandez drove the ambassador's car into the darkness of the imposing and well-defended embassy.

US Ambassador's Residence, Tel Aviv
July 19, 1:58 p.m.

The blue Ford carrying Parker was waved through the open gates of the ambassador's residence by the marines on duty at the entrance. Down the street, under a low-hanging tree, a dusty Volkswagen beetle rested by the curb. "She is here."

"Wait for night," came the reply. "Then look for weaknesses in the security. Perhaps we can secure the package while the ambassador and his security are busy elsewhere. The box must not elude us. Do not fail. You understand the consequences."

Palmyra Parker faced a dilemma. No matter how curious she was about the box inside the leather bag, her father's warnings were alarming enough to hold that curiosity in check. Her dilemma was what to do with the satchel now that she had shepherded all her father's baggage into the ambassador's residence. She remembered the Bible story from her youth—one of the guys with King David reached out his hand to steady the ark of the covenant as it was being carried back to Jerusalem. He touched the ark and—zap!—he was a fried egg.

Did she believe the box could really kill? Doubtful. But she wasn't about to risk finding out. One of her favorite sayings was: *Good judgment comes from experience; and experience comes from bad judgment.* Testing this experience could prove deadly.

Dressed in a beat-up pair of old jeans and a short-sleeved blue cotton blouse, she stood in the middle of her apartment in the south wing of the ambassador's residence and tried to figure out the most secure place to hide the bag.

There was the hide-in-plain-sight theory, that the best place to hide something was out in the open. Probably not a good idea with an object that could make your kids orphans. There was a safe in her father's room, but she didn't have the combination and didn't want to answer questions about why she would need it. Still in the midst of settling into her new living quarters, Parker's closets were a minefield of half-empty boxes of things that had yet to find a home. Hmmm . . . minefield. It would be pretty hard for anyone to navigate that walk-in closet without breaking a leg.

Parker opened the door to the closet. About seven feet off the floor, a shelf ran around the inside walls of the closet. Her clothes hung from the poles on all three sides. But good luck getting to any of them. The floor of the closet was packed, waist high, with boxes full of "our family things," those pieces of personal life that were treasures to their hearts: three boxes of her mother's china, family photos from the time she and her brothers were infants—all the things that made a home intimate for those who shared their lives within its walls. Palmyra was determined to make a real home for her and her father. So she had packed up as much of their history and memories as she could manage and shipped it all to Israel. Now it all sat in boxes in her closet, a surprise to spring on her father . . . one of these days. But not today. Today she needed to fit something else into that closet.

Among the boxes, the brown leather satchel would appear obvious. But up on the shelf were about a dozen of her handbags, some nearly as large as the satchel itself. Perfect.

She pushed her handbags to the left, along the shelf. When she started to lift the satchel, she reminded herself to be careful. The leather bag was much heavier than it appeared because of the larger wooden chest that enclosed the metal box. She grabbed it with both hands, pushed with her legs and lifted the bag to shoulder height. Resting the bag against her clavicle, she took her right hand from the handle and placed it on the bottom of the bag. With a final shove, she got its base up on the edge of the shelf—and nearly dropped it on her head when someone knocked heavily on her bedroom door.

"Mrs. Parker?"

"What!" she snapped, wrestling with the precariously balanced bag.

"My apologies, ma'am. It's Jeffrey," said the ambassador's secretary. "I apologize for disturbing you. I called out but you didn't answer. Your father is on the phone. He was very insistent that I check on you, personally, when I couldn't get you on the phone . . . to make sure you were all right. He wants to speak with you, ma'am."

God help me. "Okay." She pushed once more on the bottom of the bag, hoisting it up onto the shelf, then closed the closet and quickly walked to her bedroom door, opening it as she tucked in the tail of her blouse. "Thank you, Jeffrey. Please put through my father's call."

US Embassy, Tel Aviv
July 19, 2:45 p.m.

Cleveland returned to the meeting room feeling more confident, at least about his daughter's health and safety.

"Sorry for the interruption, everyone." Cleveland took his seat at the head of the conference table. In this moment of crisis, the ambassador's closest advisers surrounded him. He would need every one of them—their knowledge, experience, and contacts—if the United States were to effectively navigate an increasingly perplexing and conflicting array of developments throughout the region. Deputy Chief of Mission Jarrod Goldberg was a veteran of Middle Eastern diplomacy, serving two previous ambassadors to Israel along with stints in Tunisia, Yemen, and Qatar. Jon Lin, FBI station chief, was a relative novice to the area's politics but his ten-year FBI career included almost exclusive overseas assignments. Mullaney, his regional security officer, also carried impressive credentials. Not only because of his extensive experience in the Middle East, but also because of the glowing praise from Tommy Hernandez, a man whose opinion the ambassador highly trusted.

Ruth Hughes, the mission's political officer, was the fifth person at the table—perhaps the most invaluable at the moment. Hughes was the outlier. Neither a State Department nor law-enforcement veteran, she was a lawyer. In her mid-sixties, Hughes was enlisted by the State Department in 1995 after a twenty-two-year career with Aramco—the former US/Saudi oil partnership. She was corporate counsel for Aramco in 1973 when, following the Yom Kippur war, the Saudis first wrested a twenty-five percent piece of the company from the grip of American oil companies. She rose to be a corporate officer and member of the board in 1976. Hughes was considered so valuable to Aramco, she remained with the company for fifteen years after Saudi Arabia displaced Exon, Mobile, and Texaco and took complete control of the world's largest oil and gas company in 1980.

Simply put, Ruth Hughes played power politics with every government in the Middle East while negotiating contracts for Aramco. Not only did she know the players personally and intimately, she had access to back doors and private phone numbers that most westerners didn't realize existed.

Cleveland knew enough not to be fooled by her white hair, pulled back in a matronly bun. Hughes was as sharp as her pin-perfect black suit, crisp white shirt, and sparkling pearls. He was direct.

"Ruth, what can you tell us?"

"Nothing," she responded. "No one is speaking. Not off the record, not even when I call in some old, valuable past favors."

"So what is your assessment?"

"Mr. Ambassador, whatever will be announced tomorrow is huge. Big enough to shut the mouths of some normally very chatty individuals. I think we have to take Commander Abbaddi at his word, and I believe you and Agent Mullaney are correct . . . Abbaddi speaks for the king. So there is no conflict in the offing, even though Israel and each of its neighbors, plus the Saudis, are acting like they are about to go at each other's throats. What does that leave us with? If it's not war, it's peace."

"What?" Goldberg blurted out. "You think the Saudis are going to offer peace to Israel? After sixty years of conflict the Arab world is going to freely embrace the Jewish state?"

"Yes, Mr. Goldberg, that is exactly my assessment," said Hughes. "The Saudis are absolutely apoplectic about the threat from Iran . . . more so than the Israelis, if that were possible. The Persians and the Arabs have been mortal enemies for centuries, not years. The Saudis fear, and believe they see, the reemergence of the Persian confederation between Iran and Iraq. A new Persian empire, and its oil reserves, could accelerate production of oil, driving down its price on the world markets. The Saudis have a massive cash reserve, but they also manipulate a fairly restive population with universal and very expensive social policy, like free health care and free education for its citizens. Drive down the price of oil for a decade and you squeeze the Saudi royal family into the sand. Under no circumstance will King Abdullah allow that confederation to threaten his family or his nation. The only logical step is peace with Israel. And not only peace, Mr. Ambassador, but full recognition and, I believe, a mutual defense pact. The world as we know it changes tomorrow, Atticus."

Cleveland agreed with everything Hughes was saying. Still, it was difficult to pull the thought into reality.

"And no," said Hughes, apparently reading Cleveland's thoughts, "I am not prepared to make the same assertion to the secretary or the president. It's an opinion. I want more evidence before I present an argument for its validity."

Cleveland got out of his chair and walked over to the fourth-floor bulletproof window. It made sense, but . . . He turned to the room. "And what of Abbaddi's warning not to trust Abdullah? If peace is in the Saudi's national interest, why distrust him?"

Mullaney tossed down his pen on the pad where he'd been doodling for the past ten minutes. "Sir?"

"Yes?"

"I'm confused. If Abbaddi is right, then the whole geopolitical foundation of the Middle East is shifting under our feet. Can the Saudis or an Arab coalition actually be thinking about entering into a real, lasting peace with Israel? Will the Wahhabi clerics allow such a thing? If the generals in Egypt are serious about this treaty, the Muslim Brotherhood will rise up in revolt. It's just not possible . . . is it?"

"Wouldn't be the first time pragmatic politics trumped what everyone assumed is regional reality," said Cleveland. "Israel's government has always been pragmatic—whatever it takes to survive. The Israelis have worked with their enemies before when they thought it was in their best interests."

"Well, I don't care what's announced tomorrow or how big it is," said Mullaney. "Peace treaty? The most important issue is not the announcement, but Abbaddi's warning that the Saudis are about to acquire nuclear weapons. A nuclear Saudi Arabia is more of a game changer than any peace agreement. If Pakistan is ready to ship nuclear weapons to Riyadh, those weapons will be operational long before any proposed peace treaty is ratified. Then the only question left is who is going to start lobbing those nukes first—Arabs, Jews, or Persians? The end result is the same. This whole region is toast."

Goldberg leaned into the table, the pen in his hand stabbing at Mullaney like a short saber. "Can we rely on the claims of this security guard? Because that is all we have at the moment," said Goldberg. "No corroboration, no hard evidence. Nothing from CIA or FBI, right Jon?"

His back to the window, Jon Lin shook his head. "Nothing on our radar at the moment, on either subject, neither peace treaty nor an arms deal with Pakistan. But this I can tell you." All heads turned to look at Lin, his body backlit, his face in shadow. "The Saudis have bankrolled Pakistan's nuclear development program for decades. Astronomical millions of dollars. And they haven't spent that money because they love the Pakistani people. The Saudis want nukes as a deterrent against Israel. Pakistan had a head start and Family Saud didn't want to wait for its own development program. My opinion is the nukes are packed and ready to go whenever the Saudis believe the time is right. I agree with Mullaney. A nuclear Saudi Arabia is our issue."

Cleveland looked at the clock on the wall. "Time to make a phone call, people. Here's what I propose."

He walked back to his seat at the head of the table but remained standing behind his chair. He looked like a commander about to dispatch his troops into battle.

"I want all four of you on the phone, constantly, until we get this warning nailed down. I believe Abbaddi is telling us the truth and that the warning comes from his king. But my conviction alone will not be enough for either the secretary of state or the president to take any action. We need corroboration." His gaze caught Mullaney. "But we can't sit on this either. We tell the secretary what we know so far and what we suspect, especially about the nukes on their way to Saudi Arabia. And we keep working until we get actionable evidence."

Cleveland turned toward Goldberg. "Jarrod, contact Prime Minister Meir. Tell him we need to talk."

Goldberg looked as if he'd been told to fly to the moon in a milk carton. "That might be a tough sell."

Cleveland pivoted on his right elbow, which was resting on the back of his chair, and turned his full attention on the deputy chief of mission. Cleveland wondered what kind of right-hand man he'd inherited from the former ambassador. He was already having misgivings about Goldberg. "Israel just activated a third of its military reserves and has mobilized its armored divisions. Don't ask permission. Tell Prime Minister Meir that I am coming to see him today. He can pick the time, but I will see him in Jerusalem before the day is out."

Goldberg's jaw was set, his neck stiff and turning a bright shade of red. "Yes, sir," he said, his words clipped short but sharpened at the edges.

Atticus Cleveland long ago learned to trust his gut. His instincts were reliable, his assessments of people almost always accurate, even in the short term. Jarrod Goldberg just moved from adviser to adversary and Cleveland's inner circle was reduced by one.

"Jon . . . keep working CIA for information," said the ambassador. "Ruth, Brian . . . before you start making calls, I'd like to see you in my office. Thank you."

11

US Embassy, Tel Aviv
July 19, 3:26 p.m.

Cleveland and the two advisers were crowded around one end of a small table in an anteroom of the ambassador's office, so the camera for the video feed could pick up everyone at once. On the other end of the connection were Secretary of State Evan Townsend, Deputy Secretary Arthur Ravel, and Deputy Secretary of Management and Resources Noah Webster—in effect the department's COO.

"That's all we have at the moment, Mr. Secretary," said Cleveland. "Deputy Chief Goldberg is currently assigned to arrange a meeting with Prime Minister Meir; Jon Lin is connecting with CIA to pick their brains. I wish we had more."

Cleveland could see the impact of his report on each of their faces, but each face carried a different message. Secretary Townsend was deep in thought, the inner wheels of his organized mind sifting each of the elements through different shaped strainers. Secretary Ravel's eyes were full of questions, but he knew his place. Townsend would get the first questions. And Secretary Webster looked like he was about to burst a blood vessel.

"Agent Mullaney," asked Townsend, "how confident are you in this source, Commander Abbaddi?"

"I trust him completely," said Mullaney. "Sultan has been commander of the Jordanian Royal Guard Brigade, the personal bodyguards for the king and his family, for more than a decade. His father was a decorated member of the brigade, as was his father before him. More important, personally—he risked his life and his team to save a US ambassador, my crew, and me."

Secretary Townsend nodded his head. "Thank you, Agent . . ."

"Sir, if I may, there's one other thing," said Mullaney. "I've known Sultan for nearly ten years. Went to his home, had dinner with his wife and children. And I can tell you one thing for certain. Commander Abbaddi would never issue a warning like that on his own. He is devoted to his king and would never overstep his authority. That warning came from King Hussein II himself. And we can trust it."

Townsend was digesting Mullaney's information when Secretary Ravel caught his boss's eye. "Go ahead, Arthur."

"If a peace plan is announced tomorrow, what keeps it from blowing up?" asked Ravel.

It's the wrong question. Cleveland's mind was pondering questions well beyond whether a peace deal could survive. Of course it could blow up . . . probably would. But what if they did it? What if the Arabs and the Israelis really came together as allies, as trading partners, as defenders of each other's territory?

"The Palestinians will erupt into another intifada," Ravel continued. "Hamas and Hezbollah will never sign a peace with Israel. And Israeli right-wingers will never trust Egypt or the Saudis. Any peace proposal is likely to be dead on arrival."

During Ravel's comments, Cleveland watched as Ruth Hughes pushed her chair back from the table, her arms crossed and resting on her ribs, a look of frustration and disdain on her face. Hughes was an experienced and effective negotiator, trained to keep her emotions invisible. But at this moment, her scorn for Ravel's reasoning was as bright as the lights on Broadway.

She closed on the table again. "Come on, Arthur, look past the obvious for once. First of all, don't discount sovereign recognition. For the Israeli economy, a true peace with the Arab world would open up a huge market for its high-tech industries. Create normalized relations with its neighbors. And tourism would skyrocket in Israel. But the most important point is here"—Hughes turned to the map of Israel that was hanging on the wall behind them and tapped her pen on a spot in the middle of the map—"Jerusalem."

Hughes looked over her shoulder at the screen of images from Washington. "Do you really think any proposed peace agreement between the Arabs and Israel would ignore the Palestinian question? That would be ludicrous. It's a safe bet that—if this announcement is about a peace deal—the parties have already decided the future of Palestine. And this is what Palestine will look like."

Taking her pen, Hughes drew a north-south line on the map, slicing off the very eastern tip of Jerusalem to the top of the Dead Sea then turned east to the border with Jordan.

"Something like that is the only thing that makes sense," she said. "Palestine gets a sliver of East Jerusalem to call its capital and a chunk of land down to the Dead Sea. That takes the Palestinians out of the question. Hamas and Hezbollah will come into line, or Egypt and Jordan will help Israel crush them out of existence—particularly with the chaos reigning in Syria. And the Jewish ultra-orthodox and right wing? Don't be surprised, Mr. Secretary, if the peace agreement allows Israel to build its temple."

Cleveland intertwined his fingers at the back of his head and stretched his body, drawing attention to himself. "The Saudis are terrified of Iran," he said, his eyes closed. "The Egyptians are fearful of another rising of the Muslim Brotherhood. Syria would be friendless and isolated, a country ripped apart by civil war and the Islamic insurgency of ISIS. Syria is ripe for the taking. But who will move on Syria first—Turkey or Iran? New empire builders . . . Ottoman, Persian, and Islamic . . . would have their hearts and their sights set on that same slice of land–ancient Assyria–land each of them once ruled. An Arab-Israeli agreement could bring peace, but it could also be the unwitting trigger to a continental clash of empires that could throw the world into chaos." He opened his eyes and focused his attention on the camera. "That's my opinion. Opinions are not facts, but it makes sense."

The ambassador flexed his neck back and forth. "All that said—we're still missing the point. Agent Mullaney hit it square before we got on this call. Any announcement is minor league compared to the Saud getting nuclear weapons. That is our primary focus and most important question. Has Abdullah called in his nukes?"

Cleveland slapped the top of his thighs. "Okay." With a quickness that belied the groan he uttered, Cleveland got to his feet. "It's already been a long day," he said. "And it's only going to get longer. With your permission, Mr. Secretary, I need a break. We'll continue to chase down every lead we can find. Can we confer again in three hours? See where we are then?"

For the first time Deputy Secretary Webster leaned into the camera. "Mr. Ambassador," he said, his voice low and urgent, "you—and your team there—are the experts on the Middle East. You know the region; you have the contacts and the experience. You are on the ground. In three hours, we expect you to bring us some answers. No more questions. No more opinions. We need accurate intelligence. Do your jobs and get us what we need to do ours."

The transmission ended, Mullaney felt the sting of Webster's rude rebuke both personally and professionally. It was unnecessary, disrespectful to all of them, but particularly disrespectful to the ambassador in front of two of his direct subordinates. He was trying to shape words to comfort . . .

"Disrespectful buzzard, isn't he," said Hughes. "Those kind come to their own just rewards one day."

"Ruth." Cleveland turned to Hughes and laid his arm on the back of her chair. His voice was calm, gentle, considerate. "Secretary Webster is our boss. Some people, people of faith, might say he's the anointed authority that's been placed over us. It's our responsibility to respect and serve that authority. No matter what we receive in return."

Hughes held Cleveland's gaze for a long moment. "Atticus . . . if he speaks to me like that once more, what he receives in return will not be repeatable in polite company." She snatched her daily planner from the table and got to her feet. "Thank you, Mr. Ambassador. I'll report back to you as soon as I have something concrete."

The door closed with a distinctive snap as Hughes left the room with an exclamation point. Cleveland was immediately to his feet. "Call Tommy, get the car ready. We're going to the residence."

"I thought you were tired," said Mullaney.

"Just wanted to get off that call," Cleveland said over his shoulder as he walked quickly into his office. "We have work to do here. But first, we're going to the residence. I want to talk to Palmyra, Tommy, and you, together. We have work to do on that end too. Just as important . . . just as critical. Let's go."

Washington, DC
July 19, 9:18 a.m.

Noah Webster walked behind Secretary of State Evan Townsend and Deputy Secretary Arthur Ravel as they moved quickly down the seventh-floor hallway of the Truman Building toward the secretary's office. Townsend looked over his shoulder.

"You were pretty rough with them back there."

Webster bristled. *We wouldn't be in this mess if you and Boylan had any respect in the world.* His tongue longed to be a snake, with fangs that could deliver a swift, lethal strike. But he held its venom in check. "They deserve worse. We need to get in front of whatever is happening before the press finds out how clueless we are. This is a monumental failure of the Israel mission."

Townsend reached the door to his office and stopped. He didn't invite Webster to enter.

"Listen, Noah." Townsend squared his shoulders, blocking the door. "Cleveland's been in country, what, two . . . three hours?"

"Less," said Ravel, as he walked into Townsend's office.

"Give him a break. Atticus will figure out what's going on." Townsend took a step toward Webster and lowered his voice. "In the meantime, Noah, if I were you, I'd be wondering why we haven't heard a word from anyone else in the Middle East about this *big* announcement that's coming tomorrow. Is everyone asleep over there? None of our ambassadors, none of our embassy staff, none of our friends or informants has come forth with any warning or information about the announcement, let alone the Saudis going rogue with their own nukes."

Townsend was a tall man. He had more than a foot on Webster. Townsend leaned down, closing to within inches of Webster's face. "If there's a failure here, Noah," Townsend whispered, "it's a failure for which we're all responsible. Including you . . . a man who claims unfettered access to the back rooms of the world. If there is a failure, it will have your fingerprints all over it."

Townsend pulled back and looked Webster squarely in the eye. "Let's get to work, shall we? We need to brief the president. It would be nice to know what's going on when we do it."

The snake in Webster's mouth coiled, its fangs were bared, venom dripping from their points. Secretary of State Townsend turned, walked into his office, and closed the door. Webster couldn't tell if the bitter, acidic taste in his mouth was poison or bile.

12

US Ambassador's Residence, Tel Aviv
July 19, 4:43 p.m.

Both Mullaney and Cleveland were glued to their mobile phones during the entire twenty-five-minute ride from the embassy to the ambassador's residence on Galei Tchelet Street in the Herzliya Pituach section of Tel Aviv. But both put their phones away—without gaining any additional information on the coming announcement—when the car pulled through the gate in the high, white stone wall that blocked off the residence from the street.

Before exiting the car, Cleveland put his hand on Mullaney's arm. "Agent Mullaney, there must be someplace on this property where we can speak free of cameras or recording devices. You've been here the longest of any of us. Where can we talk?"

Mullaney did a quick mental survey, knowing full well that he might not yet know the location of all the cameras or recorders. "Our best bet is the gazebo out by the cliff, overlooking the sea. Probably more private than anywhere in any of the buildings."

"Okay," said Cleveland, "I'll find Palmyra and meet you and Tommy in the gazebo."

"Just give us a few minutes to sign in with the duty officer and we'll be there," said Mullaney. "Is there anything we need to bring with us?"

Cleveland was clearly agitated, anxious to get moving. He had a grip on the door handle when he turned to Mullaney. "If you have it, bring your faith with you, Agent Mullaney. You too, Tommy. You'll need faith more than anything. We've got thirty minutes. Then I want to be on the move back to the embassy . . . or on the road to Jerusalem if Goldberg gets over his offense. Let's go."

Ankara
July 19, 4:48 p.m.

Standing in the middle of Koyunpazari Street, the narrow, cobble-stone lane that wound its way farther up the mountain to Ankara's ancient Citadel, Arslan

Eroglu could look out over a panoramic view of the city, drinking in the sights of both ancient and modern Ankara. Off in the distance were the four spires of the majestic Kocatepe Mosque, elegant, elaborate spindles towering over the mosque's double dome.

Eroglu had tucked his car into a narrow opening at the corner of Karakus Street and walked down to the Gramofon Café. Though the café was a favorite destination, Eroglu had long ago abstained from hiking the long, uphill climb from downtown Ankara. But the manti and gozleme served by the Gramofon Café were as compelling as the café itself.

The Gramofon Café was a local shrine dedicated to a nostalgic view of popular music and film, its walls plastered with album covers and photos and old records, its space filled with an abundance of antique, just plain old, and modern radios and record players. Elvis had a place, along with Bob Marley, and most of the Turkish pop artists of the fifties and sixties. Even the menus in the Gramofon Café were pasted onto old vinyl LP records.

But it was the food of his youth that continued to draw Eroglu back to the Gramofon. He had just finished his meal of manti, the traditional Turkish dumplings made with ground lamb, and gozleme, a savory Turkish flatbread brushed with butter and eggs and cooked over a griddle. Eroglu's favorite was gozleme filled with spinach, parsley, and Turkish white cheese.

He sat at the table by the window, gazing down Koyunpazari Street, sipping a cup of warm tea, when his mobile phone rang. He recognized the caller's number.

"Good morning, Mr. Secretary," said Eroglu, setting his tea cup on the bright blue-and-yellow tablecloth. "I hope . . ." Eroglu left enough money on the table to amply cover his bill, stepped outside and began walking toward where his car was parked as Noah Webster breathlessly filled him in on the Jordanian report of an imminent announcement and the speculation that was percolating from the Middle East to the halls of Washington.

"This is truly disturbing news, Mr. Secretary," said Eroglu. He stopped as he reached his car and rested one hand on the roof. "You are telling me there is an announcement coming tomorrow from the Saudi king and you don't know what it is? An announcement that will . . . what were the words this security official used?" He could almost hear Webster wince through the telephone connection.

"Our source said the raised threat levels and troop mobilizations would not result in armed conflict between the countries." Webster's voice sounded strained. "He said 'a seismic shift of power and influence toward peace was about to take place' . . . that an announcement was imminent that *will change the world as you know it.*"

"Quite dramatic, this source," said Eroglu as he opened the door and settled himself in the car. "And what do you think will be this announcement that will change the world?"

"Some here believe the Jews and the Arabs will announce a peace agreement." Webster dragged each word into the light like it was a concrete ship stuck in the sand. "That a Palestinian state will be part of the bargain."

Of course they would. King Abdullah is terrified of the Persians. The enemy of my enemy is my friend. "Seems reasonable, Noah . . . don't you think? An Arab-Israel alliance? If true . . . if it ever becomes an actuality . . . a rapprochement between Jew and Arab will enrage the Persians and accelerate the attempts to unify Iraq and Iran, something we are both determined to prevent. It is a true game changer, for both of us."

Eroglu could almost taste Webster's anxiety. Surely the secretary of state must be demanding answers. They would need to brief the American president. With what?

"Arslan, you have the inside contacts to the halls of government in the Middle East and also to the dens of jihadists. You cultivate relationships with Jew, Arab, and Persian alike. Tell me, are these rumors true? I need solid information. I can't afford to remain ignorant of what is transpiring between Riyadh, Cairo, and Tel Aviv."

Webster was desperate. So sad to hear him beg.

"I must confess, my friend," said Eroglu, savoring every word along with the view of the Citadel in the distance, "that I am as clearly in the dark on this development as are you and your government. What of your new ambassador to Israel? Cleveland is a man of many talents and far-reaching relationships. Surely your ambassador would know what is about to transpire, no?"

"If he knew I wouldn't be calling you," snapped Webster. "He hasn't even gotten his bags unpacked."

"Forgive me, Noah. But I thought the ambassador had his daughter with him to take care of his household and his belongings. Has Mrs. Parker arrived in Israel?"

"Palmyra Parker is there." Eroglu could hear the petulance in Webster's response. "It seems she is already ruling in the residence, upsetting the staff with her erratic behavior. You would think Cleveland's bags were spun from gold and filled with diamonds." Webster's voice paused. "What is your interest in Palmyra Parker?"

"None, certainly," said Eroglu. "I was only concerned for you, my friend, and about the dangerous level of your ignorance."

"*Our* ignorance, Arslan," Webster snapped once more. "You are as blind on this possible alliance as I am. We need to know, Arslan. If the Arab states and the Jews come together in alliance, how will Tehran respond? Will an Arab-Israeli peace accelerate Iran's pursuit of a nuclear deal and the lifting of those crippling sanctions? That is only one of the questions that President Boylan will want answered."

The tipping points of power between Saudi Arabia and Iran were many, thought Eroglu, the importance of each shifting like sand in the wind. For decades, the family Saud enjoyed substantial power and influence in the geopolitical realm of the Middle East, almost by default. The Persians had slumbered peacefully under the shahs, enriching the Pahlavi family while the nation remained impoverished. Iran was then riven by the Islamic revolution of the Ayatollahs and its military decimated by the vicious eight-year war with Iraq.

In the meantime, Saudi Arabia assembled obscene wealth from a quirk of geology and used some of that abundance to purchase a modern air force and navy. But it was the fawning military umbrella provided by the oil-starved Americans that truly allowed the Saudis to reign with arrogant superiority over other Gulf nations.

While the Saudi royal family bankrolled and encouraged jihadists of every stripe and their Wahhabi clerics reveled in every terrorist success, the rulers at the same time helped build an American airbase on its sand and supported the coalition's wars against the deluded oligarch Saddam Hussein, happy to punish their ancient enemies, the Persians. The family Saud was a harlot, sleeping in two beds.

But revolutionary Iran under the Ayatollahs had proven to be determined and relentless in its return to regional prominence. The Islamic Republic was well on the way to building a powerful navy, was racing forward in its successful development of long-range missiles, and continued its inexorable resolve to develop and deploy nuclear weapons. Now the Shia brothers in Iran and Iraq were working together for the betterment of a new Persia. Almost as alarming, the Iranians were funneling just enough arms and money to the Houthi rebels in Yemen to make them a constant fear of the Saudis and a drain on their resources.

While Iran ascended to the cusp of dominance in the Persian Gulf area, the Saudis were suddenly vulnerable. Oil prices had plunged on the worldwide market. American entrepreneurs, showing an unexpected tenacity, were sucking oil from shale, fueling the US to energy independence. Fearful that its destitute citizens, long lulled into latency by free schools, health care, and interest-free loans to buy homes or start businesses, might join in the call for revolution that had so destabilized the region, the royal family was forced to begin drawing on its vast cash reserves to keep the generous subsidies in place.

And the apostate forces of the Islamic State—doctrinally devoted to neither Sunni nor Shia—filled the Saudis with horror, because of the savagery of their terrorism and the effectiveness of their methods.

Iran was going nuclear—whether the world liked it or not. Now Saudi Arabia appeared determined to take the same step.

"But this news of the Saudi king acquiring nuclear weapons from Pakistan is most worrisome," said Eroglu. "True . . . a nuclear Arab state would prove to be a formidable deterrent to the ambitions of the Tehran mullahs, which would line up well with our ultimate ambition, to thwart this nascent Persian Empire before it has a chance to set roots. But even more critical to us, Mr. Secretary, is that a nuclear Saudi Arabia would turn the balance of power in the Middle East on its head. I don't believe a nuclear Arab world will fit within our plans, do you?"

The silence on the phone was telling . . . every second of it. Eroglu waited.

"It would be a disaster," said Webster. "If the Saudis get their hands on nuclear weapons, our misguided president will push even harder for this deal with Iran, thinking it will stop the Iranian enrichment program. He's so blind to the truth. A deal with Iran will lift all the sanctions, have billions of dollars flowing back into Iran, and just accelerate their path to nuclear weapons."

Hmmm . . . yes. "Which would leave us with a nuclear Persia and a nuclear Islam," said Eroglu. "Not a very promising recipe for world peace, is it Noah?

I believe we must intervene in this process, Mr. Secretary. Intervene on both fronts."

Ogulbey, Turkey
July 19, 4:48 p.m.

He stood in the shadows of a darkened hulk of a building, its corrugated steel flanks rusting from neglect and only half its roof intact. Down at the end of the rubble-strewn loading dock of the abandoned warehouse, east of the intersection of State Roads 750 and 260, south of Ankara, Medir was supervising the loading of cargo into a resting convoy of trucks.

The abandoned warehouse and its ramshackle outbuildings were hidden behind a low hill of hardscrabble rock and dust. Out of sight, just like the Turk.

The Turk shifted his weight and rested himself against the warehouse door.

When the trucks were loaded and the drivers huddled at the far end with their cigarettes and coffee, the Turk took a step from the dusk of the blackened doorway. Medir immediately turned away from the group and walked the one hundred meters toward the warehouse.

Sliding back into the shadow, the Turk heard Medir's approach . . . slow, wary. He watched, silently, as Medir stood just outside the shadows, peering into the shell of the warehouse.

"The loading is complete, Master."

The Turk eased into the half-light.

"Thank you, Medir. You have done well. Join me for a moment," he gestured with his right hand, inviting Medir into the cavern of the warehouse. "There is something of extreme sensitivity about which I wish to confer."

Leading the way deeper into the shadows, the Turk pondered some information he'd just received. Events were moving more quickly than he anticipated. An Arab-Israeli détente could be seen coming for some time and would benefit his ultimate objective. But a nuclear Saudi Arabia? If true, it may require him to accelerate his time table.

Would he need Medir now? Would these new developments make the smuggler more valuable to him in the future? Perhaps. But Medir knew much. Too much for the Turk to feel comfortable. It was no longer safe to leave the gunrunner as an uncontrollable risk. The Turk had only gotten this far by limiting his risks . . . ruthlessly.

"All arrangements for this shipment are securely in place?"

"Yes, Master," said Medir, his voice tentative as they walked through the deep shadows of the warehouse. "We were able to find room for the extra crates that were hidden here. If I had known there was more than just the weapons, I would have arranged for another truck. But—"

"Do your drivers understand the route?"

The Turk's interruption silenced Medir for a moment. The smuggler started to look up, but stopped himself before the Turk could connect with his eyes.

"Yes, Master. Five-and-a-half hours to Adana. Stop at the truck depot just west of the city and wait for your contact. Then about another two hours of drive time should bring the convoy in the vicinity of Suroc, just north of the Syrian border. From there they will travel by night on the forgotten roads to reach the Peshmerga camp."

Medir paused, but the Turk knew he had more to say. "Master, altering the delivery route to the south takes the convoy through Adana, which is quite close to the American installation at Incirlik. It increases the risk. The old route would have been safer."

"And you are being handsomely compensated—perhaps exorbitantly—for shouldering the increased risk, are you not?"

"Yes . . . yes," Medir nodded.

The Turk was now certain. The risk was too great. "Tell me, Medir, how is your family? Your wife and twelve children?"

Walking to the right of the Turk, Medir slowed at the question, chancing a furtive glance. "They are well, Master."

They stopped alongside a dark shaft, dug deep into the foundation of the warehouse. The Turk turned to face Medir. "You provide faithfully for your family, Medir. You should be proud of yourself."

A draft from the darkened shaft behind him rippling up his spine, Medir's eyes searched the concrete at his feet, fearful of looking into the yellow eyes of the Turk. Those eyes swam in a sea of mayhem. "Thank—

"They will need your provision now."

Medir's head snapped up as the Turk's right arm reached out and grasped his left shoulder. A current of power, like white-hot lava, raced through Medir's veins, scorching muscle and sinew. As the boiling of his blood closed on his heart, Medir frantically looked into the face of his killer. The Turk's pale yellow pupils flared like an eruption on the surface of the sun. Medir's forehead spouted dual fountains of red. The force of the impact drove Medir back two steps as his heart muscle melted into the cavity of his chest. The second step found nothing but air and Medir dropped into the blackness of the shaft.

13

US Ambassador's Residence, Tel Aviv
July 19, 5:09 p.m.

"You'll have to humor me on this one, Palmyra." Cleveland paced back and forth across the gazebo, his suit jacket hung on the back of one of the chairs, the late-afternoon sun bathing the Mediterranean and forming a blazing blue backdrop to the visible expression of his inward anxiety. From the moment his daughter had driven out of the airport with that bag in her possession, Cleveland had been kicking himself for being foolish and shortsighted. What had he been thinking?

"I want you out of this mess." He stopped in midstride and swung his shoulders in Palmyra's direction. "I had no choice at the airport, but you are now relieved of all responsibility for the package. Mullaney and Hernandez will transport the satchel to the Hurva Synagogue first thing in the morning and then it's out of our hair. Forgive me for pulling a dad thing, but I want it out of your hands. End of story."

Parker was dressed in black slacks and a short-sleeved, pale green blouse that gave her eyes the color of Caribbean shoals. Sitting on the edge of the gazebo's railing, she let out a long sigh of exasperation. "But Dad, won't Brian and Tommy need to be with . . ."

Mullaney and Hernandez emerged from the path and entered the gazebo. "Be with whom?" Mullaney asked.

"Be with him!" Parker threw up her hands. "That's where you belong, right?"

"Well . . . I . . ."

Cleveland glanced at the watch on his wrist. There was so little time.

"Here, sit," said Cleveland, taking one of the chairs surrounding the table in the middle of the gazebo. "I've got a lot to cover in the short time we have, and I need you guys fully on board."

Mullaney was seated across the table from Cleveland, Hernandez on his right, and his daughter to his left as he launched into the events of that Tuesday that seemed like a lifetime in the past, not simply four days. "Tommy, the day we left the Neve Shalom Synagogue in Istanbul," said Cleveland, leaning to his right, "I was not the target of the attack. The satchel I carried was the target."

A twinkle came to Hernandez's eyes, a gift that Cleveland valued as precious. "Those guys were after the chocolate?"

"Not exactly." Cleveland spent the next ten minutes recounting his conversation with Rabbi Kaplan and describing the wooden box, and the metal box it protected. He was relieved that neither Mullaney nor Hernandez expressed any skepticism when he explained the history of the box and its contents, and he was grateful that neither of them flinched when he revealed the warning of the symbols on the lid of the box, the rabbi's grave caution about the lethal nature of the box, and the rabbi's belief that the message inside the box could be crucial to America's future role in the Middle East.

"So as long as the metal box remains within the wooden case holding it, there should be no danger of making contact with it," Cleveland concluded. "As a precaution, there's the Aaronic blessing that can be passed from one holder to another that serves as a protective anointing. I gave the blessing to Palmyra before asking her to bring the satchel here for safekeeping. Now we—you, I hope—need to get it to the Rabbinate Council at the Hurva Synagogue as soon as possible and get it out of our lives."

"Where's the box now?" Mullaney asked.

"It's safe," said Palmyra. "I hid it when I got back to the residence."

Cleveland saw Mullaney shoot a questioning glance at his daughter.

"Really . . . it's safe," Palmyra insisted. "No one is going to get near that satchel."

Clearly unsatisfied, Mullaney turned back to the ambassador.

"Who do you think was after the box in Istanbul?"

Good . . . Mullaney was going through a deliberate process. "I'm not sure," said Cleveland.

"The guys in the white van had Middle Eastern features," said Hernandez. "But so do the other eight million people in Istanbul. We ran a check on the van . . . stolen. None of the guys in our SUV remember any distinctive marking from the truck that T-boned them into the restaurant. We had no warning chatter. And whoever was responsible seemed to drop off the face of the earth afterward. We couldn't track down anything."

"And you think these bad guys might have followed you . . . followed the package . . . here." It was a statement from Mullaney, not a question. Cleveland didn't feel as if he was being interrogated. "You don't think you're safe, that the package is safe, in the US ambassador's residence in Israel? You live in a fortress with some of the toughest guys on this planet dedicated to your safety. Mr. Ambassador, what has you worried?"

Good man, this Mullaney, thought Cleveland. No bull. On point and direct.

Cleveland turned to his right and put his hand on Hernandez's arm. "Thank you, Tommy. You were correct in all respects."

"You're welcome . . . what? . . . Did I win a prize?"

Cleveland smiled, something he didn't think possible in the current circumstances. "No, Tommy, I won the prize when you were assigned to my detail. And now I've been given another prize, Agent Mullaney here."

"Okay . . . I'll pick up my winnings at the door. And could you make some of it chocolate? Hard to find here. Melts awfully . . ."

"Sir," Mullaney interrupted, "we don't have much time. Why are you frightened for your safety?"

The ambassador sighed and looked across the table. "It's not my safety, Agent Mullaney. It's Palmyra's safety that concerns me. The safety of all the people who work here at the residence." Cleveland leaned back in his chair, recalling the conversation in Istanbul. "Rabbi Kaplan in Istanbul told me that three terrorist attacks against the synagogue were known to the public. What isn't public is that the synagogue has survived attacks and break-in attempts that have been ongoing for decades, ever since the box arrived from Germany in 1938. There have been subtle incursions and full-blown attacks, one of which nearly destroyed the entire sanctuary. Six of the synagogue staff have been killed in these attacks, two of them rabbis. Whoever is after this box and the document it contains, they are ruthless and relentless."

Mullaney was shaking his head. "And through all these years, whoever's after the box never succeeded? Seems a bit lame for a ruthless and relentless gang of thugs."

Cleveland raised his hands, palms up. "Oh, they've succeeded," he said. "Twice the attackers breached all the synagogue's extensive security and gained control of the wooden chest."

"And they gave it back?"

"No," interjected Hernandez. "They got zapped, right?"

"Zapped . . . yes," Cleveland responded. "Both times, attackers were found, sprawled on the floor, the box not far away. Their tongues were black, they were bleeding from their eyes and their hair had fallen out."

"Ouch, that's a nasty hangover," said Hernandez, shaking his head.

"But they keep trying?" asked Mullaney.

"They keep trying," Cleveland answered. "And there's no reason for us to believe they will stop trying now that the box is here in Israel. Here in this house. We may be a well-guarded fortress, Agent Mullaney, and I'm glad for it. But a lot of people could still be hurt if we keep that box here. Besides . . . we need to get it to the Rabbinate Council. The descendants and followers of the Vilna Gaon may be the only people who can figure out what this second prophesy is all about. If the first one predicted the Russians marching into the Crimea, I think it's critical we know what the second one predicts."

Mullaney got out of his chair. "Okay, it's got to go."

Cleveland's mobile phone rattled to life. Pressed to his ear, he listened for a few moments, then clicked it off. "And we've got to go too. That was Goldberg. We meet with the prime minister in seventy-five minutes. Jerusalem is an hour's drive. So let's get crackin'."

"Are we taking the box?" asked Hernandez. "I may need my asbestos gloves."

Cleveland stopped at the threshold of the gazebo and turned first to Mullaney and then to his daughter. The adrenaline pump he got from the news of the meeting with the prime minister was overcome by an onrushing bleakness . . . helpless frustration tinged with fear and regret. What had he gotten his daughter involved in?

"I . . ."

Palmyra stepped over and grasped his hand. "It's okay, Dad. The box is safe. It's well hidden, behind tightly locked doors where no one would think to look for it or even be able to reach it if they knew where to look."

Searching his daughter's emerald eyes, Cleveland's stomach felt like the inside of an unexplored cave—dark, cold, and empty. "I haven't spoken to anyone at the synagogue." His words were an admission, whispered as if he were in a confessional box in church. "They don't know we're coming. And we've got to leave now to get there on time. I don't want to . . ."

Palmyra ran her right hand along Cleveland's cheek. "Go, Dad. It's okay. Double the guard on the front gate, if it makes you feel better. But we'll be okay. Right now, your thoughts need to be about preparing to meet with Prime Minister Meir. You need to find out what's going on. That's your job, your responsibility. I'll be fine. When you get back, we can make plans to transfer the satchel to the people at the Hurva. For the moment, though, you need to focus on the world outside the walls of this compound. Okay?"

If Cleveland could have reached inside his daughter's heart and protected her inmost being, he would have done it. Instead, he wrapped his left arm around her shoulders. "Stay away from it. Wait for us to get back, okay?"

"Yes, Dad."

Cleveland tore his gaze from his daughter's. Mullaney and Hernandez were both on their mobiles.

"Car's out front," said Hernandez. "The backup team is loading in the SUV and will be behind us before we leave."

"And the guard has been doubled," Mullaney added. "Both front and back, and patrolling the perimeter. Right now, we're Fort Knox."

With a sigh, and one more look at his daughter, Joe Cleveland drew himself to his full height, threw his shoulders back, and transformed from nervous Dad to commanding presence . . . the ambassador of the United States of America to the nation of Israel. "All right, let's move," Cleveland said. "Tommy, we need to be fast, but we need to be safe."

"Gotcha, Boss. I'll keep it under a hundred and twenty."

Cleveland held out his left hand to Palmyra. "Walk with me."

With Mullaney and Hernandez following close behind, Cleveland spoke in a low voice. "Please make sure Jeffrey cancelled any commitments for the rest of the day. And ask him to clear my agenda for tomorrow as well. I think we're going to need the time." He squeezed his daughter's hand. "Promise me you will stay away from the package. I won't be able to keep my mind focused unless . . ."

"You've got my word, Dad. I won't go near it. Just be careful out there."

With a father's prayer in his heart, he gave Palmyra's hand one more squeeze and then was around the corner of the residence, into the maelstrom of diplomatic intrigue.

14

US Ambassador's Residence, Tel Aviv
July 19, 5:31 p.m.

Jeffrey Archer, Cleveland's secretary, was in a dither. A moment earlier he had been holding his leather-bound daily planner in front of him, an imploring look in his eyes and stammering objections stumbling across his lips. Palmyra Parker empathized with Archer—she really did. But she had little comfort to offer. "Sorry, Jeffrey. Those were Dad's instructions. He's on his way to Jerusalem to meet with the prime minister. The welcome reception will just need to be postponed . . . until when, I don't know."

The pained expression on Archer's face belonged to a man with the daunting task of calling two hundred of the most powerful and influential people in Israel to tell them the party was canceled. Not a fun job.

"What do I tell them?"

Parker put her hand on Archer's shoulder as she headed toward the door of his office. "Good luck, Jeffrey."

Palmyra Parker turned out of the secretary's office and down the short corridor in the business section of the north wing, past the small, glass-walled conference room. She turned again and headed through the east wing of the residence.

Originally constructed in 1963, the ambassador's residence was extensively renovated in 1995. Located on a cliff overlooking the Mediterranean, in an affluent neighborhood of northern Tel Aviv, the residence was a large, U-shaped building that surrounded a broad patio. Its public rooms were spacious. From the north wing, Parker entered the grand oval entrance hall that was flanked by a sitting room and a living room. Farther into the house, to the west toward the expansive gardens, was a large, rectangular reception hall that was used for an endless schedule of luncheons, receptions, meetings, parties, and official functions. The western wall of the reception area was a series of movable french doors that opened into an enclosed patio that often augmented the reception room.

Parker crossed the oval entrance hall to the south wing and walked down a hallway to a stout door that looked like thick wood, but was actually a reinforced steel blast door that protected the ambassador's private wing. Access to the door was closely monitored twenty-four seven by a detachment of US Marines. Behind a one-way glass window on the left was the security center for the entire residence, where three marines were always on duty, two scanning the banks of monitors connected to the extensive security system, including the entrance to the ambassador's private quarters. In front of her was a single, armed sentry.

"Good evening, Corporal," said Parker. She gave a half wave to the unseen men on duty behind the glass window.

When the door was unlocked from inside the security office, the corporal opened the door for her. "Good afternoon, Mrs. Parker. Is there anything we can do for you today?"

"No, thank you, Corporal. Just more unpacking."

Parker entered the large, comfortably furnished living room and turned left to enter her private suite. Had she continued through the living room, she would have entered a smaller den-library that was connected to the ambassador's bedroom. The bedroom occupied the far western section of the southern wing, just as the ambassador's residential office occupied the far western end of the northern wing, and was provided a panoramic view of the gardens and Mediterranean Sea through a bank of bulletproof windows.

Parker's suite was significantly smaller but did include a full bath and two huge closets along with a sitting area in her bedroom. In spite of the size of the closets, moving boxes overflowed into the bedroom itself. Reminding herself that it was her idea to handle the unpacking of the family's personal items, Parker picked her way through the stacks of boxes and stopped outside the flanking closets. She looked at the door on her left. The satchel was tucked away on the shelf running around the top of the closet.

No, I promised Dad.

Turning away from the closet, Parker scanned the scattered pillars of moving boxes littering the floor. She shook her head, rolled up her sleeves, and pulled open the first box she could reach.

"Good morning, Mr. Secretary."

"Good afternoon, Jeffrey. How is the weather in Tel Aviv today?"

Webster intended his words to be confounding to Archer—like an oiled knife, they were slippery and often dangerous. Good to keep this little guttersnipe in his place—insecure and afraid.

"Beautiful once again, Mr. Secretary," said the ambassador's secretary. "But not everything is serene here. The ambassador has postponed his official welcoming reception. I've got two hundred disappointed and aggravated guests to disinvite."

"And the reason for this sudden postponement?"

"He's on his way to Jerusalem to meet with the prime minister, something that was not on his agenda. So I've been instructed to clear his calendar today and tomorrow," said Archer. "Something is going on. Security has been increased and the tension level around here was very high already. And now the ambassador is dumping his entire schedule and running off to Jerusalem. It's something I thought you would want to know."

Webster waited, allowing the silence to build. He wondered if he had made a mistake. Would Archer really be of value? Could he be trusted? Archer stumbled into the silence. "Cleveland's only been in the country one day, and already he's stirred up a mess.

"Is that all you can tell me, Jeffrey?"

"Well, there was one other odd thing that happened," said Archer, a conspiratorial gravity shadowing his words. "Cleveland's daughter came back from the airport with all the ambassador's bags while Cleveland and his DSS team went straight to the embassy. She . . ."

"Mrs. Parker, you mean?"

"Yes . . . yes, sir. When Mrs. Parker got out of her car she was clutching a leather bag—bigger than a briefcase, but not as big as a suitcase. She held it in her arms, like no one was going to get near it. I was standing on the steps, by the front door, and asked if I could help. She nearly jumped out of her skin. I thought she was going to fall over, so I went down the steps and reached out to steady her. It was . . . well . . . like I had the plague or something. She jumped back, pulled the bag closer to her chest and said, 'No . . . No!' And then she almost ran up the steps and into the residence. Very odd. Then, later in the day, she's in my office telling me the reception needed to be postponed, acting like nothing had happened outside. I don't know. Something was going on there. But I have no clue what it was."

"Not a terribly auspicious start for you, Jeffrey, I must say."

"I've only just been introduced to the ambassador, Mr. Secretary," Archer pleaded. "It's likely going to take some time for me to build up a level of trust with him and his family."

"Very well, Jeffrey," said Webster, a languid indifference coating his words. "Call me again as soon as you have further information. Good-bye."

Well, thought Webster, a new mystery has been added. What is in the bag, Mrs. Parker? What indeed?

"When did the ambassador leave? How many were in his security detail? Did he have a package with him?"

The gardener staggered back against the trunk of a palm tree from the onslaught of questions. In the lee of the compound's wall, shielded by the palm tree from any eyes in the residence, he pressed the phone to his ear. "I don't know, Master. I did not see him leave."

"Then what am I paying you for?" snapped the Turk.

The Palestinian gardener, a long-time staff employee of the ambassador's residence, had been recruited by this man, through the imam of his mosque, only two months ago. Still, he did not want to lose this sudden flood of cash that his extended family had so ravenously spent already.

"I was listening to the mobile telephone call of the ambassador's secretary, who was sitting in the garden. The secretary told the other party that the ambassador abruptly canceled his schedule for today and tomorrow, including the ambassador's welcome reception tonight. The secretary said the ambassador left suddenly for a trip to Jerusalem to meet with the Israeli prime minister. The secretary made his call at approximately six this evening.

"The ambassador's normal security team is comprised of two agents who ride in the limousine with him. Security was increased, and now there is a team of four additional agents who travel directly behind them in a black SUV. Since I did not see them leave, I cannot say if he used the same security protocol today. And forgive me; I did not see if he left with a package." The gardener, who had not taken a breath during his response, held it longer as he waited for a reply.

It was only when he forced air into his lungs that he realized he was on the phone alone.

Ankara
July 19, 5:48 p.m.

"We do not know the location of the package," said the Turk. His right hand held the mobile phone; his left hand fingered the wooden prayer beads of the Muslim faithful as his car moved slowly through the twisting streets of the Old City. "The American ambassador is driving to Jerusalem for a meeting with the prime minister. He left the residence about ten minutes ago. He has agents with him in his vehicle and an armed support vehicle following him. It may be in his possession. His intention may be to deliver the package to the Zionists at the Hurva Synagogue. You must stop them."

"Yes, Master."

"What is our position at the residence?"

"Security has increased significantly. It is very difficult to remain in constant surveillance of the front gate without being detected. But we have men watching and waiting at the front and the back. Perhaps when it becomes dark, we will find a way to gain access."

"You will not!" snapped the Turk. "Cleveland will be anxious to deliver the package as soon as he can. You will stop him."

US Ambassador's Residence, Tel Aviv
July 19, 5:56 p.m.

When the twelfth empty box was tossed into a corner, Parker realized she was hungry. She was also tense, frustrated, and anxious—jumpy because of that package in her closet and fearful for her father. She stretched her back and rotated her shoulders, trying to reduce the strain.

I need to get out of here for a while.

She looked in the mirror. Her short, dark hair slightly mussed, she ran her fingers through it. *That's presentable.* After emptying the second moving box, she had changed into old jeans and a Compassion International T-shirt.

Probably not the outfit for an official function, but she needed some fresh air. The outdoor market that filled the open space of the Shmu'el Tamir Garden was only a few blocks from the residence. She had discovered a vendor who prepared the most delicious pita, filled with homemade hummus and fresh Jerusalem salad.

She went into her closet for the green cardigan sweater to cover most of the T-shirt and a scarf for her hair. Her mouth was already savoring the treat to come. Pulling on the sweater, her eyes caught sight of the satchel on the upper shelf. She stopped.

No . . . I promised Dad.

She pushed her arm through the sleeve and reached for the scarf hanging on a hook . . . her eyes glued to the leather satchel.

Haisha Golden was distraught. No, she was frantic. What to do? It was nearly six o'clock, and she still hadn't finished cleaning the ambassador's private quarters at the residence. *One day! In Israel he is one day, and I don't get my work done. My job is kaput!*

Even if the sun was up, the sky was blue, and she had no bills to pay, Haisha would worry. Her mother said she was born with a scowl on her face and doubt in her heart. This was her fate. Someone had to worry.

Two decades she had worked at the ambassador's residence, first as a dishwasher. Worry begat diligence, and Haisha earned respect and greater responsibility. Which begat more worry. Only forty-two years of age, her hair was gray trending to white, her shoulders fixed in a permanent droop, the creases on her brow like dry wadis in the Negev.

As a rule, unless requested, the housekeeping staff did not enter the ambassador's private quarters if the ambassador or any of his family were still there. So for the third time, Haisha mopped the floor of the large, main reception room, hoping that Mrs. Parker would find things to do in another part of the building. Or take a nap on the terrace. Anything. She was already an hour late on her schedule and still had two rooms to finish.

Haisha was debating whether the floor needed a fourth cleaning when one of the other servants found her.

"Mrs. Parker has gone out. She's headed to the open market at the Tamir Garden."

Before the woman's words were completely out of her mouth, Haisha had secured the half-empty bucket onto the bottom of her housekeeping cart, stacked the mop next to her brooms, and was pushing the cart toward the guarded entrance to the ambassador's wing. No time to waste.

The guards waved Haisha through without delay, and she directly entered Mrs. Parker's bedroom suite. Her progress was impeded by stalagmites of moving boxes that had sprouted up in the middle of the bedroom from the stacks that once filled the closet to her right. Now she was panicked. How could she clean in this mess?

Haisha might worry, but she was diligent. And she hatched a plan.

Moving with determined desperation, she broke down flat the dozen empty boxes that were scattered around the room. She forged a path through the boxes that remained in the right closet and stashed the flat, empty boxes along a wall in the back.

In order to clean the bedroom, Haisha needed to get these moving boxes out of the way. Wondering if the stacks of boxes remaining in the bedroom were in a particular order, Haisha resolved to move them into the closet in roughly the same manner that they now sat in the bedroom. Which meant building the boxes already in the closet into higher stacks so she could make room in the closet for the ones in the bedroom. And time was escaping like air from a punctured balloon.

Her shoulders barked in pain as she lifted box upon box to make room in the closet, building stacks as high as her head. Haisha's tired and aching muscles rebelled as she pushed her body faster and faster. She still had the rooms to clean.

She hefted a heavy box and rested it against her collarbone. There was room for one more. She pushed, the weight shifted, her left shoulder gave way and the box tipped, smacking against the shelf that ran high along the closet's walls. If Haisha hadn't ducked under the precarious box to steady it, the satchel that fell from the shelf would have hit her directly in the head instead of crashing into another stack of boxes and then thudding onto the quarry tile floor of the closet. "Aaiieee . . . what a *meshuggana*!"

Determined, Haisha pushed once more against the box held up by her palms and shoved it into the space beneath the shelf. Then she turned to pick up the bag that fell from the shelf.

The bag had sprung its latch in the fall and a wooden case joined it on the floor. One corner of the wooden case was flattened. It lay on its side, its lid more than half opened, bits of purple cloth sticking out, something inside resting against the floor. A frightening vision of unemployment flashed through Haisha's mind, of the poverty her dismissal would cause, her mother opening an empty refrigerator, unpaid bills piled on the counter.

Stooping down, she pushed her hand under the wooden case and felt a metal surface. She fished around with her fingers, found a corner to the metal surface—warm against her flesh—and pushed it back into the wooden box. She set the wooden box onto the floor, closed its lid tightly and then shoved the wooden box back inside the open leather satchel that lay to her right.

Unsteady on her feet, fearful of another avalanche from the high shelf, Haisha reached into the bedroom, a frigid current of pain running across her shoulders, and pulled a straight-backed chair into the closet. Standing on the chair, Haisha hefted the satchel back onto the closet's shelf. She got light-headed and shivered as if a glacier had replaced her blood. She pushed the satchel fully onto the shelf and reached for the back of the chair to steady herself. A bolt of pain shot from her left temple to her right temple. Her mouth opened to scream when an unseen hand grabbed her heart and squeezed it like jelly.

Haisha was dead before her body hit the floor. Blood flowed from her eyes and her gray hair drifted away from her body. She had no more worries.

15

Ankara
July 19, 6:00 p.m.

The Turk exited the car, his specter-like aide drifting in his wake, and entered the narrow, darkened alley in the Old City of Ankara. Stone walls, the back ends of houses that faced the flanking streets, rose out of sight on both sides of the alley. No windows faced this alley, and the two doors that gave way into it were blocked with heavy wooden barrels. There would be no unwelcome guests at this meeting.

Before he reached the end of the alley, the Turk heard his aide come close.

"Master . . . a call for you."

Assan held out a mobile phone toward the Turk, who answered. "Yes?"

"The woman has left the residence . . . alone, empty-handed."

An interesting development. "Any word from Cerkis?"

"No, Master, not since they got on the highway."

"Very well. Gather the other disciples with you. Take her," said the Turk. "Quickly and quietly. Take her to the warehouse Cerkis uses. Perhaps the daughter is of more worth to the ambassador than the message or the box. Do it . . . now."

Handing the phone back to his aide, the Turk noticed that a large, heavy wooden door with huge metal hinges was open at the end of the alley, casting a sallow dusk onto the cobblestones. A silent sentinel held the door open. The Turk and his aide entered a tight corridor which culminated in steps rising into blackness beyond. The Turk pulled together the lapels of the long, loose coat he wore over the traditional baggy trousers and ascended each step with care, the pungent aroma of cinnamon and cardamom revealing the existence of a nearby spice merchant.

Another silent servant waited at the top of the stairs, a small oil lamp in his hand. With neither word nor gesture, he lit their way down another corridor. Outside the realm of the oil lamp, the rest of the corridor was impenetrable darkness. Only their steps pilfered the silence.

The servant came to a halt abreast a two-piece, dark wooden door. He knocked once, then stepped back. The wooden door opened in the middle and swung back on both sides, revealing a young woman in the traditional Turkish dress of a *tesettür*, a head scarf and light cover-all robe. Remnants of the woman's beauty remained, but it was ruined by a livid scar that started along the right side of her nose and extended down past her lips and over her chin to the underside of her neck. She bowed and gestured the Turk into the room.

Small oil lamps hung from the walls, provoking the dark but not dismissing it. Incense burned somewhere, masking the acrid smoke that still lifted from the hookah on a small round table on the right side of the room. Along the right wall, reclining on a cushioned divan, was his host.

The Turk walked to a cushioned chair that faced the divan and lowered himself into it without a sound. The two men relaxed, measuring each other through the smoke-filled twilight in the room.

The Turk waited. He knew that, in any negotiation, the one who spoke first, the one who broke the silence, would lose. He waited. Off in a corner, someone—probably the woman—faintly coaxed a song of lament from the strings of a zither. The Turk waited.

"It is good to see you here once again," said his host. "It's so rare that we have an opportunity to speak like this, in private."

"There is the woman," said the Turk.

"She is a mute," said his host. "She has no tongue. Only her music speaks for her."

"She can write what she can hear."

"Then speak softly, my friend."

The Turk drew the folds of his coat closer around him. *I shall not suffer this fool much longer.* "Our shipment of arms to the Kurdish fighters arrived without incident." The Turk's voice was the slither of a whisper. "The second delivery of arms, and the material necessary to transport the bombs, is on its way to Colonel Matoush. Medir, the arms dealer, fulfilled his promises. Sadly for him, Medir did not return to his home."

Over the last eight decades, ever since the box had been carried to Istanbul for safekeeping, the Turk had pursued his singular purpose with the unrelenting determination of a starving jungle cat, seducing three earlier power seekers with the fulfilled promise of limitless wealth. Still, he had gotten no closer to securing—or destroying—the box or procuring the key to dismantle the prophetic promises of the book. He had been frustrated in Turkey just as he had been frustrated in Germany before the second war. He was a brown shirt then, known as the Prussian. In 1938, he disappeared from Konigsberg like a fog on the wind, reborn in Istanbul and known only as the Turk.

His host was only the latest pawn in the Turk's plan, a pawn who dreamed himself a king. But a pawn who became more valuable when the Lithuanian's first message was revealed.

Out of necessity, the Turk remained invisible as his host grew in political power and prominence in Turkey. Since the early days of the so-called Arab Spring, when the contagion of rebellion and chaos first exploded into the Muslim world, the Turk had cultivated this relationship as if it were the rarest flower—watered with limitless wealth, fed with flattery and dreams of dominance—as he used to his advantage the anarchy that swept through so much of the Arab world.

Some, like the Muslim Brotherhood in Egypt, saw the Arab Spring as an opportunity to seize power in a land where they had been hunted as outlaws and forced to survive in hiding for decades. They were but a flame in a breeze, bright but incompetent and easily extinguished. Others were contentious and amorphous militias, roving bands of lawless marauders who, as in Libya, were handed a country without a functioning government and watched it descend into chaos.

And then there was Zarqawi. A Jordanian hoodlum, originally named Ahmad al-Khalayleh, he became radicalized during religious instruction in an Amman mosque, spent many years in Jordanian prisons, emerging as Abu Musab al-Zarqawi, a zealous convert to jihadism. He joined al-Qaeda in Afghanistan early in the new century and a few years later surfaced in Baghdad as leader of an aggressive cancer called al-Qaeda in Iraq that preached an Islamic fanaticism that frightened even Muslim leaders. Following Zarqawi's assassination-by-drone, al-Qaeda in Iraq was reborn in the power vacuum of the Syrian civil war as the Islamic State.

In reality, ISIS now ruled in the Middle East. Its self-proclaimed caliphate not only encompassed a land mass virtually erasing the border between Syria and Iraq, but it was also the single most dominant factor in the geopolitical existence of every Middle Eastern nation. Every Muslim nation lived in fear of what ISIS represented—allegiance not to a nation, but to a narrowly defined, apostate sect of Islam that controlled every aspect of life and brought it into line with a medieval and legalistic ideology celebrating heinous violence as its preferred method of evangelism.

This was not the Islam served by either the Turk or his host. Neither rebellion nor anarchy was the Turk's anticipated avenue to power. He was a ruthless adherent to the violence of jihad, but his self-serving zeal for the ascendancy of Islam emanated from him more than earthly ambition.

The Turk was not only a diligent scholar of the Koran, but he also seriously studied the writings of the other two great religions birthed from the loins of Abraham, the Jewish Tanakh and the Christian Bible. Two things were true about all three scriptural texts. Each contained a detailed, similar pronouncement on the last days of this earthly realm—a short-lived, world-wide age of peace and prosperity. But each of the three sacred books predicted a culmination of this peaceful age with differences that were striking and incompatible. Only one would be correct.

In the Hebrew Tanakh—the compilation of the Law, the Prophets, and the Writings—the Turk had learned that the end-of-time scenario would be inaugurated by the arrival of the much-prophesied Messiah, a Jewish king who would rule the entire earth, with Jerusalem as his capital. This Messiah-King would employ his divine authority and power to end all disease, bring bountiful agricultural harvests to the entire earth, and pacify all animals. Israel would be restored to its rightful prominence above all nations of the world with the Messiah-King ruling over a world united into one confederation that poured prosperity into Israel, ending all war.

The Christian Bible incorporated these same Jewish writings as the Old Testament and introduced an additional history called the New Testament. In this new text, Jesus Christ, the Nazarene prophet, was crucified by the Romans. From the Turk's study, Christians naively believed this Christ was resurrected to life after being dead for three days and was bodily lifted from this earth to sit, in human form, at the right hand of God. This New Testament predicted Jesus would one day return to earth in his human form as a warrior-king. In a climactic battle on the plains of Meggido, Christ's heavenly armies would destroy the armies of the world and usher in a millennium of peace on earth. A new, perfect Jerusalem would descend from heaven and replace its earthly predecessor. In a final judgment of all humanity throughout all history, the just would live in perfected bodies on a perfected earth for all eternity. And those who did not swear allegiance to the Nazarene would be condemned to an eternity in a blazing torture called hell.

In contrast, the sacred scripture of Islam, the Koran that the Turk and his host revered and honored, contained the words actually spoken by the prophet Muhammad, written down and organized into suras, or chapters, after his death. The Koran contained many of the same people and events as the Jewish and Christian Scripture, but established Muhammad as the last and greatest prophet. Supporting the Koran were Hadiths, written traditions of Muhammad, and Sunna, the path and practices of Muhammad. Islamic scripture predicted the coming of the Mahdi, the final and greatest caliph, who would reign for seven years over a golden age of universal peace and prosperity under Islamic Sharia law, prior to the final judgment.

Each religion believed that divine intervention would inaugurate the last days of humankind.

But only the followers of Islam believed their actions in this current world could hasten the coming of the Mahdi. What consumed the Turk, and intrigued his host, was a simple belief: that their intervention in this world could thwart all possibility for the emergence of a Judeo-Christian Messiah. They had come to a conclusion. If they could impede the fulfillment of any one Judeo-Christian prophecy, they would prevent the realization of all Messianic prophecy.

If they could manipulate the story of Scripture, they could manufacture its conclusion to fit their own ends. The Turk was convinced and committed. He could, and he would, change the Bible.

When the fulfillment of prophecy was destroyed, first would emerge a transcontinental Islamic caliphate with one ruler—one of the men in this room, but not his host, in spite of the lofty position he currently held.

But out of that caliphate would arise a ruler for whom the Turk was only a messenger. A ruler—the One—who would reign over a worldwide empire unhindered by the empty promises of a book that no longer exerted any power.

Certainly to achieve this dream, Israel must be obliterated, the West infiltrated and overthrown. But ISIS and its dream of caliphate must also be destroyed, the Persians prevented from rising once again on the crest of wanton nuclear ransom, and the once indolent Arabs prohibited from joining the limited fraternity of nuclear nations.

No, the nuclear fraternity would have a new member, but not those pleasure-sated Saudis. The Turk and his host were committed to an emerging plot that—if successful—would ensure a new Ottoman Empire once again ruling from the Indus Valley through the underbelly of Europe to the very gates of Rome, Paris, and Berlin. And the Turk had the Americans to thank for providing the tools and the opportunity for the Ottoman Empire to rise once again.

Expanding its policy of nuclear deterrence, in 2009 NATO—the North Atlantic Treaty Organization, the mutual defense alliance formed by the US and Western Europe in response to the Cold War after World War II—instituted a policy called nuclear sharing, where strategically located member countries without nuclear weapons of their own were provided nuclear weapons by NATO.

The nuclear sharing program invited these member nations to be in consultation about nuclear weapons policy. It also required each nation to store the weapons on their territory, provide or maintain the bombers necessary to deliver those weapons . . . and that the armed forces of the host countries themselves would be involved in delivering those weapons in the event of their use.

In November 2009, Turkey received an estimated fifty thermonuclear bombs from NATO. Belgium, Germany, Italy, and the Netherlands also received nuclear weapons, but fewer than Turkey, as part of NATO's nuclear sharing policy. NATO had only three nuclear powers: the United States, France, and the United Kingdom. But only the United States provided weapons for nuclear sharing.

Those fifty B61 bombs were stored in hardened bunkers at the Incirlik Air Base in the far eastern reaches of Turkey. While the American military retained ultimate authority and control over the weapons, the Turkish Air Force and its officers were intimately knowledgeable and involved with the maintenance of the weapons.

Both the Turk and his host cast a covetous eye on those weapons at Incirlik, a craving that was at the root of their conspiracy. But the Turk was determined to drive that plan one step further than his host ever dreamed.

"President Kashani's cultivation of ties with the leaders of al-Qaeda is causing significant consternation in the capitals of the West," his host said about his boss.

"There is a whispered fear that Turkey could slip into the sphere of radical jihad."

"Excellent." His host nodded his head and reached for the hookah. "The more the West fears Kashani and his plans, the better for us."

The better for you. The Turk knew the ambition that fueled this man's passion, and the steps he was contemplating to achieve that ambition. Coups to overthrow governments in Turkey were not uncommon.

"Yes, we will keep them worried," promised his host. "And what of the American's ill-conceived agreement with the mullahs in Tehran?"

The Turk rose from his chair to hide the satisfaction from his face. *Yes . . . concentrate on that, my short-sighted friend. Keep your eyes fixed on the Persians.* He guarded his voice. "Their president is determined, but he has opposition."

"And the bankers are just as determined not to lose the seven hundred million dollars a day they are stealing from the Iranians," said his host. "And the Israelis are pushing very hard against any rapprochement with the liars in Tehran. But this president appears to have very little regard for the Israelis."

"Then who does he think his friends are?" asked the Turk.

"Who can say? The outcome remains undecided. My friend in Washington says we must consider the possibility that sanctions will be lifted in the not-too-distant future."

"Then the centrifuges of Natanz and Fordo will spin night and day," said the Turk. "We must block the Persians. It is up to you, Minister, to ensure that chaos continues to reign throughout that region. Soon, our day will also come. Then we will turn the once-fertile crescent into a desert as vast as the Anbar."

His host sucked noisily on the mouthpiece fixed to the end of the hookah's hose. *Ravage your lungs.* The Turk stepped farther away from the divan. He knew that hookah smoking was one hundred times more deadly than smoking one cigarette. The smoke of either sickened him. *Die . . . so I don't need to kill you.*

"What of this coming announcement from the Saudis? And their intent to secure nuclear weapons from Pakistan?" asked his host. "This is a development that we did not anticipate. Is there to be peace between the Jew and the Arab?"

"Well informed, as always," the Turk said with a bow. "But there will be no peace. Too many stand against it, particularly in Israel, where the desire for peace is overwhelmed by distrust of the Arabs. They can announce a peace, but it will never become a reality. In the meantime, we have something the Israelis need much more desperately than peace."

His host pointed the mouthpiece toward the Turk. "Water."

"Yes, water," said the Turk. "Our stealth weapon."

Flowing out of the mountains of eastern Turkey were the headwaters of the two most important snow-fed rivers of the Middle East. The water resources of the Tigris and Euphrates river basins were critical sources of hydroelectric power generation, irrigation, and domestic use, not only in Turkey but also in Syria, Iraq, and Iran. In addition to the two great rivers, Turkey was home to one hundred and twenty natural lakes with additional water stored behind five hundred and fifty dams. And Turkey was slowly tightening the spigot.

Water was already becoming scarce across the arid Middle East during a five-year drought that ended in 2012. Iran's largest lake—Lake Urmia—once ninety miles long, thirty-five miles wide, and thirty feet deep was now a massive mud flat, containing only five percent of the water it once held. As the rains diminished and the Syrian civil war escalated, Turkey restricted even more of the flow of the Euphrates through its largest dams, the Ataturk and Keban, strangling the once-mighty river to streams through Syria and Iraq. With no international treaties requiring Turkey to keep the water flowing, Ankara now controlled the one resource most critical to life throughout the region.

"Will Iraq ask for action from the United Nations?" questioned the Turk.

"Iraq is blinded by the plague of ISIS," said his host. "That puppet government's fear is who controls the rivers, not how much water flows through them. But the farmers in Anbar are in near revolt over their barren rice fields. And the cost of importing grain is crippling the government's fragile economy. Every time we tighten the valves on the spillways of our dams brings Syria and Iraq one step closer to even greater crisis. Soon, they will be begging for help. And there is only one place they can come for that help. The plan is working. Our opportunity is near."

With the smoke dissipating, the Turk moved closer to the man on the divan. "Stay the course, Prime Minister. You have an endless supply of the one thing desperately needed by the desert dwellers in Syria and Iraq. Soon they will come and you will exact our price—a free Kurdish state carved out of Iraq and Syria and the partition of western Syria into Turkey."

"And what of the Israelis?"

"One step at a time," said the Turk. "The Israelis' turn will come. First, we build a bulwark against the Persians by crippling Iraq and empowering the fighters of the Peshmerga with their own state. There will be a time for the Israelis—when they are friendless. Be patient."

Arslan Eroglu, prime minister of Turkey, replaced the mouthpiece on the hookah. "When will Colonel Matoush move against the storage facilities at Incirlik?" he asked.

"Soon, but not until we are completely ready and certain of success. There will be one opportunity only. In this task, we must not fail." It was time to end this conversation. The Turk bowed from his waist. "*Salaam aleichem*, my friend."

"*Wa' aleichem salaam* . . . and God be with you, also," said Eroglu. "Until next time. Allahu Akbar."

16

Highway One, Israel
July 19, 6:13 p.m.

Cleveland was looking out the window of the sumptuous Maybach 57 sedan as it sped eastward along Highway One from Tel Aviv to Jerusalem. Looking, but not seeing the barren Judean landscape that occupied most of the land from the sea to the hills of Jerusalem, broken only sporadically by sterile, white communities stacked along a hillside. The scene was a blur to his right, his mind preoccupied with weighing and sifting a steady flow of information—some confirmed, some conjecture—and trying to formulate a plan for what he expected to be a difficult and challenging conversation with David Meir, the embattled Israeli prime minister.

"Forgive me for interrupting your thoughts, but I was hoping to ask you a few questions before we got to Jerusalem."

Mullaney was sitting in the back seat to the left of the ambassador. With Hernandez driving, there was only the three of them in the Mercedes limo for the trip to Jerusalem. Cleveland invited Mullaney to join him in the back of the car because he needed to get to know his regional security officer as quickly as possible and also because he was looking for a nonaligned sounding board—someone without an agenda with whom he could talk freely and not have to worry about how each word was composed. According to people Cleveland regarded as reliable, Mullaney was a man of insight, a man he could trust.

Cleveland turned away from the window. "Of course, Agent Mullaney. I'm sorry I got distracted. I wanted to talk to you also. So go ahead. Shoot."

"I have a number of questions for you, sir, but two are at the top of the list. Who do you think is after this box—after the prophecy inside the box—and is the box connected in any way to this secret announcement that's coming tomorrow? I've been trying to build a threat analysis in my mind, and those two questions keep colliding with each other."

Cleveland nodded and shifted in the leather bucket seat, swiveling on his left hip to get a better look at Mullaney. "Good questions. Do you mind if I call you Brian?"

Mullaney shook his head.

"Good," said Cleveland. "First, I have no idea who is determined to get this box and the prophecy, but they've been after it for a long time. They are relentless and ruthless. They're not going to give up. My gut tells me the second prophecy will be similar to the first—in some way connecting the geopolitical reality of today to portents of Christ's second coming, the 'last days' scenario that Hollywood loves to use for its adventure blockbusters. So I expect it will have some relevance to the politics of the Middle East, but I don't necessarily believe it will be connected to tomorrow's announcement.

"But Brian, we need to put some perspective on all that is happening around us," said Cleveland. "If we start looking at the trees before we examine the forest, we will get lost much too easily. You've been in the Middle East before, Brian. What do you see?"

"Conflict," said Mullaney. "Both obvious and subtle conflict. And the movement of great, antagonistic powers that could escalate those conflicts even more."

"Historic enemies," Cleveland agreed, nodding his head. "Enmity that spans centuries. People groups who have been adversaries for more than a thousand years. It's not a conflict of nations, but of cultures—a conflict that includes, but goes beyond, religions and moral codes. It's the ongoing conflict of three ancient empires.

"One of the core beliefs of Islam," Cleveland continued, "is that when an Islamic nation rules any portion of the earth, it rules that portion forever. One way, a simplistic way, to look at current history is to see a conflict between Judaism and Islam . . . between the existing state of Israel and the Islamic nations that surround Israel. But the core conflict of the Middle East is much more subtle, as you noted.

"The Middle East as we know it today has been ruled by one empire after another for nearly four thousand years," said Cleveland. "More than twelve hundred years before Christ walked this earth, much of the area from Eastern Europe to northern India and most of the Mediterranean basin was—for six centuries—under the dominion of the Assyrian Empire. Over time, Assyria was supplanted by the Persian or Achaemenid Empire that rose out of the central plains of Iran. Islam didn't become ascendant until after the death of Muhammad in 632, and there were several Islamic empires, or caliphates—the Umayyad, Abbasid, and Fatimid—from the mid-seventh century until the

Turks emerged at the end of the twelfth century. The Ottoman Empire ruled over the Middle East until the empire fell apart at the end of World War I.

"From a historical perspective, it is a very recent phenomenon for the Middle East to be an assortment of sovereign nations. And it's important for us, today, to remember that the Islamic faith did not exist when the Assyrian and Persian Empires were in power. Although Syria and Iran are Muslim nations now, ethnically and culturally they are not Arabs and were not Muslim States during the height of their empires. Ethnically and culturally, they are Assyrians, Persians, and Turks, and all have ruled over Palestine. They also ruled over large regions of the Persian Gulf, of what is now Saudi Arabia. Ignore for a moment, if you can, the huge schism between the Shia and Sunni Muslims. You can look at the Middle East and, except for Israel, believe it's a massive Islamic region. Which it is. But it is also a massive region where distinct cultures have been at war with each other since nearly the dawn of time.

"And to give you some sense of the scope we're talking about, the Achaemenid Persian Empire, in the fifth century before Christ, occupied over two million square miles of the earth's surface and contained the largest percentage of the world's population of any empire in history."

The lead driver in a three-vehicle convoy glanced quickly at his speedometer as slower cars flashed past on his right—180 kilometers an hour. The other two black Cadillac Escalades were in tight formation, right on his bumper. At this rate, they should rapidly close the distance on the ambassador's vehicles.

Cleveland stopped to take a breath. He wondered if he had confused or bored Mullaney with his mini-lecture. But what he hadn't shared with Mullaney was more alarming, more disturbing to his spirit than the rise and fall of empires. As a committed Christian and student of the Bible, the main question on Cleveland's mind was where did all these impending moves fit in biblical prophecy?

Personally and as a representative of his country's government, Cleveland's assessment was that a two-state solution . . . a safe and secure Israel alongside an independent Palestine . . . was apparently the best chance for peace in the Middle East. Except a two-state solution defied biblical prophecy. In the third chapter of the book of Joel, the prophet warned that all nations who tried to partition God's land—the boundaries laid out by God for the promised land, much of which was now occupied by the nation of Israel—would be judged.

On one hand, the division of Israel appeared to violate biblical prophecy. On the other hand, a peace agreement between the Jewish people and the Arab nations would end nearly four thousand years of hatred and conflict. What would an agreement like this mean in relation to the prophetic clock that started ticking in 1948? Cleveland, who had spent so many years of his life studying and believing the Bible, didn't know. And that scared him the most.

"So there are three people groups," said Mullaney, snapping Cleveland out of his thoughts, "Persians, Islamic Arabs, and Turks, who all claim ownership of the same land, who hate each other as conquerors, and live in fear that one of the others will rise again in power. Which is happening as we speak. Iran and Iraq are suddenly cozy, Turkey is part of NATO, and the Arabs are feeling vulnerable. Which is why everybody wants nukes. Sounds like the kind of looming collision that could profoundly impact the course of history for the entire world and change the nation of Israel forever."

"Precisely," said Cleveland, "and much more simply stated, thank you."

"Yeah, thanks, Brian," chipped in Hernandez from the front seat. "Atti . . . uh . . . the ambassador nearly put me to sleep with his History 101. But what does that history have to do with the box?" Hernandez asked.

"I don't know, Tommy," said Cleveland. "Perhaps it's only coincidence. But I doubt it. There are not only natural forces at work in the Middle East, but supernatural as well. As a Christian, I'm acutely aware of how important and pertinent biblical prophecy may soon become.

"One of the things Rabbi Kaplan told me in Istanbul before he transferred the box into my care was a belief that had also been passed from father to son for more than two hundred years. The protectors of the box do not know what the prophecy contains. But they do believe—and these were his words—that it will reveal the name of the man of violence, God's adversary in the last days. Now I don't see that name, that label—man of violence—in my Bible. But I do see a title for the man of lawlessness. I don't know if they are the same person, but I am filled with dread that they may be."

"Man of lawlessness . . . sounds like a WWF wrestler in a steel Cage of Death match," said Hernandez. "I'd put my money on that dude."

Cleveland took a deep breath. *If only he knew.* He reached out and put his hand on the back of Hernandez's shoulder. "I hope you never have to find out," he said. "But if there is a second prophecy in that box . . . I don't know. The first one was pretty specific. Is the Jewish Messiah's coming imminent—which would in effect be the second coming of Christ? Could it be that we are actually in some sort of "last days" scenario here?"

"Last days?" said Hernandez. "I sure hope not. I got a date with Betty . . ."

Cleveland's personal mobile phone rattled to life with a message alert. "Excuse me."

He didn't recognize the number on the incoming message, but very few people had access to his phone. It was a text message: "Mr. Ambassador, I am Mordechai Friedman, the assistant rabbi at the Neve Shalom Synagogue in Istanbul. It is urgently critical that I speak to you immediately. For your safety, please call me at this number without any delay."

Holding fast to the steering wheel, the driver in the lead vehicle thumbed the button for hands-free use of his mobile phone and connected to the driver of the second Escalade. But a gray sedan in the right lane flicked on its blinker to change lanes. He punched and held down the horn, screaming past the startled driver like a freight train through a grade crossing. Faster . . . he needed to go faster.

17

Highway One, Israel
July 19, 6:20 p.m.

Cleveland read the text message a second time as he tried to keep conjecture from rampaging over his emotions. "This can't be good," Cleveland said, as he showed the message to Mullaney and then quickly punched in the number.

"Mr. Ambassador?"

"Yes."

"Oh, thank you for calling. I am so relieved," Like a waterfall at flood stage, the words stormed through the phone into Cleveland's ear. "It's been a terrible few days and I was so confused and conflicted about what to do. The rabbi made me promise, but I couldn't sleep . . ."

"Please, Rabbi Friedman, please slow down and take a breath," said Cleveland. "I'm putting you on the speaker. Why are you contacting me?"

"You don't know? Oh, of course not, how could you? Ahhh . . . let me start from the beginning."

"Yes, please. But I don't have a great deal of time."

"Oh, yes, well . . . when you were here earlier this week, you received a package from Rabbi Kaplan. A package I believe he asked you to deliver to the Rabbinate Council at the Hurva Synagogue in Jerusalem—a wooden case with a metal box inside of it, correct?"

"Yes, Rabbi Friedman. That is correct."

"And I believe the rabbi provided you with an anointing, the Aaronic blessing, to keep you safe from the protections built into the metal box, correct?"

"Yes." Cleveland's thoughts shifted from preparing for his meeting with the prime minister to the internal warning signals that were depositing doubt and anxiety into his spirit. "Is there a prob—"

"Problem? Yes . . . well . . . following your visit to the synagogue, Rabbi Kaplan was found dead in his office."

Cleveland's heart thumped against his rib cage like a ravenous tiger at feeding time.

"He was bleeding from his eyes," said Rabbi Friedman. "His hair had fallen out and his tongue was hanging out of his mouth. It was thick and black. Three years ago, men broke into the synagogue. Two of them were found in the rabbi's office. They died in the same way."

Cleveland took a deep breath and tried to calm his fears. "What are you telling me—there is no protection?"

The silence from the other end of the call was more frightening for Cleveland than anything this man had yet said.

"Honestly, sir," said Rabbi Friedman, "I don't know. I know Rabbi Kaplan believed the Aaronic blessing protected the keeper of the box. He told me about the box, just in case my turn came. But he was keeper of the box of prophecy for twenty years without—"

"Hold on," Cleveland interrupted. "If *anyone* touches the box, the curse kills them?"

The torrent of words had dried up. For a moment, there was silence on the other end of the phone. "It's not exactly a curse," Friedman mumbled. "And there are some who will know how to open the box. Some who understand the kabbalah and how to interpret the symbols on its surface. But for the rest of us . . ."

"The wooden chest must be some kind of protection, or I'd be dead already," said Cleveland, frustration and growing anger accenting each of his words. "Tell me, Rabbi Friedman, is there anything else I need to know? Anything else that's been kept from me?"

"No, no, no," Friedman babbled. "Please, forgive me, Mr. Ambassador. I promised the rabbi I—"

"Good-bye, Rabbi."

Mullaney's thoughts were already with Palmyra Parker. "Are we turning around, sir?"

Cleveland's face was ashen as he looked at his wristwatch. "We don't have time." His voice was flat and lifeless. "We're halfway there. If we turn around now . . ."

"Brian!"

In the rearview mirror, Hernandez's eyes connected with Mullaney's. "Trouble—"

A flash of black whipped past the window. Mullaney turned to see a black

Cadillac Escalade traveling at high speed as it pulled abreast of the Mercedes limousine. Then all hell broke loose.

Mullaney grabbed the ambassador, pulled him from the seat onto the floor of the limo and threw his body on top of Cleveland as he craned his neck to see outside. "Two more coming strong," said Hernandez, but his words were cut short as the Escalade slammed into the left side of the limo and drove it onto the loose, stone berm of the highway. Mullaney heard a separate impact and the squeal of strained tires behind them, and he figured the ambassador's support vehicle was also getting rammed. By instinct, Mullaney reached for the Sig Sauer automatic at the base of his back. But he remembered the bulletproof windows of the armored Mercedes and kept it in the holster. The limo jerked left, Hernandez trying to counter the impact from the Escalade.

"Our backup is getting—" Hernandez's words were cut short when the massive Cadillac SUV slammed once more into the left side of the ambassador's car. "Ouch. Hang on!"

Mullaney could feel the car being pushed right, across the loose, stone shoulder of the highway.

"Hang on!"

Mullaney shifted his position to press Cleveland farther into the tight space between the back seat, the door, and the back of the front seat just as Hernandez jammed on the brakes, the limousine fishtailing through the flying stones.

The heavier Escalade was doing the job, pushing the ambassador's car closer and closer to the embankment on the far side of the highway's gravel shoulder. One more push should do it. As the driver turned the Cadillac harder to its right, the limo slammed on its brakes.

Looking up, Mullaney could see the Escalade whip around the front of the decelerating limo, its momentum continuing to the right as it skidded across the shoulder. But Hernandez's desperate maneuver was too late to save the limousine's slide. Mullaney felt the front right corner of the Mercedes drop off the road. In a heartbeat the limo catapulted off the shoulder, rolling and tumbling down a stone and gravel embankment. Mullaney wedged his body between the seats as he tried to protect the ambassador, but the sudden shift in relative gravity—what was up was now down; what was once right was now left—flailed Mullaney around the back seat of the Mercedes like the flicked tip of a leather bullwhip as he desperately tried to shield Cleveland.

The car rolled over twice, pounding Mullaney from roof to seat and back again. It was like being inside a cement mixer with humans instead of cement. Mullaney tried desperately to protect the ambassador, but Cleveland's body broke loose from his grasp on the first bounce and now was being tossed around like drying laundry.

Its back end swinging around, the Cadillac turned 180 degrees, its nose pointing in the opposite direction. Stones flew, but the Escalade reversed its momentum and hurtled back toward the limo, which dropped off the edge of the highway and became airborne.

Shattering its shock absorbers, the Mercedes crashed to earth on all four tires, coming to a jaw-pounding stop in a swirling cloud of dust and crushed stone.

"Tommy?" Mullaney's voice sounded as brittle as his body was battered. Gunfire was already erupting outside the limousine.

"Alive."

"Stay with the ambassador. Make sure he's okay. Lock it up and send the alarm."

"Roger that. Be careful out there, Brian."

Cleveland's body was in the well between the seats, his hands over his head, groans escaping from his mouth. Mullaney pushed his body past the ambassador. With his right hand, he pulled the Sig Sauer from its holster. With his left he grabbed the right-side door's handle and awkwardly drove his shoulder into it. Hitting the door, pain lanced across his back, but the door wasn't stuck, and Mullaney tumbled out of the car and into the dust. He scrambled on the gravel back to the side of the car, slammed shut the door, and tried to ignore a rising eruption of pain in his back that sucked the breath out of his lungs.

Gunfire was coming from several directions as Mullaney fought to clear his head and get his bearings.

Keeping the car between him and the road, Mullaney rose on his haunches and peered around the back window, over the trunk. The four DSS agents in the chase vehicle were each out of the SUV, on the ground, using Heckler & Koch 9-millimeter submachine guns to pound out a lethal and withering return fire, two on the trailing Escalades and two on the lead Cadillac that forced the limo off the road. The 9-millimeter rounds were ripping through and penetrating the doors of the Escalades, and Mullaney could see several inert bodies around the trailing Cadillacs, assailants who mistakenly thought car doors could protect them from the powerful punch of the 9-millimeter machine guns.

Turning his head to the right, Mullaney saw three black-clad hooded gunmen firing from around the Escalade nearest the Mercedes. A fourth emerged near the back of the vehicle, an RPG launcher held to his shoulder. Mullaney squeezed off two quick shots, dropping the gunman with the launcher, then squeezed off a second set to take out the hooded shooter who was firing from the driver's-side rear door. Now that he had their attention, Mullaney dropped back behind the limousine as bullets began slamming into the Mercedes.

His earpiece crackled. "Watch your back, Brian."

Mullaney spun around toward the front of the Mercedes. The pain of his movement drove him to his knees and his sight blackened for a split second. He sucked in a breath then threw himself to the right, behind the Mercedes's front right tire as bullets started ripping up the gravel around him. Someone with a machine gun had gotten into a position near the back of the Escalade with a firing angle on the limo. He had to be firing from a height advantage. On his belly, Mullaney flattened himself along the ground and shimmied beneath the undercarriage of the Mercedes. He reached the shelter of the left front tire and peeked up. The rear window of the Escalade was open, but empty. Apparently, one of the attackers was firing down on the limo from the Cadillac's cargo area. Mullaney dug his elbows into the gravel and steadied his aim on the open rear window just as a gun barrel, followed by a hooded head, emerged from the window and sighted down on the limo. Two taps on the Sig Sauer's trigger and twin red moons erupted on either side of the shooter's left temple.

Gunfire was now coming at them from under the front of the limousine, and his man fell down in a lump inside the back window of the Escalade. Three gone.

A relentless barrage from the American agents in the chase vehicle was shredding the front and the doors of the Cadillac. He could see other black-clad men sprawled in the dust on the far side of the ambassador's support vehicle. The Americans were deadly accurate and their weapons were tearing the Cadillacs to pieces. And none of their fire had breached the integrity of the Mercedes. He fired a full clip from his Uzi at the agents in the support vehicle while slamming his vehicle into reverse. Time to leave.

He floored the gas pedal, spun the steering wheel to the right and the Cadillac whipped around, facing east on Highway One. He floored it again, sending a wave of stone projectiles slamming into the Mercedes. None of those made a dent either.

In his rearview mirror, only one of the other Escalades hurtled back onto the highway.

This disaster was not going to be well received.

His head barricaded behind his arms, Mullaney was only scratched by the angry shower of rocks kicked up in the wake of the fleeing Cadillacs. Lying prone under the Mercedes, the pain in Mullaney's back increased as the threat raced into the distance. And then he noticed the blood dripping from his head down into the dust. Mullaney inched himself out from under the car.

"Wiley, what's your status," he said into his lapel mic.

"We're okay. Two wounded, but nothing serious. How's the ambassador?"

Leaning on the bullet-dented front fender, Mullaney pulled himself to his feet, his back and his neck stiffening like hour-old cement. The car's windows were spider-webbed, but none had been punctured by the assailants' bullets. He stepped closer to look inside. Tommy Hernandez had somehow worked his way into the back seat, his body positioned to protect the ambassador. His left arm was against his chest, his left hand gripping the right shoulder of his suit jacket. But his weapon was in his right hand, steady and ready to fight. Hernandez laid the gun in his lap and pushed the button on the key fob to unlock the car's doors.

Mullaney tried to open the left side back door, but it was stuck. In one of its careening bounces, the Mercedes pinwheeled on the left side of its roof, compressing down on the door. Mullaney looked into the car. Tommy's left arm looked useless. He and Cleveland were pressed against the right rear door. Mullaney's only visual on Cleveland was the back of his shoulders.

"What's his status?" asked Mullaney.

"Breathing." Hernandez grimaced. "Bashed around pretty good on the outside—like each of us."

"Don't talk about me like I'm not here."

Cleveland's voice betrayed him. He was putting on a brave face, but Mullaney could tell from his voice that the ambassador was hurt and struggling.

"He's bleeding somewhere," said Hernandez, "but not buckets."

"Okay. Let me get some help." Mullaney cocked his head to his earpiece. "Get that, Wiley?"

"Yeah . . . just cleaning a wound on Bob's arm. Be there in a minute."

Cleveland's head hurt. He felt as if he had been slipping into and out of consciousness since the car started its first flip off the road. He had a vague memory of the limousine being rammed, then a nightmare dream of being in a trash masher. After that, everything was a blur. He knew there was shooting. He knew his chest was bruised and that he didn't know if he could put weight on his left leg. Tommy said he was bleeding? Was he shot? And his head hurt.

What day was it?

And his head hurt.

With a delicate caution, Cleveland tried to shake the cobwebs out of his brain. *Owww!*

A sharp crack of rending metal speared Cleveland's foggy mind like lightning on an August afternoon.

"Easy, Atticus," Hernandez whispered. "We'll get you out of here, sir."

He rested his head in his hands and thought of how much this attempt on his life would upset Palmyra.

Palmyra!

Cleveland fought against gravity and his better judgment and turned his head to the right.

"Mullaney!" he croaked.

"Yes, sir?"

Cleveland felt utterly fatigued after just one word. His breathing labored, he struggled with getting the rest of his . . .

"Wiley . . . get around the right side . . . Tommy, here, let me help you out."

Mullaney was taking charge. Good man.

"Hold on, Mr. Ambassador. We'll have you right out of there."

No . . . wait. Cleveland felt the weight of Tommy Hernandez lift from his left side. He took a breath. And saw stars as soon as his chest expanded. No . . . wait.

"Brian . . . wait." The words came out like coughs in the night, short, staccato bursts. "Palmyra. We . . . must . . . call . . ."

Mullaney swore under his breath and pulled out his mobile phone. The ambassador could hear sirens in the distance, closing fast.

"This is Mullaney. Duty officer—now!"

Cleveland closed his eyes and tried to slow his heart.

An Israeli Defense Forces helicopter roared overhead, then banked hard to hover over the wrecked limousine. Mullaney flattened his left hand against his left ear to shut out the noise. "Pat? I want you to personally get Mrs. Parker—take three agents with you—get her over to the ambassador's quarters and stay with her. You . . ."

"She's not here, Brian. Are you guys all right? Is the ambassador safe?"

"Don't worry about us, Pat. Where's Parker?"

"She went out. Said she was heading over to the open market at the Shmu'el Tamir Garden to get something to eat. I told her we had food here. She said, 'Not like this.' That was about forty minutes after you . . . aw, shoot, the ambassador may not be the only target, right? Sorry, Brian. We'll get two squads on the street, one mobile going right to the garden, the other on foot. I'll get back to you as soon as we find her. Sorry, Boss."

"Don't apologize. Find her."

The ambassador's head began to swim. He fought to remain conscious. The only thing keeping him alert was the words he heard Mullaney speak. *Where's Parker? Find her.*

Two Israeli police cars skidded to a stop in the gravel at the side of the highway.

Palmyra!

Prime Minister's Office, Jerusalem
July 19, 6:44 p.m.

The voice outside his office, speaking to his secretary, was unmistakable. The simple sound of it carried power and, as if he was pounding on David Meir's door, demanded attention. Which, Meir knew, was Benjamin Erdad's intention.

Meir pushed the button on his telephone that connected him to his secretary. "Rebecca, if he has a moment, please ask my secretary of internal security to join me."

A momentary pause and Erdad marched into the prime minister's office with the abruptness of a man who had just lost an argument with his wife and was looking for someone—anyone—to skewer with his pent-up rage. Meir grasped for something to release the pressure already building within the room. He waited until Erdad was standing before his desk, energy shimmering off his body like heat waves on concrete in August.

"Benjamin," Meir said softly, "could you please shut the door. I would like a private word with you."

With a nearly imperceptible shake of his head and a quizzical look in his eye, Erdad turned around and marched back across Meir's thirty-meter-long office, his stride getting shorter and his pace slowing with every other step. By the time he came back to the prime minister's desk, Erdad appeared a bit less agitated.

Thin, bald, with small wire-rimmed eyeglasses resting at the bottom of his nose, Meir leaned back in his leather chair. He attempted to look relaxed but wasn't sure how well he was bringing it off. "Have a seat, Benjamin. I'm glad you stopped by. I'm expecting a visit from the new American ambassador at any minute, but I was wondering—"

"No wondering . . . we need action," Erdad demanded as he threw himself into one of the chairs facing Meir's desk. "The Arabs announce their peace offering tomorrow at noon—the long sought-after recognition of Israel's right to exist—and your cabinet may be fractured beyond repair. We need a plan, Mr. Prime Minister. We must convince the cabinet members to support this covenant of the Arabs. Or Israel will find itself more hated and more isolated than we have ever been since 1948. We will look like arrogant fools. None will stand with us. Our national security will be more threatened than at any other time in our history. What are you going to do about the cabinet?"

Rolling his Montblanc pen between his fingers, Meir slowly counted to ten, giving Erdad a chance to breathe.

"Benjamin . . . how long have we known each other?" asked Meir, already knowing the answer.

"Since we were children on the kibbutz . . . about a million years ago," said Erdad.

"And what are the three most important things that you know about me?"

Erdad smiled, and a soft laugh escaped his lips, the tension in his body vanishing.

"One—you love your country. Two—you love your wife," said Erdad. "Which one you love most, I don't know. Perhaps they go hand in hand. And three—you are the most skilled politician in Israel. Otherwise you would not still be sitting in that chair."

Fastidious and impeccable, David Meir wore expensive, well-tailored suits and remarkable ties that were bold and bright without being garish. His attire, everything about him, was calculated to remove him as far from the heat, dirt, and monotony of that kibbutz as was humanly possible. He worked hard at being an educated gentleman. He worked harder at being an effective politician. In a politically fractured country like Israel, both were critical.

Meir pushed himself closer to his desk and laid down the pen, now focusing his attention directly on his old friend. "Benjamin, do you think this Ishmael Covenant will be accepted . . . ratified . . . by the Knesset?"

Erdad's posture straightened, as if he were coming to attention. "I don't think it's likely, sir, no."

"Would it be a good thing for Israel to ratify the covenant . . . to make peace with the Arabs?"

There was a moment's reflective pause as Erdad considered the question. "I believe it would be a good thing for Israel to make peace with its neighbors," he said, "but I am not sure if it would be the right thing for Israel to commit to this covenant. We will need to read it first."

David Meir picked up the dozen sheets of paper sitting on his desktop. "It's here. I'll share it at the cabinet meeting. But I agree with you. We do need to pursue peace. Whether this is the peace we need to pursue, I'm not sure. But I can tell you one thing, Benjamin."

Meir rose from his chair, stepped around his desk, and rested on its front edge, facing Erdad. "At all costs, Israel must *appear* as if we are pursuing this peace with sincerity and determination. On the world stage, we have no other option. I don't know if this is the right peace or if this covenant can survive the Knesset. But we must try wholeheartedly to make this peace, or something like it, a reality. And the first step, my friend, is to have the prime minister's cabinet unified in accepting and supporting this peace offer."

"Good luck with that," Erdad mumbled.

Meir nodded his head. "More than luck, Benjamin. An hour ago I offered Herzl and the Shas Party the responsibility of overseeing the construction of a new Temple if this Ishmael Covenant is ratified. So Shas is on board. And our new minister of education will be a member of Yesh Atid, so our most liberal brothers are on board. With the support of Shas and Yesh Atid, Benjamin, to the world the Israeli cabinet will look unified when the Arabs make their announcement tomorrow. After that . . . well . . ."

Meir turned and pushed the button on his telephone. "Rebecca, have you received any word from Ambassador Cleveland? He should have been here by now. And please call for a cabinet meeting at eight this evening. Thank you."

18

Highway One, Israel
July 19, 7:48 p.m.

Mullaney had pulled the phone from his right ear and was punching in a number already loaded into his speed dial . . . Parker's mobile phone. After five rings, the automated voice asked if he wanted to leave a message at the beep. "We were attacked on the road to Jerusalem. Your dad's beat up a bit, but generally okay. Where are you? We're concerned. Call me."

An ambulance followed closely behind the police cars. Two EMTs jumped out, and the police directed one to the wounded agents and the other to the limo.

Mullaney stepped out of the way as the tech eased into the car and began checking Ambassador Cleveland's vital signs. Since the Mercedes had dual bucket seats both front and rear, there was no comfortable way to get Cleveland to lie down.

His eyes flashing back and forth between the ambassador and his phone, Mullaney pulled up his contacts, scrolled to the entry labeled "Levinson, Meyer," and then pushed the phone icon. The call was answered in the midst of the first ring.

"Hello, Brian. I've been waiting for your call. What's your condition?"

"Hello, Meyer. Ambassador Cleveland is banged up pretty good, but nothing fatal. But Meyer, I need your help."

"Of course. What can I do?"

During two of his tours back in Washington, Mullaney had built a close relationship with Meyer Levinson, who was, at the time, a senior operative of Shabak—or Shin Bet—Israel's internal security arm. Levinson was the agent in charge of security for the Israeli embassy in Washington. A Syrian Jew, Levinson was raised in a scientific family. Trained in theoretical physics, on a track for a professorship at the Hebrew University of Jerusalem, Levinson was plucked from academia by the Israeli Security Services and quickly advanced through the ranks of Shin Bet. Mullaney and Levinson had two things in common—their devotion to the hope of democracy and their passion for the Chelsea Football Club. It was while rooting for Chelsea during the FA Cup tournament that Mullaney and Levinson ran into each other in the Airedale sports bar in the Columbia Heights section of DC. A deep friendship was spawned under the blue-and-white lion of Chelsea.

Levinson was now director of the operations division of Shin Bet, the most prestigious and active branch of the anti-terrorism service—the home of fighters and warfare groups that pursued Israel's enemies with a relentless determination to eliminate threats before they could strike the Jewish homeland or its people.

Whether exposing terrorist rings or providing intelligence for counterterrorism operations in the West Bank and the Gaza Strip or personal protection of senior public officials, for most of its history Shin Bet generally carried out the tasks of safeguarding state security with little publicity or fanfare.

If anyone could help Mullaney find Palmyra Parker, it was Meyer Levinson.

"I'll give you the background later," said Mullaney, "but right now we need to find the ambassador's daughter, Mrs. Palmyra Parker. She left the residence about two hours ago to visit the open air market nearby."

"In the Shmu'el Tamir Garden," said Levinson.

"Yes. She is not answering her mobile phone. With this attack on the ambassador, we're concerned that she may have also been a target. We've dispatched two teams of DSS agents from the residence to search for her on foot and by car. But . . ."

"But if these were professionals," Levinson continued, "we both know that Mrs. Parker is already long gone—either being held for ransom in some dark hole or, well . . ."

Mullaney knew where Levinson was going. But they were words he didn't want to hear or speak.

"My assistant is already forming a team to start working on the tapes," Levinson said, referring to the ubiquitous network of video surveillance cameras that Shin Bet maintained and reviewed throughout the state of Israel. "We should have some information from the videos shortly. And I contacted our watchers as soon as we got word that the ambassador was under attack . . . forgive me, Brian. You *do* know that we have agents watching the US embassy and the residence twenty-four seven, correct?"

"I would expect nothing less."

"I was speaking with the team leader when you called. They saw a woman leave the compound, but she had a scarf over her head and was dressed like a worker. I'm sorry, Brian, but they are not yet familiar with the new residents. I will call you back as soon as we have more information. Please let the ambassador know: we will find her."

"Agent Mullaney?"

Brian looked up. The EMT was pushing himself out of the back seat of the Mercedes. The tech turned aside to a police officer. "Please get the stretcher from the back of the ambulance. I can't treat him here." He returned to Mullaney. "Werner." He extended his hand. "The ambassador needs to go to a hospital so he can be effectively examined . . ."

"I'm not going to any hospital." Cleveland spoke from the back of the car, his renewed voice loud, clear, and final. "Not now!"

Werner pulled in a breath, shook his head, and went on as if Cleveland hadn't spoken. "Right now, he's stable and there doesn't appear to be any damage that is life-threatening. He's got a couple of cuts that need to be stitched and a nasty bump on his head that has probably caused a concussion. In the short term, those I can deal with here. The problem is, I can't tell what's going on inside. There is a good chance of internal injuries—for you and for the other agent, as well. All three of you should go to the hospital for observation and testing. You, I want to check out as soon as I'm done with the ambassador. Oh, by the way, you're wise-guy sidekick dislocated his shoulder. We pulled it back into place. It's functional but will be sore."

"What about the other agents?"

Werner nodded his head. "Lucky, there. Two with gunshot wounds, nothing critical. One of the guys, the bullet shattered his ankle. He's going to the hospital too."

Werner was about five foot four, with a riot of sandy-colored hair exploding from his head in all directions. He was built like a boxer, steady on his feet and firm in his determination. Mullaney could tell he was well trained and accustomed to people following his direction.

"IDF?"

"Reserve," Werner said about the Israel Defense Forces. "I did three tours of active duty in and around Lebanon."

Mullaney knew about Lebanon, how the Israeli military was throttled and decimated by the Hezbollah militia, forced into a humiliating retreat after the 2006 invasion by the IDF.

"Lebanon, that was tough duty," said Mullaney. "Glad you survived. But no disrespect, Werner, I gotta tell you that the only people going to the hospital are you and the agent with the shattered ankle. We've got work to do."

Werner smiled, a signal to Mullaney that he understood. "Yeah, that's what I expected. Let me get the ambassador to the ambulance and get him stitched up and then we'll get you on your way. But that car of yours? It's pretty awesome, but it's not going anywhere either. You guys need a lift?"

"Thanks, Werner, but we've got a squad with vehicles on its way. Should be here by the time you finish with the ambassador. Let's get him on the stretcher."

19

US Ambassador's Residence, Tel Aviv
July 19, 10:15 p.m.

By the time the convoy of embassy vehicles raced into the driveway of the ambassador's residence, the battery to Mullaney's mobile phone was nearly shot and his ear was almost as sore as the rest of his bruised body. Both he and the ambassador had been on the phone nearly nonstop during the high-speed return to the residence. While Cleveland was fruitlessly trying to wrest information from the Israeli prime minister, Mullaney had been badgering both the duty officer at the residence, Pat McKeon, and Meyer Levinson at Shin Bet with urgent requests for updates. Their answers were the same—nothing yet.

McKeon was waiting on the steps of the residence as the cars came to a halt. Mullaney was barely out of the car door when the duty officer grabbed him by the arm and led him off to the side. "Listen, Brian, I've got to talk to you before we get inside."

There was an edginess to McKeon's words that prompted Mullaney to focus fully on the duty officer. "What is it, Pat?"

Pat McKeon was in her mid-thirties, athletic in build, and, by reputation and experience, solid and reliable. "First, it's my responsibility that Mrs. Parker left here without an escort. It's my mistake and I'm sorry about that. But this is not about Mrs. Parker, not directly," said McKeon. "And I didn't want to tell you this while you were in the car."

Two agents were helping Cleveland out of the car and steering him toward the entrance. McKeon ran her hand through her thick dark hair, a grimace on her face.

"When we went into the ambassador's quarters looking for Mrs. Parker," said McKeon, "well . . . the first time . . . we were doing a quick sweep through the entire building. When we couldn't find her, we doubled the team and did a more exhaustive search. Agent Barnes found the maid who cleans the ambassador's rooms. She was inside one of the closets in Mrs. Parker's suite." McKeon sighed. "She was dead. She was lying on her back in the closet with her mouth open. Brian"—she put her hand on Mullaney's arm again—"she was bleeding from her eyes. Her tongue was black and swollen, and her hair was falling out."

Mullaney turned abruptly and looked at the receding form of Ambassador Cleveland, a cold, clammy, invisible hand turning his guts into a knot.

"It's okay," McKeon tugged Mullaney's attention, "the agents are taking Cleveland to his office, not his quarters. There's a corpsman there to check out his wounds."

"Where's the body?"

"Still in the closet," said McKeon. "We've quarantined the area. Nobody touched the body, and the marines aren't allowing any access. We put a plastic tarp over her and got out of there. I didn't know . . . was she contagious? I didn't know . . ."

"That's okay, Pat," said Mullaney. "I wouldn't have known what to do at first either. Keep Cleveland in his office, and let's go take a look."

The two marine guards quickly stepped to the side as Mullaney and McKeon walked into the entry alcove for the ambassador's quarters. A heartbeat passed before one of the marines, his hand gloved, reached for the knob on the door to Palmyra's suite of rooms.

"On the right," said McKeon.

Mullaney moved to the open door of the closet. Moving boxes were stacked on either side. A brown, plastic tarp covered part of the floor. He pulled on a pair of nitrile gloves and lifted a corner of the tarp. The maid was lying on her back on the hard tile floor. Even though she looked just as McKeon had described, a rush of bile seared Mullaney's throat, and he swallowed hard to keep it in place. The woman's face was frozen in mid-scream. Her mouth was open, and a thick, black tongue jutted out from a corner. Only a few wisps of gray hair were still attached to her scalp, the rest scattered across the floor. But most unsettling were her eyes. Fear and panic were etched in the wide-open gray pupils staring blindly at the ceiling. From the corner of her eyes, rivulets of blood had run down her cheeks, into and over her ears. Her skin looked like the ashes from an old fire.

Mullaney gently replaced the tarp. "Video?"

"Nothing inside the closet," said McKeon. "From one of the cameras in the bedroom it sounded like something fell and she bent over to pick it up and put it back. An instant later there was a dull thud. No cry for help."

"When?"

"Video feed tells us it was about fifteen minutes after Mrs. Parker left the residence."

Mullaney ran his eyes around the inside of the closet. As he panned right he found the leather satchel on a high shelf, in the right corner of the closet, just above the dead woman's body.

Did Palmyra . . .

He pulled out his mobile phone and made another call to Meyer Levinson.

"Nothing, Brian," Levinson said before Mullaney could speak. "I'll let you know . . ."

"Meyer, it's something else," said Mullaney. "We have a body here at the residence. One of the maids. In Mrs. Parker's suite of rooms. And her death was . . ." Mullaney paused. "It was unusual. I need forensics and hazmat here ASAP, the works. If you can, you'd better come here and get a look at this yourself. I don't think it's contagious, but we better not take any chances."

"How is this connected?"

"I'll fill you in when you get here, Meyer, tell you what I know. But the stakes for Palmyra Parker just jumped through the roof."

20

Riyadh, Saudi Arabia
July 19, 10:31 p.m.

Prince Faisal entered his father's private study as a two-minded man. He was confident and unfailing in his duty to his family. Still, he did not enjoy lying to people outside his family . . . people he respected and who respected and trusted him. But this task was more important than keeping the respect of others outside Saudi Arabia. This task was about survival: the survival of his family, the survival of his country. And he would not fail, no matter who he needed to deceive. Faisal only hoped that dealing with the announcement of the covenant would hold the world's attention while he and his father achieved their ultimate goal.

If the Ishmael Covenant worked—if it brought peace—fine. It would help.

But the family Saud's hope was not written on some sheets of paper. His family's future was being assembled in Pakistan.

King Abdullah sat at his desk, a large pile of papers to his right. He would take one, read it, sign it, and lay it on a growing pile of papers to his left. King business. He looked up as Faisal approached.

"What of the Israelis?" the king asked, short-circuiting Faisal's attempt at greeting.

Faisal stopped in the middle of a sumptuous gold-and-black Persian rug. He bowed from the waist. "May the king live long and prosperous . . . *Inshallah*."

"Yes . . . yes," snapped the king. "What of the Israelis?"

Faisal stepped closer to the desk. Though he was certain they were alone, there was no need to risk loud speech. "Prime Minister Meir cannot control his cabinet. There are too many negative voices around the table. He will make every effort to bring the covenant before the Knesset, but I doubt he will succeed. They just don't trust us."

"As we expected." King Abdullah shook his head, the pencil-thin goatee that jutted from his chin punctuating every word. "I can understand their hesitance. But I thought David Meir could at least get it to the floor for discussion. Sad, if they miss this opportunity."

US Ambassador's Residence, Tel Aviv
July 19, 10:40 p.m.

Mullaney found Cleveland in his office, sitting on a comfortably worn leather sofa and gazing into his fears.

Thrown around inside the Mercedes during the crash, traumatized by the resultant gun battle, and then shaken to his soul by the disappearance of his daughter and the death of her maid, Cleveland was not only battered and bruised, but now he looked lost.

Mullaney needed to do something to occupy Cleveland's mind and keep him from slipping into shock.

He walked over to the sofa and, as if he were lifting a baby from a crib, put his hand under Cleveland's left arm. "C'mon, Mr. Ambassador," said Mullaney, helping to lift Cleveland from the sofa, "let's move to your study. You'll be more comfortable there, and we'll be just as accessible there if anyone needs to reach us. Levinson is on his way with a forensics team. I think we'd better get in touch with Washington first."

The telephone on the desk of Cleveland's study was on speaker so both Cleveland and his security chief could participate in his call to the State Department. Mullaney was running cold water into a towel for the ambassador in the powder room off the study.

"Atticus, I'm sorry to hear about your daughter," said Evan Townsend, the US secretary of state. "If anyone can find her it's Israeli security. But this is the second time in a month that you've been personally attacked. What's going on?"

Townsend was no fool. Mullaney came back into the study with the damp towel. Cleveland took the towel, as much to bide time as it was to wipe off his face, then laid it across the back of his neck. He needed to sharpen his mind and focus his thoughts on how best to answer his boss. And how much to divulge. He looked over toward Mullaney for support . . . advice . . . but all the RSO could give him was a shrug of his shoulders, lifting his hands, palms up. Big help.

"Yes, sir," Cleveland said toward the speakerphone. "You are right to ask why I've come under attack so often and whether there is something that links those incidents together. But so much has happened in such a short amount of time, I think we need to step back for a minute to get some perspective."

"All right, Atticus . . . I'm listening," said Townsend.

"First of all, Mr. Secretary, I'm not convinced that all the violence surrounding me is connected, particularly the embassy attack in Ankara. I don't believe we've come up with anything to contradict the original intelligence reports that the attack in Ankara was directed at Kashani, not me or the embassy. It was another act of terrorism by the People's Liberation Front, another attempt to destabilize or destroy Kashani's government."

"We might have learned more," said Townsend, "if the brother had survived his wounds or if Eroglu hadn't arbitrarily sentenced Kashani's driver to prison, where he was stabbed to death a week later. But I'll accept, for now, that Kashani was the target. Wait . . . does the rest of this have to do with that mysterious package you told me about?"

"What package?" It was another voice, one that Cleveland knew well . . . Deputy Secretary of State Noah Webster.

Cleveland took a deep breath and then jumped in with both feet. "Yes, Mr. Secretary," he said, addressing his response to Townsend. "I believe the package is the common thread to the other incidents—the car chase in Istanbul, the attack Mullaney and I survived on Highway One, and this apparent abduction of Palmyra. Secretary Webster, four days ago during my visit to the Neve Shalom Synagogue in Istanbul, the senior rabbi there asked for my help. He had a package that needed to be delivered to the chief rabbis in Jerusalem. He said the contents of the package would be of the utmost importance to the interests of the United States in the Middle East and that we should be the first to receive that information."

Cleveland glanced at Mullaney, who was nodding his head and gave Cleveland a thumbs-up.

"I don't have any concrete proof, other than the attacks themselves, but I believe it's now clear that there is a widespread, ruthless, well-resourced organization determined to gain control of this package and its contents. I expect we'll get a ransom demand soon . . . Palmyra for the package."

"So what's in this package?" asked Townsend. "What does the message say?"

"We don't know the contents of the package or of the message. What I was told in Istanbul is that the package contains a 250-year-old message from a Talmudic scholar in Lithuania to the Rabbinate Council in Jerusalem. The rabbi at the synagogue in Istanbul believed the message was in a code that only the council's scholars could break. Thus far, because of everything else that's been going on, we haven't had the opportunity to get the package to Jerusalem."

There was a prolonged pause of silence from the Washington end of the conversation. Cleveland took one end of the damp towel around his neck and wiped his face. The cool moisture heightened his alertness.

"Atticus," said Townsend, "what does this package and its message have to do with tomorrow's anticipated announcement?"

Cleveland grimaced, his head nodding. "I've wondered that myself, sir. It's hard, often deadly, to believe in coincidences. But honestly, without knowing what's in the message, I don't think we can, as yet, link a centuries-old communication from one Jewish scholar to another with tomorrow's potential peace announcement."

"Don't get sidetracked, Cleveland." It was Webster. "We"—he paused, as if he was shifting gears in his thoughts—"we're all very concerned about your daughter's safety." Disingenuous condescension dripped from every word. "But we can't lose our focus. We—you—need to find out what will be announced tomorrow."

"I'm more concerned about the possibility of a nuclear Muslim country—particularly Saudi Arabia—than I am about an Arab-Israeli peace," said the secretary of state.

Sitting on a sofa in his study, Cleveland glanced over at Mullaney, who was in a chair opposite. He smiled and raised his right hand in an *okay* gesture.

"That's been our focus as well, Mr. Secretary," Cleveland responded, anxious to get the conversation away from the box. "The senior staff here all agree that a nuclear Saudi Arabia is a game changer we want to avoid. But Riyadh and Islamabad have developed close military and economic ties over the past four decades," he added. "There's plenty of indirect evidence of a weapons agreement. Pakistan deployed soldiers inside Saudi Arabia when they were needed to strengthen the kingdom's defenses. And there is no question the Saudis bankrolled Pakistan with billions of dollars in financial aid, shipping them fifty thousand barrels of oil a day after Pakistan was slapped with international sanctions following their first nuclear weapons test. Then the Saudi's cancelled the debt, keeping the Pakistan budget afloat and pouring millions of dollars of support into Pakistan's nuclear weapons development.

"Mr. Secretary," Cleveland continued, not wanting to lose the floor, "I know some of our colleagues remain skeptical that Pakistan would directly sell or transfer atomic weapons to Saudi Arabia. There was a time when I thought the worst that could happen was Islamabad creating some kind of nuclear-defense umbrella with the Saudis. But now, with Captain Abbaddi's warning, I'm inclined to believe the Saudis have called in their debts."

"Then the Jordanians are just as frightened of a nuclear-armed Sunni nation as we are," said Townsend. "That is a valuable insight on the Jordanian position on the eve of what appears to be an Arab-Israeli peace. Any idea of when this transfer of weapons may occur?"

Cleveland nodded to Mullaney.

"No sir, but I've looped in Jon Lin. He's got the FBI and the NSA working on it."

Cleveland could hear Secretary Townsend speaking to someone in the background, but his words were unintelligible.

"Atticus," said Townsend, speaking into the phone, "this would be a national security disaster—on many levels if—"

Noah Webster abruptly cut short Townsend's words. "It's already a disaster Mr. Secretary. Which leads me to wrestle with some grave reservations about the condition and effectiveness of the entire leadership team in Tel Aviv.

"Ambassador Cleveland," Webster continued, his voice smeared with sarcasm, "you've been there less than a day and there are bodies on the highway, bodies in the residence, your daughter missing, possibly abducted . . . and no information on this ground-breaking announcement tomorrow that promises to change the course of Middle East history. You haven't even met with the prime minister. These are not the kind of results we need. We need information . . . we need infallible information about this announcement before it happens. That's why—"

"Okay, Noah," Secretary Townsend interrupted. "Tone it down a bit. As you said, Atticus has been in country less than a day, and the world is coming apart around him. This is not the time to engage in fault-finding. Atticus knows what needs to be done, and he's the right man for the job—regardless of the circumstances."

Mullaney felt the hint of a smile reach his lips and an attaboy ride through his thoughts, confirming his confidence in Townsend's character.

"Mr. Ambassador," Townsend continued, emphasizing Cleveland's title, "I want to know how we can help you. Obviously, we need to teach Pakistan a lesson on how seriously the United States views the deterrence of nuclear proliferation. More importantly, if the Saudi royal family gets its hands on nuclear weapons, then we can certainly be assured that the radical Wahhabi clerics who freely preach jihadism under the protection of the royal family will exert direct influence on when, how, and against whom those weapons are used. If the Wahhabi clerics have their way, you and I both know the pecking order for *where* those weapons will be used—Iran, Israel, and the Great Satan, right here in our own back yard. We can't allow that to happen, at all costs. Get us more information, Atticus . . . before it's too late."

21

US Ambassador's Residence, Tel Aviv
July 19, 11:25 p.m.

It came upon him like an avalanche—a roaring, sweeping, overwhelming mass of failure that buried him under heaping mounds of regret and shame. Only once before in his life had Brian Mullaney felt this devastated: when he helplessly sat beside his father's deathbed and prayed for an absolution that was impossible to receive.

Mullaney's father, Captain John Mullaney of the Virginia State Police, spent the final ten years of his life in an Alzheimer's-induced coma. At first, as the captain began forgetting things or misplacing things, both other troopers and John Mullaney's family needled him about growing older and losing it. Mullaney patiently took the ribbing, but he didn't like it.

John Mullaney was a compartmentalized machine. He went to 7:00 a.m. mass four times a week, served on the church council each Friday, and was an usher at 11:00 a.m. mass every Sunday. Every Friday was date night with his beloved Alice, and every Saturday was the time he devoted to his six children. Sunday, they all rested and watched football—the Redskins—no matter how bad the team.

Monday through Friday, 8:00 a.m. to 6:00 p.m., he served the state of Virginia and did all in his power to protect the citizens put in his care. Mullaney was commander of Division VII of the State Police Bureau of Field Operations, centering on Fairfax County. Captain Mullaney had seen many opportunities to advance his career into the higher echelons of the service. But he knew any promotion would disrupt—perhaps destroy—his routine. And he was as addicted to his routine (a place for everything and everything in its place) as he was addicted to physical fitness and the necessity of good nutrition.

Which made it all the more tragic when the symptoms became more prominent. Captain John Mullaney would sit on the edge of his bed at six thirty in the morning and ask his wife where he was supposed to be going that day. There were days when not only did he forget his keys, but he also forgot how to get home. It wasn't long before Colonel Whitcomb suggested a paid leave of absence until the captain "felt better." That time for his return to active duty never came.

Soon he had trouble remembering his children's names. While sitting in his worn-out but favorite recliner in his home's family room he began to complain about how he needed to go home. The third time John Mullaney left the house in the middle of the night and started wandering the streets of Fairfax, the police found him two miles away, waiting for a bus while wearing his pajamas.

But it was only when he became violent, when Alice felt threatened in her own home, that Brian and Doak stepped in and convinced the family a change was needed. Captain John Mullaney was admitted to All Saints Nursing Home.

The captain continually deteriorated during his years at All Saints, moving from his own room to the assisted-living wing of the facility, and finally to a sickbed where over time his body curled into a fetal position and his mind was lost forever.

Sitting by his father's bedside on that last day, Brian Mullaney suffered through several levels of anguish. His indestructible dad was only a distant memory. Though he had tried for reconciliation many times, Brian was never forgiven for leaving his dad's state police to join the US State Department's Diplomatic Security Service. And now a Pentecostal Christian, something else his father struggled to understand and accept, Brian was fearful about his dad's eternal salvation. During his life as a faithful and devout Catholic, Brian wondered, did his dad ever make that Romans 10:9–10 declaration: "That if you confess with your mouth Jesus as Lord, and believe in your heart that God raised Him from the dead, you will be saved; for with the heart a person believes, resulting in righteousness, and with the mouth he confesses, resulting in salvation"? So simple, yet so necessary. Was his dad saved? Would he go to heaven?

When his mom and sisters stepped outside to speak to the doctor, Brian got up and stood beside the bed, next to his father's head. He leaned over and whispered into his dad's ear. "Dad, I know your soul is still in your body at this moment, so I'm going to believe that you can hear me. And I know you can't speak verbally, but if you can hear me, say these words with me. I believe God can hear you, even if I can't . . . *'God, I confess with my mouth . . .'*"

Two hours later, Captain John Mullaney's soul left his body. And Brian Mullaney wept. He wept because unforgiveness was a curse that crippled his emotions even when it was buried in the deepest recess of his heart. He wept because of his loss. And he wept with the fear of failure, uncertain of his father's eternal destination.

And the avalanche of failure hit him like a roaring, sweeping, overwhelming mass of devastation, burying him under heaping mounds of regret and shame.

At one point, Mullaney believed he had dug himself clear of the wreckage of that failure. Then came his split with Abigail . . . the separation from his daughters. Now, only a few months later, he was buried under guilt and shame once more. Was there no—

"Brian?"

Mullaney emerged from his thoughts and looked across at Ambassador Cleveland, whose face was as devastated as Mullaney's emotions.

"Are you all right?"

There was a twitch in Mullaney's lower lip, which he tried to catch before it spread. A quickening of his breath, heaviness in his chest. *Not the time or place.*

"Mr. Ambassador." His words stumbled over his unreliable lips. "I've failed you. I'm so sorry, sir. I didn't protect you. I didn't protect your daughter. Someone has died inside the residence. I . . . maybe . . ."

A hand settled softly on Mullaney's arm, and he looked up to see compassion and concern being offered to him as a gift of grace.

"Brian, my friends call me Atticus. Please . . . call me Atticus," said Cleveland. "And there is no failure here. We're under attack. People get hurt in a fight. But this fight is not over. With you and Tommy, I wouldn't want anyone else fighting beside me. I trust you. I trust you with my life, and I trust you with Palmyra's life. I did before today, I still do now, and I will tomorrow—no matter what the outcome. But this fight is not over. And I think we're about to go on the offensive. I need you. I want you with me. Okay?"

Mullaney opened his mouth to speak when the phone rang. The ambassador motioned for him to pick it up.

"Yes?"

"Brian, its Tommy. Meyer Levinson is here with his team . . . a whole bunch of nasty looking guys. They are itching to get to work."

Knowing some of the man's history, Tommy Hernandez still wasn't sure what to expect as he waited to greet Meyer Levinson, director of the operations unit of Shin Bet. What he got was a Moshe Dayan clone—the rakish Israeli general with the black eye patch who was one of the heroes of the sixty-seven war and the liberator of Jerusalem. Levinson nearly launched himself out of the arriving staff car, wearing the informal and ubiquitous khaki garb of the Israeli military and security services. Levinson was lean, muscled, coppered from the Israeli sun, and bursting with barely constrained energy. All that was missing was the eye patch.

"Agent Hernandez," Tommy said by way of introduction. "The ambassador is waiting for you in his office."

"Thank you," said Levinson, shaking Hernandez's hand.

Levinson bounded up the steps of the residence two at a time, Hernandez in his wake. "If your team could wait in the reception area . . . no, right," said Hernandez, hastily trying to guide Levinson in the right direction.

When Meyer Levinson left the realm of academia, it wasn't long before he morphed into the head of the intelligence and reconnaissance units of Shin Bet. From what Mullaney had told him, Hernandez knew that Levinson was a scourge to terrorists. When the first intifada started, Levinson's field troops—operators—had a list of over four hundred wanted men. In two years, that number dropped to less than twenty. Fewer than half were in jail.

When the second intifada broke out in the fall of 2000, it was Levinson who formed the cross-departmental warfare groups who were famously effective for destroying large numbers of imminent threats in short order. Now it looked to Hernandez as if Levinson was ready to go to war once more.

"What was that cryptic comment Townsend made about the Pakistanis?" Mullaney asked as they waited for Levinson to reach Cleveland's office. "We've known about their nuclear weapons program for more than twenty years. What punishment does he have in mind? And why—"

As soon as Meyer Levinson burst into Ambassador Cleveland's office, Tommy Hernandez in tow, Mullaney's hope began to rekindle. He was out of his chair in a breath, his hand crushed in the viselike grip that was Levinson's handshake. "Hi, Meyer . . . thanks for coming over."

Levinson released Mullaney's hand, patted him on the shoulder, then turned to Cleveland. "Mr. Ambassador. I regret the reality we face, but it's a pleasure to meet you. You have been a staunch friend of Israel, and we appreciate your support. I intend to repay your faithfulness today."

Cleveland offered Levinson a seat, but he refused. "Thank you, but I won't be here long." He planted his hands on the edge of Cleveland's desk and leaned in. "We have video of your daughter as she entered the outdoor market. The stalls are too cramped for us to get any decent visuals in there. Your men and ours have both searched the market. We know she is no longer there, but I have no evidence of her leaving.

"So we know where she isn't," said Levinson. "I've got nearly half my Tel Aviv staff working every possibility to find out where she is. And we're good at this, Mr. Ambassador. We'll find your daughter. Now"—Meyer turned toward Mullaney on his left—"when you invited us to come in, you said something about a body. How can we help?"

Rehovot, Israel
July 19, 11:54 p.m.

She fell down the basement steps when she was six. She was back there in her dream—sitting on the cold, concrete cellar floor, her jeans torn at the right knee, her mind a bit foggy, momentarily uncertain how she had gotten here from the kitchen, just now beginning to identify the things that hurt.

Her mother would come to her rescue in a moment, fearful but meticulous in her examination, and she would discover the gash on the back of Palmyra's head.

Palmyra sat on the basement floor, waiting for her mother to hold her close, then pick her up and carry her back up the stairs. They were headed to the hospital . . . what was the name of that hospital? Not to worry. Her mother knew. And mother would be here. Soon, mother would be here.

It was the light that hurt.

There, just over her left eye. So bright. So close. The light hurt.

Like being hit with a wave in the ocean, Parker's body registered the cold. It penetrated to her bones.

Where was her mother?

Parker tried to look up the stairs to see if her mother was coming. But she could barely move her head. And her eyes must be closed.

It was when she couldn't move her hands that Palmyra Parker's mind and body once again joined together in the same place and time.

And she knew her mother was not coming to her rescue.

22

US Ambassador's Residence, Tel Aviv
July 20, 12:20 a.m.

For a moment, Mullaney thought the residence itself was taking a deep breath. It was as if a great gulp of the air in the building was drawn in and then a collective sigh of relief exhaled as the staff was informed that the preliminary examination could detect no evidence of disease or contamination in the death of Haisha, the maid. But that news did not dispel the escalating apprehension about the fate of Palmyra Parker and the still unknown cause of the maid's bloody demise.

While Cleveland's chief of staff, Jeffrey Archer, was meeting with the staff members one or two at a time to reassure them of their safety—and remind them of the confidentiality oath and non-disclosure agreement they signed before becoming employed at the residence—Mullaney and Cleveland stood at a side door with Meyer Levinson as a Shin Bet team dressed in anti-contamination suits rolled the plastic-encased gurney with the body of the maid to a waiting ambulance.

"So that's all you've got for me?"

Levinson was clearly not buying Mullaney's claim of ignorance as to the cause of Haisha's death. But even with his previous history with Levinson, in his official role as regional security officer for the US Mission to Israel, Mullaney agreed with Cleveland that keeping the story of the box and the Vilna Gaon to themselves was the right course of action at the moment. So the door to the closet was closed when Levinson and his team first inspected the body.

"There was sudden onslaught of multiple, severe traumas in this woman, so we can be fairly confident she did not die of some exotic, tropical plague," said Levinson, clearly fishing for more information. "Even Ebola takes time to manifest. But something triggered this explosively fatal event . . . which occurred about the same time the ambassador's daughter went missing. My skeptical mind-set makes it hard for me to believe there is not some connection, eh?"

"Director Levinson," said Cleveland, "I'm sure you and your team will be able to help us determine if there is some connection between Haisha's death and Palmyra's disappearance. But right now, we are as mystified as you are. I wish there was more we could tell you."

Levinson's right hand was tapping out a rhythm on his thigh as his head nodded. But there was doubt in his eyes. "I wish you could tell me more too." Levinson drew out the silence like an unspoken question. Neither Mullaney nor Cleveland flinched.

"All right then." Levinson made no attempt to hide the hard, calculating look he gave first to Cleveland and then to Mullaney. "I suggest you sweep the parts of the residence the maid frequented—and your quarters in particular—for any trace of a poison . . . just in case." Then he surprised them.

"When was the last time you slept?" he asked them both. "Look, this is going to take a little time, and there is nothing either you or I can do until we get some better information. My suggestion? Get some rest. I have you on speed dial, and you'll know as soon as we find out something. You're not going to be any good to us, or to yourselves, if you're walking around like zombies. Sleep while you can. You'll probably need it."

Rehovot, Israel
July 20, 12:47 a.m.

The dawning came into her darkness with a rush. The back of her head felt heavy, weighted down, hard for her neck to keep upright. She was seated on a chair, which registered before she realized her eyes were covered, something tight wrapped around her head, only the sharpened shards of light from above her left eye making any inroads into the darkness that enveloped her. Both her hands and her feet were restrained, her hands behind her . . . She could feel the chair, her feet simply immobile.

Her head throbbed, pulsating pain to nauseating heights, but the cold assaulted the rest of her body, a frigid ache that lasered through her bones and brought tears to her eyes.

Don't move. Don't speak. But her body would not obey. Her muscles issued a groan from deep in her chest, her head lolling to the right.

Sounds. In the distance. Scuffling.

Where . . . the market. She was in the market, her pita overflowing with hummus and chopped vegetables. A child called to her from the shadow at the side of a stall. She leaned down . . . she leaned down . . . then what? Then she was here. *Oohhh, so cold.*

"Ahhh . . . you've come back to us." Something was dragged along the floor in her direction. Perhaps a chair. She could smell him—lilac and orange. He was close.

"Your resurrection has made Hamid a very happy man," said the voice in front of her. It was rough edged, but there was also something liquid about it, the way his words slithered through his lips. "Had you succumbed to his very clumsy blow, it would be Hamid's future which would now be in doubt. A dead ambassador's daughter is of no value to any of us."

Fingers gently touched the scalp at the back of her head. Lightning erupted inside her skull, bouncing off the bone of her cranium and searing back into her brain. The scream that started in her chest and throttled through her throat slammed to a stop against the cloth stuffed into her mouth.

"Hamid . . . please . . . more care," said the voice in front of her. "Forgive us . . . I only want to ensure that the bleeding has stopped."

Parker fought against the pain, the cold, the urge to vomit. She focused her will to quiet her heart, to gain some return of self-control. She needed to stay alert, conscious.

"We need to cut her hair." This voice was behind her, another man, speaking in Turkish. His voice was deep, graveled by tobacco, and angry. Brutish. "She's still bleeding." Palmyra felt her hair being moved to the side. "We need to get something against it to stop the blood." Then he swore in his native tongue.

Parker tried to speak—please, don't—but all that came out was "Pluumff urtt." Vile tasting threads got caught on her tongue then slid down her throat. *Don't touch . . .*

"Forgive us, Mrs. Parker," said the slithery voice. "We need to stop the bleeding. Please hold still."

Fingers touched the back of her head and a supernova of pain exploded behind her eyes, blinding her senses to everything except the agony that sliced through her brain. Parker felt the scream rasping against her throat, but with nowhere to go, its echoes increased the torment raging inside her head. Hands grabbed each of her shoulders like Amazon constrictors, holding her steady. The fingers moved a fraction, multiplying the torture, and consciousness fled like a banshee at sunrise.

23

US Ambassador's Residence, Tel Aviv
July 20, 12:53 a.m.

Even though the door to Cleveland's office was open, Mullaney knocked on it anyway.

"Come in, Agent Mullaney . . . and please, close the door behind you."

Ambassador Cleveland's battered body was tucked into the corner of his battered, brown leather sofa, to the left of the door. He laid the book he had been reading into his lap as Mullaney sat in the leather chair opposite him.

"Your quarters were checked and cleared, sir," said Mullaney. "There's nothing in there to be afraid of."

"Hmmm." Cleveland's heart clutched at the image of Palmyra that came to his mind. "Nothing except memories," he mumbled to himself.

"Sir?"

"Oh, nothing. Just an old man struggling with faith in the face of crisis." Cleveland looked over at Mullaney and tried to force a smile to his face. "You know, Brian, it's often said that faith isn't true until it's tested. And I certainly feel like I'm being tested now. This last week . . . I don't know . . . it's like God has put me in a wringer, squeezing me to my core. I've been looking in here for solace," he said, lifting the book in his lap. "It's my great-grandfather's Bible.

"Did you know that my great-grandfather was a slave in North Carolina?"

A question registered on Mullaney's face and he appeared ready to speak, but his eyes dropped to the Bible in Cleveland's hands. He looked at it with reverence, as if it were the Magna Carta. "No, sir, I did not. You must be awfully attached to that Bible."

Cleveland leafed through the pages. The Bible was large, its cover thick and heavily weathered from years of use. But it was plain. No gilt edges. No fine binding. Leather, worn and wearied by time, but still holding firm. *Much like me.*

"There are many notes from my great-grandfather written in the margins of this Bible," said Cleveland. "He was a man whose faith was tested too. Lost his wife. Separated from his children for ten years until he was freed by the

Union soldiers. Then he went back and rescued them from the hell they were living in. Do you know what he wrote in here, before he was freed . . . before he found his children? Here . . . I'll read it . . ."

Cleveland raised the book closer to his eyes. The notes were old and faded. "He wrote it here, in the margin to Ezekiel 37"—he glanced at Mullaney—"the chapter about the valley of dry bones and how God breathed new life into those dry bones, so that they lived once again."

"Yes, sir," said Mullaney, nodding his head. "I know that passage well."

Atticus Cleveland knew his limits were being stretched, his emotions a bubbling cauldron just beneath the surface. But as his heart yearned for word of his daughter, it was also blessed by this honorable young man who was so willing to serve. Even if it cost his own life. Cleveland took a deep breath to hold his feelings in check. "Good man, Mullaney. Good man."

The ambassador looked down at his Bible. "So my great-grandfather wrote this in thc margin: *'Fear is something we teach ourselves. It can be unlearned.'* Isn't that remarkable?" He glanced for a moment at Mullaney. "He was a slave for the first forty-three years of his life. His wife was actually murdered and his children abducted while he was working for his last owner. After he was set free, he slept in barns and under trees for six months while he was searching for his children."

Cleveland rested the book in his lap once more. He closed his eyes and drew in a deep breath. A vision of his great-grandfather rose up in his mind and he felt that catch in his throat, that quiver in his chin that often led to tears on his cheeks when he thought of this man who spoke to him nearly every night. His teeth pressed down on the inside of his lip as he tried to regain his voice.

He opened his eyes. Mullaney was waiting. "You know, Brian . . . I'm scared," said Cleveland, barely hanging onto his control. "I'm so frightened about Palmyra—where she is, what she's going through, if we'll ever get her home—I'm so frightened I don't know if I can think. I don't know if I can breathe. Yet we must, right? There's no choice about thinking or breathing. It's just part of who we are as human beings."

Cleveland hefted the book in his hands. "There's no choice about faith either. Once you decide, once you put your hope and trust in a God who sacrificed his own Son to pay the blood debt for my sins, once you do that, faith is your life. Without faith, there is no life. Brian . . . I don't know how other people do it. How do they survive the tragedy that we all experience in life without faith in a fair and loving God? I don't know. All I know is that I would be lost . . . totally lost . . . without the words in this book, both my great-grandfather's and my heavenly Father's."

Mullaney was looking down at the floor, as if his shoes held some precious truth that he was trying to grasp.

"You know, sir, it's interesting how time changes your perspective on life, on the past." Mullaney's voice was low, almost whispering, as if his words were really thoughts that had leaked from his memory and dripped on the top of his shoes. "For most of my adult life I've struggled with the emptiness and disappointment of what . . . who . . . my dad wasn't when I was growing up. Never held me close to him, in his arms, said 'I love you.' A lot of years, regretting that I was never affirmed by my dad.

"One night, about three months ago, not long before he died, I was sitting in his room at the nursing home. Holding his hand. Talking to him about the past. Out of nowhere, a memory invaded. It was summer. The family was at a lake for a day outing. I was seven . . . eight . . . I can't remember. The lake had a sand beach. An area of shallow water near the shore was marked off by ropes attached to wooden pilings.

"I don't know how it happened. I was just messing around in the water by myself, probably dreaming up stories of pirates, when my foot reached for the bottom. But there was no bottom. And I couldn't swim. I went down once. Came up gasping. Went down again. Came up terrified, thrashing around, sucking in air, desperate. Somehow, I got a hand on one of the wooden pilings, dug my fingers into the wet wood. I had a moment . . . when the terror broke . . . and my eyes reached out to the beach."

Mullaney shook his head, as if his mind were still measuring the memory, sifting its importance.

"And there was my dad, galloping into the lake. He was wearing a bathing suit, but he still had his shirt on. There was a newspaper in his hand. And he was still wearing his shoes—brand-new, brown leather shoes that flashed their spit shine against the water churning under his charging feet. I don't know . . . it seemed like he reached me in two strides. If there were lifeguards, they had no time to react. My dad barreled through the water, grabbed me in his arms, held me close. 'I've got you,' he said.

"He carried me back to the beach, sat me down on the blanket. Looked me in the eyes and asked if I was all right. Then, as if a light had just gone on, he looked down at his shoes. 'Brand-new.' It was all he said . . . or at least all I remembered of the incident." Mullaney looked up at Cleveland. "But in that moment of regained memory, Mr. Ambassador, all that I felt were his strong arms around me, the safety of being held against his chest, his words in my ear . . . 'I've got you.'

"As you were speaking of faith," said Mullaney, "that moment flashed again in my memory. All these years, I was regretting the lack of something that was never lost. Now, when I think of my dad, I think of him with his arms around me. Keeping me safe. Saving my life. My only regret is that it took me so long to regain faith in my dad. In his love for me. There were an awful lot of days I could have used that faith."

His emotions were so raw, his fear so close to the surface, Cleveland was wrestling to maintain control. But Mullaney's story touched him, brought comfort to his heart, hope to his thoughts.

"I need the strength of my faith now . . . more than ever." Cleveland laid the Bible on the low table between them and faced this young man who was quickly becoming quite important in his life. "Fear is something we teach ourselves. Tonight . . . right now . . . I'm choosing not to fear." Cleveland shook his head and pushed back his shoulders. "Now . . . is there something I can do for you? Was there a specific reason you stopped in?"

The smile that dawned on Mullaney's face could have warmed the North Pole. "No, sir," said Mullaney, his eyes bright. "You've already done it. Thank you, sir."

Mullaney started to get out of his chair. "Wait . . . I did come here for a reason." He held out his right hand. "Come on, Mr. Ambassador. You need to get some rest. Even if you can't sleep, I want you lying down in your bed and getting some rest."

"Is that an order, Agent Mullaney?"

"Yes, sir," Mullaney smiled. "Yes, sir, it is. Let's get cracking."

Mullaney doubted Cleveland would get any sleep, but at least he and Hernandez had left with the ambassador stretched out on his bed, eyes closed.

"Brian," said Hernandez, as they cut through the glass-enclosed portico separating the ambassador's quarters from the staff offices in the north wing, "you look like the dazed driver of a tractor trailer full of hogs after it jackknifed and overturned on an interstate. Quite a mess. And son," he said, leaning into his friend, "you're beginning to smell like one of those old porkers too. Take a couple of hours. Get a shower. Try to rest. I'm a lot fresher than you are, so I'll stay on duty and rouse you the moment anything comes up."

Mullaney shook his head. He was on duty. This was not the time to leave his post. "I can't, Tommy. Not with all this . . ."

Hernandez stuck out his left arm and stopped Mullaney in his tracks. "Wait a minute," he said, spinning on his friend. "Are you some superhero? Are you indispensable? Let me tell you, if you don't wind down a bit, get some rest, you're going to end up being a liability to this operation and not an asset. We've got to protect the ambassador, find Mrs. Parker, find a way to move that box without anybody else getting killed, and get some intel on what's going down with this announcement tomorrow . . . no wait, today. We need you fresh, Brian. Go take a break."

Was it determination or pride driving his emotions, Mullaney wondered. Duty or arrogance? But he knew Tommy was right. He was exhausted, and he had nothing left to draw on.

"Okay . . . but call me if anything breaks. I'll have my phone . . ."

"Right next to your ear . . . I know," said Hernandez. "Take a hike."

Walking through the gardens of the residence toward the small cottage that was to be his home for the duration of his assignment, Mullaney's thoughts became more troubled with each step. The confidence he felt in his faith, the peace that rose up during his conversation with Cleveland was being pressed out of him by the crushing weight of failure that returned with a vengeance to rest on his shoulders.

In the short time he shared with Cleveland since the ambassador landed at Ben Gurion—what seemed like ages ago—Mullaney had discovered a man for whom he developed immediate respect. He could see why Tommy spoke so highly of the ambassador. Not only was Cleveland an easy man to admire, but he was also a man from whom radiated an aura of peace and confidence that engulfed all those who worked around him. And now, in less than twenty-four hours, Mullaney had twice failed to fulfill his duty. Not only was he fearful and distraught over Parker's fate, but he also had failed to prevent the ambassador from being severely wounded during the attack and had failed to protect his daughter. No one dared say the words, but Palmyra Parker, missing now for nearly six hours, could already be dead.

Mullaney felt embarrassed and angry when he got booted out of Washington. He struggled mightily with self-pity when he realized Abigail was not going to accompany him to Israel. But now he simply felt defeated. A failure. Worthless.

Stoop-shouldered, his eyes on the gravel path in front of him, Mullaney looked for hope among the stones as he trudged through the garden toward his bungalow. He saw nothing but dirt. Everything gone. What did he have left? His mind clung desperately to the hope that a shower and some rest might revive his spirits.

His spirit. There hadn't been much time to think about his spirit, his spiritual condition. Mullaney glanced up at the night sky over the Mediterranean. *Are you there? Can you help? You didn't answer my prayers that Abby and I would work things out. You didn't answer my prayers to save my dad . . . to bring his mind back before you took his life. Are you there?*

At a bend in the path, a wooden park bench looked out over the sea, blooming lilac bushes in an arc behind it, protecting it from being seen from the house. Mullaney lowered himself onto the wooden slats, propped his elbows on his knees, and dropped his head into his hands.

"Father." He found himself speaking out loud. "I don't know what you're doing. I don't know where you are. I don't feel close to you anymore. I don't feel your presence. I don't feel your protection. I don't . . ." Mullaney took a deep breath. Tried to focus his mind. Take his emotions captive and bring them in line with what he knew was the truth. So hard sometimes.

Raised in an Irish-Catholic family, he came from a heritage where men were generally expected to be strong and silent. Like his dad. There wasn't a lot of expressive emotional sharing, particularly among men. Brian knew his dad loved him, but he seldom heard those words, which made it difficult to develop a truly intimate love relationship with God, his heavenly Father, even after he became a born-again believer. For an awfully long time, Mullaney wondered if he loved God . . . the way he was supposed to love God. He didn't really feel in love with God, not the way others in his church seemed to be in love. He figured there must be some flaw in him, in his faithfulness, in his goodness.

Then he read the gospel of John. When he got to chapters 14 and 15, he went back and read them again. And again. In fact, he read chapters 14 and 15 of John's gospel exclusively for an entire year. And something remarkable became apparent.

Three times in chapter 14, Jesus used almost identical wording in speaking to his disciples. In essence, he said, "If you love me, you will obey me." And "If you obey me, you love me." In two of the passages, Jesus said, "If you obey my commands . . . if you obey my teaching." Then it slammed Mullaney right between the eyes. Here it was. Here was the one, sure way he could know that he loved God. Just obey. Obey the commands that Jesus spoke in the Scripture. Obey the words of God and obey those things that he knew God was prompting him to do—or not to do.

The struggle of obedience was one he fought daily. Probably the same battle as was being fought by every believer who was still living in a carnal body that was programmed to want what it wanted when it wanted it.

But there was something else in that fourteenth chapter of John that made the walk, this daily exercise of faith, a little easier.

After each of Jesus's assertions that "if you love me, you will obey me," Jesus followed up with a promise—the Father, Jesus himself, and the Holy Spirit would each actually *live* in every believer who professed faith in Jesus Christ as Savior. Hard to fully understand, but the promises were there in Jesus's own words in the worn-out, much-repaired NIV Study Bible Abby had given him when they first got serious. "I will ask the Father, and he will give you another advocate to help you and be with you forever—the Spirit of truth. . . . I will not leave you as orphans. . . . Anyone who loves me will obey my teaching. My Father will love them, and we will come to them and make our home with them."

Sitting on that park bench, under the same sky Jesus once gazed at, Brian Mullaney felt confidence returning to his heart, determination returning to his mind. He was confident in this: the earnest desire of his heart was to obey Jesus—obey God—in all things. He was far from perfect . . . oh, so far from reaching that goal. But he had every assurance; he had faith, that he had help. That the almighty Creator of the universe lived inside him, inside Brian Mullaney.

And it was Mullaney's job to take his emotions and the desires of his faulty flesh and shackle those feelings to the truth. Bring his thoughts as captives to his faith.

Tonight, no matter how he felt—no matter how lonely, no matter how much like a failure, no matter how far he *felt* from God—God was right inside, waiting for his prayers.

So he tried again.

"Thank you, Father, for loving me. Thank you for loving me so much that you allowed your Son, Jesus, to take on human flesh and become a man. That the Son of God offered himself to be crucified on a cross so that my sins were forgiven. And thank you, Father, Jesus, Holy Spirit, for coming and living in my heart.

"Father, I'm afraid for Palmyra. I feel like a failure in so many ways. My emotions are ready to quit. To give up. But I know you are there. I know it. And I know I can trust you. No matter what the outcome, I can trust you, that your plan is good. Better than any ideas I may have.

"So, Lord, I put myself in your hands. I put Palmyra Parker in your hands. Please keep her safe and please allow us to find her and bring her home, alive and well. And I leave Ambassador Cleveland in your hands. Give him strength. And hope. And I give you everything else—I put Abigail and our daughters in your hands; I put my job and my career in your hands; and I put that box in your hands too. Please, Lord, keep us all safe. Bring us through this mess."

Mullaney took another deep breath. He settled his beating heart. He listened for anything in his spirit. He waited.

"Amen."

Then he got up, looked at the darkened sea in the distance, and decided the best thing he could do now was get a shower, shave, and try to rest. He turned right and covered the rest of the path to his cottage at a more brisk pace than before. As he reached the door, he saw something taped to the glass window in the door. It was an envelope.

Mullaney pulled out his keys, opened the door and flipped on the light. Then he reached up and peeled off the envelope, holding it under the light. *Abby!*

Without closing the door, Mullaney ripped open the envelope, pulled out a letter, and quickly scanned it for words of hope.

"Oh . . . God . . . no."

24

US Ambassador's Residence, Tel Aviv
July 20, 1:28 a.m.

"And they didn't tell the Israeli the truth . . . didn't tell him where they really found the body."

Jeffrey Archer was in his office, door closed and locked, lights off. He didn't think he had much time, or he would have left the residence and made this call outside. But security was as tight as the lid on a half-filled bottle of honey. He felt compelled to take the risk.

"How did the maid die?" asked Webster.

"Nobody knows," Archer whispered. "But she was in Palmyra Parker's closet. The rumor mill is running at warp speed and the staff are scared out of their wits. Half of them think we've been attacked by some biological weapon. The other half believe Cleveland has come into possession of some ancient, deadly artifact with supernatural properties. If a reason isn't discovered soon, I think a bunch of the locals won't come back to work."

Jaffa, Israel
July 20, 1:34 a.m.

In a quiet, residential neighborhood just south and east of the Jaffa Port, a weather-beaten blue Opel stopped in the middle of Ohev Israel Street, its emergency flashers blinking yellow along the darkened street. A large man in workman's clothes peeled himself out from behind the steering wheel, pounded his fist on the sad car's roof, went to the front and yanked open the hood. His head disappeared into the darkness under the hood as he inspected the engine.

At the far corner, near the intersection with Rabi Nakhman Street, a white panel van rolled to a stop at the end of an alley that ran behind the houses on Ohev Israel Street. At the same time, two young men on motorcycles sat on their bikes, visors up on their helmets, where the Los Angeles Garden extended both east and west from Ohev Israel Street. They were speaking in low voices and pointing off into the distance.

While these pieces came into place, Colonel Meyer Levinson of Shin Bet was in the back of a small, black truck with the markings of a cable TV company, parked opposite Sixty-Seven Ohev Israel Street, headphones fixed on his head, eyes closed, inserting his presence into the rooms of the one-story, yellow stucco house across the street.

"Two voices . . . a man and a woman, sir," said the staff sergeant at his left who was wearing an identical set of headphones. "Both together in an inner room. No other voices. No other sounds."

"Right."

Colonel Levinson handed his headphones to the sergeant and turned to his right, toward the back of the truck. Six Shin Bet soldiers, clad all in black like Levinson, stood between the colonel and the tarp covering the back of the truck bed. All the men wore light, nearly impenetrable body armor and carried an X95 Micro-Tavor—the IDF favorite, Israeli-made, 9-millimeter assault rifle—nestled in their arms.

"There appear to be two civilians in an inner room," Levinson said to his lieutenant. He lifted his head and spoke in hushed tones to the group. "We have no information about this man, Indowi, other than he is the owner of stall number sixteen in the Shem'ul Tamir outdoor market. He may be a harmless, innocent family man. Or perhaps not." He looked at each of them. "You know the drill. Preserve life—both theirs and yours. Treat them with respect. They will be frightened with us storming into their home in the middle of the night, so keep it dialed down. We just want to talk." Levinson paused. "We do not engage unless there is evidence of a weapon and intent to use that weapon. Understood?"

Each member of his team nodded.

"Right." Levinson turned to the communications sergeant. "Put it in motion."

As Levinson and his men buckled on their helmets, the large man buried under the hood of the Opel pushed himself out and slammed shut the hood. Only one house showed light in the windows—number Sixty-Seven. He threw up his hands, muttered under his breath, crossed the sidewalk, and gently knocked on the door of Sixty-Seven Ohev Israel Street. Two men in black left the white panel van at the top of the alley and slipped through the shadows to the rear of number Sixty-Seven.

The large workman knocked on the door once more, but before his knuckles could strike for a third time, the door opened a crack, a thick security chain still in place.

"Yes?" asked a man's voice.

"Forgive me, I know it's very late. But this old beast threw a rod," said the workman, pointing a thumb over his shoulder at the Opel in the middle of the street. "Dead as a doornail. Can I use your phone to call a tow truck?"

"No mobile?"

"If I did, I wouldn't have to bother you at one thirty in the morning. But it's in my jacket pocket at home."

The man behind the door hesitated. He spoke a few words in Arabic to someone in the house. "I'm sorry," he said, "but it's much too late. It's not safe to open our—"

The workman shoved his muscular body against the door, snapping the latch and chain from its mooring, his left hand reaching around and grabbing the man's wrist in a viselike grip.

Levinson and his team were already out of the truck and moving through the doorway as the workman squashed the homeowner against the wall of the entry.

"Police . . . keep your hands in sight," Levinson called out as he rushed into the inner room. A woman was seated at a table, a backgammon board on the table between two chairs. Anger quickly replaced the surprise on her face. She raised her hands and her voice in protest but her words were drowned out by shouts, running feet, and the deadly, rapid rattle of automatic weapons toward the back of the house.

Two of his team came up on either side, their muzzles pointed at the woman's chest. "Restrain her."

Moving back into the hallway, Levinson could see that any threat had been neutralized. One man lay on the floor of the kitchen, blood pooling quickly around his head. Levinson looked to his left, into a small bedroom. His lieutenant was removing a notebook from the hand of a second man whose bullet-riddled body was draped over the footboard of the bed.

"These two came out of the bedroom with Uzis," said the lieutenant, handing the notebook to Levinson. "That one tried to escape out the back door. I saw this one duck back into the bedroom when the officers in the alley opened up. He was leaning over the bed, grabbing this notebook, while shooting through the open door. This notebook must have high value."

Levinson turned over the notebook in his hand. It was small, the size of a small calculator, about twelve centimeters long and half as wide. It was bound in rich, brown leather. Inside were ruled pages. About half the book was filled with what looked like the personal notations of an ordinary life . . . phone numbers, addresses, and directions. But this man, a terrorist doing somebody's bidding, led no ordinary life, and these were not ordinary notations. Levinson raised up a prayer of thanks, hoping they were clues.

25

US Ambassador's Residence, Tel Aviv
July 20, 1:58 a.m.

Cleveland was unable to sleep or rest. The faucet on and hot water running into the bathroom sink, he was corralling the water in his cupped hands and spreading it across his face when his mobile phone chirped. He looked down at the counter. No caller ID. He wiped his face dry with a towel and tapped his phone to take the call.

"You know what I want."

The voice was soft, the words spoken with an unintelligible accent. They seemed to leave a sheen of oil on the air, a pollution that rippled across the top of Cleveland's shoulders.

"Or what?"

"You know the answer to that also."

"I need proof of life."

"That can be arranged."

"When?"

The call disconnected. Cleveland sat down on the edge of the tub, lowered his face into the towel, and wept while he prayed.

Bewilderingly, along with a rising tide of hope, Cleveland was engulfed with warmth, as if he was in the embrace of two huge arms. The change was so startling, Cleveland lifted his head to see who was in the room with him. The bathroom was empty. But his fear had vanished.

His girls were running down the field in Lawrence Park, attacking the other team's zone. It was so good to see them again. Why would Abby take the girls from him? Why go to live with her father? What had he done that was so awful? *I'm a good man . . .*

A fan for the other team must have brought a drum. Very unusual for a soccer game, but this fan was pounding on that drum for all it was worth. Boom . . . Boom . . .

Like he was coming to the surface from the depths of a dark lake, Brian Mullaney broke out of his dream to the sound of the drum.

He was stretched out on the sofa, still dressed but his shoes off. The pounding in his heart, remembering the crushing pain of Abby's letter, was replaced by a more urgent pounding on his front door. He was two strides from the door when Tommy Hernandez pounded once more. "Brian!"

Mullaney pulled open the door for Hernandez, then went looking for his shoes.

"The ambassador got a phone call. They've got Mrs. Parker and they want the box," said Hernandez.

"We need proof of life first." Mullaney tied his shoelaces and pulled on his suit jacket. As he started toward the door, he stopped and turned to look at Hernandez. "No, Tommy," Mullaney said as he placed a hand on Hernandez's shoulder, "the first thing we need to do is pray. Will you pray with me?"

Ambassador Cleveland was pacing the floor in his study, from window to bookcase and back again, when Mullaney and Hernandez knocked on his door. The prayer he had been lifting up in his mind leaped to his lips. "Lord, please keep her safe," he whispered. Then he lifted his head and his voice. "Come in."

"You got the call, sir?" Mullaney was barely through the door when the questions started without any preamble. "What did they say? What demands?" Protocol and etiquette were often casualties in crisis. Cleveland didn't care. There was only one priority.

"Short and to the point," said Cleveland. He rested his hand on the back of a high-backed arm chair. He felt like he needed the support. "They've got Palmyra, and they want the box. I told the caller we need proof of life. The call ended."

Mullaney and Hernandez stood in the middle of the room. Cleveland could tell they felt the same nerve-stretching level of anxiety that was stoking every one of his fears.

"Did you learn anything else from the call?" asked Mullaney. "The voice . . . any sounds in the background? Anything we can give to Levinson?"

Cleveland drew in a deep breath. Oh, how he wished . . .

"I know you want facts, Brian. Something that would help us find Palmyra.

But I'm sorry, all I have for you is . . ." Looking at the floor, Cleveland shook his head. This was going to be no help. "It was a man on the phone, I believe. He spoke in English, with an accent. He spoke three sentences . . . *'You know what I want.'* I said, 'Or what?' *'You know the answer to that, also.'* I said we would need proof of life. And his last words were *'That can be arranged.'* Then the call ended."

Part of him felt foolish. Part of him felt violated. He looked up. "But what I remember most is that I felt his voice enter into my being. Beyond my body, it entered deep inside of me. And it was putrid, decaying. Like the spirit of death polluting my blood and searching for my heart." A shiver rattled his body. "We need to find her, Brian. We need to find her fast."

26

Rehovot, Israel
July 20, 2:22 a.m.

The cold penetrated both her bones and her blackness. Something wet was lying across the back of her neck. Two hands rested against her cheeks.

"We have stopped the bleeding, Mrs. Parker." It was slithery voice. "Saved your life, I believe. Now, we need your cooperation for just a few moments."

He switched to Turkish. "Remove the gag from her mouth. But be careful untying it . . . we don't want her bleeding again. And we need her alert."

The aroma of lilac and orange tricked her mind into an orchard of green trees and orange fruit, purple bushes in the distance. She breathed in then stiffened as clumsy fingers tugged at the restraint that was holding the cloth inside her mouth. The restraint fell away. One hand cupped her chin while a second gently extracted the wadded up cloth from her mouth.

Palmyra Parker stuck her tongue out, into the cold, and breathed through her mouth. She sucked in her cheeks, pulling saliva from her throat and tried to wash clean the inside of her mouth. The many thoughts in her mind wrestled for position to become words.

"You will regret this." Her voice was a raspy whisper, speaking into a darkness she knew was not empty. "They will find you. And you *will* die."

"Perhaps someone will die," he said. "But not right now. We have your phone. What is your code?"

A cough came out of her throat instead of the words she wanted to say to this beast. Parker took a breath. "I'm not helping you in any way."

"Very well," said the voice in front of her. "But if you want to see your father, we need your code."

See my father? Her mind was slow connecting the dots. *FaceTime!* "Four-seven-four-seven," she said.

Four beeps then silence.

There was a rattling vibration near her face. "See for yourself," said slithery voice, now in English.

"Palmyra?"

Her father's voice.

Tears moistened the inside of her blindfold and her chin quivered for a heartbeat, but Parker pulled in a breath and focused intensely on her words. Her time would be short, her opportunity limited.

"Palmyra . . . are you hurt?"

"Extraordinarily cold here," she raced through her words. "Low flying aircraft. Traffic hum . . ."

They tried to shove the cloth back into her mouth and she chomped down her teeth, biting deep into the fingers holding it. A cry and, for an instant, the cloth dropped away.

"Two men speaking Turkish . . ."

The slap across her face reverberated into the minefield at the back of her skull. Parker's mind spun and she grasped to hold onto her consciousness. A heavy hand pulled down on her chin and the cloth was forced back between her teeth.

"You have heard her," said slithery voice. "You see the date and time on the phone. She is alive. For now. If you cooperate."

Something clattered to the floor. Then a stomp and the crunch of glass. "Strip the phone," slithery voice said in Turkish. Then fingers grasped her throat. Iron-gripped, they began to squeeze her windpipe closed. "Such a clever infidel," said slithery voice, his fingers squeezing tighter. Parker gagged, struggled, every little move sending shards of pain through her skull. "Your life hangs by a thread. A thread that will be sliced when we have no more need of you. A pleasure I hope will be mine." A final, punctuated squeeze and the fingers loosened.

"Prepare," slithery voice said in Turkish. "And guard what you say around this . . ."

Heavy steps walked away from her. She could hear slithery voice speaking in descending volume, but his words were indistinct.

US Ambassador's Residence, Tel Aviv
July 20, 2:30 a.m.

The iPhone in the ambassador's hand went blank as the FaceTime call ended. He was holding it up so Mullaney and Hernandez could see the screen over his shoulder. Cleveland's head dropped to his chest and Mullaney placed a steadying hand against his back.

"It's okay, sir. She's alive," he said. "And we'll find her."

Mullaney looked to his right to Hernandez. "Tommy," he said softly and nodded his head toward the armchair.

"C'mon, sir," said Hernandez. "Let's sit down so we can talk this out."

Pulling his mobile phone from a jacket pocket, Mullaney tapped on Levinson's number.

Shin Bet Headquarters, Tel Aviv
July 20, 2:32 a.m.

Levinson had the notebook secured during the raid in Jaffa in his left hand and was scribbling some of the notations from it on the back of an envelope when his lieutenant came into the office.

"Yes?"

"Strange hit on the communications intercept scan, Colonel. Mossad was running word recognition software on their mobile frequency scanners and came up with this."

The lieutenant handed Levinson one sheet of paper. He was scanning the report, trying to sort through conflicting thoughts, when his phone rang.

"Good timing, Brian. We found the owner of the market stall where we think Mrs. Parker got abducted. A bit of a mess, I'm afraid, but we did find a notebook that I believe could—"

"Look, Meyer," Mullaney interrupted, "we—the ambassador—had a call from Mrs. Parker's abductors. By the time I got to his study, they called back on FaceTime. We could see her. She appeared to be hurt in some way, but she's still alive."

Levinson put the notebook and the envelope on the table. This needed his full attention. "What do they want?"

"That's a long story for another time, Meyer. What's more important is that Mrs. Parker quickly rattled off three facts before the call was cut off. She said she was extremely cold . . . that she could hear low-flying airplanes . . . and that there were two men with her who were speaking in Turkish."

"Extremely cold . . . in this heat?" Levinson pulled over a map that was lying on the table and glanced at his scribbles on the envelope. *Hmm—that's an interesting coincidence. And I don't believe in coincidence.* "Right. Brian, pull together a team and beat a path over here fast. I think we're on to something. Hurry."

Levinson tossed the notebook on the table and held the single piece of paper out toward his lieutenant. "They've checked this? Confirmed these transmissions?"

"Yes, sir. Three times."

"Right." Levinson threw the piece of paper onto the table next to the notebook. "What a bloody mess. Here, let's look over this map."

US Ambassador's Residence, Tel Aviv
July 20, 2:36 a.m.

"Tommy, call Barnes . . . no," said Mullaney, "call Pat McKeon. Tell her I want four agents armed and ready for field work, on the double. Have them bring two SUVs out front and keep the motors running."

"She didn't look good," said Cleveland. "She looked like she was hurt."

Mullaney heard a new edge of toughness in Cleveland's voice. The ambassador was still sitting in the armchair, but now he was perched on its edge. His head was no longer in his hands.

"Shaken up, maybe," said Mullaney, who walked over to stand next to the chair, "but she was still alert enough to give us those three clues. Palm—Mrs. Parker is tough. She'll be okay."

With a shake of his head, Cleveland pushed his shoulders back and stood up. "What did Levinson say? We need to get moving." There was an undercurrent of pleading to Cleveland's call for urgency. "We don't know how much time it takes"—he paused—"if she . . ."

Mullaney was wrestling with the same concerns, but fear wasn't going to help them get Parker back safely. He faced Cleveland eye to eye.

"Mr. Ambassador, there are too many things we don't know to begin running what-if games now," said Mullaney. "We don't know if Palmyra touched the box, we don't know for sure if the maid touched the box, and if she did, we don't know how long it took before—"

"So we don't know how much time she has," said Cleveland. "We don't know that either."

"No, sir, we don't. But we don't really know if what that assistant rabbi told us was true. We don't really know anything about that box except what other people have told us. Atticus," Mullaney reached out and laid a hand on Cleveland's chest, "we can't allow our emotions and our fears to run out ahead of us. We take this one step at a time. We find Mrs. Parker and make sure she's safe. Right?"

Cleveland nodded. "I hear you, Brian. And I know, intellectually, you are right. But I *am* afraid that there is not much time."

They jogged across the wide, enclosed terrace to a side door that led to the office wing, Mullaney in the lead.

"You don't believe that story you spun for Atticus, do you?" asked Hernandez. After looking at Palmyra Parker's face on the iPhone, Hernandez couldn't shake the fear that they were already too late.

"We don't know how much time she has," said Mullaney, pushing through the door to the office wing.

They covered the distance to the DSS security office in three strides. Mullaney punched in the code on the lock's keyboard, and they headed straight for the weapons locker.

"Brian, you saw how she looked," said Hernandez, but Mullaney was focused on pulling open the locker and grabbing a vest of front and back body armor. Hernandez stepped between Mullaney and the weapons locker.

"Brian . . . she looked like she was barely conscious." Hernandez felt like a member of the death squad—agents who were dispatched to the home of family members when a DSS agent was killed in the line of duty.

"We'll get there. She'll be okay," said Mullaney, strapping on the armor.

"Did you see the hair?" It was the first thing Hernandez noticed when Parker's face came up on the screen. Clumps of Parker's dark, black hair sitting on her shoulders—covered in blood. Her hair was falling out.

Mullaney pulled a Heckler & Koch MP5 9-millimeter submachine gun out of the cabinet, grabbed an ammunition bag, and dropped them on a table in the middle of the room. He finally looked at Hernandez. "Yes. I saw it. Now saddle up!"

27

Shin Bet Headquarters, Tel Aviv
July 20, 3:15 a.m.

The Shin Bet office in Tel Aviv was in the White City district of the city, over one hundred square blocks—though hardly any of the blocks in Tel Aviv were square—containing over four thousand stark, 1930s era bright white Bauhaus buildings. Designed primarily by German architects who emigrated to Israel in the formative years of Tel Aviv's existence, these austere, modern design buildings—similar in appearance to the Guggenheim Museum in New York City—had bold, sweeping, rounded corners, long narrow balconies stacked one atop another, and deep narrow windows, called thermometer windows.

Erected one after another, side by side, on the meandering streets around Dizengoff Square, the ubiquitous nature of the Bauhaus architecture and the twenty-four-hour bustle of the Old City made Ten Gillickson Street a perfect place to hide the headquarters of the nation's internal security apparatus. There was a large parking lot across the street from the four-story building with flowing balconies and a large, abandoned round kiosk on the corner of Bellinson Street, last occupied by a fruit monger, that made for a perfectly hidden observation post accessed by a tunnel under the street.

Mullaney's two SUVs squeezed into a tight little alley behind the building, off Aharonovich Street, and—with Levinson waiting at the door—his team passed quickly through the three layers of escalating security that kept unwanted visitors away from Shin Bet business. There was no conversation as Levinson led the DSS agents down a flight of stairs to an elevator.

There were two maps on top of the round table just outside the armory secured deep in the bowels of Shin Bet headquarters. Hernandez and Levinson's lieutenants were coordinating the arming of agents from both Shin Bet and the Diplomatic Security Service and working through the coming rules of engagement in the hope of eliminating friendly fire casualties. Levinson and Mullaney were stretched over the maps—one of them hastily hand drawn.

"This is the Holon industrial district, between Tel Aviv and Ben Gurion airport," said Levinson, pointing to the printed map. "It's a sprawling area of warehouses, shippers, car dealers, wholesale shops—a mishmash of everything, some of it modern, some of it decrepit and falling down. There are not that many streets running through the district but an endless number of unnamed alleys."

Hernandez came over and handed Mullaney a pocket-sized radio transmitter. A thin, stiff filament connected the earpiece with a small microphone. "We're all going to use Israeli communications gear and be hooked into their network," said Hernandez. "And they've got a nasty assortment of weapons over there, if you're interested."

Levinson looked up from the map. "You should get this briefing too, Agent Hernandez. This is not going to be an easy operation.

"All these streets," said Levinson, pointing to the map "are densely packed with small retailers and offices, along with warehouses and factories. During the day, it's a cauldron of activity. But at night, it clears out like a ghost town. That will help avoid civilian casualties, but it's not going to give us much cover."

He threw some photos on top of the table. "We pulled these off Google Maps. As you can see, some of these facilities are protected by high walls, topped with razor wire. Some look like fortresses. And this," his finger stabbed a squat, two-story, ochre-colored building, "is our target."

Mullaney cringed. "Looks like a small prison," he said, looking at the high walls and barbed wire. "What is it?"

"An abandoned meatpacking company," said Levinson. "There are huge rooms that were once used as refrigerators, others that were freezers. And that section of the Holon district is directly under the final stages of the flight path for Ben Gurion."

"Fits Palmyra's description," said Mullaney, "but how can we be sure it's the right place?"

Levinson picked up the brown leather notebook from the table. "We recovered this at the home of the man who owns the market stall where we believe Mrs. Parker was abducted. There were two armed young men, now deceased, in that house, one of whom went back into a bedroom to retrieve this notebook. There are several addresses in this book, but only one has refrigerated rooms and is on the flight path of an airport . . . this ugly building."

He pulled another photo from inside the notebook. "And then there's this. We ran a drone over the area about an hour ago." He handed the photo to Mullaney. "It's infrared, but you can see there are armed men in strategic locations in the complexes on both sides of the alley."

"Sounds like a winner," agreed Mullaney. "It's your show, Meyer. How do you want to tackle it?"

Leaning over the table, Levinson pointed to the rough drawing. "This is Ha-Banai Street, one of the main arteries through the district. Running parallel is Halahav Street over here. That street is more lightly traveled, has fewer business fronts on the street. There are few through streets running between Ha-Banai Street and Halahav Street. But our building is here, adjacent to this alley . . . more like a driveway . . . and facing onto Halahav." He picked up one of the photos.

"This building here, the one you called a fortress, contained the offices of the meatpacking company and some of the work areas. These buildings on the other side of the alley were also part of the complex. They look like larger warehouses from where the meat was shipped. That compound also has walls around it, topped with barbed wire."

Hernandez picked up the photo. "And I bet you're going to tell us we don't know which building she might be in, right? We just upped the difficulty meter."

"Precisely," nodded Levinson. "We have to hit each one of the compounds at the same time and penetrate each one of the structures as quickly and quietly as possible. I can't be certain she's there. But I can be certain of one thing. If she is there, and we're not swift and we're not silent, Mrs. Parker won't be alive when we reach her."

Mullaney thought Levinson's plan was a good one. But he didn't like their odds.

They would enter the alley from the far end, near Ha-Banai Street—four squads, twenty men, in two innocuous commercial vehicles: a small truck bearing the name of a corrugated box manufacturer and an electrician's van. Two of the DSS agents would be imbedded into each of the squads. The small truck, with two squads, would stop about two-thirds of the way down the alley, pulling behind a tractor trailer on the left that was parked against the wall of the warehouse complex. The electrician's van would enter the alley fifteen minutes after the truck and continue to near the end of the alley, pulling into a deep parking area for the building complex on the right that included the offices . . . the one that looked like a prison.

Before the van entered the alley, the two squads in the small truck would slip out of a sliding side door against the wall. They would use the fender and hood of the truck, blocked from view by the tractor trailer, to scale the wall of a complex that was adjacent to and behind the targeted meat warehouse. The two complexes were separated by only a cyclone fence. On their side, stacks of wooden pallets were up against the fence every few feet. Using the pallets as cover, they would cut the cyclone fence, then wait for the go signal. From their position they could fan out quickly. There were two single-story warehouse buildings, a huge, long one against the alley wall and a smaller, square one to the left. Six of the agents would break into pairs and find or make a way through the three doors in the side of the building. The four other agents would enter the smaller building. Their mission was to penetrate each of the warehouse buildings within seconds. Depending on the opposition.

Mullaney and Hernandez were with Levinson and seven others in the electrician's van. All of them thought it most likely that Parker would be kept in the complex that resembled a prison. As soon as the van came to a halt in a parking area between the two main buildings in the meatpacking complex, the ten men would race out of doors in the side and back of the van.

These two buildings would be more difficult. All the windows in both of the buildings were covered by thick bars. The smaller building, the offices, was two stories tall and surrounded by a ten-meter-high metal wall topped by razor wire. Along the alley side of the offices was a metal staircase that led to a fortified door on the second floor. The larger, single-story building to the right appeared to have no doors other than the loading dock door which was twenty-five meters away, down and locked. That would be their only way in.

Four men would take the office building, scaling the metal wall, up the staircase, forcing open the barred door on the second floor. Mullaney and five others would run down the side of the larger building, snap the locks on the loading dock, and gain entry that way.

They had no idea what they would find inside and no clue as to the number of armed kidnappers they would encounter.

It was a complex, challenging operation in the best of circumstances, but highly unlikely of success when thrown together at the last minute. Half its personnel had never before worked together.

As he continued to observe the urgent preparations inside Shin Bet headquarters, Mullaney tried but failed to conjure up a better plan. He had little hope and rising fear about this one. As the lieutenant and Hernandez were briefing the entire team, Levinson came alongside Mullaney and pulled him away from the table. Standing in a corridor outside the room, Mullaney could see that Levinson was struggling with something. What now?

"Brian . . . listen . . ." Levinson kept his voice low, confidential. "Once you called us in, we devoted a ton of resources to the task of finding Mrs. Parker—Shin Bet, Mossad, IDF security. We were looking everywhere and at everybody. Mossad religiously monitors all communications in Israel—into, out of, and internally. Every type of communication. We listen to it all, and we record it all. We added some keywords to these sweeps—Mrs. Parker and Palmyra Parker. We had a high number of hits, almost all of them innocent, surrounding her work to prepare the residence. But when we heard that Mrs. Parker said her abductors were speaking Turkish, we altered the scope of our search. Don't ask me how, but we intercepted these."

Levinson pulled a folded piece of paper from the breast pocket of his shirt and handed it to Mullaney. "These are excerpts of three wireless telephone conversations—the first between Turkey and the United States and the other two between Turkey and Israel. Each of these conversations occurred not long before Mrs. Parker went missing. Reaching out this far, our technology is limited and subject to outside forces, so whatever we intercept is generally incomplete and sketchy."

Facing Mullaney were snippets of three conversations. It was like looking at a verbal jigsaw puzzle, with many missing pieces on each line. But what had been captured reached out and grabbed Mullaney by the throat. All three conversations mentioned Palmyra Parker by name. And the second and third also made mention of a package.

Mullaney pulled his attention away from the words and looked at the time stamps on the conversations. The second one took place only seconds after the first one concluded. Calls to and from Turkey in the last ten hours that mentioned Palmyra Parker? This was no coincidence.

"Brian . . ." Levinson came alongside Mullaney, to his left, and pointed to the piece of paper with the first message. "Look at the originating signal."

Mullaney lifted his eyes to the top of the page. Above the disjointed, incomplete sentences were identification codes for the originator and receiver of the calls. He dismissed the codes of the calls from Turkey, which looked like a disposable, untraceable mobile. But he couldn't take his eyes off the code identifying the calling device from the US. The code was a signature address, like the signatures that computers receive when they are linked into a network. Each device has a unique signature. But similar devices, devices used by the same company or on the same network, have similar signatures. It was one way of identifying and locating the device.

He lifted his eyes from the sheet of paper and looked at his long-time friend, Meyer Levinson. He didn't want to believe what he was seeing. But Meyer's eyes told him it was true.

"This is the signature address for the State Department." The words almost stuck in Mullaney's throat. "This address is for one of the encrypted satellite phones we use at State. I know. I had one back in DC." Mullaney looked down at the sheet again, hoping to rebut the information, find a weakness in the evidence.

"I'm sorry, Brian. That doesn't look good," said Levinson. "But we can't solve that problem now. We have a tough enough job staring us in the face. So I have to ask . . . who knows about this op?"

Mullaney knew what Levinson was asking. He didn't understand a lot about what was on the sheet of paper in his hand. Figuring that out would have to wait. But he knew a lot about the DSS agents on his team in Israel. He had reviewed their files and talked to their peers extensively before he left Washington. This was a solid group of professionals with no obvious allegiances elsewhere. All of them had been vouched for by people he trusted.

"As far as I know, only my team of agents even knows we're here," said Mullaney, stuffing the folded paper into the back pocket of his pants. "But that's no guarantee. So watch your back. Let's go."

"Right," said Levinson. But he didn't turn to go back into the meeting room. Instead, he put a hand on Mullaney's shoulder. "And Brian, when this is over, you need to tell me about the box."

Mullaney's eyes opened wide and he was about to claim ignorance. Instead he smiled. Mossad was monitoring all conversations. Even his. "Okay, Meyer. I owe you that one. If . . . when . . . we come home from this, I'll tell you everything I know about the box. You won't believe that either."

28

Holon Industrial District, Tel Aviv
July 20, 4:13 a.m.

Halfway down the alley, the driver cut the lights of the electrician's van. There was enough light pollution from the surrounding area that the alley, though bordered by buildings on each side, enjoyed a sliver of dusk down the center of its length, heavy blackness on each side.

Seated in the back with the other members of the strike force, Mullaney couldn't tell if the small truck that entered the alley fifteen minutes earlier was in the right position or if the other two squads had made it over the wall and were waiting for the go order. But there was no communication on the radio and, thankfully, no gunfire, as they rolled down the alley. That was a good sign.

Outfitted with black Kevlar body armor, a black helmet with night-vision amplified goggles, and a Shin Bet windbreaker emblazoned on each side with Hebrew letters, Mullaney refocused his mind on his job. Out the door with Levinson, double-time along the side of the building to the loading dock, and then silently force open the gate that closed over the dock.

The last drone pass didn't show any sentries on this side of the building. On the pictures, there were two up front—complicating the assignment of the other squad, which was to climb the staircase and gain access to the offices through the second-floor door.

The driver nursed the electrician's van, its engine idling quietly as it rolled along in neutral gear, into the open parking area between the two buildings on the right near the end of the alley.

Showtime. Mullaney's palms itched. A trickle of perspiration rolled down his neck under his collar. It felt like someone had taken his stomach out for a walk. Always like this before a mission, even when there wasn't a potential leak in his team. Mullaney pulled in a deep breath.

The back door swung open.

"Go," Levinson whispered into his radio, the entire team getting the same message. And Mullaney jumped into the dark.

Following close behind Levinson, Mullaney sprinted along the side of the building toward the loading dock, his Heckler & Koch MP5 held closely to his chest—safety off, finger off the trigger. All DSS agents were trained like that. He wondered about the . . .

Levinson dropped to a knee, Mullaney almost running up his back. He skidded to a halt, his left shoulder scraping against the masonry wall. He could hear the heavy breathing of Tommy Hernandez behind him.

The sliding door that covered the width of the loading dock was secured by two huge padlocks halfway down each side and a third massive padlock connecting the bottom of the door, at its center, to a metal cleat cemented into the ground. Levinson reached his right arm out to the side and motioned forward. A Shin Bet officer came alongside and handed something to Levinson then hustled along the length of the door. Levinson wrapped something around the shackle of the padlock in front of him, the soldier doing the same thing to the lock in the middle of the door and then the one on the far end. The soldier took a knee, pulled something out of his pocket about the size of a cigarette lighter and squeezed it in the middle.

A light sizzle floated on the night air, a faint odor of burning metal. Levinson caught the body of the lock as it fell away from the shackle, the soldier doing the same thing on the other side. Carefully, both of them removed the remnants of the shackle from the door and its frame. The soldier came to the middle of the door, removed the pieces of the middle lock and looked in Levinson's direction. With a hand signal, both pushed upward on the door at the same time, which swung up several feet on well-oiled hinges. No sound. It took only seconds.

Levinson pressed against the corner of the loading dock and the soldier flattened against the pavement, each scanning the interior. The night remained quiet, but the radio crackled . . . and Mullaney's hopes plummeted.

"Beta team . . . no guards in the warehouse compound."

Levinson shook his head and glanced back at Mullaney. He held up his right hand, a steadying gesture, and led his party inside the larger building, the temperature dropping significantly as soon as they scuttled low through the loading dock. A corridor as wide as the loading dock itself, ran straight ahead and split the space in two—walls barely discernible to the left and right.

Mullaney flipped on his night-vision gear.

The metal walls on either side of the corridor looked like they were insulated, massive, walk-in refrigerators or freezers. Each of them had double-wide doors in the middle, ten feet across, and a single, smaller entry door at the near corner. There was no light. There was no sound. Only cold. And dark.

Levinson was in a crouch against the wall at the end of the loading dock. He reached behind him, pointed at the lieutenant, raised two fingers, then pointed down the corridor—two-man teams at the entry doors and on either side of the double-wide doors on both sides of the corridor. He pointed at Mullaney and himself and pointed to the entry door on the right. A slight wave of his fingers and the six pairs, crouching close to the floor, moved in silent harmony, surrounding the doors.

There was no visible lock on the small entry door. Levinson edged back to cover as Mullaney reached for the door's handle.

"Alpha team . . . offices are clear. No sentries."

Mullaney's hand stopped in midair, despair hanging heavy on every muscle. *We're too late.*

Levinson gave him a nudge on the shoulder.

The handle turned freely. The door was unlocked. Mullaney drew in a breath and eased it open.

The room inside, colder than Moscow in January, was a black void. Mullaney scanned the room with his night vision, turning the thick darkness into a watery shimmer of green. The meat locker was huge, hundreds of large, metal hooks hanging from a winding course of rollers that twisted above the room. The room was empty. Except for one chair in the middle of the floor. Mullaney made one more scan with his night vision then looked alongside the door for a light switch.

"This side is clear." It was Hernandez's voice.

"Clear," Mullaney replied, but blackness enveloped his voice as the cold squeezed out all hope. He stood and looked back at Levinson. Both raised their night vision gear and Mullaney flipped on the light switch.

A lone metal chair sat in the middle of the room. As he walked toward it, Mullaney saw the one thing he feared more than finding Palmyra Parker's body.

Clumps of black hair, covered in blood, on the floor surrounding the chair.

Useless!

Seated on the edge of the loading dock, his head hanging between his shoulders, Mullaney was being assaulted by every lie from his past that—for so many years—he had accepted as true. Some lies others had hurled at him. Some lies he had hurled at himself.

It's all your fault.

You're just not good enough.

What's wrong with you?

Can't you do anything right?

Ahhh, you're useless!

He was rescued from most of those lies by his diligence, meticulousness, and determination. And by his faith. But lately, his failures had been piling up. Doubt was becoming his daily companion. Maybe he wasn't . . .

He felt the arm wrap itself around his shoulders—figured it was Hernandez trying to cheer him up—as the voice spoke in his ear.

"You will find her. She is the guardian. She will be safe."

He looked to his left. No one was there.

Tommy Hernandez sat down on Mullaney's right side at the end of the loading dock.

Mullaney looked at Hernandez then turned his head back to the left. There still wasn't anyone there.

"Didn't you just . . . weren't you . . ."

"What?" asked Hernandez, looking at Mullaney as if he had two heads. He reached out and put a hand on his friend's arm. "We'll find her. She'll be okay."

If only that was true, Mullaney thought. They might find her, but Palmyra Parker would likely be far from okay. The question he didn't want to ask himself: Was she alive? He looked out through the loading dock to the alley outside. Colonel Levinson was on his mobile phone. The word would be getting out.

"Brian," said Hernandez, "if she was dead, they would have left her body."

"Somebody needs to call Atticus."

Mullaney realized he was speaking out loud.

Tommy was reaching for his phone.

"No . . . I'll do it." Mullaney was searching through his pockets for his phone when he heard Levinson call out.

"Brian!" Then he clicked his mic. "Right, boys . . . load up, on the double . . . we think we've spotted them."

Hours on the treadmill paid off. Mullaney, running at a full gallop, was only one stride behind Levinson as the team piled into the back of the electrician's van. Levinson grabbed hold of Mullaney's Kevlar vest and pulled him down next to him on the bench that ran the length of the van. "Reconnaissance picked up a four-vehicle convoy of black SUVs speeding south on Route Four, between Ashdod and Ashkelon, about ten minutes ago," Levinson yelled as the driver started up the engine and catapulted out of the alley and into Halahav Street.

Mullaney grabbed a strut to keep from being tossed across the inside of the van. "How can you be sure?"

"They're running a very tight formation, very fast," said Levinson as he turned toward the driver. "Samuel, may I have the maps?" The driver, his left hand trying to keep the accelerating van under control, reached into a bin under the dashboard and handed back a leather-bound packet.

"Samuel, are you patched into the radio?"

"Yes, sir."

"Right . . . you know what to do."

The van was heaving, like a small boat in heavy seas, rolling back and forth. In spite of the movement, Levinson pulled open the packet and turned to a topographic road map.

"This is where we are," he said, pointing at the Holon district on the western flank of Ben Gurion Airport, "and this is where the first sighting was, along this road between"—he pointed to population centers—"Ashdod and Ashkelon. The first pictures came from a stationary camera. Reconnaissance is monitoring other stationary cameras along the road, but they also redirected a drone in that direction.

"Somewhere in here," Levinson pointed south of Ashdod, "we lost them. They must have turned off . . ."

All of them were thrown off balance as the van hit something in the road very hard. For a moment, the van felt airborne.

"Sorry, sir," said the driver, still wrestling with the steering wheel.

"It's all right, Samuel. You just get us there."

Levinson steadied the maps in his lap. "They must have pulled off Highway Four here, south of Nitzan. But the drone picked up the formation again. Now they are driving without lights, very slow, down this narrow dirt road that is sometimes used by farmers."

The area Levinson was pointing to looked desolate to Mullaney. "There's nothing there," he said. "Where are they going?"

Levinson looked up from the map. "I think they're making a run for Gaza. If they can get her into the Gaza Strip before . . . well . . . it may not be possible for us to find her, let alone rescue her. Gaza is a killing field. It's like your Wild West where there was no law and too many guns."

Mullaney's mind flashed back to a past operation to rescue a kidnapped American diplomat from the war-ravaged streets of Beirut. Incredibly dangerous and unpredictable, Beirut was a rat's nest of heavily armed militia units that flip-flopped daily from implacable enemy to impassive observer, depending on the whims of the controlling imams. The mission was a disaster. They found the diplomat, dead, hanging by his thumbs in the window of a bombed out storefront. Then Mullaney and the other DSS agents had to fight their way out of Beirut under withering fire from the rooftops and blackened windows of Beirut's ravaged buildings. Two agents were killed, three others wounded, including Mullaney, who still carried the scars in his body and his memory.

"We need to get her."

"I know," said Levinson, nodding his head. Mullaney could read the determination in Levinson's eyes. The colonel pointed down at the map. "We've got a plan." He traced his finger along a faint line that ran through the barren area north of Ashkelon. "If they get into Ashkelon, we could lose them entirely. And then it's only a short run to Gaza and too many paths for us to cover all at once. This is the Nitzanim Reserve, a preserved area of sand dunes and scrub. This unpaved road they are following runs down the eastern flank of Nitzanim. Here," he tapped his finger, "it runs over a small, wooden bridge to cross this wadi." Levinson looked up into Mullaney's eyes.

"There are two squads of Shin Bet and IDF from Ashkelon heading to that bridge right now. Their orders are to tear that bridge apart, if necessary, set up a "Bridge Out" blockade and detour the SUVs down another dirt road, farther into the reserve. And here"—he tapped the map—"is where we will be waiting for them."

Mullaney was shaking his head. "We? How are we going to get there? There's not enough time."

The van swerved violently to the left, all ten men hanging on so as not to be thrown about, and then shuddered to an abrupt halt, the groaning of its distressed engine overwhelmed by a growing, throaty roar.

Levinson was first to throw open the back doors and leap out of the van. "In these," he shouted, pointing to a pair of IDF helicopters, their rotors already spinning. The other soldiers poured out of the van, running bent under the rotors. Levinson grabbed Mullaney's arm as they jogged toward the chopper. "We'll swing out over the sea and come in from the south," he shouted into Mullaney's ear. They paused in the open door in the helicopter's side. "They won't hear us coming. Don't worry. We'll be in time."

29

Nitzanim Reserve, Ashkelon, Israel
July 20, 5:30 a.m.

Mullaney knew the Mediterranean was at his back. He couldn't see it or hear its waves wash the shore. But he could smell the sea. He was also aware of the false dawn glow created by the lights of Ashkelon off to his right. But his eyes and his concentration were on a thin strip of road—unpaved light sand, actually—that was illuminated only by starlight and weaved its way through undulating dunes and scrub brush in front of him, to the east. Beyond the sand road was a massive, impenetrable black void—the mammoth opening of an abandoned stone quarry.

Along with Levinson, Hernandez, and a half dozen Shin Bet soldiers, Mullaney was lying flat on his stomach, just off the top of a dune, not twenty feet from the sandy track. More than twenty other IDF and Shin Bet soldiers were concealed in the deep shadows below the scrub brush that flanked the road, just below Mullaney's position. Another team was hidden along the top of a dune on the far side of the road, opposite Mullaney.

The two teams that had been stationed at the ruined bridge to ensure the convoy took the bait and drove farther into the desolate landscape were now inching along the detour behind the SUVs, prepared to halt any attempt at retreat. Another team was stationed to the south, Mullaney's right, where the road ran alongside the quarry opening, blocking any escape in that direction.

Levinson leaned over toward Mullaney. "They got infrared glasses on each vehicle as the SUVs made the turn into the detour," he whispered. "There was no image that looked clearly like a woman, but the third vehicle has what looked to be three people squeezed into the back seat—two bruisers pushing against the inside of the doors and a space in the middle. They couldn't see what was in that space. But I'm willing to wager that's where the ambassador's daughter is riding. We'll take the third car." Levinson paused. "We need to be—"

"I know," Mullaney whispered. "We need to be fast and ruthless."

"Yes, Brian. And lucky."

Mullaney surveyed the scene in front of him. His conclusion was simple.

They needed more than luck. He began to pray—*God help us; God help us; God help us.*

Each of the teams hiding on the high ground at the top of the dunes, flanking the road, contained snipers with scope-mounted, blackened Barak HTR 2000 long-range sniper rifles fitted with silencers. The assignment for the team of snipers on the far side was to take out the drivers. The snipers lying to either side of Mullaney were to target the person riding in the front passenger seat . . . but to fire only when they had absolute certainty that Mrs. Parker wasn't unexpectedly riding in the front seat.

It was the people in the back where things got even more risky.

The IDF soldiers had rigged a series of flashbangs, or stun grenades, in the road—nonlethal explosive devices that would temporarily disorient a person's senses.

Flashbangs are enclosed by a steel casing, intended to remain intact, which has openings to allow the light and sound of the explosion to escape but which avoids injury from shrapnel. When detonated, the blinding flash of light momentarily overwhelms all photoreceptor cells in the eye, making vision impossible until the eye can recover, usually five seconds or more. The concussive blast of the grenade causes temporary loss of hearing and disturbs the fluid in the inner ear, causing loss of balance.

When the SUVs moved within the field of stun grenades, the plan was to detonate all of them at once while the snipers took care of the kidnappers in the front seat. Then the other Israeli soldiers had only five seconds in which to move.

Eight pairs of soldiers were under cover along the side of the road. Like every member of the rescue team, these soldiers wore protective glasses and ear plugs to negate the impact of the stun grenades. One soldier of the pair would slap a small piece of plastic explosive onto the hinges of the car's back door. Detonated, the explosive would blow the door outward, off its hinges. The second soldier on each side would be pressed against the side of the SUV, gun poised. At the moment of explosion, that soldier would train his sights on the kidnapper on his side of the back seat. The plan was to haul each of the disoriented bad guys out of the vehicle and into the sand as quickly as possible. If there was any flicker of an offensive move, that perpetrator would be dead.

In the short time they had to pull a plan together, it wasn't a bad plan.

But . . . five seconds. All that had to happen in five seconds.

And if a flashbang happened to be under a fuel tank when it detonated?

Mullaney tried not to think about all the other things that could possibly go wrong. There were too many of those possibilities. And he tried to contain his frustration at being up here on this dune rather than down there beside the road. He didn't want to be the hero. Yet he desperately needed to make sure Palmyra was safe. He wanted to be closer. But those guys were the experts. They had drilled specifically for circumstances like this. The Israeli military was prepared for almost every eventuality. Parker's life was in God's hands . . . and the effectiveness of these elite soldiers.

That knowledge didn't make him worry any less.

A graying pink in the east quickened Mullaney's heartbeat even more. Night was running out on them. Soon, the stun grenades in the road, covered by a thin dusting of sand, would be visible. Then what? How would . . .

He almost felt the vibrations of the engines in the soundless dark before he recognized the low hum. Around a curve between dunes to his left, the first of the dark hulks progressed along the path, moving faster than Mullaney had expected. His heart raced. He could feel the sweat on his palms. His breath came faster. If this first part didn't work . . .

Trying to figure out where to stage the stun grenades was one of the many challenges the soldiers faced in planning the ambush, along with how to slow the SUVs—not necessarily stop them cold, but at least slow them to a crawl. Their solution was to dig a shallow, winding trench across the sandy road, about eighteen inches deep and two feet across—too big to be ignored—and then to sweep it with brush to make it look like it had been there for years. Everything hung precariously on how the first driver would respond or react to the small gulley in the road: not see it and fail to slow down, see it and still power through it, or slow down in caution?

The first SUV drove along the track, the others almost nose to bumper, still moving too fast. The lead driver didn't slow . . . until he was nearly on top of the gulley, his front tires starting to drop into the ditch. Perhaps by instinct, the lead driver applied his brakes, the red taillights of the SUV shooting out like red laser beams. Behind him, each of the other drivers mashed down the brake pedal as the SUVs jerked to an abrupt halt, the lead vehicle pushed farther into the gully when it was hit by the one behind. Without a pause, the fire and chaos of hell erupted and surrounded the SUVs.

A series of low thuds, like leather slapping leather, erupted to either side of Mullaney, the front windshields of the SUVs all shattering at once. At nearly the same instant, a chorus of low explosions blew the back doors of each SUV into the desert.

Then the plan broke down. Badly.

The metallic rattle of automatic gunfire spewed from the rear cargo area of the second and fourth SUVs in the column, hitting several of the soldiers nearest to the vehicles. In a fraction of a heartbeat, a fusillade of return fire shredded the first, second, and fourth SUV. Their windows imploded and the sheet metal was ripped apart.

At the sound of the first shot, Mullaney was on his feet, running down the side of the dune, his 9-millimeter Sig Sauer automatic held in both hands, firing at where he saw the flashes of light coming from the vehicles. But with every lunging stride, his eyes went jolting back to the third vehicle where he saw IDF soldiers heaving men out of the back seat and onto the ground.

So focused was he on the shooters and concerned about Palmyra Parker's condition in the third car, Mullaney didn't register quickly enough his rate of descent and how close he was to the bottom of the dune. His eyes up and squeezing off another two rounds into the second SUV, Mullaney's foot landed on the flat ground at the bottom of the dune, his leg buckled and he went sprawling into the sand—the pain in his back erupting, momentarily overcoming the adrenaline rush of combat.

He wasn't down long.

Mullaney was rolling over on his hip, an exposed target with his back to the gun battle, when a hand came up under his arm and dragged him into the lee of a sandy hillock. "Glad to see you could make it," said Hernandez, kneeling at Mullaney's side. "The bad guys are over there."

Mullaney risked a peek over the top of the mound. "Do you see her?"

"No," said Hernandez. "Shooters in the back of the two SUVs. The second one is between us and her. We can't get to her while . . ."

Hernandez reached toward Mullaney. "Look—it's Pat!"

The front SUV was already a smoking hulk, devoid of life. But shots were still coming from the second and fourth vehicles, firing at any visible soldier while pinning down the two IDF soldiers who had jumped into the back seat of the third SUV.

Levinson, however, was leading an assault. And running shoulder to shoulder with Levinson was DSS Agent Pat McKeon. Behind them, the Israeli soldiers moved like a deadly dance troupe. Through the twilight of early dawn, three soldiers converged on each side of both the second and fourth SUVs while the rest launched a crushing cover fire. Swiftly, exchanging positions back to front as they advanced, the soldiers came up behind the vehicles. Almost on cue, one soldier at each vehicle lifted an arm and tossed a flashbang into the back seat. After the light and blast, a split second of silence, then a soldier from each side emptied a magazine into the rear compartment of the SUV.

But McKeon didn't stop with the Israeli soldiers. She kept running, right up behind the third vehicle.

Mullaney and Hernandez were up on their feet and also running to the third SUV before the Israeli soldiers stopped firing, but Mullaney skidded to a halt beside a bullet-pocked front door, wisely not bursting in front of the missing rear door while there was still shooting going on.

"Is she okay?" he yelled into the back of the vehicle. But his apprehension and dread wouldn't allow him to wait for an answer. Mullaney stuck his head around the door strut and looked into the back seat. Pat McKeon was kneeling on the seat, her finger on the trigger of her 9 millimeter, her eyes constantly on the move. An IDF soldier, wedged into the space between the seats, was hunched over the floor area, his eyes fixed on Mullaney and the stock of his Uzi pressed into his shoulder.

McKeon glanced over at Mullaney. A smile lit up her face. "We got her back," said McKeon. "She's alive."

"But I don't know if she's okay," said Palmyra's voice from the floor of the car, under the soldier's body. "Is that the cavalry?"

The soldier lifted his body and Palmyra Parker's bloody and matted head peeked around his shoulders. There was a warrior's fire in her bright, green eyes, like she was ticked off because no one had handed her a gun. But there was also a wealth of emotion awash in the tears that formed at the corners. "I didn't think . . ."

Parker's chin was quivering as the soldier pushed himself onto the back seat, giving her a chance to move. Twice she tried to speak. But each time she stopped, bit her lip, and gasped in some shallow breaths. Mullaney reached in and took her hand.

"I . . . I thought . . ."

Mullaney holstered his gun in the small of his back. He let the soldier out of the car and then leaned in through the door, putting his hands around Parker's shoulders and lifting her into a sitting position on the back seat. "You're okay," Mullaney said, holding her gaze, trying to fill her with the reality of her safety. "We've got you. You're safe."

The tears were quietly rolling down her cheeks. It was clear to Mullaney that she was fighting valiantly not to lose her composure. "I didn't think you . . ."

Mullaney crawled onto the seat beside her, put his left arm around Parker's shoulders and allowed her to lean into him.

"Thank you," she said into his chest.

Mullaney held her. Something paternal clicked and he rocked her a little, like a baby.

"How did one of your guys get into the back of this SUV?"

"What?"

Parker pushed herself off his chest and looked into his eyes. "The guy in the back. As soon as the explosions went off, somebody reached out and slammed the heads of my guards into the side windows—at the same time. Then he got me on the floor and covered me when the shooting started."

Mullaney was having a hard time making sense of Parker's recollections. "You mean the IDF soldier who was protecting you?"

"No," Parker shook her head. "Before that . . . before he got to the car . . . before the doors were blown off. That first guy, he really saved my life."

"I don't know what . . ." Then his mind cleared. "We need to reach Atticus."

Mullaney turned to his right, toward the missing door. And Tommy Hernandez was handing him a phone.

"It's ringing," said Hernandez.

30

Nitzanim Reserve, Ashkelon
July 20, 6:23 a.m.

Parker was propped against the open door of the helicopter, wrapped in a blanket. A gauze bandage covered the ugly injury at the back of her head—a swollen knot of purple, yellow and blue bruises, crowned with an inch-and-a-half-long gash that would quickly need stitches. One medic was dressing her other scalp wounds, another checking her vitals and looking for signs of a concussion.

She was looking at Mullaney as if he had stolen her hope.

"Two died? For me?" She shook her head. "No life is more important than another. That's not right. That's not fair. How can I be responsible for . . ."

"They were doing their duty," said Mullaney. "That's what they sign up for. Shoot, that's what we all sign up for. Not that your life is more important than theirs, or more important than mine. But soldiers . . . law enforcement officers . . . we honor our duty as much as we honor our lives. Our honor *is* our lives. Innocent people would be victimized and violated if there weren't men and women who willingly put their lives at risk to maintain some semblance of order and safety. People of duty do it all the time. And sometimes it costs them dearly. But they wouldn't . . . couldn't . . . live any other way."

Mullaney sat down in the open bay by her side. "It's not your choice to make, whether someone risks their life for you. It's a choice they make. And for the same reason you mentioned. Every life is important. Every life is valuable, needs to be protected. That's the only way evil is defeated—if good men and women are willing to stand against evil and do whatever it takes to vanquish it."

They sat in the bay of the helicopter in silence, watching the last colors of sunrise leave the sky. Once the medics had finished their chores and left, Mullaney broke the silence.

"Did they say what they wanted?"

"Sure," said Parker. "They wanted the box. Why, I don't know."

They looked into the distance.

"I'm sorry about Haisha," said Parker.

"Maybe we should just give them the box."

"No," she shook her head and winced at the result. She took a deep breath. "No, there's too much going on here, a lot more than I think we understand. There's a reason my dad was given that box and the responsibility of getting the box to the rabbis at the Hurva Synagogue. I don't know why. Perhaps we'll never understand the why of it. But no . . . we protect the box and get it to its destination. Besides"—she pointed into the distance where more than a dozen bodies were laid out and covered with sheets—"I don't think we have to worry about those guys anymore."

"Not those guys, specifically," Mullaney agreed. "But I want to know who is behind all this. Any idea who those guys were?"

"I was going to ask you the same thing," said Parker. "They seemed pretty good at their profession. I was talking to a little girl between two of the stalls at the open market, and before I could react, I was down on the ground, a hand clamped over my mouth, and something injected into my neck. I came back to the world bound to a chair, blindfolded, and gagged in a freezer."

"Meat locker, actually."

"Smelled like something died in there. I was hoping it wasn't . . ."

Mullaney empathized with Parker's flashbacks to her fears, but right now he needed more information. Now that Parker was safe, he wanted to find those who were responsible.

"And they were talking to you in Turkish?"

"No!" Parker snapped. Then she took a breath. "Sorry. Still feel pretty jumpy. They were talking to me in English most of the time, asking their questions and making their threats in English. But the one behind me, Hamid, spoke Turkish. Then when the leader needed to make a phone call, he talked to Hamid in Turkish and said *Don't let her die*. Comforting. Then he walked away and made what sounded like a phone call, and on the call he was speaking in Turkish. I couldn't understand everything he said, but I could understand the language."

Parker shivered under the blanket. Mullaney considered putting his arm around her shoulders. "But then, after the call, everything changed. Suddenly," said Parker, "they got more belligerent, more animated, their threats got more vicious. That's when I really started to feel . . . well, afraid that . . ." Her hand burst from beneath the blanket and grabbed Mullaney's right arm. "What happened, Brian? What happened while I was . . . gone?"

Mullaney shook his head. *What happened?* Was it only eighteen hours ago they had landed at Ben Gurion Airport?

"Too much," said Mullaney. He turned to his right to watch Parker's face closely. "They came after us on the road to Jerusalem. The car crashed. Atticus—all of us—got shaken up. Your dad suffered a few cuts, a nasty bump on his head. But he's okay."

Parker's shoulders started to shiver. But she caught it and held his gaze with the fierce determination of a wounded warrior who knew the mission wasn't over.

"We have enemies, Palmyra, deadly enemies. And I don't even know who they are. But there's not enough time to go through it all. And we need to get you home. Your father won't be at peace until he sees you with his own eyes. But . . . first . . . I need to know everything you can tell me about what happened while you were being held. What kind of questions were they asking you?"

Parker shrugged her shoulders. "Where's the box? Does the ambassador have it? What is he going to do with it? Did anybody touch the box . . . did we look inside? I didn't understand why they asked some of those questions. Seems like they had pretty good surveillance on us from the outset, and they would have known where it was and whether Atticus had it. I kept thinking two things: What do you really want, and am I going to get out of here alive?"

A quizzical look came to Parker's face, and she turned to Mullaney. "Did they ever make a ransom demand?" she asked.

Mullaney shook his head. "Not a ransom demand. An exchange. They wanted the box. We wanted proof of life."

"Yes . . . the FaceTime call. I figured something like that." Parker pulled the blanket tighter around her, looking off into the dunes.

"Brian." Parker pushed herself farther onto the deck of the helicopter's bay and leaned against the open doorway. "When I first came to my senses in the freezer, my captors seemed . . . well . . . there was a sense of urgency to their demands. Like it was critical they got their information right away. That's when they started on this," her hand went up to the unruly tufts of hair that were sticking out between patches of bandages.

"I was going to ask you about your new hairstyle," said Mullaney, allowing himself the shadow of a smile. "Doesn't really look good on you, you know?"

"Thanks. I'll put in a complaint."

"What were they trying to do?"

Parker waved her hand in front of her face. "Oh, they had a black box with a lot of wires running out of it. They scraped off chunks of my hair and pasted electrodes on my scalp. Said they would give me one chance to tell them the location of the box or they would start killing off my brain cells a couple hundred thousand at a time. But that's not the point. They knew that box had to be in one of two places—with my father or in the residence. They weren't asking if it was *in* the residence. They wanted to know *where* in the residence it was. Like, if they knew where it was specifically, they could get to it."

Mullaney knew where this was going, and it was getting him angry.

"And there's something else," said Parker, interrupting his thoughts. "There was a second phone call, but this one was a call that came from outside. The leader answered it. There wasn't much of a conversation. *Yes . . . yes . . . I understand.*"

Parker stood to her feet and started walking away from the helicopter, her head down as if she was processing information.

Mullaney didn't need to hear anymore. He was already waving toward Hernandez and Levinson, who were talking with the helicopter crew and medics about twenty yards away.

"And then we were packing up, fast." Parker was still lost in her thoughts, kicking a stone on the ground, but her voice carried back to Mullaney. "That's the first time I realized there were more people in the room than just the leader and Hamid, the guy whose breath smelled like a dumpster. Suddenly there were a number of people moving around, gathering things up. Two came to me, untied me from the chair, picked me up under the arms, and hustled me out of that room and into the back of a vehicle."

Hernandez ran to Mullaney's side. "What's up?"

That's when Parker swung her body around toward Mullaney. The look on her face matched the rage in his heart.

"They knew you were coming, didn't they." It was a statement, not a question. Parker's eyes opened wide. "Brian . . . there's someone inside. Someone giving them infor—"

The blanket dropped from her shoulders and she moved faster than Mullaney expected, getting right in his face. "Where's my father? Please . . . I need to see my dad."

The bodies of eight dead terrorists, covered with shrouds, were stretched out in the gritty sand of the Nitzanim Reserve. Brian Mullaney's problem was that he didn't know how many more of this terrorist band remained alive. Or who their next victim would be.

"Look, Kat," Mullaney barked into his iPhone, "I don't care if the Eleventh Fleet is parked outside the residence, I don't want Cleveland left alone. I want someone I can trust—I want you—by his side every minute. And take three other agents with you. I want him covered front and back, even if he goes to the bathroom to . . ."

"Hey, Boss, that's where I draw the line!" Kat Doorley was an eleven-year veteran of the Diplomatic Security Service and one of Mullaney's most trusted agents. She took her orders seriously . . . and literally.

"You know what I meant—get a couple of guys on the team—but don't let the ambassador out of your sight. This gang we're facing, I don't know who they are. But there are a lot of them, they are resourceful, and they are determined. They snatched Mrs. Parker from just outside the residence, and I'm not about to underestimate their capacity." Mullaney almost said *again*. And perhaps that was true. But now was not the time for self-examination.

"Okay, Brian. I'm walking to his quarters now," Doorley responded, "and I've asked the marines on duty at the checkpoint to go in and sit with him until we get there. When will you be back?"

Mullaney, head of the Diplomatic Security Service contingent assigned to the protection of the staff and facilities of the American diplomatic mission to Israel, surveyed the field of battle before him in the early morning light. A line of four black SUVs—three of them bullet-ridden and burned out hulks—lay shattered and smoking in the cleft of a wadi fifty yards to the east. Agents from

Shin Bet were loading two flag-draped litters into the hold of a military helicopter. On the other side of the wadi lay the bodies of the eight dead terrorists. Six others, most of them wounded, knelt in the dust, hands and feet shackled, their grim-faced Shin Bet guards watching as the back end of a canvas-topped truck was opened to transport the prisoners.

Mullaney turned to his left and leaned away from the phone, toward Levinson. "Where are you taking them?" asked Mullaney. "Will I get a chance to question them?"

Levinson was a professional. There was grief in his eyes for the two Israeli agents killed in the dawn ambush that had rescued Parker. But there was calm resolve in his voice.

"We've got a place we can take them for questioning," said Levinson, his eyes moving from the loading truck to the helicopter that was lifting off with the bodies of his men. "Someplace a bit more secluded than Shin Bet headquarters. Give us an hour or two, then we'll give you a crack at them."

Mullaney waited until Levinson looked in his direction and then held Levinson's gaze. "Will there be anything left to question?"

Years ago, Mullaney and Levinson forged a strong friendship during Levinson's tour as head of security for the Israeli embassy in Washington. If Levinson gave his word . . .

"They'll be alive when you get there, Brian." Levinson's eyes didn't waver. "They won't be very pretty, and they may be wishing for a glorious death that will catapult them to paradise, but they'll be alive. Call me when you're ready, and I'll send a couple of my guys to pick you up. And no, we don't want you to know the location of our little hideaway. Sorry . . . but there are some things we keep rather close."

Mullaney could tell that was all he was going to get from Levinson. But it was good enough.

"Any news on the two who got away?"

"Not yet," said Levinson. "We're still looking. We'll get them, unless they make it to Ashkelon and disappear into those streets."

"Let me know if you pick them up, okay?" Mullaney nodded his head toward the second helicopter where Parker was pacing impatiently. "Can we get a lift back to the residence?"

"Sure," said Levinson. "Not a problem."

"Okay . . . Kat?" he said, turning once again to the phone.

"Yeah . . . I'm still here. We're walking into the ambassador's quarters now."

"Great, thanks, Kat. An Israeli chopper is ferrying us back to the residence. Tell Ambassador Cleveland we should be there in ten minutes. And then we've got some serious talking to do."

31

US Ambassador's Residence, Tel Aviv
July 20, 7:10 a.m.

"The first thing we need to do is get that box out of this house," said Cleveland.

Three other voices jumped on top of that comment, and the "summit meeting" in Cleveland's office teetered on the edge of anarchy.

"Dad," said Parker, "you've got a major international announcement coming in five hours. The box can wait."

"Nobody's going anywhere with that box until we're sure it's safe to move," said Mullaney.

"Yo," stammered Hernandez. "I ain't touching that—"

Cleveland held up his hands to halt the flow of words coming at him and then pointed to the leather sofa and arm chairs nestled in the corner of his office. "Please, have a seat. We're all tired." Parker settled herself on one end of the sofa while Mullaney and Hernandez lowered themselves into the matching armchairs. Cleveland's body was more than grateful to move from behind his desk to the welcome comfort of the well-worn leather sofa.

They were all on the same team . . . and he was blessed and confident that they were all on *his* team. Especially important now that they realized there was a leak, perhaps a traitor, inside the embassy or residence staff. But he had to get them all on the same page. The challenge was which page came first. There wasn't any doubt in his mind, and he was going to make that clear to them as well.

"Okay . . . okay," said Cleveland. "We have several major issues in front of us, all of them important, most of them intertwined. But getting that box out of here and into the hands of the rabbis at the Hurva Synagogue is at the top of my list. So this is what we're going to do." Reluctantly, Cleveland pushed himself out of the corner of the old, battered leather sofa and stepped out of the seating group so he could face all three of his team at once.

"I've asked Jeffrey to locate the head of the Rabbinate Council—the chief rabbi at the Hurva—and get him on the phone. I'm going to tell him I have something of urgent importance for him and request him to come here to the residence. Brian," he said, pointing to Mullaney and fixing him with his gaze, "I would like you to remain here with Palmyra to meet with the rabbi and make sure the box is transferred into his possession. I believe Palmyra, since she was the last to receive the anointing, may be necessary to make that transfer."

Cleveland turned to his left. "Tommy, you and I will leave immediately for the embassy. Jeffrey is also calling all the senior staff to make sure they all arrive early. Brian, you can join us once the rabbi leaves with the box. But we've got to be prepared for whatever comes out of this announcement today. We need to keep the secretary up to date both before and after the announcement so he can brief the president."

He was tired. More than tired. Mental, emotional, and physical exhaustion were clamoring for a foothold. Cleveland pushed his shoulders back and stretched to his full height. "As far as finding out who is behind the attacks we've come under, or discovering if there actually is someone here or at the embassy—"

"Or at the State Department," Mullaney interrupted.

"Yes . . . or at the State Department," Cleveland agreed, "who is providing information to these terrorists, all that will have to wait." He looked around at his closest confidants. "Is there anything else?"

"And we need to decide about breakfast," Hernandez mumbled. When all eyes turned toward him, Hernandez shrugged his shoulders. "Hey, I'm just sayin'. We've been up all night, and I can't remember the last time I ate anything. My stomach's been talking to me for hours. I just think it might be a good idea for all of us to get some sustenance. I think we'll need it."

Cleveland crooked his head to once again consider Hernandez, who liked to play the clown, but who so very often came up with sound ideas. "Thank you, Tommy. Now that you mention it . . ."

"I'll call the kitchen," said Parker, heading for the phone on the ambassador's desk, "and have them send up some coffee and whatever they have for breakfast."

"Okay," said the ambassador. "A few minutes break . . . and then we move."

US Ambassador's Residence, Tel Aviv
July 20, 8:52 a.m.

Israel Herzog looked like a banker. He was tall, fit, and muscular and wore a sharply tailored black suit, crisp, spread-collar white shirt, and a muted silver tie with thin, black stripes. Except for the wide-brimmed black hat on his head, there was little to indicate that Herzog was not only a rabbi, but one of the two chief rabbis of the Rabbinate Council of Israel. His beard was short and neatly trimmed, showing only a smattering of gray, and his eyes were a bright aquamarine, filled with questions and intelligence. He was not what Brian Mullaney was expecting.

And Herzog had the handshake of a bricklayer.

"Rabbi Herzog," said Mullaney, trying to free his hand and restore its circulation, "thank you for coming to Tel Aviv on such short notice."

A wide smile accented the twinkle in Rabbi Herzog's eyes. "Well, Agent Mullaney, it's not every day I get a personal, and urgent, request from the American ambassador. It's been a challenge to control my imagination on the drive from Jerusalem. What can I help you with that is of such burning importance?"

Mullaney started to lead the rabbi out of the reception room. "First . . . you came with a driver?"

"Yes, and my assistant."

"Fine. Our staff will take care of them and make sure they are comfortable. But please . . . come with me. I'm afraid the ambassador was needed at the embassy. We're going to meet in the residence with his daughter."

"And this cleaning woman died where?"

Palmyra Parker pointed over Rabbi Herzog's shoulder, toward her suite of rooms. "Just in the next room."

"And you want me to . . . ?"

Israel Herzog hadn't raised a question as Parker, with help from Mullaney, relayed Cleveland's story about acquiring the mysterious box from the rabbi at the Neve Shalom Synagogue in Istanbul—and the curse that appeared to be on the box—about the attacks on Cleveland in Turkey and Israel, Parker's kidnapping, and the strange and similar deaths suffered by Rabbi Moische Avi Kaplan in Istanbul and Haisha Golden in the ambassador's residence. But his calm exterior showed stress cracks when Parker revealed why Rabbi Herzog had been summoned to the residence—that the box supposedly contained the second prophecy from the Vilna Gaon, a coded prophecy that Herzog and his council were expected to decipher.

"We want you to take the box," said Parker, frustration and anxiety dripping from her words. Didn't Herzog understand? "Rabbi Kaplan in Istanbul said to bring it to the Rabbinate Council . . . that you would know what to do with it. That you would know how to get the Gaon's second prophecy and understand what it said. So this box is now your problem. And we want it out of here before it kills anyone else."

Rabbi Herzog held fast under Parker's withering stare. Not a whisker nor a thread was out of place. With Parker still in his sight line, Herzog turned his head to look around the room. "And where is this box you speak of?"

"It's still in the closet," said Parker. "None of us felt safe touching it."

He nodded his head. "Well then." He stood to his feet. "Let's take a look, shall we?"

The closet door was open, the leather satchel still resting on the shelf above Parker's clothes. Rabbi Herzog stood in the doorway, his hands in his pockets. He didn't seem to be in any hurry, which aggravated Palmyra Parker even more.

"Do you know," he said, turning to face Parker and Mullaney, "when the Gaon's prophecy about Messiah came to light, there was an uproar around the world. What did it mean that, centuries ago, an aged scholar from Lithuania wrote down a prophecy that Russia would invade and annex the Crimea? Now that the current Russian government has fulfilled one part of the Gaon's prophecy, does it follow that the second half of the prophecy will be fulfilled as well? Is Messiah's coming actually imminent?"

Suddenly a light flashed on in Parker's mind. A recognition of something she had overlooked . . . the Gaon's prophecy was multi-faceted. Not only were there two obvious but independent statements, one about Russia and the second about Messiah, but there were also a number of perspectives from which to view the prophecy—political, geographic, religious—and varied viewpoints within those perspectives. What did it mean to Herzog that "the Times of Messiah have started, that his steps are being heard"? If true and accurate, what did it mean to David Meir's government in Israel? What did it mean according to the eschatological clock of biblical prophecy? Didn't the coming of Messiah mean the beginning of end times, the end of the world as we know it?

"I can see from the look on your face, Mrs. Parker, that the possibilities are beginning to become clear to you." Rabbi Herzog's bright aquamarine eyes were piercing in their intensity. "In the practical, worldly perspective, if the Gaon's prophecy is accurate, does the government in Turkey need to fear an invasion from Russia? Do the Russians have plans on conquering and occupying Istanbul, modern Constantinople?"

"It would give Vartsev something the Russians have coveted since the Czars," said Mullaney, referring to the Russian president. "Control of a warm-water port for their navy. And another step in the resurrection of Russia as a world superpower." He was leaning up against the doorframe of the closet, to Parker's left.

Herzog's hat was bobbing up and down as he nodded his head in agreement. "Yes, one of many consequences *if* the Gaon's words of two hundred years ago are accurate for today. And now you tell me that inside that satchel is a box that contains another prophecy from the Gaon?"

"That's what Ambassador Cleveland was told in Istanbul," said Mullaney. "But one thing I don't understand is why you? Why did the rabbi in Istanbul insist that the box be delivered to you, to the Hurva Synagogue, to the Rabbinate Council?"

"Ahhh . . . good question. Logical. Easy to explain. The original synagogue, built on the site now occupied by the Hurva, was started by a group of Ashkenazi Jews early in the eighteenth century. Unfinished and heavily in debt, the structure was destroyed in 1720, the year the Gaon was born . . . burned to the ground by the local Arabs who controlled the debt. In 1812 another group of Ashkenazi Jews, known as Perushim, immigrated to Palestine from Lithuania. They were disciples of the Vilna Gaon and were determined to rebuild the spiritual home of the Ashkenazi. It took them over forty years to secure permission from the Ottoman Empire, and another nine years to rebuild the synagogue, which was considered the most beautiful in all Israel. Unfortunately, that synagogue was also destroyed, blown up by the Jordanian Arab Legion in 1948 during Israel's war for independence. The rebuilding of the current Hurva was delayed for decades by indecision and factional infighting. Construction finally began in 2000. Built over the ruins of its two predecessors, the new Hurva was rededicated in 2010.

"So the Hurva has always been viewed as the synagogue established by the Gaon's disciples and it's taken its place as the most revered synagogue in the country and the seat of the Chief Rabbinate Council of Israel. It's logical that Rabbi Kaplan in Istanbul would send the Gaon's new prophecy to us."

Herzog turned to face Parker. "It's interesting, Mrs. Parker, that you call the message that you believe is in this box the Gaon's second prophecy. There are actually others."

"Other prophecies?" said Mullaney. "What do you mean . . . the Vilna Gaon wrote more prophecies than just these two?"

"Oh, yes," said Herzog, the taint of surprise in his voice. "Many more. He even wrote one about the Hurva Synagogue. The Gaon prophesied that the Hurva would be destroyed and rebuilt twice. He wrote that when the Hurva Synagogue is rebuilt for the third time then construction of the third temple of God will begin. Interesting on two points—this is the third Hurva building, the second time it was rebuilt. And according to Jewish belief, a temple needs to be rebuilt in Jerusalem before Messiah can come."

"So if the Gaon is predicting Messiah's imminent arrival . . ." said Mullaney.

"Yes . . . his Hurva prophecy has made me a bit uncomfortable. But Agent Mullaney, I think that is a discussion for a different time. Still, it is interesting to wonder what else the Gaon may have predicted."

Parker's mind was spinning as fast as her stomach was churning. She hadn't thought about the potential fallout from a second prophecy. All she could focus on was getting the box out of their lives and getting her father out of the cross-hairs of the men who so desperately wanted possession of the box that they were willing to commit any crime to secure it.

"Rabbi Herzog," said Parker, "I don't know what's in that box or what it will mean—to you, me, or anyone else in the world. All I know is that people who have touched that box have died terrible deaths. And that there's a gang out there who would kill everybody in this building because they want that box or what's inside it. Will you . . . can you . . . take it away?"

32

US Embassy, Tel Aviv
July 20, 9:23 a.m.

Ruth Hughes stood to the left of the door leading out of Cleveland's inner office in the US embassy as the rest of the station's senior staff filed out, their assignments for the next two hours clearly defined by the ambassador. Her arms were crossed, her face as resolute and unreadable as if it was carved alongside Washington, Lincoln, Jefferson, and Teddy Roosevelt on Mount Rushmore.

"Yes, Ruth?" Cleveland reached for this morning's third cup of coffee, relished its warmth as it heated his palms, and leaned back in the ergonomically designed padded leather chair behind his desk. "What's on your mind?"

The embassy's political officer, Hughes had the deepest and most reliable Mideast connections of any officer on Cleveland's staff. And she had Cleveland's respect.

"What's on my mind?" asked Hughes as she moved to one of the chairs in front of Cleveland's desk. "It certainly isn't the worst-kept secret of the twenty-first century, this soon-to-be-announced treaty between Israel and its Arab neighbors. What's on my mind is how do we keep the peace once this peace treaty is finally revealed."

"Palestine?" asked Cleveland, already knowing the answer.

"Bingo! And my sources," said Hughes, "tell me part of the deal is to allow Israel to erect a platform attached to Temple Mount at the Golden Gates in order to build a Temple. Double Bingo! Well-informed people tell me there is enough in this treaty—multiple treaties, actually—to blow the lid off the Middle East six times over."

"Then how are Israel and the Arabs going to pull this off?"

Hughes, former corporate officer and board member of Aramco, the giant oil company now fully controlled by the Saudis, shook her head and looked out the window behind Cleveland's desk. "Honestly, I'm not sure either side thinks they can . . . or really wants to . . . pull this off." She pushed herself forward in her chair. "Think about it. The Saudis are driving this treaty because they are scared senseless by Iran. And if the Arabs offer peace and a mutual defense agreement, which is also in the pact, what can Israel do? Meir's government must accept and embrace the treaty. But how many in Israel are violently opposed to a two-state solution? And how many in the Arab world will be violently opposed to the building of a Jewish temple, even if it's only adjacent to Temple Mount? Pragmatically, this treaty makes a lot of sense. Realistically, some of the stuff rumored to be in this treaty will likely kill it before it takes its first breath."

Cleveland waited. He knew Hughes had only stated her preamble. She turned her gaze away from the window and stared directly at the ambassador.

"So I'm wondering, what are the Saudis really up to?" asked Hughes. "My understanding is that King Abdullah muscled a lot of people to join this covenant. That's what they're calling it, by the way. The Ishmael Covenant. The restoration of Abraham's offspring into one family. But Abdullah really strong-armed both Egypt and Jordan to join in this pact and then muscled up against all the smaller Arab gulf nations. But why? Is a fear of Iran, even a fear of an allied Iran and Iraq, enough of a reason for the Saudis to make such a bold move?"

"So what's Abdullah's game?"

"Honestly, Atticus, I don't know," Hughes admitted. "Brokering a two-state solution for the Palestinians earns Abdullah a high level of esteem in the Arab world . . . gives him a lot of swag, as they say. And that's important to him—international influence. But my instincts tell me there is more going on here than puffing up Abdullah's pride."

Hughes slid back into the depth of her chair and crossed her legs. She was about to shift gears. "But what do you think of this proposed covenant, Atticus? I know what President Boylan wants—an independent Palestine. But where do you stand on the possibility of a two-state solution?"

Once again, Cleveland considered that Hughes was excellent at her job. Either she had done her homework on her new boss or she had read him accurately. Because when it came to the Palestinian issue, Cleveland was a two-minded man. As a diplomat, the partition of Israel to make room for an independent Palestine seemed inevitable. And since both the Jews and the Palestinians had lived in the area—albeit not always peacefully—since Joshua crossed the Jordan, a two-state solution seemed the right thing to do.

But Cleveland had a second perspective on the partition of Israel that was just as vital to him as the one his diplomatic training considered inevitable.

"I'm convinced," said Cleveland, holding fast to Hughes's stare, "that any division of Israel will be a disaster—and a curse for every nation that is involved."

US Ambassador's Residence, Tel Aviv
July 20, 9:27 a.m.

Brian Mullaney took a step back from the closet, as Rabbi Herzog reached up for the leather satchel. The significance of the step back didn't touch Mullaney until he realized that Palmyra Parker had done the same thing.

Parker was looking at him with a crooked smile on her face. "Better safe than sorry?"

Mullaney shrugged his shoulders. *That's embarrassing.*

"You're safe." Israel Herzog stood in the door to the closet, holding the handles to the leather satchel in both hands. "Let's go sit down and figure this out."

The satchel sat on a coffee table, Herzog on the sofa with the satchel in front of him, Parker and Mullaney in chairs on the other side of the table.

"If you don't mind," said Herzog, "Mrs. Parker, would you be so kind as to confer the Aaronic blessing upon me before we proceed? Better safe than sorry, eh?" The rabbi removed his broad-brimmed hat and lowered his head in Parker's direction. A yarmulke still covered part of his hair.

Mullaney watched as the normally confident and unflappable Parker hesitantly placed her right hand upon Herzog's head.

"This is how my father transferred the blessing . . . the anointing . . . to me," said Parker. She took a breath. "The Lord bless you, and keep you. The Lord make His face shine on you, and be gracious to you. The Lord lift up His countenance on you, and give you peace. There . . . is that good?"

"Thank you. You would make a fine rabbi." Herzog took his hat in his hand, hesitated, and then set it on the sofa beside him. He looked up, and

Mullaney saw a subtle change in the rabbi. Up until now, Herzog had been relaxed and affable. That man was now gone. Anxiety had paid him a visit.

Herzog snapped the latch on the satchel and spread open its sides. He looked into the bag, tilted the opening more toward the light, and looked in a second time. Then he laid the bag on its side, reached in, and withdrew a wooden box about the length and width of a piece of copy paper, but about six inches high.

"Okay . . . that part was easy," said Herzog. "Now I think we come to the tricky part."

The wooden box was hinged and Herzog gently toyed with the lid, testing it to see how easily it opened. The top lifted smoothly, revealing folds of purple cloth filling the box. With his thumb and forefinger, as if he were dancing with a live crab, Herzog lifted the top fold of the heavy purple cloth. Then he peeled away the second and the third folds and draped them over the sides of the box. "Here we go." The rabbi grasped a wrinkle in the cloth of the final fold and drew it up and away. Facing him was a metal box. It looked like well-weathered bronze. Hammered into the top of the metal box were five symbols—one in the middle of the box and one in each corner.

Mullaney twisted his head to the side to get a different angle on the symbols. "What are these—" Mullaney looked up at Herzog. The question froze on his lips.

The rabbi was bending closer to the metal box on the coffee table, his eyes growing bigger with every inch closer he came, his mouth opened in a wide circle. "Ooohhh . . . I never . . ." Whack! Herzog slapped the lid of the wooden box closed and pushed his body back away from it, his head resting on the top cushion of the sofa and his eyes searching the ceiling.

"Rabbi?" said Mullaney. "Are you okay?"

Like a body rising from the grave, Rabbi Israel Herzog slowly came back to a sitting position. His face was pale and his breathing labored. Mullaney feared the rabbi may have suffered a heart attack. But his face looked worse.

Looking from one to the other, Herzog shook his head. "This . . . I . . . I must take to the council," he stammered. "It is not what I expected."

Mullaney watched as Herzog tried to steady his nerves with a long, deep breath. "But what is it?" Mullaney asked. "What are those symbols?"

Herzog shook and rotated his shoulders, as if a current of electricity had just run up his spine. "The symbols," he said, taking a deep breath, "are kabbalah, an ancient, mystical practice of Judaism."

"Kabbalah symbols on the box surprised you?" asked Parker.

"No, not that they are kabbalah," said Herzog, shaking his head. "The Gaon was a devoted believer in kabbalah, that the practice of kabbalah opened up a deeper relationship between the Creator and the created. No . . . it was the symbols themselves that surprised me."

Herzog inched closer to the table and placed his hands on the purple velvet hanging over the sides of the wooden box. "Now I have been wrong before, but I believe that what Rabbi Kaplan shared with Ambassador Cleveland in Istanbul was correct in two respects . . . it appears that the power comes from what exists inside the box, not the box itself. There is no way to tell for certain while the message remains in the box, but it follows God's pattern in the Torah. It wasn't the ark of the covenant that possessed deadly power; it was what resided inside the ark that generated that power. And it also appears to be true that the anointing, the Aaronic blessing, protects those who safeguard the box. But the anointing can only be exercised by the last person anointed . . . the current guardian. It's like the priesthood and the temple in Jerusalem. Only the high priest could enter the holy of holies. Anyone else would be struck dead . . . even a former high priest who was no longer ordained for that office. I believe that's why Rabbi Kaplan perished. He must have touched the metal box after he conferred the Aaronic blessing onto your father. Just as you conferred it upon me, Mrs. Parker. Now I am the guardian."

A gruesome thought occurred to Mullaney. What if Cleveland had touched the box after conferring the blessing on his daughter? Cleveland dead? It was hard for him to imagine . . . hard to even contemplate Cleveland suffering a death like that. Mullaney was surprised at the depth of emotion that rushed through him at the thought of Cleveland's death. His investment in Cleveland had long since passed a business relationship. It felt . . . *kinda like Dad dying.*

"But what do the symbols mean?" Parker asked again, shaking Mullaney out of his emotions. "They seemed to frighten the life out of you."

"And so they should," Herzog responded. "This combination of symbols is the most powerful death warrant in all of kabbalah. It carries the power of God in its warning, the wrath of heaven upon anyone other than the guardian who touches the metal box. It is a painful, excruciating, yet instant death . . .

judgment without mercy. Yes, I am now protected. But the power of this warning is so severe, so lethal, that it shook me to my soul."

Mullaney felt vindicated. He now looked at the wooden box as if it were a den of poisonous vipers. It was wisdom to keep a safe distance from something so deadly.

"The most powerful death warrant?" asked Mullaney. "And it's not what's on the box that's deadly, it's what is in the box?" Mullaney willed his eyes away from the viper den to face Herzog. "So Rabbi, what can be in that box? Can the words of an old man, written 250 years ago, carry the power of life and death?"

Herzog shook his head. "Not the words he wrote. Not the paper they are written on. It's the power that God has infused, imparted into the message itself." Herzog perked up and shifted on the sofa. "It's like Aaron's staff. The wood of Aaron's staff had no power. But when the power of the almighty God was imparted to that staff, it called down the plagues of Egypt and split the Red Sea in two.

"I think," the rabbi added, "that the question of greatest import, is not what's in the box, but what's in the message. What warning . . . what prediction . . . has the Gaon sent us? And why is it surrounded, protected, by so much power?"

Herzog rubbed his hands together. "So . . . I will go no further here," he said, shaking off his alarm. "I will take this box with me to the Hurva, to the council, as you requested . . . as Rabbi Kaplan desired. Because of one thing I am sure. These symbols are not the only barrier, not the only protection, for whatever is in this box. If there is a second prophecy in this box, a determined kabbalist like the Gaon would do all in his power to ensure the safety and security of that prophecy. It took the rabbis of the council and the Gaon's now deceased great-great-grandson two days to safely open the first prophecy. We have that experience to call on, so perhaps this effort will not take as long. But I will not attempt it myself."

Herzog pulled wide the opening of the satchel, but Mullaney put a restraining hand on his arm.

"Rabbi, I know this box and its contents are in their rightful place with you and the council," said Mullaney. "But I would be derelict in my duty if I didn't secure a promise from you before we allow this package to leave our control."

"You want to know what's in the box," Herzog said, nodding his head.

"And if there is a message, you want to know what it says and what it means. Correct?"

"And we want to know first," said Mullaney. "Ambassador Cleveland or me . . . we want to be the first person you contact once the box is open and the message deciphered. Agreed?"

"You have my word, Agent Mullaney. You will know what we have found as soon as we know ourselves." Herzog extended his hand.

Mullaney looked at the hand that had just unwrapped the box of death.

"It's safe," said Herzog, an amused smile on his face.

Mullaney reached out and grasped Herzog's hand. And his fingers were crushed in the viselike grip of a bricklayer. *Safe?*

33

US Embassy, Tel Aviv
July 20, 9:41 a.m.

After a quick knock, the door to Cleveland's inner office was pushed open. Jarrod Goldberg, deputy chief of mission at the US embassy, stood in the doorway, his hand still on the door handle.

"The embassy in Amman just got a tip. David Meir is in Amman," Goldberg said, his voice flat, emotionless, betraying none of his thoughts. "We're checking, but it appears King Abdullah may be in Amman also. They will be making the announcement together."

"Not surprising," said Cleveland. He relaxed in his chair and pushed back from his desk. "Thank you, Jarrod."

"Do you want me to assemble the—"

"Thank you, Jarrod," Cleveland interrupted. "Give me a few more minutes. Ruth and I have a few more issues to discuss. I'll let you know when to call together the team."

"Yes, sir," Goldberg responded, again his voice as flat as a calm sea. The door closed and latched with a soft click.

Ruth Hughes held Cleveland's gaze for a long moment. "You don't trust him. And he knows it."

"Trust? I don't know," said Cleveland. He clasped his hands behind his head and stretched his weary bones. "I know Jarrod has his own agenda. And I don't think it's the same as mine." Cleveland stood, walked around his desk, and sat in the chair next to Hughes. His words were for her ears only. "Ruth, I know you by reputation and recommendation. My gut tells me I can trust you. So I need your help."

"Anything, Mr. Ambassador. It would be my pleasure."

"Thank you." Cleveland paused . . . weighed his words. "We have a leak, Ruth. We may have a traitor in our midst, or simply someone with loose lips."

"Or an opposite agenda?"

"Don't know," said Cleveland. "But the attacks against me . . . the kidnapping of Palmyra . . . whoever is behind these things had inside information on where I was, where I was going. And they knew when Mullaney and Shin Bet were preparing to raid the warehouse in the Holon District. Our mission and our safety are compromised, at risk, until we uncover who is responsible."

"And you want me to keep my ears open."

"You have great ears, Ruth. They reach a long way. They reach into places beyond my ability. So yes . . . keep listening. Let me know what you hear."

Hughes's eyes searched Cleveland's face. "Yes, sir. I will do that. Gladly. Because I know *you* by reputation and by the uninhibited praise heaped upon you by people in whom I place the greatest trust. So yes, Atticus, I'll see what I can find out."

It usually didn't happen this quickly, developing trust. Like most in the Foreign Service, Cleveland was very select about when, and with whom, he would share those inner workings of his mind . . . open those compartments that would leave him vulnerable. For some reason, he had established an immediate intimacy with Mullaney.

He feels like a son, thought Cleveland, the realization a bit of a surprise, but a blessing nonetheless.

And now he assessed that in Hughes he had found not only an ally, but also a partner in whom he could trust.

I am a blessed man.

Cleveland sat up in his chair and arrayed himself with the full power of his position. "This information resides only at the highest level of the State Department, Ruth. Other than Mullaney, who was with me when the information was delivered, no one outside of Secretary Townsend's closest circle—at least on our side—has a hint. It's got to stay that way."

Hughes mirrored Cleveland's solemn seriousness. "Yes, sir . . . you have my word."

A bonding moment. Professional to professional. In that silence, Cleveland knew he could trust Hughes to have his back and keep his secrets. There was no greater service she could give him. And it warmed his heart.

"We have what we believe is an infallible source in King Hussein's inner circle, a man we believe speaks for the king and with his full knowledge and direction. The Jordanians are confident of two things: that King Abdullah should not be trusted and that the Saudis have called in a debt. For the past twenty years, the Saudi government has bankrolled Pakistan's development—"

"The nukes?" Hughes interrupted, bolting upright in her chair. "Abdullah has called for his nuclear weapons to be delivered?" For a moment, Cleveland could see beneath Hughes's tough exterior. Not only was she surprised, she was stunned, shocked, and shaken. "God help us, Atticus . . . a nuclear Saudi Arabia changes everything. We better start building hardened bunkers under every American foreign office in the Middle East. The Saudis get nukes . . . somebody will get antsy and start lobbing warheads in the desert. Gotta happen."

Her response echoed his own fears. But . . .

"What about the peace treaty . . . if there is a mutual defense treaty?" said Cleveland. "Is that all a smoke screen for Abdullah's real intentions? Why . . . why go to such lengths?"

Hughes was shaking her head. "No . . . Abdullah will take the peace if he can get it," she said. "There's too much benefit for the Saudis in this peace—an independent Palestine; an alliance with the most powerful military force in the region, Israel; a massive, united, military, political, and economic confederation with the power not only to thwart Iran's aggressive intentions, but perhaps also strong enough to cut the legs out from under the Iranian mullahs. No, sir, Abdullah will take the peace if he can get it. And he'll gladly sacrifice Hezbollah and Hamas to do it.

"But," said Hughes, "Abdullah doesn't think he'll get the peace. At the very least, he's hedging his bets. The odds are pretty high that David Meir won't be able to corral enough votes in the Knesset to ratify the covenant. And even if he could, which I doubt, the opposition to this treaty both inside and outside Israel will be fierce. There will be no peace with this peace. Only more upheaval. But . . . but . . . sir . . . imagine the Middle East with a nuclear Israel, nuclear Saudi Arabia, and, if President Boylan gets his accord with the government in Tehran, in the near future a nuclear Iran. The Israelis are a pragmatic bunch who will risk destruction to avoid extinction. They could be prodded into a first-strike scenario that would leave this part of the world a desolate, contaminated, radioactive wasteland."

"And leave the rest of the world starving for oil," said Cleveland. "A different kind of end days, I think."

Silence, profound in what was left unsaid, hung in Cleveland's office like a shroud on a casket, hiding the inevitability of death. A honking of horns from the street below penetrated through the windows.

Cleveland snapped the silence. "You have the sources, Ruth," he said. "We need to know."

She nodded her head. It was not only in agreement. It was a promise of determination. Of results.

"Thank you for asking for my help," Hughes said with the passion of an embrace. "I'm honored that you would trust me with this information and entrust me with this mission."

"Well, Ruth, that—"

"Sir?" Hughes interrupted. "There is one thing I've heard that I could use some clarity about."

"Certainly," said Cleveland, sensing a turn in the conversation. "What's that, Ruth?"

"Tell me about the Vilna Gaon's second prophecy and the box that is killing people."

Cleveland barely had time to register his surprise when a bellow of laughter erupted from his belly. "Oh, Ruth . . . you are good."

Cleveland looked at the clock on the wall and realized he needed to wrap up this conversation soon, regardless of how much he relished this interaction. He handed Hughes the cup of coffee he had poured from the well-used urn on the credenza and returned to his desk.

"So I don't know anything about the second prophecy," said Cleveland as he leaned into his desk and rested his body against his folded arms. "Just that I was told there was a second prophecy inside a box that has been closely guarded for over two hundred years."

"Okay, but what do you think? And what did you mean earlier when you said the division of Israel will be a curse for everyone involved?"

A door had been opened, perhaps inadvertently, but Cleveland now debated within himself whether it was appropriate, or the right time, for him to use that door. He took a step.

"Ruth, the Bible is a book full of prophecies—some fulfilled already, a great deal of those prophecies yet to come. There's a prophecy in Isaiah 19 that predicts a highway will be built from Egypt to Assyria and that the Egyptians and Assyrians will worship together. It says, 'In that day Israel will be the third, along with Egypt and Assyria, a blessing on the earth. The Lord Almighty will bless them, saying, "Blessed be Egypt my people, Assyria my handiwork, and Israel my inheritance."' Interesting, but that hasn't happened yet. And there's another prophecy that Jewish cities will grow in Egypt and Jews will worship in temples in Egypt. And that hasn't happened.

"But there are prophetic statements in the Bible that have already been fulfilled," Cleveland continued. "There are sixty-one specific prophecies in the Bible about Messiah, and three hundred references to those prophecies. Back in the fifties, a math professor gave six hundred students a math probability problem that would determine the odds of the accidental fulfillment of eight specific prophecies by one person. The answer was one-in-ten to the seventeenth power."

"The odds were one in ten, with seventeen zeroes after the ten?" said Hughes. "I don't know the name of that number."

"One hundred quadrillion. That's what I've read," said Cleveland. "But the results were confirmed by the American Scientific Association, which found that the principles of probability were applied 'in a proper and convincing way.' Ruth, Jesus fulfilled all sixty-one prophetic statements about Messiah. That possibility is impossible."

Hughes's eyes wandered around the room, unable to focus and stop on an object. It was clear to Cleveland that Hughes was carefully considering the import and impact of his words.

"Be careful, Mr. Ambassador," she said. "You might almost make me a believer."

"Is that so bad?"

Hughes smiled. "You had a point, sir. Where were you going with this? Why will the division of Israel be a curse?"

Seeds had been planted. Cleveland decided to leave it at that.

"There is another prophecy in Scripture that has not been fulfilled," said Cleveland. "It comes from the book of Joel, chapter 3. I've memorized this one. It says, 'I will gather all nations and bring them down to the Valley of Jehoshaphat. There I will put them on trial for what they did to my inheritance, my people Israel, because they scattered my people among the nations and divided up my land.' There are other translations that say 'I will put them on trial and judge them.' The valley of Jehoshaphat is the same as the Kidron Valley outside the Old City of Jerusalem. It's also known as the valley of judgment."

Cleveland got out of his chair, stretched once again, and turned to Hughes. "Ruth, in the geopolitical realm, creating a Palestinian state out of some of the land conquered by Israel in the sixty-seven war makes a lot of sense. Logically, I can understand it. But as a Christian who believes the Bible is the revealed Word of God, it shakes me to my soul to think that the United States could become a willing partner to this proposed covenant . . . to this dividing up of Israel. To me, it just doesn't make sense to ignore God's promises."

The ambassador glanced at his wristwatch. "C'mon," said Cleveland, "we need to get going and get the team together."

"One thought, Mr. Ambassador?" Hughes got up and joined Cleveland at his still-closed door. "I believe in power. I believe power resides in the hands of the strongest guy at the table. Power—the need, the hunger for power of any kind—is the most fundamental desire of the human heart. As long as there are human beings on this earth, there will be a fight for power. No disrespect, sir . . . but your Bible, your prophecies, will never prevent that battle for power."

In the world that Ruth Hughes occupied, out of her experience, Cleveland could understand her perspective.

"I believe in power too, Ruth," he said. "Just in a different realm . . . for a different purpose."

34

US Ambassador's Residence, Tel Aviv
July 20, 10:20 a.m.

Two rabbis in long black coats and wide-brimmed black hats carried a large, rectangular object between them. The object was about five feet long and two feet wide, and it was clearly heavy as the rabbis struggled under its weight. The Israeli flag was draped over and wrapped around the object, and as the rabbis carried it through the open doors of the US ambassador's residence, the marines stationed on either side of the door stood at attention and snapped a salute.

Like a funeral procession, Rabbi Israel Herzog and Mullaney slow-stepped behind the struggling rabbis, somber looks on their faces. Shifting the object in their hands, the rabbis slid the object into the back seat of their waiting automobile. Herzog and Mullaney stood by the side of the car.

"Do you think they're watching?" asked Herzog, speaking to Mullaney but keeping his eyes on the object being wrestled into the car.

"I would be surprised if they are not," said Mullaney.

"Good idea . . . making it look like a coffin," said Herzog. "And the flag was a great touch. How did you get the carton so heavy?"

"Surrounded the box with rocks," said Mullaney.

"Well, thank you for making such an effort to throw our adversaries off the scent. Although," said Herzog, "I won't feel completely in the clear until we've gotten ourselves and our cargo safely inside the Hurva."

"Please let me know when you arrive," said Mullaney, passing Herzog his business card. "This is my personal cell number. Please call when you get there . . . and let me know as soon as you have some information on what's inside the box."

Herzog turned, took Mullaney's card, and then grasped Mullaney's hand before he realized his danger. Mullaney winced at the rabbi's viselike grip and almost missed his whispered response. "Certainly . . . and thank you for making my week . . . my month. Nothing this exciting has happened since the Gaon's first prophecy was revealed. I'll contact you as soon as we have something concrete."

Mullaney watched the car pull away from the entrance. *God, help them, please. And keep them safe.*

Parker stood just inside the front door. Mullaney was beginning to read her fairly well. Now there was worry. Not fear, but anxiety surrounded her like fog on a London morning.

"Walk with me?" asked Parker.

Before Mullaney could answer, Parker had turned on her heel and started toward the back of the residence. He had to step quickly to catch up with her.

"Brian . . . what do you think is going on?" Parker said as they walked through the reception hall. She headed for the french doors to the flagstone patio that spanned the back of the entire house and led to the expansive gardens that looked out over the Mediterranean. "I mean . . . what have we gotten ourselves into? Ever since Dad got that box . . . prophecies and curses and people out to kill us to get that box back. And now this—the most dangerous kabbalah warning this rabbi has ever seen? Something that nearly gave him a heart attack? And"—she stopped on a dime and spun to face him, their bodies almost colliding—"what about all this Messiah stuff?" she said, just inches from his face. "Dad's been talking about Jesus's return since I was a little girl. I don't know what to make of it all. But . . . I'm frightened . . . frightened by all of it. Brian, what . . . where are we?"

He knew Parker's strength, but Mullaney could see the gestation of tears and fears in Parker's eyes. Over her shoulder he spied two chairs, shaded by a palm tree. "Here . . . let's sit down."

In the few moments it took to get settled, Mullaney tried to bring his own thoughts into order. He faced Parker head on. "I'll add something to your list," said Mullaney. "Does the danger surrounding the box and the prophecy have any connection to the announcement of a sudden and implausible peace treaty between the Arabs and the Jews? One of the embassy staff heard it's called the Ishmael Covenant. An interesting name in the light of biblical history. Can this covenant and the Gaon's prophecies be connected in some way?"

Mullaney rested his elbows on his knees and leaned in closer, keeping his voice low.

"I'm beginning to think it might all be somewhat connected," he said. "I'm far from an expert on these things, but I know the Bible says something about Israel getting involved with a peace treaty as part of the last days. I don't know how that squares with the idea of Messiah's or Jesus's return, depending on your faith, but there's an awful lot going on—apparently random things that are all beginning to run together. My gut intuition and my reading of the Bible makes me wonder. Perhaps it's not all random. Perhaps all that we're involved with and all that's happening around us are part of some master plan. God's master plan. Maybe we *are* in . . ."

"Don't you dare say it!" snapped Parker. "I'm feeling shaky enough already. If . . . *if* . . . what do we do? Brian, what does Dad do? How can we be safe—ever be safe—if we're staring down the end of the world?"

Ankara
July 20, 10:46 a.m.

The specter-like form of Assan levitated across the stone tile, no evidence of his feet touching the floor beneath his motionless black robes. He came to a halt beside a high, angled table where the Turk was examining a leather-bound book with thick, brittle pages. The Turk, to prove a point, allowed Assan to wait while he turned to the next page and surveyed an ancient map of Jerusalem from the time of the Byzantine Empire.

It always gave the Turk a rush of pleasure to exercise power. Even over someone as weak as Assan.

"Yes?"

Assan bowed. "There has been activity at the residence," he said. "The ambassador has left with his security detail for the embassy. He was carrying the leather satchel with him."

"He did not try to conceal the bag?"

"No, Master," said Assan, a smirk of contempt tinting his words.

"Soon after, a vendor's truck pulled up to the back entry, one who sells commercial bottled water. The driver delivered ten crates of the twenty-liter plastic bottles. He left with an old, fairly dented, dispensing device for the large water bottles. Rolled it into his delivery van using a hand truck. It must have been heavy."

Assan hesitated.

"What else?" inquired the Turk.

"Sometime after the delivery truck departed, an automobile arrived with three rabbis. They remained in the residence for quite some time. When the three rabbis left the residence," said Assan, "two were struggling to carry what looked to be a small coffin. The shape was right, but it was obscured, covered, by an Israeli flag. The guards at the door saluted when the coffin passed."

Tapping one of his long fingernails on the open page of the book, the Turk nodded. "They think us fools? Who do we have at the residence?"

"Two watchers . . . one in front, one in back."

"What did they do?" asked the Turk, a threat lingering behind the question.

"One stayed on watch. One followed the rabbis," said Assan triumphantly. "We know where we can find the ambassador. And the water delivery . . . our men thought it too obvious."

The Turk nodded. "And what of the rabbis?"

"The automobile drove to Jerusalem, to the Hurva Synagogue. We have confirmed one of them to be the chief rabbi of the Rabbinate Council. The small coffin, still wrapped in the flag, was carried into the synagogue."

The Turk looked up from the book. Assan's eyes were downcast, directed toward the stone floor. "The Hurva? Yes. That makes sense . . . descendants of the Gaon's disciples. You did well."

"Thank you, Master. And now the box is within our grasp," said Assan. "It is ours to take."

"Perhaps," said the Turk, closing the book. "If we wanted to possess the box." He turned and stared hard at the top of Assan's bald head. "And perhaps you forget your place? Is it for you to determine what steps we should take?"

The Turk was gratified to see a shiver of fear ripple across Assan's bowed shoulders. Assan bent over even farther, the upper part of his body now parallel to the floor.

"Forgive me, Excellency." The words trembled across Assan's lips. "It was not my intention. I—"

"Enough," snapped the Turk. "The two disciples who escaped to Ashkelon . . . where are they?"

"South of Ramallah, near the major intersection, equidistant between Ashkelon, Tel Aviv, and Jerusalem" said Assan. His legs were shaking as much as his voice. "Waiting for your instructions, Excellency."

The Turk eased himself off the stool. His movements were fluid and languid like a snake coming awake in the sun. He lowered his head and whispered into Assan's ear.

"Very well, my obedient one," he hissed. "Perhaps now we can remove the threat of that box and its message destroying our plans and thwart the Gaon's intentions, once and for all time."

In the dungeon-like basement, bathed in red heat, slathered with the reek of decay, the Turk bowed before the yellow eyes.

"We believe," said the Turk, "the box has been transferred to the synagogue of the Lithuanian in Jerusalem."

"Very well," slithered the voice. "That the message now resides in the Jews' house will suit our plans. Send an order to the Disciples. Obliterate the Hurva, destroy it completely, and everything that is in it . . . the synagogue, this box of plague, and the prophecy of power that hides within it. We must destroy the Lithuanian's message—his warning and the secret he obtained that could once again thwart all our designs."

There was a swelling of barbed malice in the silence. "*You* . . . must."

35

Hurva Synagogue, Jerusalem
July 20, 11:24 a.m.

Fourteen members of the rabbinate were gathered around the roughly hewn wooden table in a locked basement room of the Hurva Synagogue. In the middle of the table rested the wooden box Rabbi Herzog had acquired from the ambassador's residence. Standing at the midpoint of the table, his hands held above the box, Rabbi Herzog began chanting in Hebrew. "The Lord our God, the Lord is One." The other thirteen rabbis answered in unison with the same words, repeated over and over as Herzog lifted the lid of the wooden box and pulled away the purple velvet covering.

While the rabbis surrounding Herzog began chanting in words that were not Hebrew but Aramaic . . . incantations of the ancient rite of kabbalah . . . Herzog and the other chief rabbi spoke to each other in hushed tones.

"It was the Tree of Life symbol that stopped me," said Herzog. "The double mezuzah is a stern warning. But then I looked more closely at the Hamsa and the Tree of Life and my blood froze. I've read a lot about these symbols, particularly pounded into metal. Some are warnings, some are promises, some are deadly. I've never read of any as powerful as this. Let's pray that this ritual can open the way for us to safely access what is inside the box."

Herzog and his counterpart rabbi took hyssop branches, dipped them in a basin of ram's blood and sprinkled the blood over the top of the metal box. They dipped the hyssop branches in the blood a second time and then a third time, sprinkling the blood over the box each time. After the third sprinkling, Herzog and the other chief rabbi joined in the Aramaic chanting of the other dozen rabbis.

With the finality of a casket lid slamming shut, the chanting stopped.

Herzog picked up the still bloody pelt of ram's wool. Grasping the wooly outside, Herzog laid the bloody inside of the pelt on the top of the metal box. He pushed the pelt down along the sides of the box and covered it on all sides except its bottom.

He looked at the other chief rabbi. They knew the Aaronic blessing was effective in protecting the guardian's life if he touched the metal box. They were not as confident that this kabbalistic ritual would protect them, or any of the other twelve rabbis, if . . . when . . . they tried to open the box.

"The Gaon would have intended that the rabbinate be capable of opening the box to discover what is inside," said the other chief rabbi.

"Yes, he would," said Herzog. "But still . . ."

Herzog took a deep breath. "Only one way to find out." Halting once, just above the surface of the wool, he placed his hands on the wool along the top ridge of the box. Using his thumbs on the two corners of the top, Herzog hesitantly exerted upward pressure on the lid. It didn't budge. With a sideways glance at his colleague, Herzog pressed upward on the lid with more pressure. He felt the metal give . . . then a pop as the lid cleared from the rest of the box. Without taking his hands from the wool, or allowing the ram's pelt to lose connection with the box, Herzog eased the lid backward.

The front edge of the ram's pelt still covered the opening between the lid and the box. With a glance to the gathering of rabbis, Herzog began reciting a prayer of protection, the other rabbis following suit. And then he peeked into the shadows inside of the box.

***

The Cardo, Jerusalem
July 20, 11:38 a.m.

They stayed in the shadows under the remnant of roof as they moved through the Cardo in the blistering midday heat. Now a series of full and partial Roman columns, excavated twenty feet below the surface of Habad Street in Jerusalem, the Cardo was, in Roman and Byzantine times, the main market street of Jerusalem. Running from north to south, the original Cardo stretched from the Damascus Gate in the north to the Zion Gate in the south and was twenty-two meters wide. In the second century, shoppers would jostle past goats and sheep in the crowded Cardo market, visiting the shops of spice merchants or metal workers, trying to remain in the shade of the overhanging roof and out of the desert sun that baked the center of the street.

The columns and a replicated section of half the roof were all that remained of the Roman Cardo, no longer a wide thoroughfare that split the Old City in two but now only ruined remains that were a magnet for tourists.

Their heads covered and their faces obscured by battered, wide-brimmed hats, the two men looked like workers on a dig—their dark pants dirty and covered in dust, their laborer's shirts stained with sweat and soil. The Turk had told them this would be their way in. Other workers, other excavators had been there before them. They needed to look the part.

One wore a backpack and led the way. The other tilted slightly to the left, compensating for the heavy canvas bag he lugged in his right hand. They crossed the Cardo area that was once a market and slipped under an archway that led them back under the street level. They stopped at an iron gate that blocked any advance. The leader pointed to the chain and padlock securing the gate, then turned back toward the columns, blocking the other man from view as he withdrew a compact set of bolt cutters from the canvas bag and made quick work of the chain, pushing open the iron gate.

Once through the gate, closing it behind them, the men walked along the underground street, past shuttered shops that provided fake antiquities and useless souvenirs to some of the two million tourists who annually overran the Old City of Jerusalem. They had less than two hours to accomplish their mission, when the shops would reopen and their escape would be compromised. At the opposite end of the passage was a locked, heavy wooden door under a limestone arch. Stopping at the door, the man with the canvas bag withdrew a black, pencil-sized shape and inserted it—instead of a key—into the large lock.

The two men stepped away from the door, pressing against the wall on either side. With the push of a button, the pencil shape erupted with a short burst of blinding light, a stream of sizzling sparks falling onto the cobblestones of the passageway. When the sparks subsided, the leader pulled against an iron ring fastened to the door. It resisted, then snapped open, screeching on rusty hinges. Without a look behind them, the two men slipped inside and shut the wooden door behind them.

The two men played the intense beams of their Mini Maglites over the rubble and mountains of building materials that were scattered across the area in front of them. They were now in an area being excavated and constructed by a quasi-governmental agency with broad powers and limited oversight, the Company for the Reconstruction and Development of the Jewish Quarter. This was one of several projects the company had underway in the Old City of Jerusalem . . . reconstruction of a Byzantine underground passageway that stretched between the Cardo and the Hurva Synagogue, through a second-century archway that was uncovered in 2011.

Across a broad, open room, a wooden ladder was propped against a hole in the wall. The hole had been punched through the limestone wall that, for centuries, had sealed the Byzantine archway and hidden the tunnel that snaked beneath Jerusalem's streets to the foundation of the new Hurva Synagogue. The original Hurva, constructed in the eighteenth century, was twice destroyed and rebuilt, the new synagogue resting on the foundation stones of the earlier buildings. This new Hurva was finally dedicated in 2010. All memory of the tunnel from the Cardo to the Hurva had been buried under the rubble of centuries.

The leader held the beam of his Maglite on the ladder. Once up the ladder, through the hole, and down a tight, twisting passageway, they would be positioned under the Hurva.

Hefting the heavy canvas bag, the other man navigated around the piles of materials and approached the bottom of the ladder.

I hope we brought enough.

36

Hurva Synagogue, Jerusalem
July 20, 11:40 a.m.

The paper was thick, heavy vellum. Its edges were roughly cut, as if it had been ripped from its source. Herzog had stuck pins into each of the corners, holding the vellum in place. It sat on a piece of black velvet, tacked to a wooden board. Around Herzog, the other members of the Rabbinate Council leaned in as close as possible without pushing against Herzog's shoulders.

"The Gaon was well-versed in Torah codes," said Herzog's colleague. "Our challenge now is to determine which of the codes was used for this document."

"But what is this at the bottom?" asked Herzog. "Certainly not Torah code. And these two lines of symbols . . . what could they signify?"

"I don't know, Israel. But let's examine the message first. Perhaps the code from the Gaon's first message will give us the key."

US Embassy, Tel Aviv
July 20, 12:15 p.m.

Normal business at the US embassy had come to a standstill a few minutes before noon—a pause in life that was repeated in homes, schools, businesses, and government offices across the Middle East.

Except for the security details, nearly all the staff of the US Mission to Israel were in the cafeteria, huddled around a flat screen TV as events that would redeem the past, bring upheaval to the present, and profoundly alter the future unfolded in Amman, Jordan.

Ambassador Joseph Atticus Cleveland sat at a table near the front, some of his key staff at the same table, others scattered among the rest of the embassy's personnel. Cleveland wanted to be with his people and not sequestered in his office. This moment was life changing, particularly for those who served their country overseas in the diplomatic corps. He wanted his team to draw strength from his calm demeanor in the face of rampant uncertainty. Very soon, he would need them all . . . at the top of their game.

They were watching the international transmission of CNN, which showed a large formal meeting room, ornately decorated. The room was dominated by a long, elliptical table. Along the far side of the table sat ten men. Nine of them were the rulers or leaders of Middle Eastern countries—six in elegant, ornate versions of the traditional Arab dress of kaftan and keffiyeh and three in expensive, hand-made Western suits. The tenth man was the head of the Palestinian Authority, soon to be leader of the nation of Palestine.

The CNN transmission regularly shifted to different perspectives, at times showing the entire group, at other times focusing on the speaker . . . or the reactions of those listening to the speaker. At the moment, King Abdullah of Saudi Arabia was wrapping up the opening statements made by each of the nine participants.

Royal Palace, Amman, Jordan
July 20, 12:17 p.m.

"So, we come to this historic moment of peace," said King Abdullah, "a moment that many thought would never occur. A moment when all the sons of Abraham are joined together in the unity of the Ishmael Covenant . . . a covenant era that will heal wounds, end conflict, and usher in a new age of cooperation, security, and prosperity. The details of the two documents that create this covenant will be distributed after the signing. But these are the salient points."

Glancing up from behind his wire-rimmed glasses, King Abdullah looked directly into the camera. Furrows of wrinkles radiated from his deeply set eyes, fleshy bags drooping down to his cheeks. His beard was white, and his back was stooped, but his eyes . . . his eyes burned with the fire of a thousand suns. Abdullah was a king.

He picked up a piece of paper that rested on the table to his right, between him and the prime minister of Israel, David Meir.

"First, the Arab nations seated here today," said Abdullah, "will join with our brothers in Egypt, who years ago took this step, in signing a Declaration of Peace with the state of Israel. This Declaration of Peace specifically recognizes the validity of the state of Israel and opens the door to full diplomatic recognition and relations between all the nations represented here. Second, the nations seated here today will enter into a mutual defense treaty with Israel, encompassing the entire Middle East in a blanket of security and cooperation, each of us pledging to defend each other from any act of aggression."

King Abdullah sat in the middle of the assembled leaders. Meir was on his right, King Hussein II of Jordan on his left. Spread out on either side were the rulers from Egypt, Oman, Kuwait, United Arab Emirates, Bahrain, and Qatar, along with the head of the Palestinian Authority. Abdullah turned to his right. "Mr. Prime Minister, all of us extend to you our thanks for accepting this covenant and for your courageous willingness to also take this bold step for peace."

Meir inclined his head toward King Abdullah. "Thank you." He turned immediately to address the cameras directly. "Two generations of Israelis have lived in hope for such a day as this, a day when Israel's borders and its future are secure not only by means of its military strength, but also by means of its peaceful coexistence with its neighbors. One of the critical points that allowed this peace covenant to become a reality was a willingness of former adversaries to work together—particularly the emissaries of Israel, Jordan, and the Palestinian Authority. As part of the peace covenant, both Israel and Jordan have contributed territory for the creation of an independent state of Palestine. Jerusalem remains united under the sovereignty of Israel and will become our nation's capital, but the territory provided to Palestine includes a corner of East Jerusalem to become the Palestinian capital. Within twelve months, if all the elements of the covenant are ratified and working effectively, Israel will begin dismantling its West Bank separation barrier. And there is also a significant concession on the part of Jordan that will satisfy the hope of many religious Jews."

Meir looked to his left, past the Saudi monarch, to Jordanian King Hussein II.

Western-educated and relatively young compared to his counterparts, Jordan's king was a handsome, dapper man of the twenty-first century. Clean shaven, wearing a suit of Indian silk tailored in London, Hussein II looked more like a Hollywood movie star than a Middle Eastern monarch. Today he also wore a somber and solemn countenance.

"With great hope, and in recognition of the courage displayed by King Abdullah and Prime Minister Meir," the king announced, "the Hashemite Kingdom of Jordan will renounce any claim to territory that came under the control of Israel as a result of the sixty-seven conflict, some of that territory which will now become Palestine. Jordan will also remove the authority of the Waqf as the ruling body over the Temple Mount in Jerusalem, creating a new authority of joint responsibility with Israel. Lastly, in association with my Arab brothers, we have offered Israel the opportunity to erect a platform adjacent to the Temple Mount, attached to the Mount at, or near, the Eastern Gate. This new platform is intended to be used for construction of a place of worship for the Jewish people . . . a temple in Jerusalem."

The Cardo, Jerusalem
July 20, 12:19 p.m.

His partner rested his back against the side of the constricting passage, the large, canvas bag at his side. His clothes were now even darker from the perspiration that poured off his body. The leader had spread a letter-sized piece of paper on the floor of the passage and was intently examining its contents, looking up every few moments and shining his Maglite into one section of the darkness and then another.

"There," he whispered, pointing into the darkness with his light. "Fifteen meters farther on. There will be metal beams forming a corner. That will be the first location."

The other man nodded his head, pushed his body up from his seated position, grabbed the bag, and nearly dragged it behind him as he pushed farther along the passage.

Royal Palace, Amman
July 20, 12:32 p.m.

With a flutter of royal robes, King Abdullah stretched out his arms and reached toward the first of the two documents facing him on the table.

His heart racing, Israeli prime minister David Meir tried desperately to control his breathing and keep his hands steady. He hoped the perspiration he felt under his arms was not also visible on his face. Meir's world came to a stop as King Abdullah took the ornate, gold-plated fountain pen—an identical twin sitting before each of the rulers at the table—hesitated for a moment and, with the flourish of a stage actor, inscribed his name and the power of his position to the Ishmael Covenant . . . peace in the Middle East.

Turning to his right, Abdullah caught Meir's eyes and held his gaze. He held the document in his left hand and reached out his right toward the Israeli.

"Today, let us bury the past," said Abdullah.

Meir accepted the handshake and then the treaty. "And let's pray the past doesn't follow us into the future."

Meir felt the king's hand stiffen. In the fleeting moment of a heartbeat, a hardness crossed the king's face that made Meir feel as if he had been violated. The moment passed. Meir knew most of the civilized world was probably watching his every action.

Uncertain whether he would celebrate or regret his action, the prime minister of Israel took the pen before him and scrawled his name across the bottom of the page. *May God help us now.*

37

Hurva Synagogue, Jerusalem
July 20, 12:34 p.m.

Herzog sat in the office of the rabbinate on the west side of the Hurva Synagogue, in the shadow of the building's huge dome, his elbows planted on the top of his desk holding up his throbbing head. What had started so hopefully had quickly become torture for the council, so much so that the members of the rabbinate had asked for a break. After applying every type of kabbalistic code they knew, the rabbinate were no closer to understanding what was written on the paper that had caused so much trouble.

They had measured the writing of the Vilna Gaon against three types of Torah codes known to be used by kabbalists—Temurah, Gematria, and Notarikon—and had yet to find the correct cipher. Temurah involved rearranging letters or words: replacing the first letter of the Hebrew alphabet with the last letter, the second with the next-to-last, and so on; replacing each letter with the preceding letter; or replacing the first letter of the alphabet with the twelfth, the second with the thirteenth, and so on. Gematria involved assigning a numerical value to each Hebrew letter, and Notarikon used the first letter of a word or the final letter to stand for another.

Nothing worked. The words of the Gaon remained a mystery. Herzog didn't know what to try next.

He could smell the coffee before the cup was placed on his desk, just inches from his drooping head. His long-time assistant, Chaim, moved to a side chair, a cup of coffee in his hands as well.

"You've tried everything you know?" asked Chaim.

Herzog raised his head and nodded as he reached for the steaming cup.

"Then perhaps you should try something you don't know."

The cup suspended in his hands, the chief rabbi raised his eyes and looked to the right at his aide. "What do you mean?"

"Well, you have looked at the kabbalistic Torah codes that you expected the Gaon to use, to no avail. So were there other codes available to the Gaon in his time that were not connected to kabbalah?" Chaim drained his coffee cup and set it aside. "I met an American Jew a few years ago, David Kahn, who wrote a book called *The Codebreakers*. He told me that people have been writing in codes since antiquity. Even Caesar had his own cipher. What else would the Gaon have access to that he could expect others would know about in the future? This is a coded message that the Gaon expected to be deciphered. So there must be a way. What were the ways available to him in his time?"

Herzog was on his feet, the dropped cup spilling coffee across his desk. "Chaim, google sixteenth- and seventeenth-century ciphers and cryptologists. Then call the rabbis together," he said as he headed for the door. "We're not done yet."

The Cardo, Jerusalem
July 20, 12:46 p.m.

The fourth and last charge of Semtex explosive was lifted into a gaping crevice in one of the large foundation stones that disappeared up into the rough-hewn rock ceiling at the end of the narrow passage. The leader looked at the plastic being pushed into the hole and wondered . . . worried.

His voice was urgent, but low. "Is this enough? Will it work?" asked the leader.

"More than enough," said the bomber. "Crack the spine of the building with the first two. The others will shatter the foundation. Then it simply implodes."

The leader nodded. "Good . . . we don't want to fail."

US Embassy, Tel Aviv
July 20, 12:51 p.m.

As the TV cameras moved from face to face and signatures were added to both the covenant and the mutual defense pact, Ambassador Cleveland stood up from the table at the front of the cafeteria and turned to face his staff. "All right, let's get to work. You all know your assignments. I want to know anything and everything that even smells like it's connected to this treaty. Jarrod, send out the embassy alert. Make sure all US citizens are warned to watch for communications from the embassy. Let's go."

The Cardo, Jerusalem
July 20, 1:02 p.m.

The leader edged open the heavy wooden door, first pressing his ear against a sliver of space, listening for any sounds from the shops in the underground passageway. After thirty heartbeats, he leaned only some of his weight against the door's bulk. Other than a creak from the rusty hinges, there was no sound. He looked around the edge of the door. The shops remained closed. They had, perhaps, ten more minutes.

Hurva Synagogue, Jerusalem
July 20, 1:03 p.m.

Israel Herzog began calculating the odds. Would he truly live to see Messiah?

He looked once again at the copy of the prophecy in his hand. Possible. Perhaps more than possible.

Messiah. The end of days. The culmination of history. He read the translation of the prophecy for perhaps the hundredth time.

"You are wondering if it will be in your lifetime?"

Herzog looked up at his colleague, the other chief rabbi of the Rabbinate Council of Israel. "I'm wondering," said Herzog, "if it will be tomorrow. And I'm wondering if any of us are ready."

The rabbis, coleaders of the council, one Sephardic and the other Hasidic, sat in a corner of the rabbinate offices on the western flank of the Hurva Synagogue in Jerusalem. On a table across the room sat two boxes, one wooden and one metal, the metal box covered by the still bloody fleece of a perfect lamb. It was the metal box—the box of power that had brought so much death—that had finally surrendered the prophecy and helped the council members decipher its meaning. Now they had to live with its promise.

And Herzog needed to fulfill his promise. "I need to call Agent Mullaney."

"What will you tell him . . . how will you explain what we have discovered," asked his colleague as Herzog approached the table.

Herzog looked at the slip of paper in his hands. Amazing how such a thin fragment of paper could assign such massive, oppressive weight to his shoulders. He held a message that, if true, could alter history.

"I will tell him the truth," said Herzog, tearing his eyes away from the explosive message he held in his fingers. "I just don't know how much of the truth I'll tell him."

US Embassy, Tel Aviv
July 20, 1:08 p.m.

Mullaney was walking down the hall on the third floor of the embassy, approaching his office, when his phone rang. His caller was abrupt, his voice breathless.

"Agent Mullaney . . . this message was not in the same code as the first prophecy," rattled off Rabbi Herzog. "If anything, it's even more difficult and esoteric than the Torah codes the Gaon used in other prophecies. Nearly impossible for anyone other than the council to decipher. At first, we were completely mystified. We tried every Torah code we knew and came up with gibberish. In very short order, we were stopped dead in our tracks."

"I'm sorry to hear—"

"No . . . wait . . . we succeeded," Herzog ran on. "The Gaon left us a clue that opened a door that only we would see. Once we pierced that door, the message revealed itself like a budding rose. Agent Mullaney, I must see you so I can share with you what we discovered. When can we meet?"

Mullaney looked at the clock on the wall of his office. The announcement of the Ishmael Covenant was less than an hour old, and already Hezbollah was firing rockets into the northern settlements of Israel; Hamas was orchestrating mass demonstrations—punctuated by the hurling of Molotov cocktails—in the ragged and dusty streets of Gaza. "I can't come there, Rabbi," said Mullaney. "There's just too much going on since the announcement . . . I'm needed here."

"What announcement?"

"The Ishmael Covenant," said Mullaney, "The peace treaty between Israel and all its Arab neighbors: Egypt, Jordan, Saudi Arabia, and all the Gulf nations. You haven't heard?"

There was silence on the other end of the line.

"Yes, there were rumors," said Herzog. "Was an independent Palestine part of this covenant?"

"Yes."

"And what did Israel receive in return?"

"Recognition of its right to exist," said Mullaney. "A mutual defense pact, linking the security of Jews and Arabs together. And permission to build a temple on a platform connected to the Temple Mount."

More silence. This time the silence sounded much more profound. Mullaney could almost hear Herzog's mind twisting around the new information. "So . . . the third temple will become a reality. Interesting times we live in, Agent Mullaney. The signs of Messiah are everywhere. Which makes the information I now have in hand much more valuable to you . . . to all of us."

Mullaney could hear Herzog's voice speaking to someone else. "All right. I'll meet you at the embassy in Tel Aviv in two hours. And Agent Mullaney?"

"Yes?"

"Prepare yourself for another shock," said Herzog. "What I'm bringing to you will radically alter the meaning of what was announced today. I'll see you in two hours."

Hurva Synagogue, Jerusalem
July 20, 1:09 p.m.

Parking was a nightmare in the Old City of Jerusalem, particularly in the Jewish Quarter where narrow, twisting, cobblestone streets dominated the neighborhood, and buildings were pressed together tighter than a junior rabbi's allowance. Herzog's assistant, Chaim, exited the synagogue into Hurva Square, turned right, and worked his way south, around the synagogue. He slipped through the crowd of young office workers, wannabe musicians, and tourists who filled the square day and night, past Beit El Street, and into the serpentine shadows of Mishmarot HaKehuna Street. He avoided Ha-Yehudim Street that ran alongside the Cardo. It was more direct, but endlessly clogged with tourists. His destination was the postage-stamp public parking lot, hard against the Old City wall, east of the Zion Gate.

He didn't understand why a rabbi . . . *the chief rabbi* . . . couldn't secure a parking permit for space closer to the Hurva. And it was Chaim who always had to drop the rabbi off at the synagogue and then often waste an hour searching for a vacant parking place.

He reached the black Toyota, unlocked the car, and opened the door. Things would be different if he were the chief rabbi.

The Cardo, Jerusalem
July 20, 1:11 p.m.

They slipped out of the Cardo, crossed the Habad, and melted into the human flow of the Armenian Quarter. In the lee of the Assyrian Convent on Ararat Street, the leader withdrew a cell phone from the side pocket of his backpack. He quickly punched in the number. One ring . . . two . . .

Hurva Synagogue, Jerusalem
July 20, 1:11 p.m.

Herzog handed the slip of paper to his coleader. "Keep this one here. Chaim and I will take the other copy of the message and deliver it to Agent Mullaney. While we're in route to Tel Aviv, if you have any additional thoughts on what to divulge, call me immediately."

Such life changing—history changing—words. Herzog passed the slip of paper to his colleague. He wondered once again if he would truly live to see the arrival of the Jewish Messiah. Could that be possible?

"Of course," said Herzog. "We will need—"

The Cardo, Jerusalem
July 20, 1:11 p.m.

The ground beneath their feet heaved as if the earth were giving birth.

Two . . . three . . . four ticked off the leader as a series of lethal explosions hurled furious thunder down the echoing canyons of the Jewish Quarter. A short distance to the east, past the Cardo, a roiling eruption of smoke and debris propelled into the sky, immediately turning afternoon into dusk. A police Klaxon . . . then a second . . . ricocheted in the distance.

The leader dropped the cell phone to the stone street and ground it under his boot. They turned north toward the Muslim Quarter and the Damascus Gate, dropping broken pieces of cell phone into random trash bins along the way.

Hurva Synagogue, Jerusalem
July 20, 1:11 p.m.

For a flash of consciousness, time seemed to disengage from place . . . physics fled from reality. The earth moved. In that split second, Herzog's heart and mind jumped to the same implausible destination . . . Messiah? In the other half of the split second, a thunderous, rending explosion snapped him back to reality. As the walls of the Hurva split before his eyes, as another shattering explosion heaved the beautiful synagogue like a leaf in a hurricane, Herzog received his answer. He would not live to see the arriv—

Tons of stone and massive slabs of concrete hurtled into the basement, crashing through the council's office. Rabbi Herzog was cleaved in two by one massive shard of concrete, his colleagues buried beneath piles of stone. But two slabs formed an arch above a wooden table. Only concrete dust lightly coated the bloody lambskin draped over it.

Hurva Synagogue, Jerusalem
July 20, 1:11 p.m.

The first blast wrenched the car door out of his hands. Chaim stumbled backward and landed on his back, splayed like an offering on the shifting surface of the parking lot. He did not register the pain in his back nor the embarrassment of his position. All that registered was the echoing of one explosion after another and the mushrooming cloud of destruction from where the twice-rebuilt Hurva once stood.

Instinctively, his right hand went to his left breast. He felt the sharp edges of the envelope tucked into the inside pocket of his black suit jacket. But then Chaim was on his feet, running to the carnage, praying as he ran. Delivery of the envelope, and what it contained, would have to wait.

ACKNOWLEDGMENTS

Jesus Christ is the greatest storyteller of all time. His words have lasted longer, sold more books, and been more influential than William Shakespeare, Charles Dickens, or any writer over the last two thousand years. It may sound trite, but first I need to acknowledge the great storyteller for sharing this story with me, and the Holy Spirit for revealing characters and plotlines over the course of writing this series. As my editors can attest, I'm a gardener. I get an idea, plant it, water it, let the sun shine on it, and then see what grows, see where it goes. *All* my novels have been birthed, sustained, and completed only because God's hand was on the writing and the writer. Psalm 116:12: "How can I repay ADONAI for all his generous dealings with me?" (CJB).

The idea I had for the Empires of Armageddon series wasn't much bigger than a seedling when Pastor Nick Uva of Harvest Time Church in Greenwich, Connecticut, introduced me to the Vilna Gaon and challenged me to understand the ramifications of several end-times prophecies and how they might be pertinent to our present day. This book, and series, would be much shallower if it weren't for Pastor Nick's knowledge, wisdom, and support.

Some of the ideas about angels and their assignments came from listening to online sermons of Pastor Bill Johnson of Bethel Church in Redding, California.

It takes me a long time to write a book. So, I'm grateful to my agent, Steve Laube, who left me alone while I labored for nearly three years to write this series.

I had never intentionally written a three-book series before, so I'm grateful to all the team at Kregel Publications in Grand Rapids who extended to me an extra measure of patience and grace as they wondered, "When will the books be done?" In particular, managing editor Steve Barclift and my primary editor—Janyre Tromp—persevered through months of editing as we labored to make each of the individual books a complete story on its own merits. And much gratitude to Noelle Pedersen and Katherine Chappell of the marketing department for all your support. Thank you.

But no living human being was more vital to the coherence and conclusion of this task than my wife of forty years, Andrea. Andrea was there at the beginning, when all was excitement, and for every day thereafter during the years it took to complete this project—both the days when it flowed, and the days when I was lost and despondent. Thank you, my sweetheart, for blessing me with the time to exercise this gift.

I must extend special thanks to our daughter, Meghan, who willingly offered her time and her inventive mind for brainstorming every time I yelled "Help!" And thanks to my sister, Pat, who has been a faithful first reader.

And a special acknowledgment to Tina Heugh. Tina won a drawing—to use your name as a character in my next book—when I spoke at the Friends of the Bonita Springs Library luncheon in Florida. Tina asked me to use her mother's name, Ruth Hughes. The character of Ruth Hughes in the series is a strong woman of integrity, with a stellar business résumé. I was blessed when Tina later sent me this information about her mother that I did not know while I was writing: "My mom was a librarian for fifty-seven years, the last twenty as the first paid librarian at the Bonita Springs Public Library, where she ordered over eighty thousand books. Before that, she was head librarian for the University of Michigan Detroit branch. During World War II, she worked for Chrysler Engineering and is on the World War II commemorative wall in Washington, DC. She was civically active in Detroit as well. She became the president of the League of Women Voters after serving as membership chairperson. She also served on the boards of numerous committees. She was honored as one of Detroit's top ten working women. She is in *Who's Who of Women of the Midwest* and *Who's Who of American Women*. She was nominated to be president of the American Civil Liberties Union of the five counties of the Detroit area but had to decline because my parents were retiring to Florida." Thank you, Tina!

AUTHOR'S NOTES

I hope you enjoyed reading *Ishmael Covenant* as much as I did writing it. One of the joys I've found in writing my books, as you will see in the following notes, is injecting a lot of reality into the fiction plot—real people, real places, real events.

As a reward for getting this far, I want to offer you two free opportunities available only to readers of the Empires of Armageddon series:

- An exclusive, in-depth look at the funky Gramofon Café, a real treasure that sits in the old city of Ankara, Turkey, in the shadow of Ankara Castle . . . including traditional recipes for the Turkish delights, manti and gozleme, mentioned in the book. Plus, some photos of the café itself.
- A monthly email post that will expand upon, with greater detail, one of the topics in these author's notes.

If you're hungry to know more—or just hungry—send me an email at terrbrennan@gmail.com and I'll respond right away with these two special offers, including the recipes.

Thanks,
Terry

While *Ishmael Covenant* is a work of fiction, some plot elements are based on fact.

The story of the Vilna Gaon—Rabbi Elijah ben Shlomo Zalman (1720–1797)—is accurate in all its historical elements. He was the foremost Talmudic scholar of his age and a renowned genius on both sacred and secular learning. The story of the Gaon's prophecy about Russia and Crimea, revealed by his great-great-grandson in 2014, is true and led many to believe that the coming of the Jewish Messiah was near at hand. The Gaon did attempt three trips to Jerusalem from his native Lithuania, and the last one, only a few years before his death, ended prematurely in Konigsberg, Prussia. The story of the Gaon's *second* prophecy is a result of the author's imagination.

The Diplomatic Security Service is the federal law enforcement and security division of the US State Department. DSS agents are unique in that they are members of the US foreign service, charged with protecting diplomats and embassy personnel who are overseas, but they are also armed law enforcement officers who have the authority to investigate crime and arrest individuals both on domestic soil and in collaboration with international law enforcement overseas. With nearly twenty-five hundred agents here and abroad, DSS is the most widely represented law enforcement agency in the world. DSS also provides security for foreign dignitaries in the United States, for the annual United Nations General Assembly in New York City, and during the Olympics. Descriptions of the State Department's operations center in the Truman Building are accurate to the best of the author's resources.

Descriptions of the US embassy and the US ambassador's residence in Tel Aviv are accurate to 2014, before the US embassy was officially moved to Jerusalem in 2018. The US ambassador to Israel did host an enormous annual Fourth of July party, where over two thousand guests sprawled over the grounds of the residence and feasted on iconic American delights from McDonald's, Ben & Jerry's, and Domino's.

Over the course of nearly 2,500 years, the fertile crescent of the Middle East—from modern Turkey into the Tigris and Euphrates valleys in Iraq, down the Jordan valley of Palestine, and across the top of Egypt and the Nile delta—was but a portion of three vast, evolving, and at times competing empires: the Persian, the Muslim Arab, and the Ottoman empires. One of the fundamental beliefs of Islam is, in fact, that once an Islamic group or nation rules any portion of the earth, it rules that portion forever. Even though the Persians gradually converted to the Islamic faith only in the mid-seventh century, following the Muslim Arab invasion of Persia, if those empires were resurrected today, each would claim the same slice of the earth.

The descriptions of the last-days theology of the world's three great monotheistic religions—Judaism, Christianity, and Islam—are accurate. All three religions trace their roots back to Abraham and claim to be part (though different parts) of the Abrahamic covenant that God established with humanity. And each religion waits for a climactic time in history, birthed in peace, when the long-awaited One (either the Messiah, Jesus's second coming, or the Mahdi) will be revealed. While the Jewish Messiah will usher in an eternal time of peace for a world united into one confederation, both Christian and Islamic end times anticipate an ultimate and definitive armed conflict, followed by a final judgment of the good and the evil.

In 1979, when the shah of Iran was deposed by a theocratic revolution and fifty-two Americans were taken hostage and held in Tehran for 444 days, Iranian financial assets were frozen in banks around the world. Estimates vary, but in the neighborhood of twenty to thirty billion dollars was locked up in banks worldwide . . . including approximately two billion dollars in US banks. The two countries are still fighting over the money. In late 2018, the United States asked judges at the International Court of Justice to throw out an Iranian claim for nearly two billion in Iranian national bank assets that were frozen by US courts.

The question of accrued interest on those frozen funds, and how much interest is owed to Iran, continues to be a bone of contention. When four hundred million dollars was returned to Iran by the Obama Administration in January 2016—money the Iranians paid prior to 1979 for US military aircraft that were never delivered—the United States also sent Iran a payment of *1.3 billion dollars in accrued interest*. The money to pay that accrued interest came from the US Department of the Treasury's Judgment Fund, which pays judgments, or compromise settlements of lawsuits, against the government. In 2016, two US senators wrote in *Time* magazine:

> The Judgment Fund is a little-known account used to pay certain court judgments and settlements against the federal government. Each year, billions of dollars are disbursed from it, yet the fund does not fall under the annual appropriations process. Because of this, the Treasury

Department has no binding reporting requirements, and these funds are paid out with scant scrutiny. The executive branch decides what, if any, information is made available to the public.

Essentially, the Judgment Fund is an unlimited supply of money provided to the federal government to cover its own liability.

The history of the Hurva Synagogue in Jerusalem is accurate as related in this series. Construction of the main Ashkenazi synagogue, now known as the Hurva, commenced in 1701. The Jewish builders fell into debt to Muslim moneylenders and, in the midst of a dispute over repayment, Muslims burned down the building in 1721. After two smaller synagogues were erected on the edges of the original ruins, disciples of the Vilna Gaon were granted permission for construction of the second Hurva, which began in 1855. That building was destroyed in retaliation in 1948, blown up by the defeated Jordanian Arab Legion after withdrawal of Israeli forces from Jerusalem following the 1948 war for independence. Israel regained control of Jerusalem from Jordan following the 1967 war, but decades of internal disputes and indecision delayed reconstruction of the Hurva. The third construction of the building was begun in 2000, and the nineteenth-century-style building was dedicated on March 15, 2010. The Vilna Gaon prophesied that when the Hurva synagogue was completed for the third time, construction of the third temple would begin. Construction of the third temple of God *has not* yet begun, but many believe completion of the third temple will be an imminent harbinger of the last days.

The threat of "water wars" in the Middle East is accurate and continues to this day.

In 2014, according to the Turkish Department of Environmental Engineering, Turkey was using only thirty-six percent of its immense freshwater resources that flow from countless lakes and rivers in its central mountains. The two most important snow-fed rivers of the Middle East, the Tigris and Euphrates, originate in the mountains of central Turkey and are critical sources of hydroelectric power generation, irrigation, and domestic use, not only in

Turkey but also in Syria and Iraq. Yet in 2014 Turkey severely restricted the flow of the Euphrates through its largest dams, the Ataturk and Keban, strangling the once-mighty river. Turkey is also home to 120 natural lakes with additional water stored behind 550 dams. In 2014, it began its largest dam project ever, the Ilisu Dam on the Tigris.

International hydrologists claim that since 1975 Turkey's dam and hydropower constructions on the two rivers have cut water flow to Iraq by eighty percent and to Syria by forty percent. Both Syria and Iraq have accused Turkey of hoarding water and threatening their water supply.

At the same time, in 2014, the invaders of ISIS overran five major dams, one in Syria (Tishrin) and four in Iraq (Mosul, Haditha, Nuaimiyah, and Samarra), further threatening water stability in Syria and Iraq.

Meanwhile, Turkey had already begun water pipeline projects to export some of its *surplus* fresh water to Cyprus and the Middle East. Israel was originally included in the pipeline project for the Middle East but was removed after objections from the Arab states.

In the summer of 2014, the Islamic terrorist army called ISIS controlled more than 34,000 square miles in Syria and Iraq, from the Mediterranean coast to south of Baghdad. The major Iraqi cities of Mosul, Fallujah, and Tikrit were overrun, including key oil refineries and military bases. The Iraqi army was in retreat and disarray. The world expected another offensive thrust from ISIS that could imperil the capital of Baghdad itself. And in late July of 2014, ISIS executioners began beheading captives and broadcasting the ghastly videos. It appeared the entire Middle East was at risk of being ravaged by ISIS.

Opened in 1955, the Incirlik Airbase, located seven miles east of Adana, Turkey, includes NATO's largest nuclear weapons storage facility.

With a ten-thousand-foot runway and fifty-seven hardened aircraft shelters, Incirlik is the most strategically important base in NATO's Southern Region. At one time, the base had over five thousand NATO personnel stationed on its three thousand acres, in addition to two thousand family members. Adana, with a population of over one million, is the fourth largest city in Turkey.

NATO has operated a nuclear sharing program since the mid-1950s. Since 2009, NATO has stationed US nuclear weapons in Germany, the Netherlands, Italy, Belgium, and Turkey. While the United States and NATO maintain a "neither confirm nor deny" posture toward the numbers of its nuclear distribution, the Hoover Institute reported that the United States currently deploys somewhere between 150 and 240 air-delivered nuclear weapons (B61 gravity bombs). It is estimated that twenty-five percent of those weapons are stationed at the Incirlik Airbase in eastern Turkey, with most sources placing fifty B61 nuclear bombs at Incirlik.

Other Notes: The mission and makeup of the US military's Joint Special Operations Command (JSOC) is factually portrayed. It is a quick-strike, highly trained force composed of the best of Delta Force, SEAL Team Six, Army Rangers, and the Air Force's Special Tactics Squadron.

High-ranking US intelligence officials believe Saudi Arabia did in fact finance much of Pakistan's nuclear weapons program, pouring millions of dollars into its development. The intelligence community also believes there exists an agreement for Pakistan to provide nuclear weapons to Saudi Arabia when called for.

The Kurdish people, native to the mountainous regions of eastern Turkey, northern Syria, and northwest Iraq, are the largest people group in the world without their own nation.

The Neve Shalom Synagogue in Istanbul is one of the oldest synagogues in Turkey and caters to a significant Jewish population that was first invited to the city by the Ottoman Sultan Bayezid II following the Jews' expulsion from Spain by the Spanish Inquisition.

PERSIAN BETRAYAL

Empires of Armageddon #2

TERRY BRENNAN

PROLOGUE

Alush Gorge, Arabia
1446 BC

The sharp aroma of charcoal—a thousand fires extinguished in the dawn's first light—mingled with the desert dew and hung in the early morning air. Standing at the forefront of the vast army of Israel, Joshua looked over his right shoulder, across the valley of Rephidim. In the east, he could see the outlined bodies of Moses, Aaron, and Hur—the captain of Moses's personal guard—standing on top of a hill, the highest in the region. The sun was rising behind them, and the staff of God, raised high in Moses's hand, appeared to be shimmering, sparks leaping from it, crackling like bolts of lightning.

It was the sound of drums from across the plain that arrested Joshua's thoughts and brought his concentration back to the battle forming before him. Abner and Hiram stood at either shoulder. Behind him, aligned along an east-west axis on the southern rim of the Rephidim plain, stood half the army of Israel—thirty thousand fighting men from Joshua's tribe of Judah, each man carefully selected; another thirty thousand each from the tribes of Dan and Simeon; twenty thousand each from Reuben, Gad, Ephraim, and Asher. Behind that first phalanx stood a second wave of Jewish soldiers from the other five tribes—in total over two hundred thousand veteran fighting men.

Across the plain, Joshua estimated at least one hundred thousand sons of Amalek waited in the shadows of the dawn. Yesterday, a phalanx of these mounted desert raiders had fallen upon the last remnant of the Israelite column slowly working its way through the Alush gorge. Joshua's soldiers rallied to form a wedge of protection around the weak and defenseless stragglers and repelled these descendants of Ishmael. But the Amalekites were back, even more determined to destroy the people of Israel and the army at its head. The enemy warriors, their black, green, and brown robes flapping behind them like battle flags, were mostly mounted on swift, powerful desert stallions. From a strictly military point of view, Joshua expected he would need to employ every one of his infantry to overcome the Amalekite horsemen. But then there was Moses—and the staff of God.

After glancing once more to the hill to the east where Moses stood firm, the staff held high, Joshua lifted his right arm, his old, nicked sword sharpened to a lethal edge. "For the glory of our God and in the name of Jehovah."

Behind Joshua, in a wave that reverberated through the ranks of soldiers, two hundred thousand voices joined in the declaration, "For the glory of our God and in the name of Jehovah."

And the host of Israel stepped out to cross the plain. In the distance, a great, swirling cloud of dust rose in the north, the mounted horde of Amalek racing toward them, committed to annihilation of the Jews.

Twelve hours later, Moses still sat on a rock on the hill to the east, the staff of God held high above his head. His arms were pale, his fingers turning a shade of light blue. At times during the day, Moses actually dozed off in the heat of the sun. But the staff never faltered.

First Aaron and Hur, then in succession other teams of Moses's personal guard, took turns supporting his arms and the staff. And through the day, the army of Israel punished the bandits of Amalek, pushing them back across the field, slaughtering their horses as they fell, leaving alive no Amalekite warrior who came under their sword.

As the sun slipped behind the low hills to the west, what little was left of the Amalekite army withdrew in defeat, riding north to escape the inexorable fury of the Israelite fighters.

When the last stone was set in the altar, Moses approached and rested the staff of God on its edge. The army of Israel surrounded the altar, built at the base of the hill on which Aaron and Hur had held Moses's arms aloft during the battle. Moses lifted his left arm. "Come, Joshua."

Aware of the blood that covered his arms and his armor, conscious of the filth that crusted over his legs and his feet, Joshua held fast. He was covered with death. How could he approach an altar?

"Come, Joshua. Come . . . stand by me," said Moses.

The old man reached out his hand toward Joshua, who did not have the power or strength left to refuse. Joshua stepped to Moses's side.

Moses smiled at Joshua, then turned to the army and lifted the staff above his head.

"Today God fought for us," said Moses. "And he destroyed the army of Amalek. But know this." Moses took the staff and pointed it at the armed soldiers surrounding the altar. Deliberately, he moved the point of the staff in an arc that encompassed all the army. "While we were on the hill, the Lord spoke to me. The Lord said, 'Moses, write this on a scroll as something to be remembered and make sure that Joshua hears it, because I will completely blot out the name of Amalek from under heaven.' We will call this altar Jehovah-Nissi, the Lord is our banner, for hands were lifted up to the throne of the Lord. And the Lord has sworn here, this day, that the Lord will be at war with the Amalekites from generation to generation."

The army of Israel raised a shout and sounded the shofar so that the hills of Rephidim rained praises on the bloody plain. But Moses stepped closer to Joshua and spoke so that only he could hear.

"My son, hear my words. The Lord has a message for you, your children, and your children's children. Remember what the Amalekites did here, when our people were weary and worn out. They cut off those who were weak and lagging behind. They had no fear of God. Tell your children this . . . When the Lord your God gives you rest from your enemies and the land of the inheritance, you are still to go out and blot out the memory of Amalek from under heaven. The Lord says . . . Do not forget!"

1

Hurva Square, Jerusalem, Israel
July 20, 2014, 1:14 p.m.

Rabbi Chaim Yavod raced into Jerusalem's Hurva Square, choking on the thick, swirling stone dust that encased the square in a malevolent fog. He leaped over huge shards of fractured stone and concrete—white, arched remnants of the Hurva Synagogue's once magnificent dome. A symphony of horror filled the square nearly as thick as the stone dust—moans of the wounded and maimed, wails of survivors as they stumbled over the bodies of those who were not, shrill and urgent sirens promising help but not prevention.

Only moments earlier he had been sent to fetch Rabbi Herzog's car. Then, in a mounting tide of rumbling destruction, the world that Chaim Yavod knew best was obliterated.

The convulsions of the first explosion ripped the door of the black Toyota out of Yavod's hand and knocked him back onto the uneven surface of the small parking lot. The ground shifting under his shoulder blades, Yavod felt three additional explosions shudder the stones of the street. He looked up, above the rooftops toward the north. What looked like a volcanic eruption of smoke, stone, and debris was roiling ever higher over the square that contained the Hurva Synagogue—outside of the Western Wall, the most revered symbol of Jewish worship in Jerusalem.

Now Yavod frantically scrambled through the destruction in the Hurva Square toward the smoking, shattered remains of the synagogue. The sickening fear tearing at his heart pushed aside any concern about delivering the envelope inside his jacket pocket—the decoded second prophecy from the Vilna Gaon. Israel Herzog, chief rabbi of the Israeli Rabbinate Council, his friend and superior, was probably somewhere under the collapsed dome and crumbled walls of what had once been Israel's most beautiful synagogue. Was Herzog alive . . . any other members of the council who were with him? Could he save them? Yavod pressed on through the escalating havoc.

The Old City, Jerusalem
July 20, 1:14 p.m.

The leader consciously forced himself to keep a leisurely pace in the midst of the mayhem. The bombers were three strides north on Habad Street, headed for the souks—the three parallel covered markets of the Old City—and the Damascus Gate, beyond which they could disappear. All around them, people were racing: Israelis and Arabs alike ran toward the site of the explosions in the Hurva Square, while tourists, mothers, and children fled the dust and the terror.

The two bombers looked like worn and weary workmen headed to lunch when the leader thrust out his right arm and grabbed his partner by the sleeve of his dirty work shirt, causing a brief human pileup behind them. The leader pulled his partner close to a building facing the street.

"We need to go back."

"Risky," said his partner.

"Yes," the leader admitted, "but we need to see for ourselves. We know," he said, lowering his voice and looking side to side at the human tide moving past them, "that our work succeeded. But we need to give a report. It was a mistake not to make sure that the results were . . . effective. We don't want to make another mistake. You'll learn. Mistakes are not well tolerated. Come."

Ignoring his partner's unspoken reluctance, the leader turned to his left and began walking against the flow. He turned left on Hashalshelet, the Street of the Chain, away from the crowds, then quickly right into a narrow, curving walkway. Halfway along Tif'eret Yisrael Street the leader saw a stone walkway ascending between two buildings on his right.

"Wait."

He bounded up the stairs two at a time but stopped a head short of the top. In Israel, as was true throughout the Middle East, rooftops were often actively used as alternative living space, particularly in the cooler evening hours. It was possible this rooftop could be occupied. He peeked over the edge, left then right. No one. No chairs. No potted plants. To the right more steps led up to a second flat roof. He looked up to the higher roof, straight into the smoke and debris cloud gently settling over Hurva Square. He could hear the cacophony on the other side of the building in Hurva Square, but no sounds closer. With a quick wave to his partner, he pushed himself over the edge and moved toward the second set of stairs.

He moved up these stairs more cautiously. He took one step and paused, then another and paused. The fifth step brought his head level with the upper roof. He peeked over the edge. This roof held signs of being used, but it was unoccupied at the moment. The vast, open Hurva Square lay beyond its edge. As if he were walking on an ice bridge in the spring, his body in a crouch, he edged to a small parapet wall at the end of the roof. A slight breeze carried the smoke, dust, and cries for help off to the west, giving the leader a fairly clear view of his handiwork—carnage, destruction, chaos.

Front to back, the Hurva sat on a north-south axis, the front of the building and the large, open Hurva Square on the southern side. He and his partner were now situated on a rooftop looking northwest, catty-corner across the square, toward the ancient minaret of the Caliph Omar mosque on the far side. The Hurva, when it stood, was a massive square building of Jerusalem stone and masonry walls, almost its entire bulk covered by a huge dome. Now the Hurva looked like a squashed egg.

For maximum destruction of the synagogue, and everything and anyone inside it, the first twin explosions had cracked the spine of the building. Then another set of explosions obliterated the walls at the corners, causing the majority of the destruction to fall in upon itself, like a deflating accordion. But the blasts had also hurled huge chunks of stone wall and concrete arch in every direction around the building.

The trees in the square were shattered and stunted by the blasts, the umbrella-covered open-air restaurant tables that offered shade and respite for tourists were thrown against the walls of the adjacent buildings.

A retaining wall of Jerusalem stone, two stories high, was tied into and ran across the rear of the synagogue, accounting for the higher elevation of Ha-Yehudim Street. That retaining wall, and a square chunk of the rear of the building attached to the wall, were the only parts of the Hurva that had survived the blasts.

Below, butchery littered the vastness of the Hurva Square. Police and medical first responders were rushing around, looking for the living and covering the dead. Wails of grief battled with the still incoming sirens.

"Let's watch a moment."

US Embassy, Tel Aviv, Israel
July 20, 1:16 p.m.

In two hours, Rabbi Israel Herzog was scheduled to arrive with a secret that promised to make Brian Mullaney's life even more unpredictable and out of control.

The last two days—was it only two days?—had been relentless, seemingly endless, interrupted by only a few hours of sleep. He needed to shake off the weary exhaustion that was draining his muscles and dulling his brain. The daily security of hundreds of diplomatic staff rested squarely on his shoulders. Recently banished to Israel, his appointment as the US State Department's Middle East Regional Security Officer (RSO) was little solace for the fact that his career was on life support.

The phone rang.

"Mullaney."

"Sir, it's Floyd Bishop at the consul general's residence. There's been an explosion in the Old City. I think the Hurva's just been blown up."

Hurva Square, Jerusalem
July 20, 1:17 p.m.

Chaim skirted the eastern edge of the square. A slight breeze had begun to move some of the choking dust to the west. Scrambling his way around giant pieces of wreckage, tearing up the flesh of his hands on the knifelike edges, and avoiding the growing crowd of civilians pouring into the square to help, he fixed his eyes on his destination—an arched doorway on the north side of the synagogue, at the base of the retaining wall, that led to a lower-level hallway and the offices of the Rabbinate Council on the western flank of the Hurva.

Inside the arch, the door and its frame were no longer vertical. The doorframe canted to the right at a forty-five-degree angle, the door itself sprung open and hanging precariously from only one hinge. Chaim closed the distance, keeping a hopeful eye on the door for any sign of life and a wary eye on the still-smoldering rubble mound to his left that continued to disgorge debris onto the square. He acknowledged to himself the fear that was adding lead weights to his limbs but, with a deep breath, cast the fear aside and pressed himself through the precarious opening into the underbelly of destruction.

The Old City, Jerusalem
July 20, 1:18 p.m.

The leader of the bombers had his eyes on the square below and his mobile phone to his ear.

"The synagogue is destroyed. The rabbis and their package are now buried under tons of wreckage collapsed in upon itself."

"Where are you?" asked the leader of the Disciples.

"On a rooftop, overlooking the square."

"Remain. Make sure no one has escaped. Do not get caught."

The leader closed the phone and stuffed it in his pants pocket just as his accomplice poked him on the shoulder.

"You see . . . there is one. Looks like a rabbi," said the accomplice, as the thin, black-coated man gingerly approached a darkened archway in the retaining wall to their right.

They hunkered close to the parapet, their eyes on the slight figure who slipped into the darkness.

"He goes in," said his companion.

"Yes. And we wait until . . . if . . . he comes out."

US Embassy, Tel Aviv
July 20, 1:18 p.m.

Habit and training prompted Mullaney to swing his chair to the left toward the three-foot-square Jerusalem street map that was attached to a huge cloth board in his office at the US Embassy in Tel Aviv, Israel.

Even though he had only been "boots on the ground" in Israel for two weeks, he knew where the consul general's residence was located—on Gershon Agron Street across from the sprawling Independence Park, in an Americanized compound less than a mile from the Old City.

Floyd Bishop was a seasoned and respected agent of the Diplomatic Security Service, someone who could be trusted. But Mullaney needed all the facts. "How do you know it was the Hurva?"

"I don't. I can't be certain," said Bishop. "But as soon as I heard the explosions and felt the ground move, I grabbed a pair of binoculars and ran up to the roof. We're on a rise, and the rear of the building looks out over the Old City. There was still a cloud of debris and smoke in the air to pinpoint the location. The explosion was pretty much due east of here, north of the Zion Gate . . . sort of split the distance between St. James Cathedral and David's Tower. I can't see it clearly through the smoke and ash, even with binoculars, but the Hurva is less than two thousand yards away from here, in that very spot. And that's where the debris cloud is. If I had to make a bet—"

"Okay," said Mullaney, "take a—"

"Listen, Brian—excuse me, sir," said Bishop, acknowledging Mullaney's rank, "but that was a huge explosion—actually several explosions if I counted correctly. There's going to be a lot of dead people over there, sir. A lot of tourists. Could be some of ours."

Mullaney wiped a hand down his lined face and then scanned the map in front of him, calculating. In his nineteen years in the Diplomatic Security Service, he'd approached every assignment with constant vigilance, articulate intelligence, and an external calm that carried over to all those with whom he served.

Now the world kept blowing up around him. Mullaney was responsible for protecting the lives of every individual assigned to the US diplomatic mission to Israel and—by extension, he believed—responsible for every American soul in the land of Israel.

But he was failing miserably in fulfilling those responsibilities. First Palmyra Parker, the ambassador's daughter, was kidnapped and now—probably because of a decision he made—the historic Hurva Synagogue in the Old City of Jerusalem, Israel's most beautiful place of worship, was a smoldering pile of rubble. Only minutes earlier, Rabbi Israel Herzog called him from inside the Hurva, announcing that the Rabbinate Council had cracked the code of a two-hundred-year-old prophecy that Mullaney hoped would put an end to the death and mayhem that followed the scrap of parchment from Germany to Turkey to Israel. Was Herzog still in the synagogue when . . .

Mullaney held the phone to his ear but there was little that was holding up his hope. "All right, Floyd, how many agents on duty over there?"

"Eight, at least—could be more if some of the agents stuck around after the shift change."

"How's your exterior security?" asked Mullaney. He visualized the long,

high stone wall, topped by wrought iron fencing that ran along the front of the compound on Gershon Agron Street.

"We're solid," said Bishop. "Mostly Israeli nationals—long-time service guys who are ex-IDF—with one of our agents in charge. We're solid here, Brian, and we're the closest."

Mullaney walked to the window and looked to the east where, forty-four miles distant in the Judean hill country, the contested city of Jerusalem was located. Still a formidable physical presence in his mid-forties, the spreading streaks of gray at his temples were a testimony to the daily stress he carried on his broad shoulders. Today he also fought the twin scourges of guilt and discouragement.

"All right, Floyd. Take a team of four and get to the Hurva as quickly as you can. I'll call Shin Bet and let them know you are going to be on-site shortly. Stay there until you get some information about any victims—and whether any of the victims are American citizens. And also check into the status of the rabbis at the synagogue. The chief rabbi there, Israel Herzog, was working with us on something very important. See what you can find out and call me back."

Hurva Square, Jerusalem
July 20, 1:20 p.m.

Gray clouds of grit floated in the air, blocking out the sun as Chaim Yavod ducked under the skewed portal and entered the deeper darkness of the devastated Hurva. He left behind a swelling symphony of sirens and a frantic, growing assemblage—some with yarmulkes bobbing on their heads with every effort, others in shorts and T-shirts—frantically digging in the stony rubble that was once the most beautiful of synagogues.

Before him to the left ran a still discernable corridor, half of it collapsed, now an obstacle course of crushed stone and concrete shards, twisted reinforcing rods, and piles of rubble. Every few feet, a shaft of light sliced in through the shattered walls, now partially open to the sun, illuminating a frantic dance of dust and encasing the remnants of the corridor in a pallid fog. Yavod skittered around the fallen masonry, unaware of the blood trail left behind by his lacerated fingertips.

He had only been gone a moment to get the car requested by Rabbi Herzog.

He had only been gone a moment when the great dome was cloven down the middle, when the earth was rent from beneath his feet, when the unleashed roar of the explosions ripped past him like thunder down a valley's rift. Only a moment, but his world rested in ruins as devastating as the destruction under his feet.

He had to find the rabbi. He had to.

He reached the end of the corridor where three steps led left, to a lower level and the offices of the Rabbinate Council. What was once the ceiling had collapsed, reducing the corridor's height by half. Yavod lowered himself down the stairs, then bent over in a crouch, keeping his feet under him to navigate the ongoing debris field as he inched along the corridor toward the council's offices. The light faded. Yavod had to feel his way through the darkness. A gaping yaw of black stopped him. The front wall of the council's offices had been blown across the corridor, blocking most of it with a massive pile of ruin, leaving the interior of the offices wide open but shrouded in gloom.

Yavod scuffed his shoe through some of the rubble at his feet and found a broken piece of Shabbat candle in the dust. He lit the candle, held it in front of him at arm's length, and moved into the blackened office, pulling along an anchor of despair.